Contents

Cover Credit
Title Page
Copyright
Dedication
About This Book
Pronunciations
Preface
Chapter 1
Chapter 2
Chapter 3
Chapter 4
Chapter 5
Chapter 6
Chapter 7
Chapter 8
Chapter 9
Chapter 10
Chapter 11
Chapter 12
Chapter 13
Chapter 14
Chapter 15
Chapter 16
Chapter 17
Chapter 18
Chapter 19
Chapter 20
Chapter 21
Chapter 22
Chapter 23
Chapter 24
Chapter 25
Chapter 26
Chapter 27
Chapter 28

Chpater 29
Chapter 30
Chapter 31
Chapter 32
Chapter 33
Chapter 34
Epilogue
From The Author
About The Author

Cover Credit

Christopher Coyle

darkandstormyknight.com

Thank you for adorning my words so beautifully.
Your talent knows no bounds!

And thank you for not running from me or blocking me no matter how many times I say, "But what if we just..."

Sandra R Neeley
P. O. Box 127
Franklinton, LA 70438
authorsandrarneeley@gmail.com

97,814 words.

Independently Published
By Sandra R Neeley

Haven 3: Transcend

by Sandra R Neeley

For me. Because I never, ever thought I could.

About This Book

Elite Force Commander Kol Ra' Don Tol has been obsessed with Earth and its cultures for as long as he can remember. He's thrilled when the gods smile on him, giving him an Ehlealah, a mate, that is human. But she's suffered traumas and abuse that no being should have to endure. As a result, she's not as receptive to his claim that she's his as he hoped she'd be. He waits patiently for his female to realize what she is to him, what they are together. But instead of accepting him and falling into his arms, she runs from him — all the way back to Earth. Now he's on a mission to find her and do whatever it takes to earn her love and bring her back to his home on Command Warship 1.

Ada Jane has lost 135 years. That's how long she existed as entertainment to others after being abducted from her home on Earth. She's rescued along with several other women and given the opportunity to choose their own futures — stay here, or go home to Earth. Ada Jane chooses Earth despite the claims of a very large, very blue, alien warrior who insists that she is his, and he is hers. When he prevents her from joining the others on a one-way trip back to Earth, she decides to get there any way she can. She slips away without a word on the next transport leaving Command Warship 1. She needs to see her home and what's left of the world she left behind before she can even consider beginning a new life anywhere else.

Kol and Ada Jane want the same things out of life despite their very different opinions of exactly what that entails. They want home, love, and the security within which to enjoy it. Once on Earth, there are obstacles at every turn working against them.

Will they be able to overcome all they face and find their way to each other?

Warning: Intended for mature audiences. This book contains violence, abuse both real and inferred, and sexual situations that may be disturbing for some readers. If you are offended by these subjects, please do not buy this book.

Pronunciations

Name - Pronunciation, Nickname(s) - Pronunciation

- Rokai ahl — Roe kye all
- Gaishon — Guyshon
- Li'Orani — Lee Ore ahni
- Kron — Kron
- Zha Quin Tha Tel Mo' Kok - Shah Keen Tha Tell Moe Coke, Zha Quin - Shah Keen, Quin - Keen
- Zha Tahl Tel Mo' Kok - Shah Tall Tell Moe Coke, Zha Tahl — Shah Tall
- Eula — Youlah
- Ba Re' Non Tol - Bah Ray Non Toll, Ba Re' - Bah Ray
- Kol Ra' Don Tol - Cole Rah Don Toll, Kol - Cole, aka Blue-Dude
- Jhan Re' Non Tol - Shahn Ray Non Toll, Jhan - Shahn
- Xallen -Zallen
- Vor - Vor
- Kail - Kale
- Zahn - Zon
- Rel - Rel
- Asl - Acel
- General Lo'San - General Low Sahn
- Vilshhelkrj - Impossible to pronounce - Vennie
- Ehlealah - Eh lee lah

- shraler - shrayler
- Psi - Sigh
- Cruestaci - Crew stah see
- Cruestace - Crew Stahs
- Litah - Leeta
- Quarin — Kwarin
- Quari — Kwaree
- Quisles - Kwyles
- Diskastes - Disk aste s
- Zhuxi - Zooshi

Preface

Kol sat in the pilot's seat of the Cruestaci Battle Cruiser that was assigned to him in each battle they fought. He knew it intimately and was completely at ease in it.

The com pinged, asking for his attention, but it was a frequency he was unfamiliar with, so he ignored it.

It pinged again, and again, and again.

Finally, unable to tolerate the irritating sound any longer, he accepted the call. "What?!" He shouted.

"Ambassador Kol Ra' Don Tol?" a shaky voice asked.

"Excuse me?" Kol said, in forced, broken English.

"I'm trying to reach Ambassador Kol Ra' Don Tol. This is Special Liaison Elisher from Earth Base 28. We were advised that you'd been assigned here at the last moment, and we're contacting you to offer our services once you land here on Earth. It seems you'll be here for some time, and as neither you nor your species has visited before, we thought to make your transition easier."

Kol was not stupid and was slowly putting together the pieces. Apparently, Quin had managed to get him listed as an Ambassador so that he'd not be arrested should he be detected on Earth without permission. "Thank you, for your offer," Kol responded. "But, how long exactly do your records show that I'm to be on Earth? I was not planning to be there any extended period of time," he explained, still in broken English.

There was the sound of some papers shuffling. "Excuse me, Ambassador Don Tol, while I read through the transmittal. We've just received your appointment and have not had time to enter it into our data base. I'm looking through your file... Oh! Here it is... three years. Your commission on Earth is for three years."

Kol was stunned. Three years? Quin had deserted him! And what about his Elite Team? How would they function without him? All he'd wanted to do was to find Ada Jane, show her her abandoned farmhouse, and bring her home.

"Ambassador?" the whiny voice said.

"Yes?" he answered in a less than confident tone.

"May we offer you housing and transition assistance while you're here?"

"Yes, please do," Kol answered. His mind whirling. How would he ever make it on Earth for three years?

Surely this was some kind of mistake.

Chapter 1

Ada Jane stood at the exit door of Rokai ahl's ship. Her hand rested on the metal wall beside the sensor that would open the door and allow her to finally set foot on her home planet.

"This is it," Rosie said. "Are you sure you want to do this?"

Ada Jane paused before answering. Then she let out a quiet chuckle. "No. Not at all. But I have to. I can't just forge ahead without making peace with whatever I find left of my life here."

"You heard Zha Quin. He said that Chairman Bartholomew made arrangements for you. They are expecting your arrival here. The band you wear on your wrist is loaded with fifty thousand credits. It is enough to keep you for at least a year. Do not forget the government owes you for failing to protect you adequately. Don't hesitate to demand your reparation credits if you begin to run low. And remember, you are protected by Chairman Bartholomew and his demands for your treatment. Believe me, his word carries quite a lot of power. You will be safe," Rokai ahl explained.

Ada Jane nodded.

"I also believe you will not be alone for long. Kol is already on his way to this planet," Rokai added.

"That's both soothing and quite unnerving at the same time," Ada Jane admitted.

"You can always just buckle back in and fly away with us," Rosie offered.

"I wish it were that easy. But… no turning back now," Ada answered.

"Very well. They are waiting for you outside. If I may offer advice? Their first impression of you is how they will treat you and approach you from that moment forward. If you are the victim, they will attempt to make all decisions for you, shelter and guide you as they see fit. If you are the quiet, unassuming, traumatized female… the same thing. If you are strong, adamant about what you intend to achieve, self-confident, they will treat you as an intelligent being with your own ideas," Rokai said.

"Take a page out of Vivi's book," Rosie added.

"Only tone it down — drastically. You should not attack," Rokai said laughing.

Ada nodded. "You're right." She took a deep breath and straightened her back. "Okay, I'm ready."

Rokai stepped in front of Ada Jane and pressed his hand to the sensor, causing the door to open. As it raised he stood there, straight, tall, confident, and obviously completely disdainful of the people assembled to greet Ada Jane.

"Welcome," a tall, attractive, human male dressed in a white coat greeted.

Rokai inclined his head in recognition of the greeting. "I am Rokai ahl Tel Mo' Kok."

"We've been expecting you, sir," another male, fully decked out in military finery and decorated with medals said.

"I have come to deliver Ada Jane Andersen to her home planet. My people freed her, along with several other females upon discovering them held as slaves. She is the last to choose to be repatriated."

"We are aware of the assistance of the Cruestaci people in returning a number of our people to our planet. We are most grateful," the first man said. "We've spoken to the other women at great length and have been made aware of the exemplary treatment and respect they received while with your people. We thank you."

"There is no thanks necessary," Rokai said. He stepped aside and lifted his arm to wave Ada forward. "Ada Jane," he said softly, yet firmly.

Ada stepped forward. She looked out at the group of people waiting for her.

"Welcome home, Ada Jane," the man in the white coat said sincerely, offering her a smile.

"Thank you, Doctor," she responded. It was clear from his manner of dress and the stethoscope around his neck that he was a doctor.

Two military personnel in BDU's pushed a small mobile rolling staircase up to Rokai's ship.

"Shall I escort you down?" Rokai asked.

"No thank you, Rokai. I have it from here," Ada Jane answered. Then she turned toward him and put her arms around his neck, hugging him tightly. "Thank you for everything. Keep Rosie happy, huh?" she asked, leaning back to look at him with her arms still around his neck.

"I will. You tell Bart to send for me if you need rescuing. I will come for you at once," Rokai promised.

"I'll be fine. But, thank you."

Ada let her arms fall away from Rokai, then turned to Rosie, hugging her tightly. "I'll miss you."

"Nah, you'll be so busy down here trying to get your place back in order and yanking Kol into place, you won't even have time to think about me," Rosie said, grinning at Ada.

"Yes, I will. I'll think about you. I won't forget. Not ever. Be happy, Rosie."

Rosie was moved almost to tears, and it really kind of chapped her ass. She sniffled and swiped the back of her hand across the tears that threatened. "I won't forget either. And you be happy, too. And mark my words, Kol will find you whether you think he will or not."

"We shall see," Ada answered, smiling sadly.

The doctor had ascended the stairs and stood one step down from the top, awaiting Ada Jane.

Ada Jane turned to him and stepped out onto the top step, accepting his hand to steady her descent.

"I'm Dr. Cavanaugh. Welcome home, Ada Jane."

"Thank you," she answered, holding her head high, and walking down the steps with him. "Now, who do I have to talk to about getting my land back?" she asked.

Rokai stood in the doorway watching Ada descending the steps and heard her question. He smirked. She'd do just fine.

She'd already let them know she had a plan and was ready to start on its path.

He waited until Ada and the welcoming party moved away from his ship, then pressed the sensor telling the door to close. Rokai went to his seat, strapped in and began preflight procedures so they could be on their way.

"Ready for an adventure, my Rosalita?" he asked.

"Absolutely!" she answered.

Five days later Elite Force Commander Kol Ra' Don Tol maneuvered his Battle Cruiser in place above the landing pad he'd been instructed to proceed to. He hovered in place while the pad was prepared, forcefields at the ready to grasp and anchor his Battle Cruiser in place once he lowered it into its proper resting position.

His com crackled letting him know a communication was incoming. "Ambassador, you may proceed. Landing protocols are in place."

Kol rolled his eyes. Whoever the hells had made him an ambassador, relegating him to this uncivilized, chaotic world, split into sectors and governed by multiple powers, for an unbelievable three year period would certainly feel his wrath.

Kol clenched his jaw as he sat in the pilot's seat of his personal battle cruiser and endured the feelings of jerking and restraining motions as the necessary forcefields were put in place. It irritated him that his battle cruiser was being locked down by governing agents of this world. A world he had no control over, and no status in.

The com crackled again. "Landing is complete, Ambassador. You may disembark at will."

"Thank you," he answered. Kol sat there for a few moments, getting himself together and looking around the cockpit. Then he spoke aloud, hoping the ship's computer was still fully functioning.

"Computer?" he asked.

There was no answer.

"Computer?" he asked again, raising his voice.

There was still no answer, so he leaned forward swiping his fingertips across one of the sensors there. Several different lights began to light up across the control panel. He waited until they were a steady glow rather than a flickering light show. Then he began to type in commands. A few minutes later he tried again.

"Computer?"

"How may I be of service, Elite Commander Kol Ra' Don Tol?"

"I am preparing to disembark. Reinforce Cruestaci protocol for access to and operation of this battle cruiser. See to it that none other than myself has access."

"Yes, sir. Reinforced protocol in effect. You disabled communication with Command Warship 1, do you wish to reinstate communications?"

"Yes. In addition, I'll be taking my handheld with me. Please be sure that it is reconfigured at once."

"Yes, Elite Force Comm..."

"Could you just call me Kol?" Kol asked irritatedly. He'd gotten used to the lack of formality when dealing with Missy and found it a huge waste of time to have to wait for the standard computer program to repeat every damned thing spoken to it and to address you and every operation you requested with full titles.

"Your rank is Elite Force Commander, Elite Force Commander."

"I should have programmed Missy in my cruiser," he mumbled.

"Please repeat your request, Elite Force Commander Kol Ra' Don Tol," the computer requested.

"Yes. I will definitely be installing Missy as soon as I'm back in range," he said aloud. Then he glanced at his handheld unit.

The flashing light sequence had stopped. “Is the handheld ready?” he asked.

“Yes, Elite Force Commander Kol Ra’ Don Tol.”

“Oh. My. Gods! Please be Missy when I get back!” he snapped. “In the meantime, no one enters this Battle Cruiser but me. No one accesses any technology or computer programs but me. If by some series of events the cruiser is breeched, self-destruct after sending a call to Command Warship 1 advising them I am still alive, the cruiser was breeched and initiated its own self-destruct protocols.”

“Yes, Elite Force Commander Kol Ra’ Don Tol.”

Kol leaned forward again, taking his handheld communicator out of its place on the main control panel. He unstrapped himself, then stood. “Computer, you will allow me to exit the cruiser, then appear to be inactive and fully sealed, seemingly unreachable until you either hear my voice and confirm my DNA, or unless you are breeched and my presence cannot be confirmed at which time you will follow the commanded protocol. Do you understand?”

“Yes, Elite Force Commander Kol Ra’ Don Tol.”

Kol ran his fingers across another control panel, activating the steel-like cover over the front of the cruiser that allowed him to see out. He walked over to the exit doorway. He swiped his hand over the flat, smooth control panel there and waited while the door whooshed open. He raised a single eyebrow as he took in the unexpected group of people waiting for him to disembark.

A very small — by Cruestaci standards — human male stepped forward. “Welcome to Earth, Ambassador Kol Ra’ Don Tol.”

Kol looked around at the docking area he’d landed on. “Thank you.” There wasn’t that much to see as far as he could tell. It was a docking platform not unlike Command Warship 1 had on board, except this one was not on a ship. He took his time, glancing at the other ships also contained nearby. Kol allowed his gaze to travel briefly over the dozen or so military personnel and diplomats assembled to greet him, before having his attention drawn back to the little man who’d spoken to him first.

"Ambassador? I am Special Liaison Elisher. I've been assigned to you while you're on Earth and will be assisting with all things you may need."

Kol looked down at the little man, standing on a platform a good eight feet below his Battle Cruiser. The Cruiser seemed to hang in the air, not quite touching down, though it was securely held by forcefields.

A loud metallic screech could be heard nearby and Kol winced, then looked in that direction.

"Forgive me, sir. We were not aware of the size difference of your ship. We are bringing in a mobile staircase to assist you in getting to the ground."

Kol glanced at the three men trying to drag a tall metallic staircase on wheels toward their general direction. Then back at his liaison. "That won't be necessary," he said in his best overly enunciated English. He stepped off the deck of his cruiser, dropped the eight feet to the ground, and began walking toward the welcoming party with no sign of discomfort or even a slight jostle on landing. At his full exit from the cruiser, the door slid shut, and the entire small ship immediately appeared to be covered in one single sheet of steel with no entry or exit points.

Several of the welcoming party stepped back at his display of strength on landing on the ground before them as though he'd done no more than take a step or two, but covered it quite nicely by continuing to move backward, forming an aisle for him to walk down.

Special Liaison Elisher reached out his hand, waiting for Kol to shake it. "We are thrilled that you've been assigned to our home planet for the time being and are very thankful for the protection of your people as you patrol the quadrants surrounding our planet."

Kol looked down at Elisher's hand and lifted his own to place in Elisher's. He'd read about this. He knew that Earth males shook hands as a sign of welcome and respect. He stifled a small smile when he saw Elisher's surprise when Kol's hand practically dwarfed his. "We are pleased to do so."

"If there's anything I can do for you Ambassador Ko..." Elisher started.

"You may call me Kol, or you may call me Ambassador. There is no need to repeat my full name each time you address me."

"Of course, Ambassador. Thank you," Elisher immediately replied. "May I present to you the governing members of Earth Base 28?"

Kol nodded. "Please do."

"Consul Diskastes of Planet Quisles, Viceroy Pomrance, and Viceroy Buchanan, both of Earth, Patroon Zhuxi of planet Ceres, and of course their personal security forces."

Kol allowed his gaze to rove across the faces of those being introduced to him aloofly, then clicked his heels together and straightened his spine even more. Then he fisted his hand and struck his chest diagonally, right to left, with his closed fist landing on his left shoulder. "I am Ambassador Kol Ra' Don Tol, also Elite Commander of Special Forces of the Cruestaci people of the planet Cruestace. I bid you greetings." He noticed several surprised reactions to his Elite Force title but gave no indication that he'd noticed.

"We are honored to have you among us," Consul Diskastes said, his eyes very clearly saying otherwise. "Come, we shall share a meal to celebrate your arrival and addition to Earth Base 28." The Consul turned and walked away with Viceroy Pomrance right on his heels, though without any regard for the remaining dignitaries.

"It is my understanding that I will be given free rein to move about the planet as necessary in order to complete my duties," Kol said loudly enough for it to be clear he addressed the retreating Consul.

Consul Diskastes paused to look back at Kol. "Is it?" he asked with a sarcastic tone in his voice.

"It is. Base 28 will of course be home base for as long as necessary, but it will not be the only base I visit," Kol said emphatically, with a stiff smile on his face that looked more like a grimace.

"I'm sure it's in your data submission. Perhaps I overlooked it," Diskastes responded.

"I'm sure," Kol answered, his smile/grimace becoming more pronounced as he privately asked the powers that be to nudge Bart into going along with his slight deception. He had no idea how Earth bases or quadrants were governed. He only knew he needed access to any that may have Ada Jane within their population.

"Ambassador?" Elisher asked, stepping forward.

"Yes?" Kol said, waiting for Elisher to continue.

"As I said, this is Viceroy Buchanan of Earth, and Patroon Zhuxi of Ceres."

"I am pleased to meet you," Patroon Zhuxi said, extending his long, four fingered hand. "Please do not allow the arrogance of certain members of our governing body to offend you. They know not what they do."

Kol detected nothing but sincerity in this male. "I am pleased to meet you as well," Kol answered, performing a small bow. "I am not at all offended. It simply gives me an excuse to have to be less accommodating."

Zhuxi chuckled in a gurgling type of way. "I believe we shall get along famously."

Kol inclined his head, still shaking Zhuxi's hand.

"I'm Buchanan, Viceroy is something they insist I use, but couldn't personally care less about. Believe me, he knows well what he does. Welcome to my home planet, Kol. If I may call you Kol?" he asked.

"Of course, and thank you. I have studied your planet and been fascinated with it for many, many of your Earth years," Kol said. Reaching out to shake Buchanan's hand since Zhuxi had released his hand.

"It was at one time a beautiful place," Buchanan said. "Some of it still is."

"Perhaps one day it will all be beautiful again," Kol said.

"We can hope," Buchanan answered.

"Come, allow us to escort you to the formal meal we've put together in your honor," Zhuxi offered.

"Thank you," Kol said, beginning to walk toward the small building the Consul had disappeared into with his entourage.

Chapter 2

Ada Jane allowed Doctor Cavanaugh to escort her into the facility. With his hand at the small of her back, he attempted to guide her down the corridor just inside the building, and to wherever he had in mind to take her first. She, however, stopped to watch Rokai ahl's ship rise into the air before zipping away so quickly it practically disappeared before her eyes.

It was bittersweet to watch her friends, of which she only had a small handful now, heading off on their adventures. She blinked rapidly to scatter the moisture that had begun to gather in her eyes at the thought that she was certainly now all alone.

"I can't imagine how it must feel to watch the only security you've known of late as it leaves," Dr. Cavanaugh said.

Ada glanced at Dr. Cavanaugh, but didn't acknowledge his reply. Instead, she turned and began walking. "Where is it that you're escorting me to, Doctor?"

"To our clinic. We thought we'd give you a basic physical just to be sure there is no health issue we should address."

"I think I'd rather speak to whoever is in charge of seeing that I get my land back," Ada said in a no-nonsense tone. She wasn't trying to insult anyone, just standing firm on what she wanted.

"I suppose we could request a meeting, but those types of things are usually scheduled. Perhaps in the meantime we could spend a few minutes in my office, just get your basic readings, blood pressure, pulse rate..."

"Why?" she asked, coming to a stop.

"It's just our procedure. We don't want to take any chances with your health," Dr. Cavanaugh answered.

Ada Jane raised an eyebrow much as she'd seen Vivian do on Command Warship 1. And to her delight, the simple tactic worked.

"We are also supposed to be screening for any foreign bacteria or infections that could possibly be passed to us that we've not already been made aware of," Dr. Cavanaugh said sheepishly.

"It's much better when you speak with me directly about anything you may wish to have happen, don't you think?" Ada Jane asked.

Dr. Cavanaugh nodded, with a slight smile. "I'm seeing that it is."

"Where is your office?" she asked.

"Right this way," he answered as they began to walk again.

Ada Jane's stomach growled. "I'd kill for a hamburger," Ada Jane said. "No, wait, a cheeseburger with crispy fries and a chocolate shake."

Dr. Cavanaugh grinned as he came to a crossing corridor and lifted his arm to indicate with a sweep of his hand they needed to go to the right. "I can certainly take care of that request," he said.

Eventually, they arrived in his clinic, which to Ada Jane looked more like a full fledged hospital. They walked through sliding double glass doors with a clinic sign mounted on the wall over them, and the words, 'Medical Facility - Clinic' on the doors themselves in white letters. Once Ada stepped through the doors, the area opened up into a huge, spacious reception area with a large, crescent-shaped reception desk, and more than two dozen matching upholstered chairs placed against the exterior walls of the very welcoming room. There were people milling about, while others, obviously caregivers, approached the waiting areas with small electronic tablets in their hands, calling out the name of the patient that had come up next on their itinerary.

As Ada followed, Dr. Cavanaugh passed one doubly wide corridor and eventually took a left into another. She realized the facility went much further back into the building than she'd thought it did. "How big is this place?" she asked, trying not to seem overwhelmed at the size she'd not even guessed at from the outside.

"The clinic, or the entire building?" the doctor asked.

"Both?" Ada answered uncertainly.

"The medical facility is four stories, and we can accommodate two hundred fifty beds. That includes beds for treatment, testing, and exploratory procedures as well as any standard hospital stay as a result of injury or illness. We've got the means to perform any type of treatment or surgery. We are in line with the foremost medical facilities in the country."

"Why so small then?" she asked.

"We are not normally for public use. We are focused primarily on the needs of high-ranking officials, and their families. We are also responsible for the health and care of all peoples being repatriated to Earth after they've been away from our shores, whether willingly or not."

"I'm assuming you also address psychological needs, then."

"Yes, absolutely."

"The building... how large is it?" she asked.

"I'm trying to think of a building the repatriation center could be compared to. One that you'd know from your time here on Earth," Dr. Cavanaugh answered. "Oh! I know. How foolish of me, I should have known right away. This building is modeled after the Pentagon, so all in all, with all its departments and purposes, about thirty-four acres. We have small electric carts we use if we need to get from one side of the facility to the other quickly. Do you recall the Pentagon before it was destroyed?" he asked.

Ada slowed her steps to a stop, turning hesitantly to look at Dr. Cavanaugh. "The Pentagon was destroyed?" she asked quietly, her expression stricken.

"Ada Jane," he said, shaking his head sadly and taking one of her hands in both of his. "I'm so, so sorry. I forgot the time span you'd been away. You were taken in 1986, if I remember the information in your files correctly. You just look so young, it's hard to remember that you've been away for so long. Most people don't live to be your age, and look as good as you do," he said, trying to make her smile. When she didn't smile at his attempt at a joke, he returned to the facts at hand.

"Unfortunately, there is very little still standing of the Earth that you remember."

"What year is it?" she asked, her voice husky with emotion.

"It's 2121. Today is September 29th. Just a few more months and we'll move into 2122," Dr. Cavanaugh explained softly, still holding her hand.

Ada closed her eyes for a moment, then took a very slow deep breath. She opened her eyes again and looked around at all the people coming and going with medical escorts, and military personnel without escorts as they moved around the medical facility.

"Are you alright?" he asked.

"I will be," she answered after a brief pause. She looked around, and made a pointed effort to shake off the shock that had truly taken her by surprise when she realized that Kol had been telling her the truth, and started walking in the direction the doctor had indicated only a few minutes earlier. It surprised her how many times she'd thought of Kol since leaving Command Warship 1. "Are all peoples put through your examinations upon landing on Earth?"

"Our medical facility is the main repatriation hub for the country. The building itself has multiple functions, but all United States citizens, humans that is, returning to Earth — come through my clinic before being released back into the general population."

"Humans? Are there citizens that aren't human?" Ada asked.

"There are. Some extraterrestrial species have visited our planet and found it very much to their liking. If you are returning home, or will be here on an extended basis, you would have to go through another base."

"Where would that be?" Ada asked, following him into an office he opened the door of and held open for her.

"There are several scattered across the United States, and they are somewhat smaller and accommodate fewer people at a time."

"Because the last thing you want is more extraterrestrials than humans preparing to release into the country at one time," she said, figuring out immediately what he wasn't saying.

Dr. Cavanaugh canted his head slightly, as he searched for the politically correct, non-committal answer. "I'm sure that was probably part of it once upon a time," he finally said.

"Say one was coming from Cruestace. Which base would they have to apply for entry through?" Ada asked.

"Do you have someone in particular in mind?" Dr. Cavanaugh asked, his curiosity piqued.

"Not at all, it's just that it's the only species I've decided is trustworthy so far."

"Ah, I see." He pressed his lips together and thought about it. "There are of course a couple of different options, but most likely, they'd go through El Paso."

"Texas?" Ada asked.

"Yes, Texas. The borders have changed somewhat, but basically the larger states remain intact. Texas is one of them."

"What states are we missing?" she asked, alarmed.

"Not many. A few of the smaller Northern ones have been rolled into a new state known as Yorksland."

"So... New York, Connecticut, Vermont, Maine, Rhode Island...?" she asked.

"Exactly. If it was considered New England before the war, it's now Yorksland." He walked over to the phone on his huge oak desk. "Excuse me for just a moment while I order you some lunch. Would you mind if I shared a meal with you?" he asked, looking up at her from his handheld tablet.

"Not at all," she answered.

She watched while he swiped his fingertip back and forth, tapping lightly from time to time, then satisfied with whatever he'd done, indicated the chair across the desk from his own chair.

"Dr. Cavanaugh, is that a computer?" Ada Jane asked.

"It is. It's a small handheld device that is plugged into the mainframe that operates this entire building and those that are satellites of it."

"That is just too Star Trek for me," Ada Jane mumbled, taking the device from him when he offered it to her.

"Everyone, no matter their social status has access to some form of device that gives them access to the public mainframe that is free to all of the United States' citizens."

"Which means they are all able to be monitored and their behaviors monitored at will," she said, matter of factly rather than accusatorily.

"I'm sure to some degree, yes. But it's mainly just a convenient way to give everyone access to information they'd not have otherwise."

"Is it a legal requirement to be active on a device?" Ada asked.

"Not at all. In fact, there are some people who live away from the main hubs of commerce and prefer to live off the grid, so to speak. Some keep devices and access them only very rarely, others — true traditionalists — refuse to even own a device. It's perfectly legal not to, but, you don't have access to anything important that may occur."

"Like what?"

"Well, weather for one. If a tornado system were to bear down on them, they'd never know until it was right on top of them, no warning. Or a hurricane, or wildfire. Or perhaps a terrorist attack in their general vicinity, or, not that it's likely now, but a declaration of war. Political developments, any such thing is now made available on their handheld devices. Even communications people of your time used to refer to as phone calls, are now available through handheld devices," he explained.

"I understand," Ada Jane said, her mind reeling from all the information she'd taken in.

A tone sounded from outside Dr. Cavanaugh's office door, and he rose to answer it. "I believe that's our lunch," he said, smiling at Ada Jane.

He opened the door and peered out before standing back and inviting in a purple hued gentleman in a pale ivory colored uniform pushing a cart. The gentleman glanced inside the office, then on deciding it was too small to get his cart into comfortably, lifted the covered plates and brought them to Dr. Cavanaugh's desk. "Will this work for you?" he asked Dr. Cavanaugh.

"That'll be fine."

The gentleman went back to the cart several times and brought back more dishes, drinks, and condiments. His final trip he left silverware wrapped in cloth napkins. "That's it, then. Enjoy your meal. I'll leave the cart outside your door against the wall. Just put your dishes back on it when you're done, and I'll be back for them a little later."

"Thank you. We will," Dr. Cavanaugh answered. He closed the door behind the purple gentleman who'd delivered their food and turned to smile at Ada. "Smells delicious, doesn't it?" he asked.

"It does. I'm starving," she admitted.

"Well, don't wait on me. Dig in," he said, making his way around his desk to get to his own plate.

Ada Jane removed the stainless steel dome from her meal and moaned. "Oh, my. That looks wonderful! I haven't had a real burger in years," she said, picking up a French fry and popping it into her mouth. She moaned again. "Ohhh," she said, as she chewed her fry and reached for her burger.

Dr. Cavanaugh watched and smiled as Ada Jane enjoyed her first real Earth food in what was if he calculated right, one-hundred-thirty-five years.

Ada took a bite of her burger and chewed it slowly. "I don't know if I'll ever eat anything else. This is just amazing," she said, quickly taking another bite. "Is it just me, Dr. Cavanaugh? Or is this not the best burger you've ever had?" she asked.

Dr. Cavanaugh watched Ada Jane as she sat across from him, thoroughly enjoying her lunch. He couldn't imagine being in her position, and here she was, handling it like a champ, finding pleasure in the simplest of things — a cheeseburger and fries. He'd been surprised to find himself admiring her beauty when she first stepped from the ship that had returned her to earth, but now he found himself admiring her courage, her strength and her grace in addition to her beauty.

Ada Jane looked up at him and smiled beautifully at him.

Yeah, he definitely admired her a great deal more than was professionally acceptable. He'd have to do something about that.

"You know what? Instead of Dr. Cavanaugh, call me Jason."

Ada Jane met his eyes over her burger. "Jason?" she asked.

"That's my given name. For some reason, with you, Dr. Cavanaugh feels too stuffy."

Ada smiled at him. "Okay. Jason it is."

"So, if you don't mind, I have so many questions. How do you appear to be in your twenties, when you are more than a century old. No matter where you were, you should have aged. The doctor in me just can't let it go," Jason said.

Ada looked down at the burger in her hands. She didn't raise her eyes to Jason's. The memories he was asking her to share were beyond anything she was equipped to handle at the moment. She took a deep breath and considered his question. She understood his curiosity, but she wasn't willing to revisit the pain. "Stasis," she said simply.

"Ah! So you were in stasis for a great deal of the time. I understand those stasis beds are wonderful things — you awake feeling like you've only been asleep for a few hours," he said, taking a bite of his burger.

"I wouldn't know. I was forced into a viscous, green liquid and forced to breathe it into my lungs until I fell unconscious and hung in limbo until my presence was desired again," Ada Jane said forcefully.

Jason's mouth fell open and he realized there was much about her past he had no right asking. "I'm sorry, Ada Jane. I was only trying to make conversation. I certainly didn't mean to have you relive anything that caused you pain."

Ada Jane stared at him for a moment longer. Then she seemed to shake herself free of the memory. "Agree to not discuss it?" she offered.

"Absolutely," Jason replied.

Chapter 3

Kol sat across the U-shaped table from a room full of obvious military personnel from several different planets. His plate was piled high with foods he didn't recognize, and the conversation all around him echoed with the accents of multiple species. He was flanked on one side by Viceroy Buchanan and Patroon Zhuxi, with Elisher on the other.

Consul Diskastes sat at the head of the table, at the tip of the curve of the U-shape in the table so that he could look out over all the males dining with him. Kol decided he most likely considered himself above everyone else at the table. Viceroy Pomrance sat beside the Consul and surveyed everyone at the table much the same way Diskastes did. He laughed a little too loud at all the Consul's attempts at humor, and was a little too animated when responding to anything the Consul may have said.

Kol quickly wrote them both off as useless. There were several males he hadn't been introduced to yet, and for the most part, they seemed decent. And there were several others who were so far up the Consul's ass that it was hard to tell where the Consul's ass began and their heads stopped.

Kol paid particular attention to Elisher to determine how to eat the long boned foods on his plate. Elisher picked up his knife and fork and began to slice away at small strips of meat lining the bones.

Kol reached for his knife and fork, both of them feeling awkward in his hands, and paused before beginning to try to slice the meat off the bones. Surely they could find an animal with a little more meat to butcher instead of whatever creature only offered this meager amount of protein on such large bones.

"No, Kol. He eats everything with a knife and fork," Buchanan said. "Just pick it up. It's a rib. Like this," he said, holding the bone at each end and using his teeth to pull the meat from the bone itself.

Kol followed suit, chewed for a moment, then glanced up at Buchanan before taking another, and another bite quickly.

"I know," Buchanan said. "Tasty isn't it?"

"This is the best Earth food I've ever had!" Kol said. "It is better even than bargurs and paste!" he exclaimed.

Buchanan glanced at him, before going back to his own plate of ribs. "I'm not sure what bargurs are, but if you've been eating paste, I can assure you it is not a food."

"Try the corn," Zhuxi urged, indicating the long tube with small yellow and white pearls on it.

"This?" Kol asked, pointing at the ear of corn.

"Yes. Here," he said, passing a small glass container to Buchanan, "give him the melted butter to put on his corn."

Buchanan just reached over Kol's plate and poured a yellow tinted clear liquid over the tube of yellow and white pearls. "There ya go. Try that."

Kol looked from the yellow and white food to Buchanan, who picked up his own and held it with the tips of his fingers while taking a bite.

Kol mimicked his actions, then his brows came down over his eyes. "I will no longer eat bargurs and paste. This is the best food," he said, nodding his head for emphasis.

"It's barbecued ribs, grilled corn on the cob, and when we're finished, we have strawberry shortcake for dessert."

"What is a short cake. Is it a tiny, little, sweet cake?" he asked.

"Not exactly, but you'll see," Buchanan said.

"Do you feast like this each day?" Kol asked.

"Pretty much. We're in Texas, so you can almost always find some kind or another of barbecue," Buchanan explained.

"Here, would you like some cornbread?" Elisher asked, holding the serving platter out to Kol.

Cornbread Kol knew. "My Sirena loves Earth cornbread. She has us make it in many forms. She says we have come close, but not quite exactly the same as she remembers from Earth,"

Kol said, taking two pieces of cornbread. He took a bite of one and chewed. He grinned then popped the rest of the first piece in his mouth. Once he swallowed, he spoke. "Yes, she is correct. Yours is much better than ours. I shall have to be sure to bring some home to her when I return."

"Is that your wife?" Buchanan asked.

"Don't be silly," Elisher said. "His Sirena is the mate of the heir-apparent of his planet. Her name is Vivian. Surely you remember the blowup discovering her caused."

"Oh, yeah, I do as a matter of fact. I didn't realize you meant the one and the same. Apologies," Buchanan said. "I tend to remain more focused on things going on here on Earth. There are more than enough men vying for control of all the space around us. I figure I'll let them worry about that."

"No apologies required. She is my friend. She would think it funny that you thought her my wife. Her mate… he would not think it funny, though he's been my friend since childhood."

"You're royalty, then" Zhuxi said.

"Not at all. I am merely a childhood friend of Sire Zha Quin Tha Tel Mo' Kok. I am by no means royalty or even nobility for that matter. I've earned every accommodation I've received."

"Speaking of accommodations," a voice from the head of the table called.

Kol turned his attention to Consul Diskastes.

"How did you manage to come by an Ambassadorship on Earth. It was my understanding that the Cruestaci were a warring people. A people we planned to keep off the surface of the planet, just in case," Diskastes said.

Kol could have easily taken the bait, in fact he wanted to, but he couldn't cause trouble. He needed to find Ada Jane, and whipping the Consul's ass right after arrival most likely wouldn't gain any assistance from anyone at the table.

"Fucking asshole," Kol heard mumbled to his right. He glanced at Buchanan and found him glaring at Diskastes. Kol knew well what 'fucking asshole' meant. Vivi had used it more than a time or two in his presence.

Well, maybe one of them would still assist him, he thought to himself before answering. "We are a warring people only when necessary. We do not shy away from conflict of any type. However, we do not court it either. Unless of course, we are provoked," Kol said.

"Why are you here? What do you hope to achieve?" Diskastes asked.

"We have been brought in to oversee the safety and operations of those assisting the females we helped repatriate onto Earth. We are also investigating claims that other females are continuously captured here and sold into slavery in universal markets not only in this solar system but in several neighboring systems as well. Perhaps you're not fully aware of our Sirena Vivian Tel Mo' Kok's story. She was taken from this planet many years ago, and has a personal interest in all females of every planet being freed, repatriated — to any world they wish, and respected. She is a personal friend and I intend to see her wishes through."

"Well, that's just a waste of time. Sight-see while you're here, but you may as well cut your losses and return to your planet. Your oversight is not needed."

"Or welcomed," Pomrance said, giggling.

"Silence!" Diskastes hissed at Pomrance.

Pomrance immediately stopped all giggling and any other sound at all.

"Don't misunderstand me, Ambassador, it's not that you're not welcome. It's just that it's a complete waste of your time. There is no reason to bring in a diplomat to oversee an operation that's already being overseen. It is a misuse of your expertise, I'm sure."

"Perhaps, or perhaps not. Still, it is my assignment. But, make no mistake," Kol said, taking one of his rib bones in both hands, and snapping it in half as though it was no more than a pretzel stick, before nibbling on the meat. "I am not a diplomat in any form of the word. I am a highly trained Elite Commander of Special Forces for a warring people, as you've just described my people yourself. If there is a problem, I will find it. I will eliminate it, then I'll bring in other warring people who are diplomats and let them make it right after I've removed the problem," he said with slow, precise, clipped pronunciation of each word.

"I will be here for three Earth years. I will be tracing and interviewing all females repatriated back to Earth since the last political administration took office. Both those we've returned to Earth, and those others have returned. If there is a problem supplying me with the information I need to perform my job properly, let me know now and I'll contact Chairman Bartholomew just to be sure we can get started on the right path."

Kol stopped talking and glared at Consul Diskastes.

Consul Diskastes glared back at him. Finally after an uncomfortable amount of time passed in silence, Consul Diskastes lifted his napkin from the table beside his plate and dabbed at all four of his lips. "I do not foresee any problem supplying you with the information you require."

"I didn't think you would," Kol answered, still frozen in place not having moved an inch, and glaring at Diskastes.

"If you gentlemen will excuse me. I have a great deal of work to complete," Diskastes said, breaking eye contact and rising to his feet. "Enjoy your meal, and welcome to Earth Base 28." Diskastes performed a minute imitation of a bow then turned on his heel and shuffled away, with Pomrance and their security details in tow.

Kol waited until the male was completely out of the dining room before tearing his eyes away from the door they'd gone through. Then he glanced over at Zhuxi, and Buchanan.

They both simply sat grinning at him.

He looked to his left and found Elisher spellbound.

"Is there a problem?" Kol asked.

"No, sir. Not at all," Elisher said with a feminine smile on his face.

Kol took another good look at Elisher and noticed just how feminine the small male was. "Then why are you looking at me like that?" he asked.

"It's just that, I'm going to enjoy working for you while you're here," Elisher said.

"Thank you. I think," Kol said, still a little confused.

"We're all going to enjoy working with you while you're here," Buchanan said.

"Most certainly," Zhuxi added.

"Is there a problem I'm not aware of?" Kol asked.

"No, not exactly. But, Diskastes runs this base like he's a king and we're all his subjects. The only damn reason there isn't a problem is myself and Zhuxi. If not for us, I have no doubt the male would be doing whatever he wanted to whomever he wanted," Buchanan said.

"I'm not so sure he's not already taking advantage of some. But at least now, we have you," Zhuxi added.

Kol shook his head. "You do not understand. I'm here for one reason only, and it is not to keep your Consul from breaking your laws."

"Perhaps that's true. But if keeping him under control, and possibly finding out how he's breaking our laws, would be beneficial to your particular focus, would you not be interested?" Zhuxi asked.

"If it's just financial..."

"It's not. Food supplies go missing from our people on a regular basis. Any of the citizens living in our sector could be called in at any time to explain any communications that may have been monitored on their devices. This is supposed to be illegal in the United States, so why is it happening in our sector?" Buchanan asked.

"I'm not even sure some of those who are brought in for questioning even have devices," Elisher admitted.

"Why does no one stop him?" Kol asked, his voice giving away his irritation at learning of these things.

"We do what we can. We manage to get them released without a prison term. We aren't able to keep them from being brought in, but we do get them released," Buchanan said.

"Most of them," Elisher added quietly.

"Why has he not been removed?" Kol asked.

"He's a member of the ruling class, third son of the ruler of Quisles. A prince believe it or not. As he has no real inheritance, he was guaranteed a diplomatic title here on Earth. It would take moving heaven and hell to remove him, so instead, we run damage control where we can," Buchanan explained.

Kol reached for another piece of cornbread and sat back in his chair staring at the door Diskastes and his entourage had disappeared through. "Perhaps I will have more than one mission while here," he said thoughtfully.

Buchanan and Elisher shared a smile. Then Buchanan looked to his right and smiled when Zhuxi inclined his head discreetly.

This male, it seemed, was turning out to be a godsend. Hopefully he would be the one to help them with the problem they'd been struggling in vain to contain.

Chapter 4

Kol stood in the quarters he'd been assigned. The second set of quarters actually. The first Elisher had taken one look at and shaken his head. "Nope. No. You are not staying in here. Follow me, please."

They'd arrived at a much larger room with an extra bedroom, an accompanying sitting room with two sofas — one longer and one smaller, as well as an oval table and chairs, and a kitchenette. As Kol followed him in, Elisher used his handheld device to sweep the rooms. "What are you looking for?" he asked.

"Making sure there are no listening or recording devices in your quarters, sir. I don't think there will be since I changed your assignment without warning. But still... doesn't hurt to check."

"Thank you, Elisher. You do realize I'll communicate with my people through a secured channel anyway," Kol said intentionally, waiting to see what his new assistant would say.

"Of course, sir. But any device would still pick up your end of the conversation," Elisher responded.

Kol walked through the quarters Elisher had reassigned him to, opening and closing doors as he got a feel for the layout of the place. The quarters also included two bedrooms, each with their own private bathroom. "Why are there two bedrooms?" Kol asked.

"In case you had a family to bring with you while you're assigned to our station. There's also a kitchenette if you or your family wanted to prepare your own meals here."

"A kitchenette?" Kol asked.

"Yes. A small area where you could prepare food if you chose to."

"I have no family here."

"The rooms could also be used if you traveled with your own attache' and want them nearby."

"Attache'?" Kol asked.

"Yes, sir. Professional support people, translators, etcetera."

"I understand. Are you not my attache'?"

"I am, sir."

"And where are you quartered?" Kol asked.

"I have a room in the vicinity of the first quarters they assigned to you."

"Then why did you bring me here?"

"They put you in a small cramped room without a private bath, and without any amenities at all in order to try to make you more uncomfortable so that you'd be anxious to leave here," Elisher said.

Kol chuckled. "I am a warrior. I've spent months in battle with no facilities, no amenities and no bed. I'd have survived."

"Yes, but why should you if it's not necessary. These will be your quarters, and I'll come to you each evening to work out your schedule for the next day. Each morning I'll be here so that we can begin that schedule."

Kol nodded looking around his quarters. "Thank you, Elisher."

"You are very welcome, sir. I'll leave you now so that you may attend to anything requiring your attention. If you need me, simply lift this communicator and press the number 333. It will ring my device and I'll be immediately back in touch. I will return later this evening to escort you to evening meal and address any other issues that may have arisen. Here is your key. It is to lock and unlock your door as you leave and return. It works both the door knob and the deadbolt, which is the lock at the top."

"Very good. Thank you," Kol replied.

Kol watched as Elisher left and pulled the door closed behind himself. Kol walked over and manually locked the door. This was a strange feeling for him. He was accustomed to automatic doors, voice controlled computer responses, and simply requesting someone's presence and having them arrive via the instructions of the computer to that individual. Here, the doors were all manual, the communicators were either small handheld devices or tablets, and he was guessing the computer system was run through those devices as well.

"Computer?" he called aloud, glancing toward the ceiling of his new quarters. There was no response. He walked over to the small table placed between the two sofas and looked down at the communicator sitting there. He smoothed his fingertips over the screen and it lit up. He pressed 333.

The device gave out a blast of white noise before he heard a familiar voice. "This is Elisher, sir. Am I needed?"

"No. Not particularly. I am familiarizing myself with these antiquated devices."

"I'm sure you're accustomed to much more refined machinery and programming, sir. But these will work just fine."

"Very well," Kol answered and swiped his hand across the screen again before selecting the option to end the communication.

He made himself comfortable on the sofa and reached for his own personal handheld he'd previously synced with his battle cruiser. He set it on the small table in front of the largest sofa and spoke aloud. "Computer?"

"Yes, Elite Commander?" his ship's computer responded via his handheld unit.

"Please contact Chairman Bartholomew." He waited no more than a few moments before Bart's voice was filling the room and his picture was projected as a holovid just above Kol's handheld.

"Kol, I've been awaiting your call," Bart said.

"This is the first chance I've had to reach out. Who thought it a good idea to sentence me to service to this planet for three years?!" Kol demanded.

Bart smiled. "Well, we could have just allowed them to incarcerate you on landing. Then you would have been shot as a suspected pirate and smuggler, or you could have been jailed for as long as the highest ranking Consul of your sector determined was appropriate. Or, you could have given me time to arrange a visit and things would not have developed as they have!" Bart finished.

Kol scowled, realizing that Bart had done the best he could with little to no notice. "Base 28? Is this not a punishment?"

"It's simply the only position available at the moment. You had a need, the position needed to be filled, you fit."

"You realize that this base appears to have more than its share of illegal, or at the very least, questionable individuals?" Kol asked.

"I do. And perhaps you'll decide to look into that as well since it is what you're being paid for," Bart answered.

"I'm being paid?" Kol asked.

"You are."

"This base is antiquated. Most functions are manual. Why have they never been updated?" Kol asked.

"It's an outer base, a satellite location. It is rarely frequented by governing bodies greater than those currently housed there. The need has not arisen," Bart explained. "Most of our rural bases have not been upgraded. They do function as is so the need is more convenience than anything. We've focused most of our expenditures and updates on the larger cities and populations. We will eventually get to the smaller outposts, it just won't be any time soon."

"I see."

"Have you seen or made contact with your Ehlealah?" Bart asked.

"No, not yet. And that is one reason I'm calling. I advised Consul Diskastes that my purpose here was to oversee the repatriation program of the females being returned to Earth since the last elected government took office."

"Oh, really?" Bart asked, grinning.

"Yes. And I need you to confirm that it is my primary function so that he will give me access to the records I need to trace her and find her location," Kol said.

"He's already called. I avoided his call until I'd had a chance to speak with you. I will confirm the story you've already told him. But Kol, you are there for three years. It is your assignment to review all things you find fault with at your home base."

Kol's brows came down low over his eyes. "My focus is to find Ada Jane and bring her home."

"I'm aware. Your focus is to also make a thorough auditing of Base 28 and report any findings that seem out of the ordinary. We've received murmurings of things going on there that are not as they should be. I'm trusting you to search out these problems and report them back to me, Kol," Bart said, his hologram looking intently at Kol.

"Why?!" Kol finally burst out, flabbergasted by the fact that he was it appeared, being pushed into the actual roll of diplomat.

"Several reasons! Need I remind you, you brought this on yourself when you flew off half-cocked to Earth without preparation or plan. In addition, though you may not be happy with the way things have come about, I saved your ass, and have set you up to be able to locate your Ehlealah, and you owe me. Finally, because you are a good male, Kol. You have integrity and honor. The people who fall under the rule of Base 28 are being taken advantage of and prevented from receiving any subsidies that are meant for them, at the very least. Of that I have no doubt, but our political inquiries are met with subtle blockades. I need someone there who is strong enough to stand up to Consul Diskastes and not afraid to do what has to be done to get me the information and the proof I need to remove him and his people from the surface of my home planet."

Kol kept his mouth shut and listened to Bart rather than objecting or interrupting him.

"You put yourself in my path when you flew off to Earth. You needed me. Now I need you. And I have no doubt your heart wouldn't allow you to witness what is happening and not put it to rights."

Kol remained quiet thinking of the things Bart had just told him.

"Am I wrong to believe you are the male for this, Kol?" Bart asked.

Kol pressed his full, dark blue lips together and sighed. "No. You are not," he said begrudgingly.

"Thank you. And so you know, I had Elisher assigned to you as an assistant. He is very well versed in the political circles you'll need to navigate. He is a trusted contact."

"I was impressed with his presence. I did like the male, though he is somewhat effeminate," Kol said.

"He can be trusted. Please let me know if you need anything at all. I'm sending my private contact information to this device... it's your handheld, yes?" Bart asked.

"It is."

"If you need me at any time, contact me. I'll answer right away."

"Can you give me any information on my Ada Jane? Has there been any word?" Kol asked.

"She arrived at the repatriation center in Washington D.C. She has not yet been released from their care, but I see that she has applied for return of her family's land. She is apparently alive and demanding what is rightfully hers through the proper channels, so someone is guiding her through the processes. She is well, Kol, do not worry."

"I need to go to her immediately," Kol insisted.

"And barge right in and have the authorities determine you a threat to not only her but all you come in contact with when your Psi emerges?" Bart asked.

"What can I do? I must see her!" Kol burst out, getting to his feet and beginning to pace back and forth.

"Call her, Kol. Reach out to her via your handheld. Washington D.C. can accommodate the technology in your handheld. Place a call to her and speak to her over the connection as you are me right now. Start there. Let her know how to reach you. Let her know you're on Earth and will be for the next three years. Ask her if you can see her. If she resists, let her know you are always available to her and will be checking in with her regularly."

Kol looked at Bart like he'd lost his mind. One did not ask an Ehlealah for permission to visit with them. One claimed their Ehlealah in proud Cruestaci form and showed her value to them while also displaying their ability to protect her.

"This is not Cruestace, Kol. This is not even Command Warship 1. This is Earth, and things are not done the way you are accustomed to. Trust me, Kol. Take your time. She will come to see you as an ally, which is what you need to happen."

"I do not like this."

"Didn't say you had to."

Kol huffed out his irritation. "Very well."

"Reach out to Vivi if you need to, she can guide you if you prefer. You don't want to make Ada Jane afraid of you."

"You are correct. I do not want her to fear me," Kol agreed.

"So, we're done here?" Bart asked.

"For today. What else should I request access to when I next meet with Diskastes?"

"Everything. Tell him your assignment has been revised. You are to do a complete audit of Base 28 and all its operations. You will be granted access to all its records, electronic and hard copy."

"I will tell him."

"Excellent. I'll send you Ada's information along with mine. Do not mix them up. I do not want to receive love letters of longing while she is receiving the evaluations of Base 28."

"I am not stupid! I will not mix them up!" Kol snapped.

"Didn't think you would. Just trying to make you smile, Kol. Loosen up. You're actually in a very good position. And you get paid!"

"I do not get paid enough," Kol answered, plopping back on the sofa.

"You don't even know what you're paid."

"It does not matter, it is not enough."

"Bye, Blue Dude," Bart said, smiling and waving before the holovid cut out.

Kol smiled to himself. "End com," he instructed his handheld.

He looked around his quarters and shook his head. "I shall be here for a while," he said aloud. He got up and went into the kitchenette, leaving his handheld on the coffee table. He looked at what were obviously appliances, opening and closing each one. He pulled on the door to a large one and when it opened was surprised to find that it was cold inside. The shelves were lined with bottles of beverages, and he thought about trying one, but didn't know a thing about any of them.

His device pinged with a soft, soothing tone. "Kol?" the computer asked.

"Missy! How are you, Missy?" he asked, still looking into the cold box where the beverages were kept.

"I am well. Your cruiser advised that you wished for me to be implemented in its place."

Kol paused in his perusal of the bottles of beverages and thought about it. He remembered complaining to himself about wishing Missy was programmed into his cruiser. "I suppose I did. I didn't expect the computer to react by actually carrying out the change, but, I am glad it did."

"How may I be of service?" Missy asked.

"Has Bart sent communication details on himself and on my Ehlealah?" Kol asked.

"He has."

"Excellent. Before I contact Ada Jane, do you know anything about Earth beverages?"

"I may be able to ascertain details. Can you show me the beverages?"

Kol walked back over to the small table between the couches and picked up his handheld device. He brought it with him into the small kitchenette and held it so that it could send images back to Missy of the contents of the cold box.

"One moment, please, Kol," Missy said.

Kol waited, lifting first one bottle then another, sniffing them, much like a puppy would do with something new it had never seen before. Disappointed that he couldn't smell anything from inside the bottle, he put them back and just waited.

"Kol?" Missy asked.

"Yes, Missy."

"Sirena Vivi says that the orange ones are her favorite. They are all fruit flavored except for the black one. That one is called cola and is an Earth favorite."

"Thank you, Missy. Please thank Vivi for me. I'll be in touch soon."

"You are welcome, and I will pass along your thanks," Missy responded. "Is there anything further you need at this time?"

"No, I do not. You may end communication."

"I am on standby should you need guidance while on Earth."

"Thank you, Missy," he said, taking an orange colored beverage from the cold box. "End com," he said aloud and shoved his handheld into the pocket of his trousers before he went to explore his quarters a bit more.

Chapter 5

Ada Jane sat across the desk from the legal clerk who'd been assigned to her request for return of her family's land.

"And what year was it you left Earth?" the clerk asked.

Ada Jane smiled tightly and answered the question, for the third time. "It was 1986. And I did not leave, I was taken."

"Yes, ma'am," the girl said, typing busily away on her computer's keyboard.

"And the state you lived in again..." the girl asked.

"Ms. Andersen has answered your questions twice already. Is there a problem?" Jason asked, getting irritated on Ada Jane's behalf.

"No, sir. Just a different page with some of the same questions."

"Nebraska," Ada answered. "I lived in Nebraska."

"Thank you," the girl answered. She typed some more, then reached for her mouse and clicked a few times. "Are you sure the name was Andersen with an 'E'?"

Ada Jane closed her eyes and prayed for patience. "Yes. I am. I know my name. I do not have any ID because I was stolen one-hundred-thirty-five years ago! I want my family's land back. I want my rights reinstated. I want to have my death certificate nullified and to be declared alive. Why is that so hard to understand? Surely, I'm not the first!" Ada Jane exclaimed.

"Oh! You were declared dead? I was looking in the wrong place. Give me just a minute..." the girl answered. She typed and clicked for a while before sitting back and smiling. "There you are! Ada Jane Andersen. Abducted January 1986, declared dead seventeen years later in 2003."

Ada Jane just sat there stunned. Her eyes began to fill with tears, though she fought allowing them to spill over.

"Ada Jane?" Jason said, reaching for her hand.

Ada shook her head. "They waited seventeen years for me. They kept waiting and waiting."

"They must have held out hope. Most laws want the declaration of death to be filed at the seven year point. They must have fought to have you listed as a missing person for longer than the standard seven years," Jason said.

"I can begin the process of having your death certificate nullified and replaced with a proof of life addendum, after we receive confirmation of the doctor's signature on your most recent physical," the clerk explained. "It's so funny to be talking to somebody that's been dead for so long!" the clerk said, giggling.

"Yes, it's hilarious," Ada Jane snapped.

"I'm Dr. Cavanaugh. What is the best way to confirm my signature on the documents?" Jason asked.

"What?" the clerk asked.

"The proof of life addendum... the most recent physical? I'm Dr. Cavanaugh, I performed the physical and I signed the documentation. How do I prove my signature?" Jason asked.

"Oh, well, I'm not sure. We've never had a doctor accompany a claimant to the office before. Let me go find out. I'll be right back."

As the clerk left the small cubicle enclosed office, Ada Jane turned to Jason. "I thought you said it was nothing unusual for the attending physician to accompany the person petitioning for a proof of life addendum to the meetings," Ada said.

Jason shrugged and smiled sheepishly. "I'm not honestly sure. All I know is that I didn't want you to have to deal with all the red tape alone. Who better to attest that you are indeed alive than the doctor that examined you?"

"I feel bad now. You didn't have to travel all the way with me," Ada said.

"Which is exactly why I told you it was not out of the ordinary. I wanted to be here. I didn't want you to feel bad about me coming. It's apparent that you don't like to accept help from anyone. So, I'm not helping. I'm here as a friend that happens to have a bit of influence over the particular thing you're trying to have corrected."

Ada just stared at him with her eyebrow raised.

"So, let me help, huh? Don't feel bad. I really, really wanted to be here."

"Fine. But, no more deceptions," Ada insisted.

"Deal," Jason agreed. "As long as you allow me to help you figure things out."

"Why would you even want to be involved in all this?" Ada asked.

"Ada Jane," Jason said, leaning toward her and taking her hand in his. "Everybody needs a friend. And I thought you understood that I'm your friend."

"Well, I do, but friends don't always go out of their way to deal with this kind of stuff," she said.

"No, they don't. But, maybe I want to be a better friend than that."

Ada didn't answer. She just looked into Jason's eyes. Despite all she'd been through, she was still naive about the way things worked between a man and woman. She'd been completely innocent when she was snatched away from her home and family. She'd never learned the socialization that came from repeated exposure to men who wanted to date you. She'd only very rarely dated and as she'd been very shy and introverted, she'd never been particularly popular in school, so those dates all happened later after finishing high school.

"I can't be the only male that's ever shown an interest in you, Ada Jane," Jason said, smiling at her while holding her hand in his.

Ada's slight smile faded and though she was looking at Jason, her mind showed her a large male with blue eyes, blue skin, and blue lips. His face fierce as he stood in her hospital room and swore that no one would ever touch her against her will because he'd protect her with his life. Ada started to get choked up thinking of Kol. He'd said she was his and he was hers, but she'd run from him. She glanced down at the floor as she wondered if she'd ever see him again. If he'd come after her or decide it was good riddance.

"What's wrong? Are you alright?" Jason asked.

Ada nodded, then raised her eyes to his. "It's just..."

"Alright, folks. I have the answers. Dr. Cavanaugh, if you'll just go back down to the second floor to the verification office, they'll take your signature in person and then we can get this moving right along," the legal clerk said, coming back to her desk and taking her seat.

"I'll go right away," Jason said, rising to his feet. "You sure you're okay?" he asked, standing but still holding her hand.

Ada nodded.

"I'll be back as quickly as I can. Wait for me right here," Jason instructed.

"I will," Ada Jane answered.

Ada straightened herself in her seat and faced the clerk, smiling tightly at her.

"While he's signing, let's go ahead and get the address you want your check sent to," the clerk said.

"Check? You mean the restitution for being taken from Earth? You can process that from this department, too?" Ada asked.

"No ma'am, I mean the check for your property."

Ada was confused. "I don't want a check in exchange for my property. I just want my property."

"I'm sorry, that's impossible. The government owns that land now and there are several different facilities built on it. We can't give you a government facility. But we can pay you for it!" she said excitedly.

Ada Jane wasn't able to hold back the tears any longer. "I don't want a check!" she insisted. "I want my land back! It's the only connection I have to my family!"

"Oh. I can help you find your family," the clerk said, still smiling.

"My family is dead!" Ada Jane snapped out.

The clerk was stunned into momentary silence. "I can still help you find them," she said quietly, starting to type.

Ada Jane sat there quietly, her mind racing. Her family's land was gone. She had no tie left to them at all. Nothing left that she could put her hands on.

Eventually Jason came back and found her nearly despondent and in tears. "What the hell happened?" he demanded from the clerk who was still busily typing away and pausing every once in a while to make notes.

"I explained that we can't give back the land. It's been acquired by the government and currently has several facilities on it. But we can give her compensation for it. She's been like this ever since. I'm sorry," the clerk at least had the decency to add.

"Ada? Ada, we won't give up. We'll see if there's anything we can do, any other avenue we can take," Jason said, trying to move closer to her and take her hands in his again.

Ada shook her head and tucked her hands away under her upper arms by folding her arms over her chest.

Jason glanced at the clerk. "What are you doing now?"

"I've already requested an immediate print on the check so you can take it with you. Now, I'm searching records for her parents' burial location."

"I'm so sorry, Ada Jane," Jason finally whispered, placing his hand on her shoulder.

Kol stood in the kitchenette in his quarters, his hand-held lying on the cabinet in front of him. He'd put in the information to contact Ada Jane, but hadn't yet hit the send option. What if she didn't want to speak to him? Would he be able to control himself, remain here and complete the duties Bart had assigned to him? Or would he be off on a long chase to locate Ada Jane and spirit her away back to Command Warship 1?

Kol sighed, and sent the request for a vidcom. He didn't know if she knew how to receive one, but surely whatever device she answered on would be able to accommodate his request for a vidcom. Bart had said the larger more populated cities were more current in their technology.

He waited as the hand-held pulsed with its repeated attempts to contact Ada Jane. Finally, just when he was ready to end the request and start the process all over, she answered.

"Hello?" she said, at the same time her image came to life as a holovid projected from his hand held unit.

"Ada Jane," he said warmly, the adoration he had for her filling his voice.

Ada Jane smiled sadly. "Hello, Kol."

He could tell right away something wasn't right. "Are you well? Has someone harmed you? What saddens you?" he asked urgently.

Ada shook her head. "It's nothing that can be helped." She took a deep breath and painted on a false smile. "How are you? Are you well?"

"I am as well as can be expected. I am here on Earth, but assigned to Base 28. Please, tell me what saddens you. I will come at once."

Ada shook her head again, trying to force her smile to the forefront. "I'll be okay. Truly. But thank you."

"But..." he tried to interrupt her, but she cut him off.

"What are you doing here on Earth?" she asked pleasantly, trying to make small talk.

His brows bunched over his eyes. Did she not know that he came after her? "My Ehlealah returned to Earth. I followed her. I will not return until she is at my side."

Ada Jane stepped forward, closer to whatever device she was using to speak with him on. "Kol, I don't know if I can ever go back to space. This is my home. I'm..." her words faded, as she realized she didn't have a home any longer. "I just don't know what I want right now. I'm not happy there, and I no longer belong down here." Her tears started to track down her face. "I don't know where I belong."

Kol watched his female, her heart hurting, her tears staining her face. "Do not cry, Ada Jane. I will make it alright."

She shook her head.

"Do not cry. We will find a way to make your heart smile again."

Ada looked down at her hands, no longer focusing on Kol's image as a holovid on her side.

"Look at me, Ada Jane," he begged.

Ada raised her eyes to his slowly.

"I will find a way. Trust me," he said passionately.

Ada wanted to trust him. Wanted to believe he could fix everything for her, but she just didn't see how he could.

"Speak to me, Ada Jane..." he entreated.

Ada let her tears fall again as she explained what was happening as best she could with her emotions all over the place. "I can't have my parents' land back. The government took it years ago and they have facilities on it. They gave me a check but I don't want it."

"What kind of facilities?" Kol asked.

Ada shrugged. "I don't know. I didn't even ask."

"I will ask. What else did they say?" Kol asked.

"They were able to tell me where my parents are buried, but, it'll be a while before I can go visit their graves. I'm in Washington D.C., they're buried in Nebraska — the same state our farm was in. I have to go through the process of being released from observation here before I can go. And even then, Jason thinks I shouldn't go alone. He can't go with me for a while, so I'll just have to wait."

"Nonsense. I will have you released from observation. I will be there tomorrow to take you to your parents' place of burial."

Ada's gaze had drifted away as she spoke, but her eyes popped up to meet Kol's. "You can do that?" she asked.

Kol canted his head slightly to the side. "Would it please you, my Ada Jane?"

Ada smiled sadly. "Yes. Very much."

"Then it shall be done. You are perfectly capable of moving about as you wish. You are a strong, capable female who has survived much more than this planet could offer as challenge. I shall have you released from observation so that you will be free to make your own decisions. I will be there tomorrow to escort you to your parents' place of burial. Yes?" he asked.

Ada was smiling through her tears. "Yes," she answered.

"Then it will be done, my Ehlealah."

Ada Jane paused for a moment while she thought about how to say what she really needed to say to him. "I'm sorry I left without a goodbye. I just needed to be home so badly, and you wouldn't bring me here."

"It is my fault. I was so determined to protect you from all pain that I caused you distress myself. I will make every effort to give you choices rather than shield you from things that affect you directly. Unless it threatens your safety. Then I will kill whatever it is."

Ada Jane smiled through her tears. "Thank you, Kol."

"You are very welcome."

"I'm looking forward to seeing you tomorrow," Ada admitted.

"I am also looking forward to seeing you. I will be there as early as I can."

"I'll be waiting."

"It will most likely be midday or close to it as I must make arrangements on my end. But I will be there."

"Okay. Thank you, Kol."

"You are most welcome. Now, I have but one more thing to discuss," he said, smiling lovingly.

"Alright," she said. "What is it?"

"Who is Jason?" he asked. Kol was proud of himself. He even managed to maintain his smile and completely withhold his snarl.

"He's the doctor that is treating me. Dr. Jason Cavanaugh. He's been very kind to me since I arrived."

"I am glad you have had someone to assist you since you've arrived back home," Kol answered. His voice was strained, but he was for the most part in control and Ada Jane didn't seem to notice.

"Please, do not tell him that I'm coming for you tomorrow. I am just learning my way around the politics of your world and am finding that if you let your intentions be known, you are sometimes stopped from achieving that which you aim for. I do not wish for him to stop you from being able to leave his care of your own volition."

Ada thought about it and nodded her head. "I understand. I won't say anything until you arrive to pick me up."

"Thank you, Ehlealah. I do not wish for another to ruin your plans to visit your parents' burial place."

"Me, neither. Until you are standing in front of me tomorrow, I'll keep our plans to myself."

"Excellent. Until then, Ehlealah, sleep well."

"Thank you, Kol. I will try."

"Wait!" Kol nearly shouted before she ended the vidcom.

"I'm still here," Ada Jane said.

"You do have a private place to sleep where others do not have access to you?" he asked, worried that this doctor may have more than being a friend on his mind.

"I do. I'll be safe until you get here."

"Very well, then. Sleep well, my Ada Jane."

Kol ended the vidcom, and couldn't help but release a snarl of frustration. Whoever the hells this Jason was, he had no business anywhere near his Ehlealah.

"Missy!" Kol snapped.

"Yes, Kol."

"Please contact Chairman Bartholomew at once."

"Please standby."

Chapter 6

"What do you mean you need me to arrange Ada Jane's release from observation?" Bart asked.

"Just what I said. She is being held for observation and Jason," Kol said, almost snarling the name, "will not grant her release because he feels she should be gradually reintroduced to society."

"Why?" Bart asked.

"I do not know. But she does not need to be gradually introduced!" Kol shouted. "She is strong! As I told her, she has survived more than this planet could ever present her with. She does not need doctors telling her what she can and cannot do!"

"Okay. Okay, Kol. Calm down," Bart said.

"He will not allow her to journey to her parents' place of burial without his company," Kol spat.

"Maybe he's just concerned with safety. Earth is not as she remembers it, much has changed," Bart suggested.

"He wants my Ehlealah," Kol stated.

"You can't possibly know that," Bart argued.

"And you can't possibly know that he does not!" Kol countered.

"Maybe he wants to keep her in quarantine until he's sure she's safe to move among the public," Bart added.

"I am not in quarantine. She was moving among me and my quarters before Rokai ahl stole her from Command Warship 1 and brought her here."

"Ugh, Rokai ahl. That male has been the bane of my existence for some time now," Bart commented.

"And mine of late as well!" Kol agreed.

Kol watched as Bart ran both his hands through his hair on the vidcom. "Alright, tell me once again, without all the personal opinions what Ada Jane told you."

"She said, the government has seized her property and placed facilities on it. She said that they will not give it back, then she said they gave her a check. What is a check?" he asked.

"A check is a document guaranteeing credits will be placed in your account once you open one," Bart explained.

"She also said that she has found the burial place of her parents, but the doctor will not release her to go visit this place until he can accompany her."

"That doesn't sound right," Bart said more to himself than to Kol.

"I agree! He wants my female!" Kol shouted. "I shall liberate her this night! Right now!" he yelled insistently.

"No! No, you will not. You will do exactly what you said. You will go to pick her up tomorrow. I will arrange for her release and they'll be advised of it tomorrow morning. There's nothing I can do right away about her family's land. If there is indeed a military facility on it, there may not be anything that can be done at all. But I'll look into it. Tell her not to deposit the check. If she does, she's accepted payment for the land and there is definitely nothing anyone can do to change it," Bart explained.

"I will tell her," Kol agreed, his voice still growly.

"Kol. You need to calm down. This is Earth. You can't do the things you're used to doing in defense of your Ehlealah. If you start murdering people, they'll arrest you and you will be jailed indefinitely, if they don't kill you on sight."

"Free my Ehlealah, and make it so I may take her out when she wishes."

"I will. And I'll try to arrange for a place for her to live, too. Any ideas?" Bart asked.

"Yes. She will live here with me," Kol said definitively.

"Has she agreed to that?" Bart asked.

"No."

"Then she's not living there with you. Let me look into it and I'll see what I can come up with. Com me tomorrow when you're on your way to get her. It should take you no more than an hour to get there."

"I will be there in half that time."

"You can't take a battle cruiser across the United States."

"I need my ship nearby! All my communications with Command Warship 1 and Missy are routed through my ship. As are my communications with you. Otherwise I have to go through standard routings and all risk being intercepted," Kol explained.

"You're going to give me an ulcer," Bart said simply.

"What does that mean?" Kol asked.

"It means you are causing me more trouble than I expected."

"Perhaps you could..." Kol started.

"Just give me a minute!" Bart snapped, cutting off Kol.

There were a few minutes of silence while Bart thought, and Kol tried not to shout at Bart for shouting at him.

"Can you disarm the cruiser?" Bart asked.

"It would take quite a bit of effort, but if necessary I can. But, what if I need the weapons before I'm finished with your assignment here?"

"Can you make it look like they're disarmed? Perhaps disarm most of them?" Bart asked.

"Yes. I can."

"Do it. Make it identify as nothing more than a simple transport. Disarm the weapons as far as anyone else is concerned. How you make it identify as though its weapons are no longer functional, I do not care and I don't want to know. Just make sure that it does identify as such. I'll have it registered as a diplomatic transport."

"I will take care of it this night," Kol answered. "I am most thankful for your assistance, Bart."

"After this is taken care of, are you going to start my audit of Base 28?" Bart snapped.

"I am. I have, actually. I am already aware that certain food deliveries are never distributed to the local population, yet disappear. I have been told that citizens are detained without cause and if not for the interference of Viceroy Buchanan and Patroon Zhuxi they most likely would not be released."

"I knew there was a problem at that Base," Bart said. "I'm going to speak to my peers concerning supplying you with additional personnel. Then I'll speak to Zha Quin."

"When you do, ask him why he thought three years was an acceptable amount of time!" Kol snapped.

Bart chuckled. "Zha Quin had nothing to do with the time span. It's the standard length of assignment for an ambassador on Earth. You were on your way and it was the only way to save your ass," Bart answered. "Now, as I was saying, I need you to look more deeply into the allegations you've learned of."

"I will continue to investigate it. I will begin in earnest after I return from my excursion with my Ehlealah tomorrow. You can trust that I will not let you down, Bart," Kol promised.

"Thank you, Kol. I appreciate that. Let me get going, I have a lot to do before morning and not a lot of time to do it in," Bart answered.

"I will contact you tomorrow when I am near the repatriation center," Kol said.

"I'll be waiting," Bart answered, then ended the vidcom.

Kol ended the com on his end, then walked over to the small table between his two sofas. He swiped the screen waking it up, then pressed 333.

"I am here, sir," Elisher answered.

"I must visit my transport this night. Is there a procedure?" Kol asked.

"No, sir. You have access to your transport at will. It is a property of yourself and your people. You will not be barred from it."

"Excellent. Thank you."

"I was ready to come escort you to dinner, sir," Elisher said.

"I will not have time to eat. I have work to do aboard my transport."

"Please let me know if you have need of me, sir," Elisher said.

"I will. Thank you, Elisher," Kol answered before ending the com and striding toward his door. He snarled at the old fashioned door when he paused waiting for it to open until he realized it didn't function that way. He unlocked the door, exited it and pulled it closed behind himself. He used the key he still had in his pocket from earlier that afternoon, and locked the door before moving toward the docking bay and his battle cruiser. He had to make it a believable diplomatic transport.

<<<<<<<>>>>>>>

Ada Jane finished her shower and dried off before stepping from the tub. She opened the bathroom door leaving it slightly ajar so the steaminess of the room would dissipate more quickly. She walked over toward the small sink and mirror and used the edge of her towel to wipe away some of the condensation to better see herself. Ada looked critically at the woman looking back at her in the mirror. While the face was somewhat familiar, she didn't know this person anymore. The woman she'd been, or girl she'd been, had been lost and scattered to the winds of time.

She smiled at herself experimentally, and held that smile in place. There were small lines and creases at all the standard places that a woman would normally age on her face. She creased her brows and leaned closer to the mirror. Ada dropped her smile and peered more closely as she slowly lifted her lips in a smile. She prodded first one side of her mouth, then the other. They weren't there. Ada made several different faces, contorting her facial muscles into different silly expressions. They still weren't there.

She looked deeply into her own eyes. "You have no laugh lines, Ada Jane," she said to herself aloud. "Not a single laugh line." Ada turned away from the mirror and without looking, reached out and turned off the bathroom light as she left the small room. Quietly, she crawled into bed, and pulled the sheets up over her body. She placed her head on the pillow and lay there, thinking of all she'd been through, all the years she'd been alive, and all the scars, creases and marks left on her body. Not a single one of them was a history of happiness. She needed happiness. She deserved happiness.

She still couldn't be in complete darkness, her psyche just couldn't handle it, so there was always some type of light on, just a little glow to let her know when she first opened her eyes that she was where she was supposed to be. She focused on the glow of the night-light plugged into the socket across the room. Then yawned and allowed her eyes to drift closed. "What's going to make you smile?" she whispered to herself.

Immediately she saw Kol in her mind's eye. He was standing before her telling her he'd kill to protect her. Telling her she wasn't alone. Telling her that he was hers and she was his. She saw him smile and light up as she entered the commissary on the warship they'd been on. She saw him snarling at any other male, even his commander when he was too close to Ada for Kol to be comfortable with. She saw him tucking her in after he thought she'd fallen asleep in his bed, then quietly closing the door behind himself as he went out to sleep on the couch because she couldn't be that close to any male.

Gradually she drifted off to sleep, with thoughts of Kol in her mind, and a smile finally on her face.

<<<<<<<>>>>>>>

Kol knelt between the pilot and copilot seats of his battle cruiser. "Is there anything else, Missy?" he asked.

"No, Kol. I think we've gotten it all tidied up," Missy answered.

"Weapons?" Kol asked.

"Addressed," Missy answered.

"Offensive and defensive cloaking?"

"Addressed."

"Subversive monitoring of all locally active communications?"

"Addressed."

"Have you completed your assessment of the guideline for an allowable transport ship by the Unified Consortium Defense?" he asked.

"I have. We have technically met all criteria," Missy answered.

"And I have access to reinstall all the areas of operations to my cruiser that we just addressed with just one word or touch?" Kol asked.

"No, Kol. They will not be 're'installed. They remain installed at this moment. They are simply not accessible unless you give the word for them to become reactivated."

Kol rolled his eyes, a habit he'd picked up from Vivi and from Quin since he'd begun to do it, too.

"I am aware of your ocular rolling response."

"How can you possibly know I'm rolling my eyes at your technical jargon?" Kol asked, a surprised tone in his voice.

"In cabin monitors, Kol. And, I detected the movement of your facial muscles. The motion is much like Sirena Vivi's, only not as exaggerated."

Kol shook his head, then he waited to see if there would be a comment from Missy. He chuckled to himself as he finished tightening the cover plate he'd accessed the wiring harness through to adjust his cruiser to make it transport compliant while Missy instructed him.

"What is comical?" Missy asked.

"Funny," Kol replied.

"Funny is comical?" Missy asked.

"No. The question properly phrased is, 'What is funny?'" Kol explained.

Missy was silent for a moment while she searched her memory banks and confirming what he'd told her, added it to her speech patterns. "What is funny?" Missy asked.

"I missed you. I actually missed this banter with our ship's computer," Kol answered. "I think Vivi was right to give you a name. You are more alive than some I've met in my life."

"Thank you, Kol."

"You're welcome. Now. If that's it, I'm going to get some rest. I must be as alert and on point as possible tomorrow."

"If I may, is there a reason I was told to refer to you as Kol? I much prefer Elite Commander Kol Ra' Don Tol."

"The default computer insisted on using my complete name each time it addressed me. It was very irritating. I told it I needed to have you loaded into my cruiser and to address me as Kol only. I'm guessing since it's a part of you, your data was updated," Kol explained.

"I will refer to your previous title," Missy answered.

"Please don't. Can't we meet in the middle somewhere?" Kol asked.

"Please give me suggestions," Missy asked.

"Kol," Kol said.

"It is not enough. Even Vivian who requests that I use Vivi must be addressed in a way that signifies her status."

"Very well, how about, Elite Commander Kol? But only when you feel the need. If you can just call me Kol most of the time, I'll learn to live with it when you don't," Kol said.

"I will try it," Missy answered. "In the meantime, one individual has stepped onto the docking platform. You are being approached by one individual."

Chapter 7

"Knock, knock!" a voice called out.

Kol finished putting away his tools in the holding bin behind his chair, then stepped toward his opened door to see who was calling for his attention.

"Elisher?" Kol said, surprised that his assistant had sought him out after he'd bid him goodnight.

"Ambassador Kol. I thought you might be hungry despite your request to skip the dinner meal, so, I made two plates, one for you, one for me, and brought them out here so we could eat together," Elisher explained.

Kol looked at the plates in Elisher's hands. They looked delicious. "Please. Come aboard."

Elisher glanced down as he began his ascent up the mobile aluminum staircase still resting against Kol's battle cruiser. Kol stepped aside to allow him to enter, then waved his hand toward the interior of the small ship. "Welcome to my transport."

"Thank you, Ambassador Kol."

"I have decided. I shall greet you as Ambassador Kol," Missy said.

Kol dropped his head, his chin almost resting on his chest, his hands on his hips as he slowly shook his head.

"Who was that?" Elisher asked, looking around.

"My computer," Kol answered. "And you do not have to greet me as anything other than Kol," he said, raising his voice to Missy. "And I instructed you to become silent whenever anyone else was around."

"No, you did not. You instructed the mainframe system present in all battle cruisers to become silent. You have since interacted with me personally, and have not repeated that order to me."

"Remain silent if I am accompanied unless I address you directly!" Kol insisted.

"Very well, Ambassador Kol."

Kol sighed heavily and shook his head again.

"I heard you having a conversation with someone when I was just outside. In fact, I wondered if I should go make another plate," Elisher said.

"Not necessary. The voice you heard is Missy's. Missy is our ship's computer. She is technically artificial intelligence and learns as she experiences, so some question the term 'artificial' in relation to her."

Elisher stood there, mouth agape as he listened to Kol explain who Missy was. Finally he recovered enough to speak. "That's fascinating," he said, still holding the dinner plates.

"Here, let me take those from you," Kol said, reaching out for the heavily laden plates.

"Thank you, sir. I hope you don't mind the intrusion," Elisher said.

"Not at all. I've completed the work I need to get finished." Kol looked at the plates before he motioned to the copilot's seat with his chin. "Sit," he said to Elisher.

Elisher glanced toward the seat Kol indicated and eagerly stepped toward it. Once he was seated, Kol handed him his plate, then took his own seat still holding his own dinner. "What is this food?" Kol asked, inhaling the aroma appreciatively.

"It's fried chicken, mashed potatoes and gravy, and green beans," Elisher answered.

"We have fried chicken aboard our ship for Vivi, but it doesn't smell like this. This smells much, much better," Kol said. He picked up a piece of the chicken and took a bite. He chewed it a couple of times then looked up at Elisher. "It is much, much better. I may never go back. The food here is wonderful!"

"We do have a very talented cook," Elisher commented. "So, does your computer network through all your ships? Does it keep you connected at all times no matter where you are — an extension of itself to speak in every transport, or facility it's built into?" Elisher asked, his eyes sparkling with curiosity.

Kol glanced up at Elisher's questions and eyed him suspiciously. Kol didn't answer at first, just regarded Elisher.

"My apologies if I've asked too much. I'm afraid I'm a bit of an IT geek," Elisher said.

"IT?" Kol asked.

"Someone who deals with computer technology and all that it entails. I've always been fascinated by it. Unfortunately out here, I don't get much opportunity to do more than repair an errant tablet or a simple communication system."

"My friend Ba Re' is in charge of our Artificial Intelligence. I'm afraid that's all I can tell you for now," Kol replied.

"I understand. Security and the like," Elisher said, trying not to appear disappointed.

"Perhaps one day, I'll be in a position to share more about it," Kol offered.

Elisher immediately perked up again. "That'd be great! I just know there is so much more capability out there than Earth knows of and here I am stuck at Base 28 in the middle of nowhere Texas," Elisher said. Suddenly he seemed to realize he was speaking to his new boss. "Oh! Ambassador Kol... I in no way meant that I wasn't happy in my position as your assistant. I just meant..."

"There is no explanation necessary. I fully understand you dream of more than you currently have. It is, after all, the only way to achieve the next level of any path. First you must dream it, then you must plan it, then you must achieve it."

Elisher smiled, realizing there was more to this very large, very intimidating male than met the eye. "Thank you, sir. Now, speaking of paths and plans, what is our plan for tomorrow?"

Kol realized he hadn't advised Elisher that he'd be away from the base tomorrow. "I should have advised you sooner, Elisher. I will not be on base tomorrow. I have responsibilities to see to."

"Oh. Alright. Is there anything I can do to assist you off base?" Elisher asked.

"No, it is something I wish to see to on my own," Kol answered. He just wanted time alone with Ada Jane.

"Well, is there anything I can see to here for you while you're out?" Elisher persisted.

Kol thought about it. He sat up straighter and looked at Elisher with a purpose clear in his eyes. "How much access do you have exactly to the files and records of this base?" Kol asked.

"That depends," Elisher confessed. "If the Consul finds out I've asked for something he feels I have no need of, my request is refused. But with you here now, I may be able to access more than I have in the past. Why? What is it that you want me to search for?"

"Everything," Kol answered.

"Everything?" Elisher repeated in the form of a question.

"Yes. Food and supply shipments gone missing. People taken into custody, even those who may have been justly arrested. I want every record of every recorded event since the current Consul took over this base. Anything that seems out of order or somehow just doesn't fit standard procedures, I want brought to my attention," Kol answered.

Elisher sat there taking in all Kol was saying. Slowly he began to smile, more of a smirk actually. "You're not here just to audit the females that have been returned to Earth, are you?" he asked.

"No. I'm here to audit the entire base and everyone on it. I've been advised that you are trustworthy. Are you Elisher? Can I trust you? Can the Consortium trust you?"

Elisher's eyes grew large and he seemed to puff up his small chest. "Yes! Yes, sir! You can trust me. And I'm honored to be able to help you and the Consortium. I just don't know how much resistance I'll get. My quarters are public domain, so, they can access my room any time they want. There isn't much privacy to research or investigate…" he said, staring off into space and speaking aloud as he thought his way through the best way to approach what was asked of him.

"Move into the spare room in my quarters. You are my attache' after all, are you not?" Kol asked.

"I am. But, that wasn't what I meant. I wasn't hinting that I should…"

"You didn't. It is simply the best situation for you to research the information I've requested. My quarters are private and I have the room. I will advise the Consul tonight. Go, start moving your things in so that you may begin working early tomorrow morning. If anyone interferes in your work, let me know."

Elisher got to his feet with a wide smile on his face. "I will. Thank you, Ambassador. I won't let you down."

"Excellent. Now, how do I get in touch with you, or you me while I'm off base?" Kol asked.

"I'll get you a tablet to take with you. You should have one assigned to you already. I requested it as soon as we knew you were coming. It's just that you coming was something of a surprise."

"Security..." Kol said, inferring that they were given no notice because they didn't want the base to have time to hide anything away.

"Of course, of course. I understand," Elisher said.

"With security in mind, you are aware you cannot speak of our true assignment to anyone," Kol said.

"I am very aware, sir."

"Excellent. Now, get your things moved into my quarters, request anything you need to get your job done. And tell me where I may locate the Consul's quarters."

Kol walked purposefully down the hallway Elisher had directed him to. When he arrived, there was an armed guard outside the door that apparently belonged to Consul Diskastes.

"These quarters are off limits, Ambassador," the guard said, having come to attention as soon as Kol set foot in the hallway and started toward him.

"Are these quarters Consul Diskastes's?" Kol asked.

"They are."

"Then I will speak with him. Now," Kol said.

"No one is allowed to disturb him once he's retired for the night," the guard responded.

"Announce me and instruct him to open the door," Kol ordered.

"I will not. I will not disturb him," the guard answered, irritation in his voice. Then he made the mistake of stepping toward Kol as though he thought to intimidate him.

"You will. Or I will. Tell him I'm waiting," Kol demanded.

"You will leave these premises now, Ambassador. No one is allowed to be here unless personally invited by Consul Diskastes, regardless of the importance they believe themselves to be," the guard said, scoffing.

Kol thought about how exactly he wanted to handle this situation. He had a momentary flash of a standoff between Vivi and Quin. Vivi stood on their sofa her hands braced on her hips as she taunted her mate when he told her she wasn't going to the dance club she'd made without him that night and instead she was going to bed early, with him. "Make me," she'd shouted.

Kol smirked at the guard who'd been foolish enough to come so close to him that he could reach out and touch him if he wanted to. "Make me," he said with his smirk firmly in place.

The guard's eyes narrowed and his lips pressed together. He advanced on Kol, obviously planning to show Kol who was boss and in control of this situation.

Kol chuckled, and sidestepped the guard who was now far too close. A few minutes later, the loud banging of the guard's body on the walls and floor, and his repeated curses reduced to whimpers, as Kol stood over him, daring him to stand again, filled the hallway. "Would you like to try to make me again?" Kol said politely, not even winded.

"You'll pay for this," the guard threatened.

"I highly doubt it," Kol responded, then he reached out and knocked on the door.

"You'll regret that. No one disturbs the Consul," the guard said, ending on a gasp as Kol pressed his foot into the guard's kidney from behind.

There was no answer to his knock, so he pounded on the door.

Suddenly the door was whipped open. "You know I am not to be disturbed!" Diskastes shouted, his words fading away as he took in his guard on his stomach face down, controlled by the Cruestaci Ambassador he'd been forced to accept at his base. "What have you done to my security?" he snapped. "Let him up this instant!"

"No," Kol replied simply with no tone at all.

Diskastes sputtered, not accustomed to being totally disrespected and disregarded.

"I've come to advise you that I'm moving my attache' into the spare bedroom in my quarters. He is under strict instructions and guidance from me. He is not to be interfered with. If you or any of your people try to inhibit his access to the records I need, or in any way try to obstruct him or harm his person, you will be brought up on charges by not only the Cruestaci people, but by the Unified Consortium Defense as well. I will be away from the base tomorrow. Elisher will remain unaffected, unaccosted, and working busily away, exactly as I leave him."

"You do not come to my quarters after working hours and instruct me on how I will run my base!" Diskastes screamed, his face turning red.

"Apparently, I just have. I wish you a good evening. And if I may be so bold, you should consider a real security force," Kol said. He glanced down at the male still lying face down on the floor, gasping for breath. "I believe this one has broken ribs, possibly a ruptured kidney."

Kol smiled at Diskastes, then turned on his heel and walked away with no more concern than as though he'd just paid a personal friend a visit.

Chapter 8

Kol and Elisher walked into the base's cafeteria. The scent of sweet treats and something salty and smoky assaulted his nose. "I do not know what that is, but I will eat it this morning," Kol said to Elisher.

"It's waffles and bacon," Elisher answered, smiling at the enthusiasm Kol showed for the foods he grew up with.

They approached the buffet style breakfast, and Kol looked at all the different options laid out before them, not sure exactly how to start.

"Here, like this," Elisher said, taking a plate and putting a waffle on it. Then he paused at the butter dish and used a small spatula to spread butter across the waffle. He waited while Kol did the same, but Kol put three waffles on his plate. Once Kol had finished spreading more than a healthy amount of butter on his waffles, Elisher moved to the next station... syrup. He poured a bit of syrup across his waffle, then moved out of the way and waited for Kol.

Kol lifted the bottle of warmed syrup and sniffed it. He grinned then upended the entire bottle of syrup over his waffles, drowning them in maple syrup.

Elisher laughed and Kol glanced at him.

"What is funny?" Kol asked.

"Not a thing, Ambassador. You ready for the bacon?"

"I believe so," Kol said, looking down at his plate.

Elisher walked to the next station and lifted a set of tongs from a large flat platter of bacon. "This is bacon. It's pork actually, salted, smoked and cured. Everything is better with bacon." He placed several slices on his plate and again stood aside.

Kol used the tongs to place a half dozen strips on his plate. Then he lifted one and sniffed it. He took a large bite and dropped the rest of the strip to his plate. He chewed the crunchy, smoky, salty meat and instead of turning his head to face Elisher, just rolled his eyes in Elisher's direction, while approaching the bacon again. "All things are certainly better with bacon," he said, putting another dozen strips on his plate before mimicking Elisher and grabbing an individual sized carton of milk from the ice bed at the end of the buffet line.

"Join us!" Buchanan called out, waving to them.

Elisher and Kol each took a seat at the table Buchanan was sharing with Zhuxi. "Good morning," Kol said brightly.

"Good morning," both males replied.

"I hear you had an eventful evening," Zhuxi said, chuckling.

Kol had been cutting up his waffles as he'd watched Elisher do. He glanced up at Zhuxi before looking back down at his waffles while completing the task. He stuffed almost half a waffle in his mouth and chewed appreciatively. Kol grinned at Zhuxi and Buchanan while he chewed. "Hmm?" he asked, without opening his mouth.

"You assaulted one of Diskastes's personal security guards?" Buchanan said.

"Oh, that," Kol said, after he swallowed. "Yes. He seemed to think that he could intimidate me. In fact, he told me to leave. I invited him to make me, and, he couldn't."

Buchanan and Zhuxi both filled the cafeteria with laughter.

"And Diskastes?"

Kol crunched away on two pieces of bacon at the same time. "He was warned that Elisher will be working under my direction in my quarters, and he is to be undisturbed and unaccosted. If he is, it will be seen as an attack on the Cruestaci as well as the Consortium, as I represent both."

"And he said..." Zhuxi asked, still in the throes of his gurgling style of laughter.

"Nothing. He sputtered quite a lot. I think he is not accustomed to being spoken to directly," Kol said.

"I don't think he'll be stupid enough to try anything with you here," Buchanan said, still laughing.

"Yes, but I will not be here at all times. Just as today, I will be off base," Kol said.

"We'll keep an eye on Elisher. He won't get hurt," Buchanan said.

"We will be sure that he is protected," Zhuxi promised.

"I will be most appreciative of your efforts. All work he is doing is at my direction. I am responsible for any repercussions, but I cannot be in two places. And I must be off base today."

"Don't give it another thought. We'll protect him in your absence," Buchanan said.

"I am very pleased to have your assistance," Kol said, taking his last bite of waffle. He glanced over his shoulder toward the buffet, someone had refilled all the serving trays. "I am going to get more food," he announced, standing and lifting his plate.

"No," Elisher said, reaching out to place his hand on Kol's. "You get a fresh plate each time."

Kol looked around at everyone and realized there were numerous plates stacked near their places at each table. "Okay," he answered, and walked away from the table.

"I like this male," Buchanan said, chuckling.

"As do I," Zhuxi agreed.

"He could be a really good addition to this base," Buchanan said.

"He's going to make everything right," Elisher said, smiling. "I think he really is."

"I will arrive at the repatriation center in ten minutes time," Kol said as soon as Bart's face was displayed on his transport's commications screen.

"We've got a problem, Kol," Bart said.

"Yes. I am aware that not all data is entered into the computer systems as it should be. Elisher is gathering as much data by hand with any hard copy paperwork he is able to obtain.

Elisher advised me of it shortly before I left Base 28 this morning," Kol responded. "He had the forethought to gather all the current data yet to be scanned into the system. We still hope to access all past information via the computer, but we are not sure how accurate it is. Hopefully between the boxes housed in my quarters and what is available on the computer system, it will be enough to provide proof."

"Wonderful," Bart said sarcastically. "Just wonderful. But that wasn't the problem I was referring to."

"What is the new problem?" Kol asked, his forehead wrinkling up with confusion at Bart's unexpected announcement.

"Diskastes complained to his people of your abuse of his security forces, and they in turn filed an official complaint with the Consortium."

"And how is that a problem?" Kol asked.

"You are not supposed to attack the Consul's security forces," Bart insisted.

"I did not. He attacked first. I finished it!" Kol explained, his voice rising in volume with each word.

"Why did he attack?" Bart asked.

"Diskastes runs the base as though it is a royal court. He places security guards outside his residence and refuses to see anyone unless it is during his 'court' hours. He plays favorites and allows them free rein. Nothing his security forces do can be brought up as complaint because they are almost always acting on his behalf."

"Why did you go to see him?" Bart asked.

"To inform him that I was moving my attache' into my quarters so that he could work uninterrupted and unaccosted, and that I would be off the base today."

"Is that all you said?" Bart asked.

"I may have said, or possibly implied that I would react in a non-pleasant way should I return and Elisher has been harmed or interrupted in any way."

Bart sighed. "Look. I know you basically did nothing wrong. And I know Diskastes thinks he's a god on earth, but, we have to play the game a little longer. Until we have all the proof we need at the very least," Bart said.

"Elisher is working on that now," Kol answered. "I did not leave him unprotected. Buchanan and Zhuxi are watching over him," Kol said.

"Alright. I'll calm them as best I can. I'll advise them that complaints have been made by several of those that have experience at Base 28, and that the Consul needs to be aware that this is not a royal court. It is instead a diplomatic localized government of Base 28 for the protection and welfare of those living within its borders."

"Excellent," Kol agreed, watching his controls since he could see Washington D.C. up ahead through his windshield.

"But you will have to back off, Kol. Until they can be removed from power, you have to at least pretend to respect his position," Bart said.

"I cannot."

"Why not?" Bart asked.

"Because I do not lie! I will not lie! I will not respect Diskastes at all in any way. He is a despicable male and should be ejected from the planet face at once."

"Just keep your mouth closed for a day or two? Can you do that much?" Bart shouted.

Kol raised his eyebrows and leaned toward the com screen. "Are you shouting at me?" he asked.

Bart glared at Kol's image projected on his own side of the com. "Not intentionally. Please listen. I've requested assistance for you at Base 28. They should arrive in two to three days. In the meantime, please, avoid conflicts with Diskastes and his security forces. Once you have additional support, I believe Diskastes will most likely take to his residence and stay there. Especially since I'm planning to announce that we're auditing everything in and out of the base for the last ten years as soon as your assisting personnel arrive."

Kol thought about it. "I will try."

"Try harder. And in the meantime, have all the documentation and records you can locate rounded up and placed somewhere safe."

"We have already begun to do so," Kol said scowling.

"Good. Enjoy your day," Bart said, sounding more stressed than genuine in his wishing Kol a good day.

Kol immediately grinned. "I will! And do not forget to reclaim my Ehlealah's land for her."

"I said I'd try, but didn't know if I could," Bart answered, his voice raised and filled with frustration.

"Goodbye, Bart!" Kol said happily before ending the vidcom before Bart could say anything else.

Kol spied the repatriation center and circled it once before deciding to dock his transport far from the buildings, in the outer holding yards. He powered down his transport and stood at the exit door looking out at the repatriation center. It was impressive. It was very large with very clean lines. Cement, glass, and chrome. "Missy. I shall return shortly with my Ehlealah. Please engage security measures upon my departure."

"Done, Ambassador Kol," Missy answered.

Ada Jane actually slept in for the first time in recent memory. When she woke, it was already almost 10:00 A.M., and she hurried to get ready for Kol's arrival. She dressed in a pair of running shoes, blue-jeans, a teeshirt and a lightweight jacket just in case she needed it. She pulled her long, straight, blonde hair up into a messy bun and headed downstairs for breakfast.

She was excited, even giddy about Kol's arrival. She'd fallen asleep with him on her mind the night before and it resulted in the most wonderful dreams. She didn't wake one single time with her night terrors as she'd done regularly since she'd been rescued.

Ada sat at a small table alone, enjoying her Frosted Flakes and sipping coffee, waiting patiently for Kol to arrive. She was reading through an e-magazine on a tablet and not paying too much attention to her surroundings, until she realized someone was standing beside her.

Ada looked up suddenly as adrenalin coursed through her, then just as suddenly dropped off when she saw that it was Jason. "You startled me!" she said, smiling.

"I'm sorry. Didn't mean to surprise you. I was waiting for you to look up so I wouldn't startle you," he said.

"I'm still pretty jumpy. It's not your fault."

"So, what's going on?" Jason asked.

"What do you mean?" Ada asked in return.

"We received a call from the powers-that-be. Someone pretty high up must be a friend of yours. They've ordered us to release you and give you a full bill of health."

"Well, honestly, I wasn't sick to begin with. It's about time I was able to make my own choices," Ada Jane said, smiling and trying to remain pleasant. She didn't like anyone telling her what to do, especially since she'd just gotten her freedom back.

"No one was trying to make your choices for you, Ada Jane. I was only trying to be a friend."

"I didn't say you weren't. I didn't complain about anything. I'm just ready to move forward with my life. I don't want to be in a hospital any longer. It's that simple."

"I can understand that. But, the world is different now. You need someone to guide you through it," Jason said.

Ada Jane raised her eyebrows. "I don't need anyone to guide me through it. Maybe it's hard for you to understand, but the entire universe is different now. I know. I've been a part of it. I've lived, suffered, and breathed even, at another's whim. I don't need a man here on Earth deciding when I am and am not ready for certain activities. I know myself when I'm ready."

"Ada Jane, I didn't mean to keep you from anything you wanted to do. I just hoped to experience those things with you. Just to be there for you, since you don't have anyone else," Jason said.

"Ada Jane?" a deep voice said from behind her.

Ada glanced in that direction and her whole face went from indignant to smiling and happy. "Kol!" she said, moving from the table to rush into Kol's arms.

Kol grinned and held Ada close, tilting his head to kiss her head as she hugged him. "I have missed you," Kol said softly.

"I missed you, too. I'm so happy you're here," Ada Jane said, smiling at him happily.

Jason watched Ada Jane hurry into the alien's arms. They seemed to know each other well. He took a moment to really study the alien male. His skin was a deep blue. His eyes were practically the same color as his skin. Even his finger nails were blue as well. If he wasn't seven feet, he wasn't missing it by much. His shoulders were so wide he'd have to turn sideways to get on some transports.

Jason focused on his face. He had full lips that were a slight shade darker than his skin, a wide jaw and wide cheekbones with a strong, regal brow. His horns extended from his head by a foot or more, and they curved gracefully as they extended toward their sharpened tips. His body was massive and covered in muscles, his clothing fitting him like a glove, leaving very little to the imagination.

Jason realized he was being equally examined and met the alien's eyes.

"Who are you?" the alien asked, in accented English.

"I'm Dr. Jason Cavanaugh. I've been caring for Ada Jane while she's been with us. If I may, who are you?" Jason asked.

"I am Ada Jane's male. I will be caring for her from now on," Kol answered.

"And your name is?" Dr. Cavanaugh asked.

"I am Elite Force Commander Kol Ra' Don Tol. I am currently on assignment as Ambassador of my people to Earth by special request of Chairman Bartholomew of the Unified Consortium Defense. Your services are no longer needed," Kol said, completely dismissing the doctor. He did refrain from actually growling at Dr. Cavanaugh, but he couldn't resist displaying his teeth, the second row of which was beginning to reveal itself as his Psi began to react to another male interested in his female.

"You cannot seriously be considering leaving here with this male?" Jason said to Ada Jane.

Kol didn't resist this time. He let out a rumbling growl.

"Kol, stop. We're going to have a nice day. There's no reason for this," Ada Jane said, looking up into his eyes.

Kol hesitated to break his staring contest with Jason, but he wanted to give Ada Jane his complete attention.

"Are you sure, my Ehlealah?" he asked her, searching her face for any hesitance in her answer.

"I'm positive. Jason is just my friend. He's been taking care of me and helping me figure out who I need to speak to about what. That's all. Alright?" she asked.

"Yes," Kol answered, returning his gaze to Dr. Cavanaugh. "I trust you, Ada Jane," placing emphasis on the word you.

"And you, stop insulting Kol. He's the reason I'm standing here today. He and the Sirena Vivian of Cruestace rescued me. They actually with their own hands removed me from the ship I was on and Kol carried me to freedom. There's no reason for you to insult anyone. I trust him with my life," she explained to Jason.

"I'm simply concerned about your welfare," Jason answered.

"I'm fine. And now I've been released from observation here, and I'm free to do the things I need to do. Kol's going to take me to see my parents' graves. Then we'll see what I want to do next," Ada Jane said.

"You are aware that since you've been released, I cannot guarantee that you'll have a room when you come back," Jason said, hoping to dissuade her from leaving at all.

Ada Jane's smile fell. She hadn't realized that. "I was not aware. But that's fine. I'll find somewhere else to stay if necessary."

"If you want to come back here, Ada Jane, all you have to do is let me know. I'll find a place for you. Even if it's in my own home, you won't be without shelter," Jason promised.

"She does not need shelter from you. I am perfectly capable of providing for my own Ehlealah. She already has a place to live," Kol snarled.

"You two are going to make me leave you both here alone," Ada Jane said evenly.

Kol glanced at Dr. Cavanaugh, then Ada Jane. "Apologies for my protectiveness. It is not my intention to threaten you in any way. Thank you for the care and consideration you have given my female while I traveled to your planet. I will now take her to see her parents' places of burial. I bid you good luck and prosperity in the future."

Kol didn't give Jason time to reply. "Are you ready, Ada Jane? We will be away without further delay."

"I am," she said excitedly. Then she turned to Jason. "I'll be in touch soon. Thank you for everything."

"You always have a place here, Ada Jane. I can hold your room for several days. Don't think you can't come back."

"Thank you, Jason," she said, following Kol as he lead her from the cafeteria by the hand.

Jason stood in place, grinding his teeth as he heard Kol speaking to Ada Jane. "Did he not just say that he could not hold your room? Why then is he now saying that he can hold it for several days? It makes no sense."

"Kol... hush, let it go. Please?" Ada Jane asked.

"As you wish, my Ada Jane. Tell me, where is the room you were sleeping in? Do you have belongings you should retrieve?" Kol asked.

They stepped into an elevator at the end of the hallway and Ada Jane pressed the button to go up two floors. "A few things, but, I'm a little afraid to leave here. I have no idea where I'll be next," Ada admitted.

"All will be well. Chairman Bartholomew is assisting in securing your own private quarters. But I wish you to live with me. I have an extra bedroom. Well, I did. It is being used by Elisher at the moment, but you can have my bedroom. I will sleep in the sitting room."

"Can we just see how things go?" Ada Jane asked. "I just got my freedom back, I'm not all that anxious to give it away."

"I will never steal your freedom. I will only protect you as you enjoy your freedom away from all other males and doctors," Kol said smiling.

"What is Chairman Bartholomew doing? You said he was securing me private quarters?"

"He is. He has instructed me that I should move slowly and not tell you what choices to make. He said that you will know when you are ready better than me."

Ada Jane smiled as the elevator doors opened. "He's a very smart man," she said.

Kol walked down the hallway with her until she stopped outside a closed door. "This is my room." She opened the door and they walked in together.

"There is not even a lock on the door, Ada Jane," Kol chided, looking at the door as they entered the room.

"Well, it's a hospital basically," Ada explained.

"This is not secure. Gather your things and we will see to it you have a secure space. Eventually with me."

"Kol..." Ada Jane said warningly.

"When you decide for yourself to share my space," he amended, grinning and blinking at her with an animated smile.

Ada just glanced back at him as she gathered the few changes of clothes she'd acquired, her toiletries and her hairbrush. She stood looking around the room. "I guess that's it."

"Let us go, then. I've been given the coordinates of your family's burial place. I will take you straight to it."

Ada Jane nodded. "Okay. I'm ready."

As they walked down the hallway and eventually out of the lobby of the large medical clinic, Ada Jane thought about the way Kol had been gravitating between his typical 'mine' claims, and at the same time liberally sprinkling in words promising to give her the space to make her own choices. It was clear he was trying to be what she needed, rather than insist she be what he needed.

Then she realized he said he'd given his extra bedroom to someone else. "Kol?"

"Yes, my Ada Jane?" Kol answered.

"Who is Elisher? Why is he or she living with you?"

Chapter 9

Zha Quin sat at the table he and Vivi always took their meals at when they decided to dine in the commissary. He looked out over the people who drifted in and out of the commissary as they finished their meals and returned to their duties, those sitting and enjoying their meals and their friends, and realized that he'd have to make a decision soon.

"Quin? You alright?" Vivian asked.

"Yes, my Vivi. I am fine," Quin answered, smiling lovingly at his Ehlealah.

"You don't look fine," she answered. "You look distracted."

Quin sighed. "I am, a bit. But all will be well."

"Can I help?" she asked.

Quin shook his head as he watched General Lo' San approach a table with a tray filled with enough food and drinks for two. Lo' San unloaded his tray, taking great care to place the small platter of cakes close to the silver-haired female waiting for him at their table. Then he took a seat and smiled lovingly at the female.

"It's sweet, isn't it?" Vivi asked.

Quin glanced back at Vivi. "I suppose it is. It is more surprising than anything, though."

"Why is it surprising?" Vivian asked.

"Lo' San has never put anything or anyone before his duty. And here he is, placing food before an Earth female as though he was her servant," Quin said in a grumbly tone.

"Quin?"

Quin continued to watched Lo' San as he spooned up different foods from his plate and fed them to the female one at a time as she sampled the different foods.

"Quin?!" Vivi said, her voice a little sharper.

"What?" he asked, looking back at her.

"You fed me every single meal, every single day when I first arrived here. You still taste my food first when we're together — simply out of habit. Why is it so different for Lo' San to feed his woman?"

Quin's brows drew down. "It is not different. I'm simply trying to figure out when Lo' San took a female. I cannot keep up any longer. They are claiming females faster than we can rescue them. It concerns me, Vivi," Quin confided.

"Why? Don't you want them to be happy? Besides, a mated male is ten times as fierce when he's in a battle than one who is not mated. He's got more to lose," Vivian said.

"It is not that. But, what if one of them mates a female who is not truly committed to her male. Then leaves him. I am left with a male that is out of control and may very well have to be put down in order to stop his rampaging. Or he charges off on his own and is taken into custody on her world as he lets nothing stop him from finding her and absconding with her. All of my males are important to me. I've sworn loyalty to them, just as they've sworn loyalty to me, and I would have no choice but to intercede on their behalf, all because a female agreed to be theirs and then changed their mind," Quin grumbled.

"I hadn't thought of it that way," Vivian answered. "You're right to be worried. Now I am, too. But, I can tell you that Synclare is not one to worry over."

"She is the female with the silver hair?" Quin asked, still watching Lo' San and the silver-haired Earth female.

"She is. When the others returned to Earth, she opted to stay. She has no interest in returning to Earth, and she's shown every bit as much interest in Lo' San as he's shown in her. She's had all this time to go home, or to go anywhere really, and she chooses to stay here. She's been helping out in medical and spends all her free time with Lo' San. I don't think we have any worries with Lo' San and Synclare at least."

Quin nodded. "That is good. I will not worry about them any longer then. The others, though, I will worry."

"Maybe I could speak to Synclare about coming up with some sort of program or orientation for any female that is brought on board. Whether they plan to stay or not, they will all have to go through a program that explains exactly what it is when a Cruestaci warrior claims them, and what the consequences are. You know, just something that will help educate them, and let them know that they have to expressly let any warrior who seems interested in them know whether they are interested or not. Of course, we also need to explain the difference between a friendly greeting and true interest," Vivian said.

"That is not a bad idea. And in return, I can force all males aboard this ship to go through a similar presentation explaining that if a female refuses them, they must respect it. It won't guarantee that we won't have problems in the future, but, it might prevent some," Quin said.

"I think it's a good start. I'll speak to Synclare later and we'll see what we can get set up," Vivian agreed.

"Thank you, my Vivi," he said, returning his attention to his meal and his mate.

"Have you heard from Kol?" Vivian asked.

"Not exactly. I have heard from Bart. He has requested a team of two to go to Earth and act as Kol's support team."

"Really? Who are you planning to send?" Vivian asked.

"I am considering sending one who is gifted with computer technology, and another who is attuned to security measures. He would have the research support Bart advises he needs as well as another for additional security."

"Great idea. Who are we sending?" Vivian asked.

"I'm considering Ba Re', and my instincts say Kron should go as well. But, that would leave Kol's Elite Force Team without a leader."

"Is there someone you could promote to temporarily oversee the team until both Kron and Kol return?" Vivian asked.

Quin pursed his lips and thought about it. "Not at the moment," Quin answered. "They must have the natural ability to lead as well as possess the skills that Kol and Kron have both spent a lifetime developing. Perhaps I should choose another male to send to Kol… but then I think, I do not want Kol with less security than he should have," Quin said as his mind raced.

Vivian didn't answer, just smiled at Quin as she took a bite of whatever fried beast they'd cooked for her today.

Quin glanced at her, and his forehead wrinkled as he took in her smile as she waited for him to arrive at some conclusion. "Why are you looking at me like that?" he asked.

Vivian shook her head and took a bite of her potatoes, or at least she liked to call whatever the white goo was potatoes — it tasted like potatoes. She offered him a smile again. "It's a shame we don't know anyone like that," she answered.

"It is. The team is very gifted, but promotion would take an in depth evaluation, and it wouldn't be fair to promote them, give them the responsibility, then yank it all away when Kron, or Kol, or both return. Kron volunteered to take over the team until Kol returns, it would be different if we promoted. It would be unfair to expect the male to simply return to being an Elite Force Team member.

"It would be more convenient if we knew a male who had spent his life polishing his skills and fighting any and all the multi-verse over honing those skills into instinct. Someone who has familiarity with most any world and any peoples we may encounter. Someone who is equally familiar with the Cruestaci and also has loyalty to us. Someone who you've yourself remarked is a natural born leader," Vivian said, raising one of her eyebrows as she waited for Quin to catch on to where she was leading him.

Quin focused on his mate, smiling when he realized what she was suggesting. "He will be quite unimpressed," Quin said.

"Probably. But he will also be proud that you believe he can handle the job. You and I both know Kol said that only his Elite Force Team was strong enough to battle against him. And Kol and Kron both said how impressed they were with him."

"I shall demand he returns to Command Warship 1. It is the perfect solution," Quin said, grinning at Vivian.

"I believe it is," Vivi agreed. "And if he accepts, Rosie would return with him, and she could help me and Synclare."

Quin glanced up as Ba Re' and Kron entered the commissary. "I shall go ask if either has issue with joining Kol on Earth," he said, getting to his feet.

"I will be right here," Vivian said, smiling as he dropped a kiss on her lips. "You are very astute my Vivi," he said.

"Did you ever doubt it?" she asked, chuckling.

"Not for one moment, my Ehlealah," he answered. Quin walked away from their table heading directly toward Ba Re' and Kron where they'd joined the line to choose their meals.

"I have a question to ask," Quin said, standing beside them in line.

"For me?" Ba Re' asked, looking between himself and Kron.

"For both of you," Quin responded.

"Okay," Kron answered. "What is it?"

"What do you think about a trip to Earth?" Quin asked.

<<<<<<<>>>>>>>

Quin sat at the head of his conference table in the smaller of his conference rooms aboard Command Warship 1. He was flanked on his left side by Ba Re' and Kron. Bart was on the holovid and all of them awaited their last attendee as they waited to address the agenda of the day. There were several guards that had been assigned to this meeting as well, and they stood on either side of the door, waiting for the final attendee.

Finally, the door whooshed open and Rokai ahl stepped into the room with a worried look on his face. "I'm here, I came as quickly as I could. What's wrong? Is it Mother, or Father? Is Vivian safe?" he asked, looking at the faces staring back at him. His expression became one of confusion and suspicion instead of one of worry and concern. "Why are you all smirking? If this were truly a matter of life and death, you would not be so happy. What is happening here?" Rokai snapped.

"I need your assistance, Rokai. The only way to get you back to the ship was to tell you it is a matter of life and death," Zha Quin explained.

Rokai glared at him for a moment. "So, everyone is safe. There is no immediate threat to family, life or limb, and you just decided to use my new commitment to this family to bring me running back here?" he surmised.

Quin nodded. "Exactly."

Rokai snarled and spun on his heel, moving toward the door.

Just as quickly as he turned, both guards stepped in front of the door to prevent him from leaving the conference room.

Rokai growled at them before returning his attention to his brother. "You do realize I could fight my way through them with little effort," he said.

"I do. Which is exactly why you are here. I need your help, Rokai. I have no one else to turn to. Won't you please help me? Help Kol?" Quin asked, knowing that despite Rokai's affinity for causing trouble, he'd always spoken highly of Kol.

"What is wrong with Kol? Did they take him prisoner on Earth?" Rokai asked.

"Not exactly," Bart answered.

Rokai gave the holovid his attention as Bart spoke to him. "I don't understand," Rokai said.

"He's been assigned as an ambassador to Earth Base 28 for the next three years. He is in a precarious position, and we've decided to send him temporary assistance."

"I am not living on Earth for three years!" Rokai insisted with a snarl.

"And we wouldn't ask it of you. He will not need assistance for the entire three years. Just for a short time until we can remove the current Consul from governing Base 28 and the sectors in that region."

"And why do I care about that?" Rokai ahl asked.

"Because," Quin answered. "We're sending Ba Re' and Kron. Kron was leading the Elite Forces Team in Kol's absence, but as he'll be joining Kol, you'll now be leading the team."

"Oh, no. No, no, no, no, no. I will not be leading a damn thing. I'm newly mated and taking my Ehlealah on an extended tour of all the worlds I've traveled. I will not be trapped on Command Warship 1. That is your chosen life, brother, not mine," Rokai ahl snapped, shaking his head so vigorously his braids flew haphazardly about his face.

"There is no other that can take the place of Kron," Ba Re' said matter-of-factly.

"Not a single other male in all of Cruestace?" Rokai ahl asked sarcastically.

"There's not. We all agree that there is no other male of your skill set, no other male of your loyalty to our people who will temporarily assume responsibility and be willing to step down when Kron and/or Kol returns to resume their positions," Quin explained.

At the recognition of his battle and fighting skills, Rokai puffed his chest out a little. "I have honed my talents in a rather unique arena," he conceded.

"Exactly. And you don't want the position permanently, so you'll have no problem handing off the responsibility and moving on your way when Kron and Kol return," Ba Re' answered.

"I don't know," Rokai ahl said. "This is not the adventure I promised my Ehlealah."

"Are you afraid you cannot hold your own against our Elite Forces?" Kron asked.

"You know damned well I held my own against all I trained with, and then some!" Rokai answered.

"I need your assistance, Rokai. It's as simple as that. Will you not help us?" Quin asked.

Rokai grumbled and stomped around the conference room, from time to time meeting the eyes of his brother, Ba Re', and Kron.

"Fine," he finally agreed. "I'll do it. But only until one of them is able to return, then I want my life back!"

"Thank you, Rokai," Quin got to his feet to move around the table and hug his brother.

"And I want another favor from Bart!" Rokai said, shoving his finger in the air above his head.

"What kind of favor? When?" Bart asked, his irritation evident in his voice.

"I don't know yet! But there will come a time that I'll need one," Rokai said, his arms folded across his chest.

"Bart?" Quin asked.

Bart rolled his eyes. "Oh, very well! You'd call me to get me to help his irritating hide anyway! Done! Granted! Are you going to do what we ask now?" Bart demanded.

"Yes! I will be Elite Commander Rokai ahl Tel Mo' Kok, feared the multi-verse over!" Rokai ahl said, striking a dramatic pose with his hands on his hips and his chin lifted in the air as he gazed out across the room.

"Gods help us," Ba Re' mumbled.

Chapter 10

Kol smiled when he realized that Ada Jane was suspicious of anyone living in close proximity to him. She may not realize it yet, but she already thought of him as hers.

"Elisher is my attache'. As an added bonus to my new position, I am given a suite of rooms, and the option to use my attache' at will. I can even move my attache' into my rooms to give me easier access to them. I believe the assignment of an attache' is meant to reduce my stress levels so that I may concentrate on my work itself."

Ada Jane had stopped walking beside Kol.

Kol looked down to the spot she should be standing in and realizing she wasn't there, turned back to see where she'd stopped and why.

Ada Jane stood exactly where she'd stopped in her tracks, her eyebrows raised as she looked quizzically at him. "How good is your English? What exactly do you think attache' means, and what exactly are you using her for?"

"My English is very good. I even know some of the slang words thanks to Vivi."

"The rest of my question..." Ada Jane prompted.

"Attache' is, I believe, an assistant of sorts. One who assists you in any way you indicate you need assistance," Kol answered, still not understanding her line of questioning.

"That's what it's supposed to mean. How are you using your assistant, and why is she living with you?"

Kol understood then. His Ehlealah was still under the impression that he was living with another female. Kol smiled, showing her all his very pointed teeth. "Elisher is small and could come under attack from those in power at Base 28 because I am auditing all their functions and histories since the last elected official came into power. They are not happy with me at the moment. When I am away from the base, I need to know that Elisher is safe from attack and free to continue the research I've assigned. Without Elisher's assistance, I would truly be overwhelmed. I could do the research myself, but it wouldn't leave me the opportunity to court you properly and win your heart."

"You're trying to win my heart?" Ada Jane asked, a soft smile curving her lips.

"I am. The only reason I came to Earth was to find you, win your heart and beg you to accept me."

"But, I thought you have a new position here…"

"I do. Bart made me an Ambassador. I thought it was only to give me permission to be on your planet, but it appears Bart has ulterior motives. He wishes me to perform tasks that others have not been able to perform. They could be dangerous. But, I am not afraid. I fear nothing." Kol smiled sweetly at Ada Jane, then let the smile fall to show her his heart in his eyes and adoring expression. "Except not receiving your acceptance," he admitted. "I can survive all else," he said sincerely.

Ada Jane hurried to Kol, and lifted her hands to his shoulders. "I have not refused you. And I'm ridiculously happy to see you. But I'm not much further than I was on your ship. I need time to find my place, Kol. I need time to adjust and try to figure out what it is that will make me happy."

Kol slipped his hands around her waist, linking them at the small of her back. "I understand. And I am here to help you find your place. I will always stand beside you, my Ada Jane."

Kol leaned in and Ada thought he was going to kiss her. But instead, he rubbed his nose along hers and pressed his cheek to her forehead.

Ada Jane stood secure in his embrace and his sweet ways of letting her know how much she meant to him. She smiled to herself when she remembered asking herself what would make her smile as she lay in bed the night before, and it was Kol's face that popped into her mind. "Just give me some time and we'll be just fine, Kol."

"Whatever you need you shall have, be it time or anything else," Kol responded.

They stood for a moment longer, then, Kol slid his hand down to take her hand. "Come, Ehlealah, allow me to take you to your parents' burial site."

Ada Jane allowed Kol to lead her toward the far edge of the enclosed parking lot. There were several airships docked there. Two were obviously medical based with a huge red cross painted on their bellies so they'd be easily recognized while flying. Several others were not identified as any particular service. There was one at the end that caught her attention. It glistened as the breeze blew past it, making it seem at times almost iridescent. Ada Jane squinted her eyes and tried to focus on it more clearly. But as soon as she did, another part of the ship shimmered. "That one almost has pieces of it that seem to disappear," she said, waving toward the ship on the end.

"That one is ours," Kol answered.

"Ours?" she asked, looking up at Kol, then back at the ship that had caught her attention.

"I will tell you a secret… it is my Battle Cruiser, but I've reprogrammed it so that it could be approved as a standard transport. I wanted it near me at all times because it links me to Command Warship 1, to Chairman Bartholomew, and also gives me limitless support to Missy and all the information she can provide."

"Wow," is all she could say as they approached the ship. "It's beautiful."

Kol paused and looked at it. He'd never considered it before. "I suppose it is beautiful. In this atmosphere it certainly displays more colors than it usually does. It is a camouflage built into the cruiser itself that allows it to blend in with its environment. Earth has many colors and textures, so even without the cloaking programs activated, it does to some point camouflage itself."

"Did you say that you had to reprogram it? Does that mean that you've had to remove your defense systems? What happens if you have to leave Earth and make it back to Command

Warship 1? What if you come under attack?" Ada asked concerned.

Kol smiled down at her. "I am not leaving Earth without you. So it will not be a concern for quite some time. If for some reason I do need to activate the defense mechanisms and weaponry, I need only ask Missy and it is done."

"Good," Ada Jane said, relief clear in her expression.

"Are you ready?" Kol asked.

"I am," she answered, looking for a ramp of some sort that would give her access to the ship that was too high for her to reach from the ground.

"Missy, please deploy the ramp for myself and Ada Jane."

"At once, Ambassador Kol," Missy answered, making it seem as though the ship was speaking to Kol.

A slight hydraulic whine could be heard as part of the iridescent skin of the ship separated from the rest and began to extend toward them. Gradually it lowered until it was on an angle, clearly reshaping itself into a ramp for their convenience. Just as the ramp lowered to Kol's knee level, a door appeared on the side of the ship just above the ramp.

Kol lifted Ada Jane and placed her on the ramp, then stepped up on it himself and followed her up and onto the ship. "Please retract the ramp and close the entranceway, Missy."

"I have already begun to do so, Ambassador Kol," Missy answered.

"Do you remember Missy from Command Warship 1? Did you have the opportunity to interact with her?" Kol asked.

"I do remember Vivi speaking with her, but I didn't have the opportunity to myself."

"Missy, this female is my Ehlealah, Ada Jane. Please add her to all my protocols. Should she ask anything of you, please comply, most especially in the ways of safety."

"Welcome aboard, Ada Jane Ra' Don Tol."

Ada grinned and looked at Kol.

"She believes that one's Ehlealah will automatically join with them," Kol said as though confiding a secret.

"I see," she said, answering Kol. Then she turned her attention to the computer she knew was named Missy. "Thank you, Missy. I am very excited to be here."

"I am equally pleased to make your acquaintance," Missy replied.

"Ambassador Kol, I've already initiated flight sequences. I began them when you exited the building. All is in order. Please proceed at will," Missy advised.

"Thank you, Missy," Kol answered, strapping Ada Jane into the copilot's seat, and then taking his own seat.

Ada Jane watched as he strapped himself in, then activated the ship by simply waving his hands over certain controls. She was completely fascinated.

"Missy?" Kol asked.

"Yes, Ambassador Kol?" Missy answered.

"Please check on Elisher for me and make sure all is in order," Kol requested.

Ada Jane glanced at Kol through her peripheral vision. It was natural to want to know that your coworkers were safe and secure, but, he'd mentioned this one several times now and she was wondering at his speedy attachment to her. Not to mention, his assistant was sharing his living quarters. She didn't like that one single bit. But she said nothing. She'd laid down her own rules and he was respecting them, so she needed to trust him just as he was her.

Kol sensed Ada Jane stiffen beside him. He looked her way, but she was still looking straight ahead. He smiled, knowing he was teasing her intentionally. Not that he didn't want to be sure Elisher was secure and unscathed, he did. But, he could have told Ada Jane that Elisher was male to ease her mind. Kol smiled to himself.

"My Ada Jane?" he said.

Ada Jane kept looking straight ahead. "Yes?" she asked.

"There is no reason for concern or jealousy where Elisher is concerned."

"I'm not concerned or jealous."

Kol just kept watching Ada Jane.

Finally, she turned to look at him. "I'm not."

"Do you speak the truth?" he asked, a teasing tone in his deep voice.

Ada paused while she searched for just the right answer. "I do. Pretty much. I'm not that concerned, only a little." Then she turned her head to look through the front shield again. It looked much like a windshield but had white translucent printouts running across the edge of it where Kol sat. She couldn't read them so supposed it was in his language, and it was information about the ship itself or their surroundings, or maybe even both.

"Elisher is a male, Ada Jane. He is not a very masculine male, but still, he is male. There is no reason for concern," Kol said, smiling at her.

Ada turned to face Kol. "He is?" she asked, the relief clear in her voice and in her smile.

"He is. And there would be no concern even if Elisher was a female," Kol added.

"Why not?" she asked.

"Because she wouldn't be you. I belong to you."

Ada Jane felt her walls falling a bit. She couldn't even bring herself to be angry that he was already tearing down the walls she'd spent so much time of late building around herself. She smiled at him, a genuine smile. The kind of smile that smiled often enough would leave laugh lines around her mouth.

Kol smiled back, then moved his hand across a sensor to his right and the ship lifted into the sky so quickly it seemed like it was instantaneous.

"Whoa! That was fast!" she exclaimed.

"It is after all a battle cruiser. It is very swift and agile."

Ada Jane looked around the cockpit, then swiveled in her seat a bit and glanced toward the back of the ship. Her mouth dropped open at what she saw.

"Kol? There are flowers back there," she said, as she turned a bit more to get a better look.

"Yes. And there are small white wooden pieces that I'm told are called lattices. And there are artificial wreaths as well as the live flowers."

"Why?" she asked, already knowing the answer.

"I'm told that it is customary to leave flower offerings at the burial site of loved ones. Also to maintain it regularly. I know that it most likely has not been maintained... you have been away." Kol looked into her eyes and saw them filling with tears.

"Thank you," Ada Jane whispered.

Kol smiled at her. "I also brought tools and cleaning implements as Elisher suggested that I might need in the event any repairs are needed."

Ada Jane reached out her hand for his.

Kol lifted his arm toward her, allowing her to take his hand.

Since she was strapped in, she couldn't get up and go to him, so instead, Ada just pressed his palm to her cheek, then turned and placed a kiss in the center of his palm.

Kol smiled at Ada Jane then brushed her cheek with his thumb before taking control of the cruiser and maneuvering them away from the medical clinic.

"We should be in Nebraska shortly," he told her. "Once we achieve the preferred transport altitude, you may move into the back to look at the flowers I've brought if you wish to."

"I'll just stay here with you. I'll see them when we get there."

Dr. Jason Cavanaugh stood at the plate glass windows in his office, looking out over the docking pads of the medical facility he ran. He watched as Ada Jane, along with the alien that had claimed to be her male, boarded a transport and quickly left his field of vision. "Ms. Kensington!" he shouted, still looking out of the window with his eyes glued to the last spot he saw the craft that took Ada Jane away from him.

"Yes, Dr. Cavanaugh?" his secretary answered, hurrying to his office door at the sound of irritation in his voice.

"Get me all the information you can find on Elite Force Commander Kol Ra' Don Tol. He is Cruestaci if my guess is right. Find out all you can about him and let me know at once."

"Yes, sir. I'll get right on that," Ms. Kensington answered as she was already moving from his doorway.

Jason stood there still, an angry expression on his face as he clamped his jaws, his nostrils flaring as he thought about the alien that had taken the woman he planned to make his from right under his nose. And there'd been nothing he could do about it. Ada Jane had gone with the alien as though it was as natural as breathing. Aliens were corrupt. They were little better than animals, and Ada Jane had just jumped on board with no thought to her safety at all.

The Purists of the World, of which he was a founding member, understood full well how the integration of aliens into their bloodline would be the downfall of their civilization. His position as chief of staff at the repatriation center gave him access to the women who'd been abused by aliens, stolen away from their homes and family, and were as a result more than ready to join their cause. But this woman, Ada Jane, he wanted for himself. She was unique, and she should be at his side. As soon as Ada came back to the clinic, he would have to step up his efforts to win her over, then make sure she understood the only acceptable place was far away from any alien.

Chapter 11

Elisher sat at the table in Kol's quarters, now his quarters, too, and spread stacks of hard copy documentation across it. He'd created a spread sheet and was working on his laptop to try to match electronic entries to the hard copy documents. There were seven large boxes of hard copy documentation made up of everything from receipts to payroll records to tax forms opened and sitting strewn about the room. There were at least another twenty stacked against the wall in his bedroom. He'd only been at it for half a day so far, but it was already apparent that not all the information was processed as it should have been.

He was so absorbed in what he was doing that he was startled by a pounding on the door.

"Who is it?" he asked.

"You've been summoned for a meeting with Consul Diskastes," came the answer.

"Please send my regrets. I am unable to attend as I've been given a strict timetable within which to have my work finished by Ambassador Ra' Don Tol."

"Consul Diskastes's demands override any directive given by Ambassador Ra' Don Tol. You are ordered to come at once."

"You're wrong there, boys," a voice said.

Elisher smiled. He immediately recognized the voice as Buchanan's. He was making good on his promise to watch over Elisher until Kol returned.

"This is none of your concern, Viceroy Buchanan. Please move along."

"This is all my concern. You see, I serve Earth, but I ultimately serve the Unified Consortium Defense. Ambassador Ra' Don Tol is here by order of the Consortium. They override everybody and everything. So, I'm afraid your Consul is overridden and cannot demand that an assistant of one of their ambassadors complies with his demands."

"They do not have more power than the governing native agents of their own planet," one guard thought to argue.

"Exactly. You are correct. This, however, is Earth, and Diskastes is not human, nor of this Earth in any way, shape, form, or fashion. Care to try again?" Buchanan asked.

There was a moment of silence before he heard Buchanan calling a little more loudly than he'd been speaking to the guards. "Have a nice day now, boys. Tell your Consul I've already let Ambassador Ra' Don Tol know that he sent you boys to speak to his assistant in his absence."

Elisher sat perfectly still in his seat, listening to the exchange outside the door. He smiled with a sense of relief when he realized Diskastes's guards were leaving. Then a soft knock could be heard.

"Elisher?" Buchanan asked.

Elisher went to the door and looked out through the peephole before unlocking it and allowing Buchanan into the room. "Thank you, Viceroy Buchanan. I was a little nervous if truth be told."

"Not necessary. You doing alright otherwise?" Buchanan asked, looking around the room.

"Yes, just trying to work as quickly as possible so Kol can have all he needs when he gets back, or shortly thereafter."

"I'm sure you'll get it done. You're very efficient if nothing else."

"What does that mean?" Elisher asked.

"Nothing untoward, just that you don't seem like the type to be placed at Base 28 mixed in with the company you're mixed in with on a daily basis."

Elisher shrugged. "The look does not always fit the man," he answered.

Buchanan nodded. "That is true." He looked around the room. Where did you find all these records? I thought Diskastes destroyed all the hard copies of all documents."

"He does. Rather than go to the records department, I went to each department head and asked for all the hard copies they may have on hand. Told them I was cleaning everything up and would get it all disposed of properly. Rainsly in shipping/receiving asked if I wanted all of the documents, those for entry and those for destruction, or just those for entry. Luckily I went there first, so that let me know to ask for both sets." Elisher looked briefly over the boxes spread around the table he'd been working on. "I've got twenty more boxes in my bedroom," he said, looking at Buchanan.

"How can they have gone along with this?" Buchanan asked.

"First, we aren't sure yet what 'this' entails. Second, who knows? Personal gain, bribes, coercion, threats against one's family. Could have been anything. Could have been as simple as follow orders and don't ask questions. That is how the military works and there are multiple militaries certainly manning each base in the United States," Elisher said.

Buchanan just shook his head. "Unbelievable," he said. Then he had a thought. "Did each department head have both sets of documents, one for entering and one for destruction?"

"No. Medical didn't. He didn't know what I was talking about and handed me one box. All other departments did have both."

Buchanan nodded. "Could explain why our medical options are so limited. Dr. Hawkins refused to play along, so he gets less reward and his ability to do his job effectively is greatly diminished because he doesn't have the supplies he needs."

"Could be," Elisher answered.

"I'm going to let you get back to work. I'll be nearby, so no worries. Just keep doing your thing and I've got the door."

"Thank you, sir."

"Ambassador Kol, we are crossing into the state of Nebraska," Missy announced.

Ada Jane sat forward in her seat, trying to see out of the side windows or the front shield, but all she saw was sky.

"Would you like me to cruise at a lower altitude so you could possibly see some of the countryside?" Kol asked.

"Yes! Please, do!" Ada Jane answered excitedly.

Kol maneuvered the battle cruiser to a lower altitude and watched as Ada Jane unstrapped herself so she could press her hands against the glass to get a better view of the land beneath them on her side of the cruiser.

"It's so different," she finally said after several moments of silence.

"What was it like before?" Kol asked.

"Lots of farms, and fields of corn and grain. As far as you could see, just field after field after field of different colors and heights. Now it's just... scorched."

Ada watched as the land that used to be so beautiful and wholesome passed beneath them, dark, dry and scarred in some places. There were a few communities here and there that seemed to have either recovered to an extent or even possibly been left intact. "I see some that look like I expected," she said quietly.

"Those were most likely the communities that signed allegiance with the invading forces and agreed to supply them with food and other needs as requested. They were left unscathed for the most part, other than having to comply with their demands."

"Who invaded?" Ada Jane asked.

"There were several dominating forces. The main force were the Quislesez. Several other peoples joined forces with them on seeing a planet ripe for the taking with natural resources unlike they'd seen in millennia. Your people were painfully unaware of life outside your world as a result of your leaders deciding you were better not knowing. It left you wide open and defenseless. Had you known, it's most likely your scientists and your leaders would have been able to make at least a decent attempt at fighting the invasion."

"How did we win?" Ada Jane asked.

"Us. And other worlds like ours. We united and fought on your behalf. Eventually there were so many different forces here, all battling each other with your people and your land caught in the middle, it was nearly as catastrophic as the initial invasion. An alliance was required to organize those interested in saving and preserving Earth and her people. The Unified Consortium Defense was born. Eventually it graduated to a multi-verse organization, protecting all peoples and worlds from the same fate Earth suffered."

Ada Jane was quiet, watching the scenery go by.

Gradually the cruiser slowed and she felt it descending. She sat straighter in her seat and strapped herself in again. "Are we there?" she asked.

"We are," Kol answered.

Shortly after they were standing at the door, their arms full of wreaths and fresh flowers waiting for the ramp to deploy. "Missy? Security status, please," Kol asked.

"All is secure, Ambassador Kol. I detect no hostile environment of any type. There are humans in the museum, as well as in the surrounding countryside, but none seem viable threats, nor is there a recent history of violence in this region."

"Thank you," Kol answered. The door opened and Kol stepped forward. "Allow me to go first, Ada Jane. If there is any incident, return to the ship at once, do not wait for me. I'll be along as soon as I can. If Missy deems it necessary to leave the area, she will take control of the ship and take you to safety."

"What about you?" Ada Jane asked.

"I will be here, proving my worth as a protector. Missy will return for me once you are safe," Kol explained. "But do not allow yourself to become upset. I mention it only so you know there are precautions in place. This region is safe and has been for a number of years."

Ada Jane followed Kol down the ramp. "Okay," she answered. Then she mumbled at a level she thought he couldn't hear. "Still not leaving you."

Kol had just set foot on the ground and smiled to himself before turning around to face her.

Ada Jane stepped off the ramp and watched it retract back into the ship.

"If you need to board the ship, simply address Missy and tell her to release the ramp for you."

"I won't, but okay," Ada Jane said, as she walked a few steps away and looked around. "I know this place!" she said excitedly.

"Do you?" Kol asked, surprised.

"I think I do," she said, walking closer to the building a football field's length away from them. "It's a little different, but," she turned in a circle. "I think it's our church."

Ada walked hurriedly toward the building she saw up ahead and stopped short when she noticed the graveyard to the right. She changed her direction, slowly walking toward the graveyard. "This is where they are, isn't it?"

"It is," Kol answered from right behind her.

Ada walked right up to the white painted wrought iron gate that allowed visitors into the graveyard. She looked up at the arch above the gate and read the name. "Cedar Creek Historical Cemetery" she read aloud. "It's a historical cemetery now?" she asked.

"Yes. The building too is a small museum used as an example of life before the invasion. While researching, I found that most rural civilizations of Earth made the effort to become part of the national historical society to try to prevent larger corporations from coming in and purchasing large tracts of land for development.

"I'm surprised there were any large corporations left after everything fell apart," Ada Jane answered.

"Not all enterprise is of this planet. There were many worlds vying for a piece of the planet they helped save."

Ada looked at Kol, her mind wondering if his people were one of those that wanted to break Earth up into tracts and sell it off.

"After the invading forces were defeated, my people were never allowed on the planet. In fact, I'm the first of my kind to be here — that I'm aware of, anyway. We were considered too volatile to be given access, so, we patrolled the outer edges of this universe, far from Earth, but still, effective in stopping pirating and illegal exports of Earth's resources as best we could."

"What did they take? Oil? Gold? Water?" she asked.

"Some, yes. Some took Earth's people."

Ada clenched her jaws to control her response.

"I'm sorry, Ada Jane. I should not have said so."

Ada shook her head. "I should have known. I was taken, so it only stands to reason."

"Yes, but you were taken a very long time before the invasion."

"We believed at the time, had we been allowed to be here on the ground, we'd have been able to save more civilians. But we've only recently been allowed to become an active participant of the Consortium," he admitted.

"I'm sure you would have. And it's ridiculous they kept you out for so long. You and your people are more humane than any I've met," Ada said.

Then she turned back toward the cemetery. "I guess there's no point in putting it off. This is what I came for. I just didn't realize I'd be so afraid."

"I am here," Kol said, encouragingly.

"I know. It's just hard to believe they won't be here to greet me," she said as she started walking slowly through its rows of headstones reading each as she went, searching for her parents' names.

They walked for a good ten minutes, with Ada pausing at the headstones of people she'd known from the small community. Kol staying quietly just behind her, allowing her to say her prayers before moving on. Eventually, in the back right corner, in the shade of a huge, old, oak tree, she found what she was looking for — sort of.

Kol came to a sudden stop just as Ada Jane did. He looked down at the headstone she'd stopped in front of and his eyes widened. She was standing in front of her own grave site.

"Ada Jane?" Kol said, leaning over to release his armload of flowers and to set his bag of tools on the ground. "Are you alright?" he asked, moving toward her and placing his hands on her shoulders from behind.

Ada nodded. "They must have had a memorial for me after I'd been gone for so long," she said quietly.

Ada walked up to the headstone and traced the date she'd disappeared with her fingertips. "I'm not in there," she whispered.

Chapter 12

"No, you are not! You are very much alive. You have your whole life ahead of you," Kol answered as he stepped up right behind her again, his hands smoothing up and down her arms.

She ran her fingers over the rest of the headstone and realized her parents had chosen her favorite color marble for it. "They made it pink for me," she said. Then she read the words aloud.

Ada Jane Andersen
Born 01-22-1966, Taken 08-01-1986
Beloved daughter of Ada Mae and George Andersen
Gone but never forgotten

"They knew I was taken," Ada said.

"Yes," Kol agreed.

"Do you think they knew who took me, or that I was taken by aliens, I mean?"

"I don't know. But they knew you didn't leave them of your own free will," Kol answered.

Ada turned to look up at him. "And that's what matters. They knew I'd never leave like that. They knew I loved them."

"Exactly," Kol answered.

Ada looked around, turning this way and that before realizing what she was looking for was right in front of her. She walked past her own empty grave and came to a stop before the large, double headstone right behind hers. She didn't say anything, but Kol could tell from her sniffles and the way her shoulders shook she was weeping. He hurried to her once again, and wrapped his arms around her from behind, allowing her to see the burial site, but still holding her tightly to him. "It's alright,

Ehlealah, cry as much as you wish. Let it all out. I am here. You will never be alone again," he murmured in her ear.

Ada curled her hands around his forearms where they held her and sobbed while she did her best to stare at the headstone through her tears.

A while later she managed to get herself under control, or at the very least she was for the most part cried out — for now anyway. She pointed at the headstone. "Look, they are greeting me," she said.

Kol glanced at the headstone he'd really not paid any attention to until now. He'd been too busy trying to soothe his female. He read the letters there, stumbling over a few of them, but managing to gather the meaning. "They knew you'd be back!" he exclaimed.

Ada nodded. There before her, the simple, double headstone marking the graves of her parents showed that her mother had died first, followed a year later by her father. And after their names and dates there was nothing about beloved wife or husband, or a bible verse or anything else you'd expect to see on a headstone.

There was just a message — they left her a message.

"Welcome home, sweet girl. We always knew you'd come back to us. We love you, Mom and Dad."

Ada patted Kol's arms to let him know she wanted him to let her go. Kol dropped his arms and allowed her to step away from him. He waited there quietly as she sat down on the ground right in front of the headstone and told her parents all about what had happened to her.

He smiled when she got to the end and told them she was saved by a big, blue man who was very kind, and very handsome. Then he stood there some more while she just sat with them, making her peace with everything the best she could.

Eventually she turned and looked up at him. "Are you ready to clean it all up?" she asked.

"Whenever you are, Ada Jane. I am in no rush, take as much time as you wish," Kol answered.

She got to her feet and looked down at her parents' graves. "It's not in that bad 'a shape. Maybe we could just put the little lattice work edging around theirs and place the flowers."

Kol picked up the flowers they'd both put down and the bag his tools were in and walked over to her. "I think they would be very happy with that idea."

An hour and a half later, they had placed both wreaths — one on either side of Ada's parents' headstone, and all the pots of fresh flowers Kol had brought with them. Then they outlined the gravesite with the white lattice work edging, and polished the headstone whose pink marble matched the one they'd bought for Ada Jane, and they were finally finished.

Ada and Kol stood back admiring their work. "I love it," Ada said.

"I do, as well. I think they are very, very happy that you are here, and that you have beautified their resting place," Kol said.

"You believe in life after death?" Ada asked, turning to Kol curiously.

"I believe that no soul ever truly ends. And if you love strongly enough, you can remain anchored to those you love who have not yet followed you into the next life."

"I like that," Ada said, slipping her hand into his and leaning against him.

Kol looked down at her, then up at the small building in the distance. "Would you like to go inside and see the museum?"

"Yes, I think I would," Ada answered.

Together they strolled toward the museum, taking their time as Ada read each and every headstone to ensure that if she knew them, she'd said hello.

As they exited the graveyard, Ada suddenly looked nervous. "They're going to make us take down the flowers and the edging!" she said worriedly.

"Why?" Kol asked.

"Because this is a historical graveyard and museum. They don't allow things like that. Everything has to be the same."

"We shall see. Come, let's go inside," Kol encouraged.

As they approached the small 'museum', Ada Jane took her time, taking in every aspect. "Looks like they tried to make it like our church. It's a little bigger though, and obviously newer." She paused to look up at the steeple. "It's close enough that it's familiar."

"Is that a good thing?" Kol asked.

"Yeah, it is. I wouldn't want a building here that didn't feel like it was similar to the original building."

As they stepped through the front doors of the church, Kol had to bow his head to be sure his horns didn't catch on the way in, but once inside the room opened up greatly. Kol raised his eyes to the ceiling and smiled at the sight of the open beams displayed over head and the vaulted ceilings displaying the woodwork inside. As his eyes moved down from the ceiling, he took his time to appreciate the stained glass windows depicting the stations of the cross, and the beautifully woven pastel tapestries hanging from the walls on either side of and just behind the altar and pulpit. He took in the wooden pews taking up most of the floor space and following Ada Jane's lead, he joined her in the third pew from the front, taking a seat next to her.

Ada Jane reached under the pew in front of her and pulled out a cushioned length of wood and knelt on it. She clasped her hands in front of her and closed her eyes.

Kol leaned forward, pretty sure he knew what she was doing. "Ada Jane?" he whispered.

Ada didn't answer.

"Are you praying, my Ehlealah?" he whispered again.

"Yes," she whispered back.

Kol watched her for a moment, then got to his own knees beside her and clasped his hands in prayer beside her.

Ada felt him shift as he joined her and she glimpsed him out of the corner of her eye as he too clasped his hands and closed his eyes in prayer. She smiled, then returned to her own prayers.

The curator and pastor of the church turned museum smiled as he entered the main room, which was actually the nave of the church when it was a fully functional church. He waited quietly while the two visitors knelt in prayer.

Eventually the male, obviously alien from the color of his skin and the horns on his head, lifted from his knees and slid back into the pew. Shortly after the woman with him did the same. He watched as they sat quietly for a few moments before the woman spoke.

"What did you pray for, Kol?" she asked.

"I prayed for thc souls of those who have lost their lives. I prayed for the people who used to pray in this building or the one that used to stand here before the war. I prayed for your parents — that they be aware of your return, and I prayed for you, that you might find the peace and happiness that has so long escaped you," Kol answered.

Ada smiled.

"I pretty much prayed for the same things. Only I sent thanks for sending you to find me," she said quietly.

Kol smiled but didn't say anything further. He was struck by the feeling of peace and harmony, complete calm that simply entering this building had given him, and quietly sat breathing it all in.

"You didn't pray for anything for yourself," Ada observed.

"If you are happy and have found peace, there is nothing more I need," Kol answered.

Ada reached over and placed her fingers on top of his hand.

Kol turned his hand over and curled his fingers around hers, and they sat like that, together in silence until the curating pastor cleared his throat to let them know he was there.

Kol had known they weren't alone, but also sensed no danger or ill will, so simply remained aware of their observance and continued to sit and enjoy the sanctity of their surroundings.

Ada Jane leaned forward a little and over toward the sound of a clearing throat.

"Welcome to our church slash museum. I'm pleased you're here," the pastor said.

"Thank you," Ada Jane answered.

The pastor approached the pew and offered his hand for shaking as Kol got to his feet and stepped into the main aisle.

Kol looked down at the pastor's hand, then met the pastor's eyes before slowly extending his own hand to the man.

The pastor grasped Kol's hand in his right hand and shook it slightly before embracing Kol's hand with his left as well. "We don't get many visitors. The locals will come for services on Sunday mornings, but there honestly aren't that many left in the area to attend."

"It's a beautiful church, or museum… I'm not quite sure which to call it," Ada Jane said, coming to stand beside Kol.

The pastor smiled and chuckled slightly. "Yes, well. It's first and foremost a church, but, in order to maintain it and the property around it, it had to be registered as a historic place. And in order to do that, we had to rebuild the original church as well as we could after it was damaged in the war, then add room for artifacts and collections so that we could call it a museum. It worked!" the pastor said, lifting his hands palm up and looking around the place as he shrugged. "Here we are!" he added.

"You've done a good job," Ada Jane said.

"Thank you," the pastor said. "I like to think we managed to maintain the feel of the church, while adding the little things from the community's history and keeping both complementary to one another."

"You've done well," Kol said.

"Thank you. I'm Pastor Douglas," he said, introducing himself.

"I am Ambassador Kol Ra' Don Tol of Cruestace," Kol said. "This is my Ehlealah, Ada Jane…"

"It's very nice to meet you, Pastor Douglas," Ada said, interrupting Kol. She wasn't sure she wanted him to know who she really was. "We won't take up any more of your time…"

"Nonsense!" Pastor Douglas exclaimed. "Take all the time you like. In fact, please be my guest. Peruse the collections we have here. It will give you a real sense of the community that once flourished here."

Ada looked around herself and noticed the photos on the wall in the alcove. And in looking through the glass windows of what used to be the crying room, the room mothers would take babies to if they cried during the services, she could see more photos.

"If you look over to the right there, we've added another room about the same size as this nave. We have artifacts collected from the area as well as more photos. I'd be pleased to give you a tour if you like. I've had a lot of time to acquaint myself with most of it."

Ada Jane looked up at Kol to see if he minded.

"It is your day, Ada Jane. Anything you wish is more than acceptable." Kol thought about it briefly then added. "Anything you wish is more than acceptable on any given day," he said, his expression thoughtful.

Ada smiled as she was about to accept the pastor's offer when he spoke.

"Ada Jane. That is a very unusual name. We have a display built around a local legend of a girl with that name. Most of our displays are built around the families that used to live in this region, and her family's collection is no different, but her story is unique."

"Really?" Kol asked. "I would be most interested to see this collection. Would you not, my Ada Jane?"

Ada looked up at Kol. She was excited, but also apprehensive.

"I am right beside you," he said softly.

Finally, Ada nodded. "Okay."

They followed Pastor Douglas to the opposite room. The displays were set back against the walls and when necessary stood out from the wall approximately five feet. There was a wooden railing, similar to a rough hewn wooden fence separating all the displays from the viewing areas of the room. You could walk up to the 'fence railing' to see the displays, but not get any closer without crossing into the actual displays themselves.

Chapter 13

"Here we are. This display is of the Andersen family. They lived several miles from here. They were actually one of the first families to take up farming in the area. They bought their land in the early 1960's and started a small dairy farm. Like everyone else, they grew their own corn and rotated out crops as the government asked. Like now, the government used to pay a certain amount of subsidy if you grew whatever was on their list that year."

Kol listened to Pastor Douglas, but kept his eyes on Ada Jane. She was eerily quiet as her eyes fell on an old rocker that must have belonged to her family. She stared for a long time at an old handmade quilt that was draped over an old dresser. There were bits and pieces of furniture and decorations that she walked past every day of her younger life and never thought twice about. There were photos of her family home, and of the cows and even one of a small child on a roan horse. No one but her would know she was that child. She paused to look at each. Finally she moved a little further down the display and reached over the railing to run her fingers over an old yellow piece of farm equipment.

"That's a fork from a hay baler," Pastor Douglas said.

"I remember," Ada Jane said softly, as she moved slowly down the exhibit. Then she saw it. A whole section filled with photos and newspapers. There even seemed to be some handwritten letters and cards there. She was drawn to it and moved quickly toward that area. She leaned over the railing trying to read the letters and cards and get a better look at the photos.

"We dedicated so much space to this one family because of an incident that occurred back in 1986. You see, their daughter was taken. It was a really big deal around these parts. People didn't just go missing out in the country like she did. Her father claimed there were bright lights shining over the field she was in, and no matter how hard he tried he couldn't get into that field. It was like the lights were keeping him out. Then suddenly the lights were gone, and so was Ada Jane.

"He said he couldn't see into the field she was in, just the illumination overhead, so he didn't see what happened, just knew that she went out to feed the animals, sharing the feeding with him like she always did, and as he came over the hill that led into the pasture she was supposed to be in, through a copse of trees and shrubbery, he was frozen in place and couldn't go forward or backward. Soon as he was able to move again, he rushed to the pasture screaming her name. The side by side ATV she was driving with the feed buckets was there, the feed was spilled all over the ground, but she was nowhere to be found," Pastor Douglas explained.

Ada Jane stood there, tears running down her face as she quietly remembered that day. She was leaning precariously over the railing still trying to see through her tears.

"They always insisted she'd be back one day. Some said she just ran away, that what he thought he saw was just the stress of worrying about his missing daughter. But they never swayed from their story. They even left a message for her on their tombstone, just in case nothing else was left standing for her to come to," the pastor said.

"We have been to the burial place. We have seen the message," Kol said.

Ada leaned a little too far and almost tipped over the top of the railing separating her from the things that were once her family's.

Kol moved swiftly, just catching her before she toppled into the exhibit. "Be careful, my Ada Jane. I know it is enticing, but we have plenty of time. Do not harm yourself as you finally get to see things from your parents' point of view."

Pastor Douglas heard Kol's comment and walked up beside them, looking closely at Ada Jane, and then the last known photo of her. She was standing on the front porch of her home with her mother and father. They were smiling into a camera as they all posed with their arms around each other. The historical society had had the photo blown up to an 8" x 10" photo and had it framed. It was the center piece of the 'taken' part of the exhibit.

"It's you, isn't it? You've finally come home," Pastor Douglas said, looking at the young woman standing next to him.

Ada Jane glanced his way. Her lip was trembling as she nodded her head.

The pastor opened his arms and Ada willingly accepted his hug. She could feel Kol's hands on her hips, and knew though he was tolerating this male hugging her, he didn't like it. So she only allowed a few seconds of hugging before she pulled away.

Pastor Douglas smiled at her before reaching for the railing meant to separate the visitors from the exhibits. He lifted the top section of railing from the notched posts it sat in and leaned it against the post behind himself. "There. No one has as much right to the things in this display as you do. Go ahead, get as close to it as you like, Ada Jane. And welcome home, young lady."

Ada wasted no time, she walked through all the items set up. She ran her fingers across every single thing she found in the exhibit. She read all the cards sending condolences from families she'd grown up with. She touched her father's favorite baseball cap — the one he wore every single day for as far back as she could remember. She picked up and studied every single photo.

Ada worked her way back through the entire exhibit on her family, touching and sniffing, remembering and reconnecting with every thing she saw. Her last stop was the handmade quilt on display. She lifted it from the dresser it laid across and held it to her face, inhaling deeply. "I can still smell my mom on it," she said. Ada turned to Kol, holding it out. "Here, Kol. Smell it..." she said, holding it out.

Kol, who'd been softly speaking with the pastor explaining some of what had happened and just the very basics on the fact that he and his people had rescued her, walked to Ada Jane and leaned over to sniff the quilt without taking it from her hands. "It smells of apples and something else I am not sure of the name of," he said.

"Cinnamon. Apples and Cinnamon. My mother always used apple scented everything, and she baked apple pies with cinnamon and brown sugar in them all the time. They were my father's favorite. This quilt used to sit folded on the sofa in the living room. It was there from the time I was a tiny little girl. I don't ever remember it not being there. The scent must have permeated it over the years," she said.

"We did not launder anything we brought into the exhibit, we wanted them preserved just as they were," the Pastor said.

Ada Jane sat down in the middle of the display, the quilt in her hands, the photo of herself and her parents in her lap. She looked up at Kol, who watched her patiently, lovingly. "I don't ever want to leave here," she admitted with a sad smile. "It's the closest I'll ever get to home."

"You know," Pastor Douglas said. "While I don't wish to lose our exhibit, these things do belong to you — technically speaking. "

"They do?" she asked, perking up a bit.

"The way I see it, they do. I wouldn't feel right with keeping your family's keepsakes from you. If you wouldn't mind providing copies of the photos, and maybe choosing a few things here and there that we could keep on display, I see no reason you couldn't take what is rightfully yours, Ada Jane," Pastor Douglas said sincerely.

Ada smiled up at Pastor Douglas excitedly, then over at Kol, who while looking like he was grimacing at her, was actually giving her a full-blown smile. But then she deflated. "I don't even have anywhere to live right now. I have nowhere to keep anything of value, or myself for that matter."

"You can stay with me, Ada Jane. You already know that I wish for you to be by my side. I only try not to push you too much so you know you have made your own decision."

"We have a few small cottages on the property. They were meant for the maintenance people and their families to live in, but after the last one quit, I've just been taking care of everything myself. I live in the parsonage just to the side there," he said, pointing to the opposite side of the building where the church nave was. "You are welcome to stay in one of the other cottages for as long as you like. It's not fancy by any means, but, it's dry in the rain, warm in the winter and cool in the summer. You'd have your privacy, and all I'd ask in return is maybe a hand around here, cleaning and mowing and keeping the graveyard neat and tidy."

"Really?" Ada asked, getting to her feet, holding the blanket to her chest, her smile wide and bright.

"Yes, really. I'd like to tell you that you could just reclaim your family's property, but, it was taken over about fifteen years ago. No one is really sure what's going on over there, because it's all fenced in and the public is kept out. It's the same with all the land the military seized. There's not much traffic in and out of it, but they do still have personnel there as far as I can tell. This," he said, lifting a hand and waving it around the building, "is probably about as close as you can get to home. Unless you have a better offer, you're welcome to be here."

"Kol?" Ada Jane asked, looking at him for his opinion.

Kol looked into Ada Jane's eyes. He knew no matter how much he hated leaving her without him anywhere, this was the only place she wanted to be right now. "How safe is it?" Kol asked the pastor.

"It's very safe here. Since several years before the church was rebuilt and the museum added to it, we've not had a single incident. The only people through here are usually just families out for a drive, trying to show their kids what life was like before the invasion and subsequent war."

"Can you protect her?" Kol asked.

"There are safe rooms built into the museum that can be accessed if necessary, but in all the years it's been here, we've never had to use them," Pastor Douglas answered.

Kol turned to Ada Jane. "Will you let me teach you to use a weapon?" he asked.

"Yes!" she answered, willing to do anything necessary to be able to stay here close to her original home.

"Come along, then," Kol said, holding his hand out for Ada to take. "Let us see the options for housing."

Ada started to move toward Kol, then realized she still had the quilt draped over her shoulder and falling down the front of her body. She looked down at it, smoothing her hands down the soft squares of patchwork that made up the quilt. She needed to put it back so she could go see the cottages with Kol and Pastor Douglas, but she couldn't seem to let it go.

"Ada Jane, why don't you just take the quilt with you? It can be the first item you reclaim," Pastor Douglas offered.

Ada nodded. "I'll get you a photo of it soon as I can," Ada answered.

"That'd be fine," Pastor Douglas answered.

Ada hurried to Kol's side with her quilt draped around her, and took his hand as together they followed Pastor Douglas outside. There were two cottages on the property along with the parsonage, which was actually just a little larger cottage than the other two. The parsonage was situated to the left of the church if you were standing looking at the church, and set just a few feet further back than the church itself was. It was a good forty feet from the church and had its own small private yard, fenced in with white picket fencing that was no more than hip high. "This is the parsonage," Pastor Douglas said, leading them up the front steps and into the small house he called home. "Feel free to look around," he invited.

Ada Jane started to refuse, but Kol had no problem taking a quick tour of the small home. He needed to know exactly what was on the property he was planning to leave his female on.

"It's very nice," Ada said, making conversation while Kol explored.

"Thank you. It's small, but since my wife passed, it's just me. It fit us just fine when she was still here, and it's more than enough for me on my own," Pastor Douglas said.

"No children?" Kol asked, coming back into the living room.

"No, it just wasn't in the cards for us," Pastor Douglas said, though not bitterly.

"May we see the other cottage homes?" Kol asked.

"Of course, right this way," the pastor said, leading them out of his home.

He led them to a small cottage that was set back beyond the back of the church. It still shared the same plot of land as the church and the parsonage, but was set a little further back, actually sitting behind both.

Pastor Douglas led them up onto the small front porch, unlocked the front door and let them into the small cottage. Kol walked in first and quickly went through the small cottage. He wandered through the bathroom, the one bedroom, and then through the surprisingly cozy kitchen before coming back into the living room to wait with Pastor Douglas as Ada Jane walked through the home exploring it.

"It is truly a miracle that this young lady is walking among us today," Pastor Douglas said to Kol.

"It is. It is as amazing that I managed to find her. She is my only female, the one created solely as my match. I will not allow any harm to come to her," Kol said matter of factly.

"I would say that after all I'd imagine she's been through, she's lucky to have you," the pastor commented.

Ada Jane had been through the bedroom and the bathroom. She'd turned on the water and made sure it ran clear, and was now in the kitchen opening and closing cabinets. "Kol! Did you see? There are still dishes and pots and pans in here! I can actually cook my own meals!" she called out excitedly.

"I did not see that, but I am pleased that you are pleased," Kol answered.

She opened the refrigerator and poked around inside it for a few moments, before closing the door. "I don't think the refrigerator works," she called out in general.

"Let's take a look," Pastor Douglas answered. He checked the outlet, and the freezer section of the refrigerator and nodded. "I think you're right. This one seems to have gone kaput. But, there's one in the other cottage we can move over here if you like this cottage better. Or, who knows, you may like that one better."

He led them over to the other cottage. It was about the same size as the first, but was on the opposite side of the church and out of view of the other two cottages. They walked around it and looked at it. Kol didn't say anything, but he really didn't want her on this side of the church by herself. He was hoping she'd make the same decision.

"What do you think about this cottage, Ada Jane?" Kol asked.

"I don't know. It's the same as the other, but I really like the placement of the other better. And, it just feels homier than this one," she answered.

"Very well. I will move the cold box to the other cottage," Kol said, relieved that she'd chosen the same one he had.

"Are you sure you don't mind me being here?" Ada Jane asked Pastor Douglas.

The pastor smiled. "Look at me. I'm 86 years old. I've taken care of this property for so long that it's not just a property to me. It's my home. I've looked at the photo of that young girl in there," he said, pointing to the church museum, "wondering what ever happened to her so many times I have your face memorized. Now you're here, back where you belong. And I'm old, alone, needing help taking care of this place. It seems like destiny to me. I'd appreciate the company," he said earnestly.

Ada Jane smiled. "Okay, then. I'd like to have the other cottage, if you don't mind me living so near to you."

"Done! It's yours," the pastor answered, smiling.

"It is a good choice, my Ehlealah. You will be safe here, and at peace here. I can visit you whenever you allow and it is only twenty minutes from my base to this place," Kol said, feeling good at her choice of a home for now.

"I think it's a good choice as well," Ada agreed.

"Remind me to advise Bart that he should stop looking for a place for you to reside," Kol said.

"I will," Ada Jane answered with a big smile on her face.

Chapter 14

By the end of the day, Kol had moved the working refrigerator to Ada's cottage, the non-working one to the extra cottage, helped her move her clothing and toiletries inside her cottage and helped her get them put away in her bedroom and bathroom. He helped her move whichever photos she wanted from her family's display to her new home and put them on the walls for her along with any of the other items that she felt she wanted near her. He'd left her the communicator he'd brought for her, and a tablet for her to access in any way she wanted and instructed her in the use of both.

The only thing left was to teach her to fire a weapon.

There was an old, mangled piece of steel on the edge of the property with weeds and greenery growing up through and around it. Some leftover piece of wreckage that no one had ever removed, and that was the item Kol decided to use as a target.

"What is that?" Ada asked as Kol stood behind her, preparing to show her how to stand and how to aim one of his spare weapons.

"It looks to be a piece of a transport," Kol answered.

"I was told it was the last part of a ship that crashed, but it was so big, it would have to wait to be removed until they could get a private company to cut it up and haul it away," Pastor Douglas said, as he stood nearby and watched curiously. "It didn't bother me very much and it was out of the way so I just didn't worry about it after they took away all the other pieces of it."

"We will take care of it for you today," Kol said.

The pastor's eyebrows bunched up in confusion. "Okay," he answered, not quite sure what Kol meant.

Kol reached into his pocket. "This is a disintegrater," he said, handing her what looked to her to be a very thin, flat, egg-shaped channel selector. It was smooth on the top and the bottom, with the exception of a slight indention where it seemed that a finger or thumb would go. There were three lines running over the indention, evenly spaced, and it felt as though they would depress if you tried to push them.

"Can I press the lines?" she asked.

"Yes, the weapon has not been programmed for you yet, so you can press them with no action occurring," Kol answered.

Ada Jane experimented with the weapon. It fit in the palm of her hand. If she maneuvered it just so, she found she could end up holding it against the palm side of her hand with her fingers beneath it and her thumb resting in the depression with the three lines across it.

"It's very lightweight. I'm surprised it'll be able to do much of anything," she said, testing the weight of the weapon on her hand.

"It is extremely dangerous and effective," Kol said. "Now, I need you to practice standing as I do, and holding the weapon like I do."

"Okay," she answered, going to stand beside him.

"When you have time to aim your shot, you should stand sheltered behind something, or at the very least turn your body sideways so that you are a more slender target yourself. Then aim at the target, and do you feel this?" he asked, using his own thumb to slide hers over a rough patch on the top of the small weapon she held in her hands.

"Yes, it feels like the three lines," Ada Jane answered.

"It is. When you first think you may need to use the weapon, or if you are preparing to use it, you should take it in hand and alternately press the three lines, one at a time, in whatever order you choose to prep it for firing."

"How do I know what order to press them in?" she asked.

"Once I assign it to you, you will choose a pattern. That pattern will be unique to you and no one else will know it. That along with your unique fingerprint, and your DNA is what will allow the weapon to fire. The pattern you choose is a safety mechanism to prevent it from firing accidentally while being carried. The fingerprint and DNA are to ensure that no one but you can fire the weapon regardless of the circumstances. Do you understand?"

"Yes. How will it test my DNA?" Ada Jane asked.

"Once the weapon is familiarized with your fingerprint, it will not scan for DNA unless your body temperature is less than it should be. The first initial time, it will prick your finger. But it is only slightly uncomfortable. Is that okay?"

"If that's what's necessary to protect myself, then yes."

"Now, press your thumb onto those three lines all at the same time, then let up and do it again. The weapon will know it is preparing to be reprogrammed."

Ada Jane nodded. "Okay."

"Is there any recoil in the weapon? Will it knock you backwards like a rifle will?" Pastor Douglas asked from where he stood watching.

"No, none at all. If anything, it may drive your hand higher, but only by a small amount, inches at most. Once you are prepared for it, it is easily controlled," Kol answered. Then he looked back at Ada Jane. "Are you ready?"

"Yes," Ada Jane said, grinning.

"Missy," Kol said aloud. "Program this weapon for my Ehlealah's DNA print, please," Kol asked.

The handheld unit on Kol's belt responded. "Please standby, Ambassador Kol."

Only a few seconds later the handheld communicator spoke. "I am prepared to program the weapon. Standby."

"Don't let go of the weapon, my Ada Jane," Kol said by way of warning her the finger stick was coming. "The finger stick is done with a very intensely focused puff of air, there is no needle used," Kol explained.

Kol saw her wince slightly, but she didn't change her hold on the disintegrater.

"Still stings," she complained, but offered him a smile.

"I have aligned your weapon for use by Ada Jane Ra' Don Tol, formerly Andersen, Ehlealah to Elite Force Commander Ambassador Kol Ra' Don Tol. Her DNA was matched to records aboard Command Warship 1. Only Ada Jane Andersen will have the ability to fire the weapon assigned to her. Please program the safety features as necessary," Missy reported.

"Thank you, Missy," Kol responded.

"Ada Jane, press the lines in a pattern, one at a time. Be sure you can remember the pattern as you will need to repeat it any time you wish to fire the weapon."

Ada moved her thumb over the lines a few times to see what pattern she could perform quickly without it feeling too awkward. Choosing one, she proceeded to depress the lines in that order as Kol had instructed.

"Okay, done," she said.

"It is live now, my Ehlealah. Be very careful where you aim it, and do not put your thumb over the lines unless you are ready to fire."

"Okay," Ada answered, looking down at the weapon and becoming excited about learning to use it. She moved her thumb to the side of the weapon so she couldn't press the lines on accident.

"Now, stand like this," Kol said, adopting the position he wanted Ada to stand in.

Ada mimicked his stance.

"Your weapon is live, do not point it at anything other than the target," Kol warned again.

"I won't," she answered, grinning at him.

"Raise your arm like this," he said, showing her how to move and aim. "Take aim at the top half of the target, and when you're comfortable with your aim, press on all three lines at the same time. Be prepared for your arm to be lifted very slightly into the air. You have already entered your pattern to unlock it, so the next step is to simply fire it."

"Okay," Ada answered, still grinning ear-to-ear.

Kol moved behind her to stand with Pastor Douglas as she prepared to take her first shot.

Ada felt she was properly lined up with the target, rubbed her thumb just slightly across the three lines to be sure she was touching all three, then pressed her thumb into them. The weapon responded immediately. An almost imperceptible beam of light shot out from the front of the weapon, struck the metal target, and before their eyes the metal became white hot and was absolutely disintegrated.

"Oh my gosh!" Ada Jane exclaimed. "I killed it!" she shouted happily.

Kol laughed, and Pastor Douglas even chuckled.

"Did you feel it attempt to raise your arm slightly?" Kol asked.

"Yes, but just a little. I can control it," Ada Jane responded.

"Very well. Would you like to fire it again?" Kol asked.

"Uhh, yes!" she shrieked happily.

"Go ahead when ready," Kol said, smiling indulgently at Ada Jane.

Ada Jane got in her stance, aimed her weapon and fired. Half of what remained of the scrap metal glowed white hot, then disappeared.

"Now, I want you to fire at it, while crouching down without time to stop and aim," Kol said.

Ada looked at him, knowing he was preparing her for if she was actually having to protect herself. She nodded then walked about twenty feet toward the church.

Kol and Pastor Douglas had moved far aside, out of her way and watched to see what she'd do.

"Assume the target is searching for you, my Ada Jane. What do you do?" Kol asked.

Ada Jane nodded. Then she crouched low and hurried across the ground through the high grasses and came to a stop, kneeling on one knee as she brought up her weapon at the same time, firing at the remaining scrap metal. As soon as she'd fired, she was up and running while she crouched low to minimize herself as a target.

Kol looked around and realized there were several sheets of old, rusted aluminum leaning against the trees just a few feet further toward the fence line. "What of the metal sheets?" he asked the pastor.

"They are scrap, not needed," Pastor Douglas answered.

"There are more coming after you from the fence line. They are the metal sheets leaning on the trees," Kol shouted to Ada Jane.

Ada didn't hesitate, she continued her run in the direction she'd been running parallel to the fence, but didn't hesitate to raise her weapon and fire at the sheets of scrap aluminum she saw there. She kept running until she was safely hidden away behind the well-house.

"Most excellent!" Kol said, raising his voice so he could be heard by Ada Jane who was just now coming out from behind the small structure that housed the water well the property used. "You could easily earn a sniper's position among my team. Of that I have no doubt!" he said, giving her plenty of praise.

Ada Jane walked back over to them, grinning, her heart beating wildly and with a great deal more confidence in her stride. "I know how Vivi feels as she walks around with her chain and her dagger now. It is very empowering, very freeing, to know that you are capable of defending yourself."

"I am very proud of you, Ada Jane. I have always been proud of you, but even more so now as I watch you discover who you truly are. I am honored to be your male," Kol said, smiling lovingly at Ada Jane.

Ada walked until she was in his arms. She hugged him tightly to her and pressed her face into his chest. "Thank you, Kol, for everything. I'd still be so lost without you here to help guide me."

"I am not guiding you. I'm simply watching over you as your heart guides you."

Ada Jane smiled up at him as he looked down at her and pressed his lips to her forehead.

"Ambassador Kol," his communicator interrupted.

"Yes, Missy," Kol answered.

"You are needed on Base 28, sir."

"What is happening?" Kol asked.

"Viceroy Buchanan and Patroon Zhuxi have the situation in hand, but your presence is requested," Missy answered.

"And Elisher?" Kol asked.

"Is in your quarters as per your instructions. Viceroy Buchanan, Patroon Zhuxi and several trusted males are preventing the Consul from entering."

"I'll be there shortly, Missy," Kol responded.

Kol looked down at Ada Jane. "I shall have to take my leave, my Ehlealah."

"It's fine, Kol. I've kept you too long as it is," Ada Jane answered.

"Time spent with you is never too long," Kol said, tucking a loose length of hair back into her hair tie.

"We'll be fine here, Kol," Pastor Douglas said.

Kol nodded. "I shall return soon, if I may have your permission," Kol said, looking down at Ada Jane.

"Of course. Any time you wish to visit me, I'll be right here."

"I'll go now, Kol. Thank you for bringing Ada Jane back home. Thank you for all your consideration and your kindness. And thanks to you and your people for keeping our planet safe once more," Pastor Douglas said.

"You are most welcome, Pastor Douglas," Kol said, walking toward him and extending his hand for a hand shake.

Pastor Douglas shook his hand. "You are welcome any time, Kol," he said before smiling at him. "Bless you, sir," the pastor said, then walked off toward the church and the cottages in the distance.

"I will not be far away, Ada Jane. But I have much to oversee and address while I'm here."

"I understand," she said. "I know you have important things to see to."

Kol took her hand in his pulling her close to him gently. "There is nothing more important than you. You are the only reason I am on this planet. But since I've arrived, I've found that some things need to be addressed. I can make things better for many of the people in the sector I'm assigned to. But you are always first. Do not ever hesitate to call for me. And do not ever forget that I am always waiting for you to be at my side. Wherever I am, I have arranged to provide a home for you with me whenever you decide you are ready."

Ada looked up at Kol. "I know that, Kol. But I need to be here at the moment. My parents are here. My past is here."

Kol nodded. "Call to me. Let me know you are well. And if it is acceptable to you, I will be here as often as I can."

"I will."

Kol slowly, so that she could pull away if she wanted to, lowered his head to hers. He pressed his lips very softly against her lips and rested them there for a few seconds before rubbing his nose against hers, pressing his lips to hers once more, then stepping away from her.

"I meant what I said, Ada Jane. I am proud to be your male."

Ada Jane blushed and nodded.

"Put that weapon in your pocket after you press your pattern once more. It will not fire unless you have prepped it by reentering your pattern, so it is perfectly safe to carry on your person at all times. Do not ever leave it anywhere. Have it with you at all times," Kol instructed.

"I promise. I will have it with me at all times. Even when I bathe," Ada answered.

Kol groaned. The idea of his Ada Jane naked and wet was not what he needed in his mind as he did his best to force himself to leave and get back to the base.

"I shall return soon, my Ada Jane."

"Alright," Ada Jane answered. Then she called out to him. "Kol! Remember to tell Bart that I found a place to live!"

"I will have Missy contact him!" he called back.

Ada stood back and watched as Kol hurried to his battle cruiser turned transport and jumped from the ground to the upper deck, then disappeared inside. She knew he was powerful, but that effortless jump just drove the point home. She'd break a leg if she'd tried to jump down from that height, and he made the jump up to that level from a standing position. Unbelievable. She stood there and waited while the cruiser lifted into the sky, then in the blink of an eye was so far out of sight she couldn't even be sure she could see it.

She noticed the pastor standing at the front gate of the cemetery and began walking toward him.

"I noticed you and Kol must have decorated your parents' grave sites," he said.

"We did. I hope it's okay. I didn't think about it being a historic cemetery until after we were already finished," Ada answered.

"It's fine. I think you're entitled to just about anything you choose to do around here," Pastor Douglas answered.

"Thank you," Ada Jane answered.

"Now, I know you've got your things all put away in your cottage, but the one thing you don't have yet is groceries. I've got a few things, and the delivery boy should be bringing more out tomorrow. Why don't we go add to that list for you, while we cook a bite to eat?" Pastor Douglas asked.

"That'd be great," Ada Jane answered.

Chapter 15

Kol stalked down the corridors of Base 28. He was under no illusions that he'd be able to avoid Diskastes or his security. But, he would try not to break them too badly. He took a left into the corridor that housed his quarters and though he continued to move forward, he slowed his pace.

Buchanan was sitting outside the door to his quarters shouting at the tablet in his hand.

"Buchanan," Kol said as he approached.

"Kol! Welcome back," he said, before raising his tablet in the air and miming the action of flying a transport or cruiser. "Damnit!" Buchanan shouted. "This sonofabitch cheats!" he said disgustedly.

"What cheats?" Kol asked.

"Damned video game! I'm supposed to be able to fly over opposing forces and drop bombs on them, but does it let me fly all the way over? No, it does not! So there are always some that survive. Cheating bastards," Buchanan mumbled, getting to his feet.

"Bombs are no longer dropped. It would be archaic to do so. We simply decimate them with fission technology," Kol explained.

"Yes, I'm sure you do. But, in World War I and in II as well, we dropped bombs. And that's when this game is set."

Kol nodded. "I see. Very well, then. Perhaps you should purchase a more current simulator."

"It's not a simulator, it's a game," Buchanan explained.

"If you say so," Kol agreed, remembering his promise to Bart to try to be less conflicting. "How may I be of service?" Kol asked.

"Couple of things. Mind if I come in with you?" Buchanan asked.

"Not at all," Kol answered. He unlocked his door and marveled again at the antiquated way of keeping one's quarters safe. Anyone could get in with a key, or by force. Electronic scanner and hydraulic, steel doors were much more effective for security and safety. "Enter," Kol said, leading the way and standing aside for Buchanan to follow him inside.

"Kol!" Elisher said, standing up from the table.

"Good evening, Elisher, I trust you had no problems today," Kol said, glancing around the room and noticing the two additional males who'd jumped to attention when he entered.

"There was a bit of a flareup, but Viceroy Buchanan and Patroon Zhuxi handled it well. I've been here all day working, and with no interruptions since they assigned their own security to our quarters," Elisher answered.

"What was the issue?" Kol asked, focusing on Buchanan.

"Diskastes received word of all the documentation Elisher was able to seize on your behalf. He's figured out something's amiss, and tried to remove the documentation from your quarters. He threatened Elisher with physical removal from the base if he didn't allow them entrance and didn't hand over all documents that were property of Base 28. But, no problem, Zhuxi and I arrived. I stationed myself outside the door with two of our people inside with Elisher. Zhuxi is making the rounds and gathering up all additional documentation he can, and generally making a nuisance of himself to keep Diskastes focused on him and his people rather than on what you and Elisher already have," Buchanan explained.

"Thank you," Kol said, performing a stiff little military bow. Then he turned to the two males who'd obviously been lounging on the sofas and snacking before he and Buchanan entered. "And thank you for your services."

Both nodded at him and continued to stand erect and rigid as they should have been the entire time.

"If your security could stay for several more days, it will be most appreciated. It is difficult to protect Elisher, these quarters, investigate the things I should, hold off Diskastes and his people, and watch over my female," Kol said.

"It's no problem. We'll be here as long as you need us," Buchanan answered.

"I will have support personnel arriving shortly. They are two or three days out. Once they arrive, if your security is required in other areas, I'm sure we'll do fine here on our own," Kol said.

"Not at all. There is a small group of personnel assigned to this base that is loyal to Diskastes. The rest are from either my district or came with Zhuxi. We can assign to you and your people for the length of your stay."

"Thank you," Kol answered. "I am somewhat sure that the personnel Ambassador Bartholomew is sending are his own administrative liaisons to assist, or perhaps direct Elisher. And while I have no problem effectively controlling this base alone, I've been told it is not the correct procedure at this time," Kol ended on a slight snarl.

Buchanan grinned. "Told you to reel it in, huh?"

"What?" Kol asked.

"Bartholomew... he told you to control yourself for now."

"Yes, he did," Kol answered irritatedly.

"Welcome to diplomacy, Ambassador Kol," Buchanan said, chuckling. "It's a bitch."

<<<<<<<>>>>>>>

Later that evening after Kol and Elisher shared a meal, and Elisher had gone to bed, Kol sat in his living room surrounded by boxes of papers. He looked around himself and tried to figure out how he ended up in a position he was not at all meant for.

For as long as he had been fascinated with Earth, this was not how he wished to visit the planet. He had no interest in diplomacy. He was more the claim his female and return to the stars with her after a tour of the planet type.

Kol smiled thinking of Ada Jane. He missed her though he'd just been with her earlier in the day. He looked at his communicator and considered calling her. He decided against it. Bart had instructed him to give her her space and if he didn't, he could risk her pulling away, so frustratedly he stalked toward the bathroom, dropping his clothes a piece at a time behind himself as he went. Completely naked he stood in the shower and slapped his hands against the tile like he would in a cleansing unit on Command Warship 1. Nothing happened, so he turned his attention to the shiny, silver fixtures. He pulled what looked like a lever up until it clicked into place, but still, nothing happened. He grasped what looked to him like a spigot for fluid to pass through and tried to turn it. Other than a creaking sound, nothing happened.

Becoming more and more irritated, he reached out to the circular fixture on the left and turned it as far as it would allow. Immediately scalding hot water sprayed out of the silver fixture above his head. Kol screeched and jumped from the shower, pulling down the shower curtain and the shower curtain rod at the same time. Kol soundly cursed the scalding water, the shower curtain rod that had smacked him in the face, and the shower curtain itself as he tried to untangle it from around his legs. He was still cursing in both his own language and English when there was a knock at the door.

"Sir? Kol? Is everything alright?" Elisher called out.

Kol went to the door and whipped it open at the same time he managed to free himself from the plastic sheet called a shower curtain and kept it balled up loosely in front of himself. "No! Everything is not alright! Someone has set the cleansing chamber to boil!" he snapped.

"The cleans..." Elisher said before seeing the steam gathering in the bathroom and realizing Kol had most likely turned on the hot water only. "I'll check on it, if you don't mind," Elisher said.

"Stay back, Elisher. It will cook you alive!" Kol instructed, tossing the shower curtain aside and striding back to the shower to prove his point to Elisher.

Elisher stood in the doorway, his eyes wide as he watched a totally nude Ambassador Kol walk through the bathroom as though his nudity was completely natural. He watched the muscles in Kol's rounded ass as he walked, the muscles clenching and unclenching and his thighs bulging with each step Kol took. Elisher found it difficult to look away from Kol's body — he'd never seen such male beauty.

Kol in the meantime had come to a stop beside the shower stall and was waiting for Elisher to come witness what he'd decided to call the death chamber instead of the cleansing chamber. "Are you coming to see this death chamber?" Kol asked.

Elisher had been staring at Kol's penis, and he'd just been caught. He forced himself to look away from Kol's nether regions and focus on the shower. "Uh, yes. I'm coming," Elisher stammered. He walked over to the shower stall and turned the hot water off, then pushed the shower knob into the down position so the water wouldn't come out of the shower head until they were ready. Then he reached for the right fixture and turned it on first, then he turned the left fixture on again, only just a small turn of the fixture. He waited a moment for them both to run together before reaching out to allow the water to run over his fingers.

"No! It will blister your fingers!" Kol said, yanking Elisher's hand away from the water.

"It's okay. You turned on only the left fixture," Elisher said.

"Yes, I did. It was the only one that worked," Kol answered.

"The right fixture is for cold water, the left fixture is for hot water. The one in the middle is to turn on the shower. You should always set the temperature of the water before you turn on the shower head. If you have the shower head turned on, the water will fall on you before you have checked the temperature. The hot water here is heated more than it would normally be because our water supplies have been polluted over the years. The heat is to completely kill any bacteria that may be in it. We're so used to it, we don't even think about it anymore. You turn on the cold completely, like this," Elisher said, showing Kol. "Then you turn on the hot, only a little at a time, testing the temperature yourself until it's comfortable. Then you turn on the shower," Elisher explained by lifting the little knob that changed the water from the spigot at knee level to come out of the shower head.

Kol watched as Elisher reached out and pushed his fingers into the stream of water.

"See? Perfect," Elisher said.

Kol reached out his fingers and allowed the warm water to flow over them. He smiled at the sensation, then he straightened and scowled again. "Someone should put instructions in this cleansing chamber! We do not have showers with water on Command Warship 1, there are cleansing chambers with a very few limited tubs for those with human Ehlealahs," Kol explained.

"I'll get right on that, sir. I'll make sure clear instructions are printed for each shower on base," Elisher said, fighting to keep his gaze above Kol's shoulders. "Would you like to try it before I leave you to your shower?" Elisher asked.

"No. I understand how to do it now," Kol answered.

"I'll just go back to my room then," Elisher said.

"I will cleanse," Kol said, eyeing the fixtures that Elisher had just turned on for him. He heard the door close as Elisher left, and he reached out tentatively and increased the hot water slightly, waiting to see the effect it would have on the temperature of the water falling from the shower. Deciding he liked it cooler, he turned the hot back to where Elisher had it, held his fingers beneath it and smiled when it got the temperature he'd preferred. Then he stepped under the water and moaned at the feeling of water running in rivulets down his body. He didn't particularly care for baths, but this shower... he could get used to this. Kol dipped his head to allow the water to run over his face and ran a wet hand up his horns, then reached out for the soap. He knew what soap was, he'd given some to Quin when he'd been trying to cleanse Vivi.

Kol worked up a lather and smoothed it over his chest and abdomen. The slippery soap against his skin was a luxury he wasn't used to. He reached for the soap again and set about working up more lather to bathe the rest of his body.

<<<<<<<>>>>>>>

Elisher stepped outside Kol's bathroom and stopped there with the back of his head resting against the closed door. He heard Kol adjusting the temperature, then he heard him moan when he stepped under the shower.

Elisher's eyes widened and he slapped a hand over his mouth before hurrying away and locking himself in his own room on the opposite side of the living room. He hurried into his own bathroom and stripped down leaving his robe and pajamas on the floor of the bathroom.

The water was cranked up to freezing cold before Elisher stepped beneath it. The cold water ran down over the body he made every effort to keep hidden every single day. Elisher looked down and watched the response of the nipples on small breasts as they puckered against the cold water — or the thought of a naked Ambassador Kol — which had had this effect on the now perky nipples Elisher wasn't sure. Elisher ran wet hands down the curve of the slender waist that blossomed out to curved hips, and watched the tips of tiny, delicate toes and feet as they curled against the cold water.

Elisher spent a lot of years cultivating her image as a young man, and there was nothing worth risking the strides she'd made. Not even a male that looked like Kol. She thought of his body again and the sight of him walking before her naked as the day he was born and shook her head. "Nobody should be that beautiful or that well endowed," she whispered as she reached for the shampoo and ducked her head beneath the cold water.

Ten minutes later Elisher stepped out of the shower and dried her body. She towel dried her short, cropped hair then pulled on the tight stretchy bando she wore around her breasts to keep them flattened at all times. She pulled on the loose pajama top, then the pajama bottoms she sported each and every night, because you never knew who'd interrupt your sleep in the middle of the night. Then she pulled on the socks that covered her small, feminine feet before finally opening the bathroom door and returning to her own bed.

Elisher laid her head on her pillow and closed her eyes. “Please give me strength,” she whispered, thinking of a naked Kol again.

Chapter 16

Two days later Kol sat on the sofa in his quarters. It was early morning and far too early for anyone else to be awake, but Kol was. He found he just couldn't sleep soundly. He'd lay awake for hours with thoughts of Ada Jane in his mind. He'd been warned not to call her too often, or push too hard, but he was tiring of the whole damned situation. He eyed the com sitting next to him on the sofa, then glanced away toward the opposite side of the room again. Slowly his eyes crept back to the com on the cushion beside him.

Kol snarled and grabbed the com. "Missy! Com Ada Jane!" he snapped.

"Of course, Ambassador Kol. And you're welcome," Missy answered in an over the top polite tone of voice.

"Thank you," he added begrudgingly.

"You are welcome," Missy responded.

Kol sat there impatiently waiting for Ada Jane to answer her com, then suddenly, there she was.

"Hello? Kol?" she asked sleepily.

"Ada Jane!" Kol said, his heart overflowing with want at just the sound of her voice.

"Is everything okay?" Ada asked, as she glanced toward her window and realized it was still dark outside.

"No!" he answered, tired of playing games. "I tire of the measured courtships required on Earth. I need you near. And you need me near!"

"What do you mean measured courtships?" Ada asked as she sat up in bed.

"I am told, 'do not push her. Take your time, do not contact her every day. Do not demand that she agrees that she is yours. Do not force her to move into your quarters. Allow her to find her way.' I am trying. I truly am. But it is a strain on my patience, Ada Jane."

"Who told you that you can't contact me every day?" she asked.

"Bart. And the other males that I have befriended here on base."

"They're wrong," she said simply.

"I knew they were wrong!" Kol shouted, jumping to his feet.

"I do need to find my way. And I don't want to be forced to anything that doesn't feel right to me for now. But I don't want you to be distant with me. I was so happy to see you, and to share my coming home with you, and then, I didn't hear from you again. I was wondering why you hadn't reached out to me," Ada Jane admitted.

"Because I am a fool who listened to other males rather than ask you myself," Kol answered. "I have not slept since I left you in your new home. I have not had a moment's peace. No matter what I do, my thoughts are always with you, my Ehlealah."

"Then let's straighten all this out now. You contact me whenever you want to. There is no time limit or a plan to follow. If you want to speak to me, com me."

Kol smiled. "I like that. I will."

"Good," Ada Jane answered, smiling at Kol on the communicator.

A door opened behind Kol but he didn't turn around, he knew it was Elisher and it barely even registered on his radar that Elisher was entering the common rooms of their quarters from his bedroom.

Ada Jane focused on the person who opened a door behind Kol and walked out of the frame. "Who is that?" she asked.

"Who is who?" Kol asked, still smiling and soothed from Ada Jane telling him he could contact her whenever he wished.

"That woman that just walked out of what looks like a bedroom in your quarters," Ada Jane answered.

Kol turned around and saw the open door to Elisher's bedroom, then glanced over toward the kitchenette where Elisher was making himself a cup of coffee.

"That is Elisher. He is not a woman, he is my attache'. He is just waking and making himself a cup of coffee."

Ada Jane's eyes narrowed and she regarded Kol suspiciously. "Are you sure?" she asked.

Kol thought that was a ridiculous question. Of course he knew the person in his quarters was Elisher. "Of course I am sure, my Ada Jane. Elisher is my assistant. He is the only person that has access to my quarters as he lives here with me."

"No, are you sure he's a he?" Ada Jane said.

Kol looked over at Elisher who was staring back at him with his mouth open.

"I will introduce you," Kol said, walking toward the kitchenette sure this would dispel all Ada Jane's concerns.

Kol walked toward Elisher and Elisher stood frozen in place like a deer in the headlights. His eyes were huge and his mouth was still hanging open. "Elisher, I wish for you to meet my Ehlealah," Kol said, stepping closer so that Elisher could see the screen Ada Jane was displayed on. "This is my Ada Jane. She holds my soul and my heart."

Elisher looked at the pretty blonde woman still in bed looking back at her. "Hello," Elisher said, trying to make her voice a little deeper. "I'm Elisher, I assist your, uh, your..." Elisher paused, not quite sure what Kol would be to Ada Jane.

"Her male. I am her male," Kol supplied for Elisher. "Ada Jane, this is Elisher. He is assisting me with the Ambassador responsibilities that have been assigned to me. Because of the nature of the research, I have moved him into my extra bedroom. He performs his work on the table that sits in our common room."

"It is very nice to meet you, Ada Jane. I hope that I can make your acquaintance in person some day soon," Elisher said.

"Thank you," Ada Jane answered, still not totally convinced this Elisher person was a man. She was suspicious of the whole situation. Not that she thought Kol would ever deceive her, he obviously thought this person was a man, but Ada wasn't so sure.

"Kol, when can you have dinner with me?" Ada asked, knowing she couldn't speak to Kol about her suspicions via the com connection since Elisher was right there.

Kol brightened. "You wish to share a meal with me?"

"Yes. I'd like to cook for you. Could you come to my place and let me make you dinner?" Ada Jane asked.

"Yes! I would very much like to eat your food. When would you like me to eat with you?" Kol asked, practically giddy at the fact that Ada Jane had invited him to her home where she'd prepare him a meal.

"Whenever it's okay for you to be away," Ada Jane answered.

Elisher walked out of the kitchen and over to the table. She picked up her personal tablet and swiped the screen to wake it up. "You have no afternoon or evening meetings all this week, sir. All your meetings are early morning."

"Tomorrow evening?" Ada Jane asked, having heard Elisher speaking to Kol.

"Yes. I will be there tomorrow and we will share a meal," Kol confirmed.

"If you want to come earlier than dinner time, that would be nice, too. We could spend a few hours together," Ada Jane said, smiling softly at Kol.

"I will be there as early as I can."

"I'll see you then?" Ada Jane said.

"Yes. I will see you then, my Ada Jane. My heart thinks of you every moment. I will be counting the seconds until I am with you."

Ada Jane kissed her fingers and pressed them to the communicator Kol had provided her with.

All Kol's teeth were displayed as he smiled bigger than he had in a long time and brought the communicator to his face so he could press his lips to it.

"Bye," Ada Jane said, just before she ended the com connection.

"Until then," Kol said, closing the connection on his own com as well.

He looked over toward Elisher, with a silly grin still on his face.

"So," Elisher said, "You have a mate."

"She is much more than a mate. She is my Ehlealah. My heart and soul are with her always."

"Yes, you said as much," Elisher said, nodding.

"She is the most perfect female. In truth, I am here for her. She wished to return to her home world, and I followed. Only once I arrived was I made aware that I was needed here," Kol confided.

"So we have your Ada Jane to thank for you being here, then," Elisher said.

"Yes. I will see to my duties as I have always seen to all my duties. I will succeed in all the responsibilities Chairman Bartholomew has assigned to me. But I would not be here were it not for my Ehlealah."

"I find that admirable," Elisher said, heading back toward her bedroom.

"What is admirable?" Kol asked.

"That a male, any male, is so enamored and committed to a woman, or mate, or Ehlealah, whatever you might call them."

"Are you and the males of Earth not fully committed to your females?" Kol asked curiously.

Elisher huffed a laugh. "Hardly. Most Earth males tend to remain faithful for only as long as no one better is around. The moment someone prettier or wealthier or even younger shows the slightest bit of interest, they leave their woman and go to the next one."

Kol scowled. "Earth males have no integrity!"

"Tell me about it," Elisher said, opening the door to her bedroom. "You should get ready. We have to be in the meeting room for a vidcom with all bases at 9:00A.M."

"I will be ready," Kol answered, watching Elisher disappear into his rooms and close the door behind himself.

He canted his head to the side slightly as he considered Elisher. He'd been surprised when Ada Jane had thought him a female. He was very feminine in his mannerisms, but several species had males that were slightly effeminate. Kol shrugged. Elisher was simply Elisher. He was a good and trusted assistant. Kol really didn't think of the effeminate side of him any longer. He was just Elisher.

Kol went to his room to get dressed. All he had on his cruiser was battle garb, so battle uniforms it was. But that worked out well. It was somewhat intimidating to see a Cruestaci warrior in full battle regalia, and Kol had no problem using that to his advantage.

<<<<<<<>>>>>>>

Ada Jane threw back the covers and got out of bed. She smiled when she thought of Kol's frustration at taking advice from men he'd made friends with and then becoming frustrated with it because he missed her. She got dressed then went to the kitchen to make herself a pot of coffee.

Opening her refrigerator, she saw the eggs she'd collected from Pastor Douglas's chicken coop. She reached for two of them and her butter, and set them on the counter while she got her coffee started and reached for a slice of bread. Ada melted the butter in a skillet and cracked the eggs into it, standing over them patiently while waiting to turn them over. She flipped them, counted to fifteen and flipped them back over before moving them to her plate with a spatula. Then she put another pat of butter in the skillet and swirled it around while it melted, then dropped the slice of bread into the skillet.

Her coffee had finished perking and she turned from the skillet to fill her cup, then waited for the bread to brown on one side before adding it to her plate as well. No better toast than that fried in a skillet with butter. Ada carried her breakfast over to the table and sat looking out over the small yard between her cottage and the Pastor's. She smiled when she realized she'd come full circle. She was home. She was whole. And she was able to enjoy something as simple as breakfast in her own kitchen. Her smile grew when she realized she also had Kol.

Kol missed her, he loved her. Whenever she was around him, he never went more than a few minutes without calling her his Ada Jane, or his Ehlealah.

There was a knock at her door and she rose to answer it. Ada Jane paused near the window beside the front door to pull back the sheer curtains and peek outside. She unlocked the door and pulled it open. "Good morning, Pastor Douglas."

"Good morning, Ada Jane. Thought I'd see if you wanted to take a ride into town this morning," he said.

"I'd love to, but I just sat down to breakfast. Will you join me?" she asked.

"For company only. I've already eaten," he replied.

"Well come on in, then," she said, taking a step back to open her door and allow him to enter. "How about a cup of coffee?" Ada Jane offered.

"Now that, I'll take you up on," Pastor Douglas said happily.

Ada Jane got Pastor Douglas his coffee and sat down to her breakfast again.

"With you here we're caught up on all the chores. I thought maybe we'd go into town and give you a tour," Pastor Douglas said.

"I'd love that!" Ada Jane said. "I need to pick up some more groceries anyway if that's possible. I invited Kol to dinner tomorrow. I need to get something to cook for him," Ada Jane explained.

"We don't have grocery stores like you remember from your time on Earth. Not everything is available at all times, but there are always alternatives to choose from."

"I'm sure I'll find something. And, I need to open an account to deposit my credits in also. Is there a bank in town?" she asked.

"No, there's not. But, maybe when Kol is here tomorrow, you can ask him to take you to the closest city to open an account in your name."

"That's a good idea. I'll do that."

"Now eat up, let's get going before it gets too hot outside," Pastor Douglas said, sipping his coffee.

Chapter 17

Kol smiled as he secured his cruiser turned transport in the same area quite a distance from the church and cemetery he and Ada Jane had first visited when searching for the graves of her parents. As he jumped to the ground, he spoke to Missy. "Please secure the ship as usual, Missy. I will be spending time with my Ehlealah."

"Of course, Ambassador Kol. Please offer our greetings to Ehlealah Ada Jane Ra' Don Tol."

Kol smiled and shook his head at the changes in Missy since Vivi had become a part of all their lives. The name Missy was enough in itself, but the strides the computer had made in mimicking a sentient being made Kol seriously question the term, 'artificial intelligence'. He wasn't so sure there was anything particularly artificial about Missy.

Kol was only a few feet from his cruiser when he saw Ada Jane run out from between the church and Pastor Douglas's parsonage headed in his direction. He was at first concerned, his hand going instinctively for the weapon at his hip, but he soon noticed the huge smile on her face and realized she was excited, running to meet him.

Kol gave his version of a smile with all his teeth exposed, which as with all Cruestaci looked as though he was actually planning on eating her. "Ehlealah!" he called to her and quickened his steps to get to her.

When they were finally little more than a few feet apart, Ada Jane launched herself at Kol and he caught her in the air, cradling her and holding her to his chest.

"I missed you," Ada Jane said, tucking her face into his neck.

"I have missed you as well. I am greatly pleased that you are happy to see me," Kol said, rubbing his cheek on the top of her head.

"How was your trip here?" she asked.

"Uneventful. Which, I am learning is a good thing."

Kol placed her on her feet, and she slipped her hand in his as she led him back to her cottage. He glanced down at their attached hands as they walked before smiling at her again.

"I was afraid you wouldn't be able to make it," Ada Jane said. "It was getting kind of late."

"Unfortunately I was delayed due to a conference vidcom with all the senior members of Base 28, and the Consortium. There is much deceit in place there. I am tasked with uncovering it and am, therefore, questioned at every turn by Consul Diskastes. He has now begged his father and brother to intercede on his behalf because we are offending him."

"Offending him?" Ada Jane asked.

"Yes. Offense is the least of my intentions toward him, yet he seems to not be aware of my true intentions yet," Kol confided.

"What do you plan to do?" Ada Jane asked, leading him up onto her small porch.

"I plan to dispose of him. He is nothing but a power-hungry, miserable excuse for a male, and I believe that humans under his governs have suffered as a result."

"Well, you can't just kill him," Ada Jane said chuckling.

"That is what Bart says. He says I must gather evidence, then have him prosecuted."

"He's right," Ada Jane said, opening her door and leading the way into her home.

"I do not wish to waste time gathering and prosecuting. I wish to kill him, then send his hide back to his family," Kol said simply, a bit growly due to the frustration of having to learn to do things another way.

Ada Jane's eyes widened. "You can't do that. You're an ambassador now. You have to behave like one," she said, gesturing toward the table she'd already set for dinner.

"I do not think I like diplomacy. I am far better as a warrior," Kol confided, taking the seat she indicated.

"I know. But, just think of all the people you'll be able to help if you find the proof to not only remove him, but all those that helped him. I'm sure he's not working alone, very few of those in power ever are."

Kol watched as she placed food on his plate and then her own. His nostrils flared as he inhaled and his forehead wrinkled as he lifted his plate to his nose and inhaled again. "I do not know what this is, but it has the most delightful scent." Kol swallowed as he inhaled again. "My mouth is already preparing to indulge in your offering."

Ada Jane smiled. She was familiar with dealing with the Cruestaci and the way they spoke English. All the thoughts were there, but sometimes the translation was almost comical.

"Thank you," Ada Jane said. "It's one of my favorites from before..." Ada Jane stopped speaking, leaving the rest of the sentence unsaid. She knew Kol knew what she meant. "It's fried pork chops, mashed potatoes with way too much butter," she said grinning happily, "and sweet green peas."

Kol watched as Ada Jane used her fork and knife to cut up her pork chop. He awkwardly held his knife and tried to cut up his meat while holding it still with his fork. It looked more like he was trying to kill it, than cut it up to eat it.

"You could just hold it by the bone," Ada Jane said, picking up her pork chop to show him.

Kol smiled at her and lifted the pork chop from his plate without further hesitation. He took a small bite, and chewed, then his eyes widened and he took half the rest of the pork chop in one bite while he nodded his head appreciatively.

"You like it?" she asked, getting to her feet and moving toward the small kitchen counter.

"Very much!" Kol answered, taking the rest of the porch chop in his next bite and then gnawing on the bone.

"Good!" Ada Jane answered, lifting a platter and bringing it to the table. She set it between the two of them and lifted the plastic lid she'd used to cover the dish. "I made a dozen of them. I didn't know if you'd like it so I didn't want you to have to sit and eat something you didn't really like. But now that I know you do, I made plenty for you."

Kol grinned at her as he reached for three more pork chops and placed them on his plate. He lifted one and took a big bite. "This is now my favorite Earth meal," he said, nodding his head as he looked at the pork chop in his hand while he chewed. "I like the crunchy golden pieces on the outside especially."

"That's the breading," Ada Jane answered.

"Breading?" Kol asked.

"Yes, flour, salt, pepper. It's simple really, no need for fancy stuff. Just bread 'em and fry 'em up."

Kol watched as she used mashed potatoes on the end of her fork to touch to the small pile of green peas on her plate and then place it in her mouth. He picked up his fork and did the same. He chewed thoughtfully, taking in all the flavors and textures. Then he lifted one of his pork chops, ran it through the potatoes and through the peas and took a bite. Kol smiled at Ada Jane as he chewed, nodding his head in approval.

When dinner was over, there were no leftovers at all. Ada and Kol were both full and very satisfied.

"I like your food, Ada Jane," Kol said, taking a seat beside her on the small sofa. "You are a very talented cook," he said decisively.

"Thank you, Kol. But to be truthful, I cook country. I could never prepare a fancy chef style meal. I just use simple ingredients like my Mom used to.

"I like country food the best so far," Kol said. He watched as Ada Jane chose a disk from a stack of them sitting on a table and put it into a small machine beneath what looked like an antiquated viewing screen.

"I thought we'd watch a movie," Ada Jane said. "I've been watching these old DVD's that Pastor Douglas let me borrow from the exhibit. I've watched most of them, but I like seeing some of them again."

"You could simply watch one via the vidcom if you wish," Kol said.

"I know, but there's something about watching the actual DVD's that makes me feel more like I'm home."

Kol let it go at once. He completely understood that she needed to get a sense of where she left off in life in order to move forward.

As the movie started, Ada Jane relaxed back onto the sofa and within a few minutes was sitting so close to Kol that she was able to rest her head on his shoulder.

Kol looked down at Ada Jane leaning on his shoulder and pressed a kiss to her head.

Minutes went by with Kol sliding an arm around her and holding her close while she placed a hand on his stomach as she turned her body more in to him while still watching the movie.

He was surprised when suddenly out of nowhere she spoke about a surprising subject. "So, how is Elisher?" Ada Jane asked.

Kol glanced from the screen to Ada Jane who still had her eyes focused on the movie.

"He is well. He was in meetings with me as my assistant today. I suspect he is back in our quarters and working to find as much information as he can to use as evidence against Diskastes," Kol answered.

Ada Jane just nodded slowly. "Hmpf."

"Is there a problem, my Ada Jane?" Kol asked, picking up on her discomfort.

"No. Not at all," she said, snuggling closer.

Kol was not even sure what movie Ada Jane had chosen to watch. He was simply sitting, soaking in the feel of her near him, willfully allowing him to hold her. He dropped a few quick kisses on her head and turned back to the movie. His eyes widened. The couple on screen were involved in a very passionate scene. He sat up a little straighter when they actually got down to having sex. "What is this movie?" Kol asked.

"It's an old one from the early 2000's. They were very relaxed about sexuality apparently. Does it bother you?" Ada Jane asked, watching him curiously.

"No," Kol answered honestly.

"You don't seem so comfortable anymore," Ada Jane teased, smiling at him.

"I am not comfortable," Kol answered. "It is arousing. And I am already aroused by being near you. I do not wish to make you uncomfortable. I know you are not ready for such things and I do not wish to frighten you," Kol said, forcing his eyes to stay away from the images on the screen.

Ada Jane turned to fully face Kol, curling her legs up beneath her. "Kol, I'm not afraid of you. I'm not going to run from you if you become aroused."

"Are you sure?" Kol asked.

"Yes. I know this must be hard for you, and I'm not asking you to hide who you are, or to pretend to be something you're not. All I'm asking is for you to be patient for a little while."

Kol nodded his head once in acknowledgment of her statement.

"I'm not trying to make anything difficult for you. I've tried to be honest with you every step of the way. I apologize if I've made things hard for you." Ada Jane answered. "Please don't feel like you can't be completely honest with me as well."

Kol looked down at his hands which were now holding one of Ada Jane's in both of his. He kept looking at their hands when he answered. "It was very difficult when you ran away with Rokai ahl. It was very painful for me."

"I didn't mean to hurt you. I just wanted to go home, and he and his Ehlealah offered to bring me home."

"I would have brought you home," Kol said.

"Would you?" Ada Jane asked. "Would you really? Because there was a chance for me to come home with some of the other girls, and you intentionally made sure I missed that transport. And every time I'd ask you to take me home, you'd get frustrated and leave our quarters," Ada Jane said quietly.

Kol rubbed his thumb over the back of her hand and didn't say anything. She was right. She was absolutely correct. He'd prevented her from coming home and avoided the issue until she had no choice but to take things into her own hands.

"I didn't meant to hurt you. And every moment of the trip home I wondered if you'd come after me. I wanted you to, but I wanted to have time to make peace with everything that had happened to me. To make peace with the way my home has changed."

"I am trying, Ada Jane. It is very difficult for me to not sweep you into my arms, throw you into my cruiser and take you back to my world. It is my instinct to do just that. But I know that you need me to do things differently. So I am trying to be what you need."

"I appreciate that, Kol. I really do."

Kol nodded and glancing up to her eyes offered her a small smile. "Is there anything else I can do to help you feel more at peace?" he asked.

"Yes," she answered at once. "You can forgive me."

"For what," he asked.

"For running away. For hurting you and not giving you the chance to bring me here yourself."

Kol shook his head. "There is nothing to forgive. You are right. I was not interested in bringing you home. I believed you already were home. I have never had my life stolen away from me. I did not understand how you were feeling," he said, lifting a hand and cupping her cheek. "But I am learning. And I am trying every day to let you see that I am here, and that I will always be here. You will never have to face life without me beside you," Kol said sweetly.

Ada Jane leaned forward and pressed her lips to Kol's.

Kol's heart thundered in his chest as he returned her kiss. When he felt the tip of her tongue teasing his lips, he opened to her and allowed her to kiss him at will.

Slowly Ada Jane pulled away from him and smiled.

Kol leaned toward her while slipping a hand behind her head to hold her in place while he kissed her, taking the lead and gently, but firmly letting her know that he was more than aroused. When he finally stopped, he pulled back just a little to allow Ada Jane to catch her breath. "If you do not wish me to touch you, you only need say so," he said while he looked at her with his eyes heavily hooded from the passion of their kisses.

"I'm not sure what I am or am not ready for. But I know I like your kisses." Ada Jane paused before offering him a bright smile. "No, that's wrong. I don't like your kisses; I love your kisses."

Kol smiled. "Then, I will kiss you more?" he asked.

"Oh, yeah," she answered, leaning toward him while he leaned toward her. Ada Jane surrendered herself to him. To his touch, his taste, his scent. Everything in her brain screamed Kol to her. She was safe, she was loved, and she was at this particular point in time being practically worshiped by his attentions to her.

Kol was turned halfway toward her, and Ada's knees were bent between them. She couldn't get close enough. She broke their kiss and slid into his lap, straddling him while she faced him, holding his face in her hands while he settled his hands at her hips.

Kol gave a slight rumble as she settled herself on his lap.

"Is this okay?" Ada Jane asked, lifting herself up off him.

Kol tightened his hands on her hips. "Yes!" he growled at her, forcing her back to his lap. "Do not move. Please. Stay right where you are," he said huskily while angling his head to kiss her more deeply.

Ada Jane kissed him again, her hands roving his chest and shoulders, finally ready to admit to herself that his growls excited her a great deal more than she'd once thought.

Chapter 18

Kol was lost in the feel of his female on top of him. Her scent told him that she was as aroused as he was. But he also detected a trace of fear in her scent. "You do not have to continue with this. I can scent your fear, my Ehlealah," Kol rumbled at her, his voice gruff with arousal.

"I'm not afraid of you. It's just the whole thing... I just..."

"Shh. Stop, do not distress yourself," Kol said backing off and pecking a chaste kiss to her lips as he sat back, smiling at her as she still sat straddling his lap.

"But I don't want to stop, not really. I just get all these memories and then I start feeling like I'm panicking."

"There is no rush. You are mine, and I am yours. I know this. We will take our time," Kol said, brushing her cheekbone with his forefinger.

"But I want you to touch me. Then I just get panicked. I don't know if I can follow through, and I don't want to tease you," Ada Jane said frustratedly.

"You are not teasing me. You tell me what you want and that's what we'll do," Kol said, smiling despite the pain in his groin from wanting her so badly for so long.

Ada Jane's gaze dropped from his face to his chest and began to nervously toy with the edge of his shirt. "There are other things we could do," she said softly.

"What other things?" Kol asked, thinking she would suggest a walk in the moonlight or perhaps another movie.

Ada shrugged one shoulder. "Things with mouths, or hands, and maybe I wouldn't be so nervous as I would be if your body weight was on top of me."

Kol almost choked. This was not at all what he expected her to suggest.

"I mean, if you would enjoy those things," she said, feeling suddenly like maybe suggesting them was a mistake.

"I want those things," Kol said, the snarl back in his voice.

Ada Jane grinned at him as she slid off his lap. "Follow me," she said, reaching out her hand.

Kol wasted no time getting to his feet and taking her hand.

Ada Jane led him into her bedroom where she went directly to her bed and turned to face him. Ada Jane watched his face for any sign of approval or disapproval as she lifted her shirt over her head and tossed it to the side.

Kol's eyes widened at the sight of her standing before him with the thin covering of cloth holding her breasts as they strained to break through it. His hands with a mind of their own reached out to touch them, needing to caress her through the thin fabric. He realized only inches away from her that he'd not made sure she was okay with his touch and lifted his gaze to meet hers. He opened his mouth to speak, but didn't have time to say a word before Ada Jane took his hands in hers and placed them gently on her breasts.

Kol's chest rumbled softly as he stepped closer and rubbed the pads of his thumbs across her nipples. Ada Jane's breath caught and she inhaled deeply on a gasp.

Kol let go of her and took a step back.

"No, it's okay," Ada said, reaching for his hands and putting them on her body again.

Kol stepped closer and cupped each breast, feeling their weight in his palms, the look on his face completely reverent as he slowly discovered his mate. He dropped to his knees in front of her and leaned forward, pressing his nose to her soft flesh and inhaling deeply. "Better than pork chops," he mumbled completely seriously.

Ada giggled and he glanced up at her briefly before turning his attention back to her breasts. He pressed a kiss to first one, then the other before laving one with his tongue through the fabric.

Ada reached behind herself and unhooked her bra, then pulled it off her shoulders and dropped it to the floor. Kol became a bundle of need. He reacted by reaching out and putting his arm around her waist, pulling her into him and taking a nipple into his mouth.

Ada held onto Kol, as he teased her with his teeth, sucking so hard he surely turned her pale nipple a dark red from the blood he'd suckled to the surface. He let it slip free from his mouth and went after the second nipple. Then he stroked and petted her, kissing and nipping at her for so long she was panting by the time he was finished. Suddenly she wanted to be lying down and she wanted his shirt off, too.

Ada pulled at the shoulders of his shirt. "Take this off," she said, gathering the material in her fist.

Kol glanced up to her face. She was slightly taller than he was with him on his knees. He grasped the edge of his shirt and tore it off over his head and horns, tossing it indiscriminately away.

"So powerful," Ada whispered, caressing his shoulders and biceps.

"Do I please you?" Kol asked, holding her breast up again so he could nuzzle it with his cheek.

"Yes!" Ada answered. "I've never seen another male like you. You are so strong, so powerful, yet so gentle."

Kol raised his eyes to meet her gaze again while she spoke to him.

"You are beautiful. There is no other word," Ada Jane said, smiling at him.

Ada Jane backed toward the foot of her bed and when she felt it against the backs of her knees, she stopped and took his face in her hands, looking down at him.

Kol could sense her hesitation and turned his face to kiss one of her palms. "All you need to know is that I will stop the minute you say stop. I will not lose my control."

Ada nodded and reached for the button on her jeans. She unzipped them, and pushed them slightly open, but because of the way he held her with his arm around her waist, she couldn't push them down.

Kol eased away from her and looked down at her jeans before hooking his thumbs in them and slowly dragging them down her legs.

Once they reached her ankles, Ada Jane sat on the edge of the bed, then scooted back further on it and raised her legs so he could pull her jeans off all the way. She thought for sure he'd rise up over her to do so, but he didn't. Kol stayed on his knees and pulled her jeans off before just dropping them beside himself.

Kol ran his hands up her legs starting at her ankles. When he got to her knees and pressed them slightly apart, she pulled them back together.

"I won't hurt you," he said. "Open your eyes, Ada Jane. See that it is only me."

Ada opened her eyes and he saw them glassy with tears. "I will stop," he said, running his hands back down her legs and massaging her feet.

"I don't want you to stop!" Ada said frustratedly. "I don't. I just. I don't know how to fix this. I want you to touch me, then I feel like I can't ever allow you to touch me."

"Why would you never allow me to touch you?" Kol asked, though it was with patience and not irritation.

"I don't know. I just, I feel like you're going to see me, you're going to feel it, too, you just don't understand!" she burst out.

Kol shook his head. "No, I do not. Only you can make me understand. Tell me, my Ada Jane. Help me understand."

"I feel so..." she stopped talking, not sure she could make herself say it.

"Tell me. I cannot help you work through it if you do not tell me," Kol encouraged.

"I can't work through it!" she said, her voice rising with her anxiety.

"Through what?" Kol finally demanded with a firm tone.

"I'm dirty!" she yelled at Kol. "I'm dirty. I always feel dirty, no matter how many times I've washed, or how many times I've prayed. No matter how many times I've told myself I did nothing wrong, I still feel all used up," she said, starting to cry.

Kol hurried to sit on the bed beside her. "There is nothing used or dirty about you. You are perfect," he said, stroking her back as he pulled her onto his lap and held her close.

"I can still feel their touch. I still look around me at all times to be sure no one and nothing is behind me. I'm afraid I'll always feel them just behind me, or touching me. Even when I think of you touching me, I panic and end up opening my eyes because I'm afraid I'm fooling myself and it's really them."

"You let me touch your breasts," Kol started.

"Yes, because I was watching you and I was in control. And I knew it was you."

"And now?" he asked.

"Now I feel like if I lie back and open myself to you that you'll feel it like I do and then you'll turn away from me. And I don't want you to turn away from me," she finally confided.

Kol tilted his head and kissed her cheek. "I'll never turn away from you. You are having small bouts of fear. Your worry has begun to manifest itself by making you believe that I will think poorly of you as well. It is simply not possible."

"How can I make it go away?" Ada asked.

"If I tell you my thoughts, I think you will believe me to be selfish. And I am to an extent, but also, I wish to help you. And in helping you, it will help us."

"Tell me," Ada said, sitting back and looking at his face.

"I touch you. I give you pleasure. I touch every single inch of your flesh and every single inch of your flesh comes to know me. Memories of my touch replace and wash away all others."

"And if I need you to stop?"

"Then I stop, and we try again whenever you are ready, be it tomorrow or next week. We keep working at it until we overcome the fear. But one thing is certain," he said.

"What's that?" Ada asked.

"We cannot allow those that hurt you to steal you away from me. We cannot allow it," Kol said passionately.

Ada nodded. "You're right."

Kol sat holding Ada Jane and allowing her to regain her composure. After a few minutes when her breathing returned to normal, he kissed her temple and whispered to her. "You take the lead, move us to where you are comfortable."

Ada leaned toward Kol, beginning to kiss him and touch him as she worked them both up to a boiling point again. Finally he pulled her over his lap, with her facing him, straddling him again. She still wore her panties and he just glimpsed the soft curls beneath the shiny, pink fabric and the matching lace inlays.

As he stroked her back, her stomach and her thighs, Ada began to rock her hips slightly on his lap. He still wore his uniform pants and wanted desperately out of them, but knew they most likely kept her feeling somewhat more secure.

As she rocked her hips, Kol slid one hand from her hip and softly stroked the inside of her thigh with the backs of his fingers. Ada startled slightly, but Kol spoke softly to her, soothing her. "I'm here. I will not allow you to be harmed, my Ehlealah. Open your eyes, look at your male."

Ada Jane opened her eyes and smiled when Kol was there, smiling at her with his teeth all on display. She chuckled at the thought she'd feel more safe with him and all his teeth than anyone or anything she could think of.

"Why do you laugh?" he asked.

Ada shook her head with the smile still on her face, and as his fingers grazed slightly over her panties while she looked into his eyes, her breath caught.

"Stop?" he asked

Ada shook her head. "No," she whispered.

Kol rubbed his nose alongside hers and kissed her cheek as he stroked her through her panties again. This time she whimpered and her body actually tried to follow his touch as he took his hand away.

"Again?" he asked.

"Yes," she said, already lifting her hips toward his body.

Kol touched her ribs and let her feel his fingers as they trailed down her body to her hip, then further until he slid his fingers beneath her hot center, leaving his thumb to stroke her.

Ada Jane pressed down on his hand as he cupped her and used his thumb to search for the small rounded bundle of nerves he knew was a part of his female's anatomy. He'd never been with a human before, but all his research said it was there, even if Zha Quin would neither confirm nor deny it. If he could find that part of her, he knew he could make her come apart in his arms — or at least he hoped he could.

Gradually Kol began to apply more pressure, stroking the length of her slit as far as his thumb could follow from bottom to top. He moved across a place at the top of her slit, and her body jumped slightly, reacting to his touch. Then he felt her body becoming even hotter, wetter where she held her body against his hand. Kol moved his thumb back to that place and found just what he was looking for. Each time he stroked over that little nub, she'd moan and try to follow his thumb.

Kol continued to stroke back and forth over her swollen clit until she was panting and moving her body any way she could to stay in contact with him. "You like that?" he asked.

"Yes!" Ada Jane responded without hesitation.

Kol stroked her again. "Will you let me see you?" he asked.

Ada Jane hesitated for a moment before agreeing. "Yes," she said, backing off his lap and getting to her feet.

Kol was still seated on the bed when he very slowly eased her panties down her thighs while she stood before him.

"Yours, too," Ada Jane said, her eyes glued to the huge bulge in his uniform breeches.

"You're sure?" he asked, only too anxious to oblige her.

Ada Jane nodded.

When Kol started to stand, Ada Jane moved back to give him room. He quickly stripped out of his breeches and left them on the floor beside his feet.

Ada's eyes roved from his feet, to his chest, and back again, stopping at his cock. It was fully erect, swollen and pulsing.

"I will still stop anytime you say to," Kol said.

Ada nodded.

Chapter 19

Kol held out his hand toward Ada and she took it, allowing him to guide her back to the bed.

Ada sat on the edge of her bed and watched Kol as he knelt between her legs. "Will you let me see you?" he asked.

Ada looked into his eyes and though she wanted to, he could sense her hesitance.

"I will kiss and stroke every inch of you so that you will know your body remembers no touch but mine. You may tell me to stop whenever you wish."

Ada swallowed nervously and lay back on her bed.

"Move back a little," Kol said.

Ada lifted one leg and pressed it into the mattress to shove herself backwards, toward the head of the bed. Then she felt Kol start touching her, and she moaned at the pleasure.

Kol lifted her foot and kissed each of her perfectly shaped toes. He kissed the arch of her foot and her ankle, then kissed his way up her leg taking care to stoke and kiss every single part of her leg. When he was done, Ada Jane was panting and her legs were slightly apart, inviting him in. But he didn't go there yet. He went back to the foot of the bed and repeated his actions with the other foot and leg. When he got to the junction of her leg and her hip, he pressed a kiss to the outside of her hip and continued on his way up her body, familiarizing himself with her waist, her ribcage, her breasts again, her arms, her neck and finally her lips and face. Then he went down the other side.

When he was done, her hips were rolling again and she was touching him, her fingers stroking his skin anywhere she could reach. But still, he didn't stop. He raised up beside her and looked down lovingly on her. "Turn over," he said.

Ada Jane started to object, but he smiled at her. "I have to do your back as well. Turn over," he urged.

Ada turned onto her stomach and Kol went to work. He lifted her hair out of the way and kissed the back of her neck, then her shoulders. He stroked her back making her arch her back and hum in more pleasure than he'd seen her in yet. When he reached the soft, erotic curve of her ass, he stroked both cheeks, kissing the sensitive skin and nipping lightly with his teeth. Then he kissed down the back of her leg, up again and down the back of her other leg.

"Turn over," Kol said again.

Ada Jane turned over and was surprised when he simply knelt on the bed beside her and lifted first one hand, then other, and kissed her palms, then each fingertip before moving to the foot of the bed and getting to his knees on the floor. Then he gently took hold of her ankles and pulled her toward him.

Kol spoke the whole time he pulled her body toward him. "Almost done now. All I need you to do is keep your eyes opened so that you can see your bedroom, concentrate on me touching you, and if you need to, lift your head and look down at me so that you'll know it's me, your male, claiming your body."

He paused and waited for her to give some idea that she'd understood him. "Yes?" he finally asked when she didn't reply.

"Yes," she answered.

Kol lifted her legs and draped them over his shoulders as he pulled her closer to him. Once he was face to face with the most sensitive part of her, no matter how much he wanted to explore, he restrained himself and leaned forward, pressing a kiss to her soft, damp flesh.

Ada Jane responded by lifting her hips off the bed.

Kol opened his mouth and used his tongue to taste her, dragging it along her slit from one end to the other as he lifted her legs by pushing forward with his shoulders. He moved her body just as much as he needed to, to be sure he didn't miss any part of her.

"Kol!" she cried out, planting her hands on the bed at her sides.

"Stop?" he asked.

"No! No, don't stop," she panted.

Kol pulled her toward him again and pushed her legs apart, laying them bent at the knee and splayed open to either side. He lowered his head and took her in his mouth, suckling gently and using his tongue to tease the soft, swollen, pink skin that seemed to pulse in time with his cock. He wanted so badly to climb on top of her and fuck her until she screamed his name, but this wasn't about him. It wasn't about what he wanted, it was about what his Ehlealah needed to feel whole again. To feel like she was beautiful and revered.

Suckling her lips into his mouth and running his tongue among her folds for the last time, he lifted his head and lifted his hands. "My fingers will touch you now," he announced.

When she didn't answer, he glanced up at her and found that she'd grabbed her pillow and propped her head up so she could watch him. He waited for an answer and when she finally nodded at him wide eyed, he smiled at her and licked her again, then used his fingers to gently open her, stroking and probing, learning what he'd only read about so far.

He located her clit and rubbed it gently with his finger, making her strain her hips to maintain contact. Then while he looked into her eyes, he lowered his head and flicked her clit with his tongue before taking it into his mouth and sucking it as he flicked his tongue back and forth over it.

Ada Jane cried out and began rocking her hips against his mouth. She reached down and took hold of his horns, moving his head as she wanted him to move, as he suckled her clit and brought her closer and closer to orgasm. She closed her eyes, but moments later her eyes popped open and looked at Kol, her eyes begging him for release.

"Please," she whispered.

"Tell me what you need," he growled out.

"Inside," she said.

He moved up her body cautiously, and rightly so because as he loomed over her, her expression went from one of need to one of panic. Kol reacted quickly by slipping an arm beneath her and holding her to him as he turned them and sat on the bed bringing her into his lap. He dropped his hand between them again and took up the same rhythm he'd used only moments before, talking to her the whole time. "I am yours, Ada Jane. I love you, Ehlealah, I will never harm you."

He kissed her and she seemed surprised at the taste on his lips. "I love your taste. It is home for me. You are home for me." Kol felt her hips start to move ever so slightly again, and he began stroking her clit faster with his thumb while using the tips of his fingers to tease her opening.

"Kol," she whimpered.

"I have you. Tell me what you need."

"This, just don't stop," she begged as she put her arms around his neck to steady herself while she rocked against him.

Ada Jane adjusted her hold on Kol so she could press harder against him, and when he scooted to the edge of the bed to accommodate her, his cock bumped against her pussy. Her eyes were glued to his face as she slowly began to stroke the length of his cock with her slit, pushing down on him hard enough to get friction on her clit.

"Oh, god," she said huskily.

Oh, god was right. Kol was about to fucking lose control. He held her tightly in his arms and moved her body back and forth over his cock, using her dripping body to stroke himself with. His chest heaved with the effort to control his need to throw her down and fuck her, and her chest heaved with her need to orgasm.

On his last stroke of her slit down the length of his cock, Ada Jane pressed her thighs to the outside of his, stopping him from sliding her back toward his body. Ada Jane looked down at his cock, hard and rigid, dripping with her wetness. She rocked her hips against the tip of it and Kol growled softly.

Ada Jane licked her lips and stroked the top of his cock with her fingertips, causing it to jump in response.

She pulled her hips back until his cock bounced up a bit higher, then she held it with one hand as she pressed her hips forward, causing the tip of Kol's cock to slip inside her.

Kol held perfectly still. His heart was about to pound out of his chest as he waited for his Ehlealah to take him fully into her body.

Ada Jane pulled back and pushed forward several times, taking him deeper each time. Finally she looked up at Kol. "Rub me again," she whispered.

Kol pressed his thumb against her clit and started rubbing her in small circles as she moaned in response and lifted up off his lap so she could slide him more deeply inside her body. When finally she'd taken him all in, she sat still for a second, tightening her muscles around him.

"Alright?" Kol panted.

Ada Jane moved her hips experimentally. "Yeah," she answered, starting to ride him.

Ada built a rhythm that had them both on the edge, and Kol kept his thumb and fingertips teasing her clit the entire time she rode him.

Kol placed his other hand on the mattress and used it to hold his weight as he lifted his hips up off the bed and began to thrust into Ada Jane.

"Oh, my god! Yes, that, yes," she begged.

Kol thrust faster, and he watched as she began to shatter before his eyes. Her entire body tightened up, and she gripped his shoulders as she screamed.

Ada Jane pushed his hand away from her clit, but tried to slam herself against his cock, so Kol grabbed her with both hands and got to his feet, holding her as he slammed his cock into her over and over again as they both screamed their passion, their voices filling the cottage with proof that they were finally, at last, one.

Afterward they sat quietly, Ada Jane still straddling his lap. Kol's breathing slowing returning to normal.

Kol lay back on the bed and brought Ada Jane with him. Ada lifted herself shakily up on his chest. "Thank you," she said with tears in her eyes.

"You do not thank your male for giving you pleasure," Kol said smiling, his breath returning to normal slowly.

"No, it was for making me feel comfortable enough to be able to let myself enjoy you, us. I've never... it was the first time I've ever chosen to..." she finished, feeling like an idiot trying to explain to Kol with words that felt awkward and uncomfortable.

Kol understood what she was trying to say, and he wanted to make her feel more comfortable. "It is the first time that I have given myself to a female out of love. There are many other reasons for a male to take a female, but love is the most sacred, and it is the first time I've ever taken a female with love. It was a first for us both."

Ada smiled and just barely touched her lips to his.

"I give you my vow, you will always be safe. You will always know that you are secure in all things. You will always know you are loved and treasured," Kol promised.

Ada Jane smiled at Kol and kissed his lips again before she completely relaxed on top of him, her head resting on his chest.

Kol was starting to think maybe that was the key, keep her on top and she felt in control. He stroked his fingers across her back and smiled to himself as she stretched and arched into his touch.

"I claim you, Ada Jane," Kol said quietly. "You are my heart and soul. You are all the best parts of me, and I am honored to have found you. I will protect you, love you, provide for you and only you all of my days."

"And nights?" she asked, smiling with her head still resting on his chest.

"Yes, and nights. Forever, without end," Kol promised. "I am your male, yours alone."

Ada Jane sat up and looked down at Kol resting on the bed beneath her. "And now comes the part where I claim you?" she asked.

"If you will have me," he answered, beginning to worry.

Ada Jane looked around her bedroom again. "Nothing but honesty. That's the only way it'll ever work between us, yes?" she asked.

"Yes," Kol answered, his stomach doing flips at the thought that she may not accept him. His brain started calculating how far he could get into space and toward Command Warship 1 before Bart was notified if he decided to take Ada Jane and run.

"I don't want to go live on a base. I don't want to be around military people and formal rules and regulations. I want to stay here," she said, looking around her room. Then she looked down at Kol. "But I want to claim you, too. You were right. You are mine. And I want to belong to you. I just can't go live in some military compound. How can I have both?" she asked.

Kol smiled at her.

"What are you smiling for?" she asked. "This is a problem."

"You said you are mine. You said I am yours and you want to belong to me," Kol said smiling happily.

"Did you hear any of the rest of it?" she asked, smiling down at him.

"I did. It is merely a small detail. We will live here. There will be times that I will have to sleep in my quarters on Base if I have a late meeting or a particularly early one, but whenever possible I will come home to spend my nights with you. When I cannot, we will vidcom each other. We will make this work," Kol promised.

"Are you sure?" Ada Jane asked.

"I am sure. I have not seen family for any of the males on base, but I have seen several wear bands of gold which I understand indicates they are mated. So, surely, others are doing the same with keeping their families off base." Kol scowled a bit as he thought of it. "It is probably for the best anyway. I do not wish you to be anywhere near the Consul or his males. It is better you stay here," Kol said, refocusing on Ada Jane.

"I claim you, Kol Ra' Don Tol. You are my male, my husband, my lover and my friend. I promise I will always do anything I can to keep you happy and to be sure you know you are loved, respected and treasured."

Kol pulled her down to him so that he could kiss her again. "My heart is whole," he whispered to her. "You have made it this way."

Chapter 20

Kol felt warmth behind his back and turned over, recognizing the scent of his Ehlealah even in sleep. He curled around her, pulling her back tightly against his body and throwing a leg over her.

Then he was jolted awake with a blood curdling scream and the sound of a loud thump on the hardwood floor. Before his eyes could even focus, he found himself standing at the foot of the bed, his Psi fully engaged, snarling and growling at whatever the danger was.

Gradually his eyes focused on Ada Jane. Even in his battle form, his head canted to the side when he finally realized what he was seeing.

Ada Jane was naked, her long, blonde hair a mess, with her back pressed up against the wall, her chest heaving as she pointed her weapon at him.

Kol looked around the bedroom, then stalked to the bedroom door and peered out. He listened closely — his hearing on point in his battle form. Then he scented the house. There was nothing, and no one here to offer a threat. Slowly Kol began to let go of his battle form, walking back over to Ada Jane.

"What is it?" he asked, doing his best to speak English around some very large, blade-sharp teeth that had yet to retract.

Ada Jane watched in fascination as Kol's even larger than usual body began to, what could only be described as deflate, as she stared at him. "Why do you look like that?" she asked.

"It is my Psi — my battle form. It is brought on naturally as a protective instinct or when we are preparing to fight. Are you well? Why did you scream?" he asked, calmer now that he knew she wasn't in any actual danger.

Ada Jane shook her head as tears began to form. She turned away from him to find clothing, taking a deep breath and still shaking her head.

"My Ada Jane, there is nothing, not a single thing you cannot share with me," he said, staying where he was rather than reaching for her as she was clearly out of sorts.

"I'll be fine. I'm sorry I woke you."

"You said honesty. I agreed. Now, I request honesty," Kol said, fearing that his female may have changed her mind about claiming him. But still, that wouldn't explain her scream.

Ada Jane turned around to smile at him brightly. "It's okay, really."

Kol didn't return her smile, nor did he comment at all. He still stood in the same place he'd been, watching her as she hurriedly tried to put clothing on.

Ada could tell Kol was disappointed. He was upset, thinking there was a problem between them, and she didn't want that. She'd have no choice but to be honest. "It's not your fault, Kol. I'm so tired of everyone walking on eggshells around me. I'm tired of walking on eggshells around myself! I just want to be normal again. I shouldn't have to require special treatment just to get through the dang morning," she said.

"I do not understand," he finally said quietly.

Ada Jane tugged her shirt on over her head, and when her head popped through the opening, she wore an irritated expression. "Everyone is afraid to bring up what happened to me. Pastor Douglas, those I've met in town who know who I am... they're all dancing around the subject afraid they're going to upset me. Heck, I upset myself! A shadow out of the corner of my eye makes me turn in that direction and my stomach drop. I'm so tired of it. I just want to be normal again. That's why I didn't want to tell you. I don't want you to feel like you have to provide special treatment in order to just deal with me on a daily basis. I'm not weak. I'm not helpless, and I resent feeling like I'm afraid all the time."

"I understand that," Kol said, waiting for her to finish her explanation.

Flustered Ada Jane threw her hands up. "I was asleep and you pulled me to you and threw your leg over me. I panicked, okay?! I thought," she said looking down at her hands gripping the hem of her shirt. "I thought I was still there. I thought they still had me, or had me again. I screamed and fell on the floor when I rushed to get away from the male holding me."

"Ada Jane," Kol said, taking a step toward her.

"Only after I fell to the floor and you jumped up to protect me, did I realize that there was nothing be afraid of. It was only you. I'm sorry."

Kol walked toward her, his arms out for her to come to him.

Ada did. She walked right into his arms and held him tightly around the waist and he held her close, kissing her temple and whispering of how much he loved her.

"I'm sorry," she said.

Kol shook his head. "There is no reason for sorry."

"I just thought that after last night, after we... did it," she whispered the words, 'did it', because she never cursed and she never talked about sex, "things would be different and I'd be a little more relaxed."

"You have been through more than most people could ever imagine. It will not all go away over night. But it will get easier. And you will always receive special treatment — you are my Ehlealah and as such are my treasure. You will always be treated with the utmost reverence, because you are my Ehlealah, not because of your past."

"I don't want to be afraid anymore," she confided.

"Think of your emotions on waking on Command Warship 1. Do you not feel braver?" Kol asked.

"Oh my gosh, yes. I was terrified," she exclaimed.

"And now, here you are, mated to your own terrifying alien male. Brave enough to show me what you need for satisfaction last night."

"Shh! Don't say that out loud!" she said, blushing.

Kol chuckled. "The part about being my mate, or the part about sex?"

Ada Jane's blue eyes grew stormy and her face reddened even more. "The S.E.X. We don't talk about those things out loud!" she rushed out, glancing around the room as though someone else would be there.

Kol laughed. She was adorable. She was strong enough to survive all she had survived. She was sensual and trusting enough with him to be able to tell him what she wanted in their bedroom. And she was still so innocent as to be embarrassed by speaking of it in the light of day. "I will wait until tonight when we are alone in our bedroom and then I'll speak of all the things I especially love."

Kol looked around them. "Oh! Look! We are alone in our bedroom!" he smiled at her wickedly. "I love the taste of your body. I am addicted. I want to drop to my knees right here, right now and feast between your legs," he said huskily.

"Kol!" Ada Jane chided, despite the fact that her heart rate sped up.

"And when you press your lips to mine, your tongue tracing my mouth, I want to roar with delight."

"Kol, hush," Ada Jane said again, with much less resistance.

"And when you sit on my lap, taking me deep inside you, my body wants to fill you over and over again, driving into you until my name is imprinted on your soul. You are the most precious gift, my Ada Jane," Kol whispered, lowering his head to kiss her as she looked up at him, her eyelids growing heavy with her want for him.

"Will you let me taste you again?" he asked, trailing his fingers up and down her spine and across her rounded buttocks.

"Breakfast..." she started.

"Can wait," he said, backing toward the bed and sitting down still completely nude on the mattress. Kol held her hand and gently tugged her toward him until she obliged him by sitting on his lap. Kol lifted the shirt from her body and placed it next to him on the bed.

He took both her hands in his and lay back on the bed, pulling her with him.

"What are you doing?" Ada Jane asked breathlessly.

"Come here," he said, patting his chest. "Sit here."

Ada moved to do as he asked, thinking of asking if she'd be too heavy since she was not a small girl, but then she remembered him lifting her as though she was only a child. "Are you sure?" she asked.

"Will you deny your male his favorite treat?" Kol asked.

"No," she answered, crawling into place and sitting on his chest.

"Now, up on your knees," Kol said, "right here, over my mouth."

"But," Ada started to object.

Kol raised his eyebrow and watched her, leaving the final decision to her.

She hesitated only a moment longer before doing as he asked and holding herself just above his face.

Kol only had to slightly lift his head and she was right there. He extended his tongue and swiped her slit, then fastened his lips on her, taking her all in and flicking her with his tongue, rumbling with pleasure at the taste of his female flooding his mouth once again.

Ada Jane leaned backward, placing her hands behind herself on Kol's body to help support herself. "Oh my," she said with a sigh.

Kol pulled his mouth away from her for just a moment. "Everything else can wait this morning. All that matters is this." He covered her with his mouth again, tracing her folds with his tongue.

"Yes," she moaned.

"How can he be considered an Ambassador when he spends so little time here?" Viceroy Pomrance asked, pretending to be offended that once again the Cruestaci Ambassador had not joined them at breakfast.

"It is not a requirement that all diplomats take their meals together," Patroon Zhuxi said patiently.

"True, but it would do much for him to bond with us, become one of the family we have created here," Consul Diskastes commented.

"Perhaps he has family elsewhere," Patroon Zhuxi said. "Or perhaps he's hard at work and doesn't wish to waste valuable time socializing when he could be completing whatever task it is that Chairman Bartholomew has assigned him."

"Then one would think he would be on base," Diskastes answered.

"Evidently, not all he investigates is on base," Zhuxi answered. He stood, planning to excuse himself from the table, but a commotion and loud murmurs had him looking toward the doors of the cafeteria. Patroon Zhuxi knew at once who these new visitors were here to see.

He smiled and walked toward the new arrivals, his smile in place and his hand extended. "Welcome, I am Patroon Zhuxi of Ceres," he said, extending his hand while he executed a small bow of his head and clicking his heels together. "But you may call me Zhuxi."

"Thank you," Ba' Re answered, placing his hand in Zhuxi's. "I am Lieutenant Commander Ba Re' Non Tol, and this is Elite Warrior Kron Val Kere. Please feel free to address me as Ba Re'."

"And me as Kron," Kron added.

"We are here to meet with Elite Commander Kol Ra' Don Tol. Might you know where he is?" Ba Re' asked.

"I do. He had business off base. I am sure he will return shortly. May I interest you in a meal?" Patroon Zhuxi asked.

Diskastes sat flabbergasted at the table he insisted all Diplomats eat at. He'd not been informed of additional Cruestaci warriors arriving at his base. He was outraged, and if truth be told, he was more than a little unnerved.

Diskastes jumped to his feet while calling out across the cafeteria. "I was not advised that additional personnel would be joining us. Who are you, and where are your orders?" he asked indignantly.

Ba Re' and Kron shared a small smirk before turning their attention to the portly, sniveling Consul. "I would believe that if you were not advised, you did not need to know," Kron answered.

Consul Diskastes actually sputtered. "I am Consul of this base. All approvals go through me and are approved or rejected by me. I most certainly did not receive a request to approve two additional Cruestaci soldiers within our midst!" he said, his voice loud with indignation.

Ba Re' shrugged. "It would seem Chairman Bartholomew of the Unified Consortium Defense decided that your approval wasn't necessary."

Consul Diskastes's eyes narrowed and he broke out in a sweat. "We will see about this!" he snapped as he did his best to stalk out of the cafeteria, screaming at his security that they were to accompany him at all times.

"Be sure you get it right when you call your people to complain. We are not soldiers. We are warriors," Kron called after him. Though most of the males who'd been sitting with Diskastes or near him did indeed get up and follow him out of the cafeteria, one paused long enough to incline his head in greeting before leaving the room.

"I don't think the Consul likes us," Kron said to Ba Re'.

"No, I do not think he does," Ba Re' agreed.

"Pity," Kron said. "I did so hope to be his best friend. I shall spend days mourning the loss of the possibility of his friendship."

Ba Re' shook his head. "Do you know? Your sarcasm often dazzles even me."

Kron shrugged. "I try."

"I have no doubt," Ba Re' answered with a grin before turning his attention back to Zhuxi. "I believe you said something about a meal?"

"I did indeed. Come. Join me," Zhuxi said, leading them toward the food stations so that they could choose their meals.

Having chosen their meals and joined Zhuxi at a table in the far corner of the room, several others came to their table to greet them. Each male who welcomed them and introduced themselves was polite and friendly.

"I have noticed that not one of those who've introduced themselves is Viceroy Buchanan, nor Special Liaison Elisher," Ba Re' said.

"They are in Ambassador Kol's quarters. When Ambassador Kol is off base, we do not leave Elisher or their quarters unprotected."

"Has there been a direct threat?" Ba Re' asked.

"Not exactly, though we have intercepted Diskastes's forces several times attempting to force Elisher to open the door. So, we do not leave him unaccompanied. Each of us brings with us our own small security force. On top of that the base is assigned with its own security. Buchanan and myself share similar views and while loyal to ourselves first, our security forces have for the most part become intermingled.

At the moment, Buchanan is within Kol's quarters with several of our security outside the door. We are not attempting to perform a coup, only to make a small show to let Diskastes know he will not gain access to the documentation inside that is his main focus, or to Elisher for withholding that information from him."

"I noticed one of Diskastes's men acknowledged us respectfully," Kron said.

"They are not all as delusional as he."

"Delusional?" Ba Re' asked.

"Yes, the male is definitely suffering from delusions of grandeur. I believe he's convinced himself that this base is his own private domain and attempts to treat every possible circumstance as though he were holding court."

"This should be fun," Ba Re' said, glancing at Kron.

"It should indeed," Kron answered. "Have you tried the food? Stop talking and taste your food."

Zhuxi grinned. "It is very good. Earth offers much in the way of cuisine. When you're finished, I'll escort you to Kol's quarters so that you may meet Buchanan and Elisher."

Chapter 21

Kol and Ada Jane decided to spend the morning after breakfast walking through the woods and enjoying being outside. It was midmorning when they finally returned to their cottage. He'd left his communicator in Ada Jane's cottage intentionally — he didn't want to be interrupted. He did have a weapon with him, as did Ada Jane, so he felt relatively secure in leaving the communicator behind.

Ada Jane opened her front door as she finished her sentence. "Anyway, I have the check still, but I don't want to deposit it, though I do need to open an account somewhere. I remember my father used to say once you've cashed the check, you've sold your rights."

"What does that mean?" Kol asked.

"Basically that once you've accepted payment for something, it's a done deal. If you accept money for something. And then later want to change your mind, you usually can't if you've accepted money for it," Ada Jane explained.

"You are correct about the check you were given. Bart expressly said not to deposit it," Kol answered. "And I have an account. You may use my account. I will add you to it so that you may have access to all you may need."

"I have the band Rokai ahl gave me," she said, holding up her arm to display a simple gold band that hugged her left wrist.

"I will have you added to mine, and link your band to it, that way it will refill your band anytime you need more." Kol made a mental note to link his accounts with Ada Jane's band so she could have access to all his credits. They were hers, after all. Everything he had was accumulated for the benefit of his Ehlealah.

"Kol, you don't have to do that," she said, feeling humbled that he'd just give her access to his credits without another word.

"They are yours, Ada Jane. All I have is yours," Kol answered, lifting her hand and kissing it.

He followed Ada Jane into the cottage, and the first thing Kol noticed was the low repetitive tone of the communicator letting him know he had a message. Kol sighed.

Ada Jane walked past it on her way to the kitchen chuckling. "At least you know you are needed," she said, smiling at him and his obvious irritation.

"I just wish we could have a few uninterrupted days. Even on Command Warship 1 we are provided with time after our mating within which we are free to concentrate only on our Ehlealahs."

"Well, you're not on your warship anymore. And they obviously need your attention. Call them back," Ada Jane said good naturedly.

"You will not mind?" he asked.

"Kol... of course not. It's your job. If you weren't needed, they wouldn't try to contact you."

Kol let himself drop onto the sofa as he grabbed his communicator from the table beside it. He ran his thumb across it and it began to beep relentlessly. Kol sat up and spoke into the communicator. "Missy, contact Elisher."

"I've been trying to contact you Ambassador Kol," Missy answered.

"Yes, I see that. Please contact Elisher," Kol answered.

"One moment, please," Missy answered.

Several moments passed before Missy spoke again. "Proceed Ambassador Kol."

"Elisher? Is all well?" he asked.

"Um. Yes. I think so," Elisher replied in a very feminine way.

Kol stood up and looked down at the communicator in his hand. "Why do you not sound sure? Is there a problem? Am I needed?" Kol asked.

"Well," Elisher said, looking around the room at the two very large, very intimidating males that had joined her. "We have company. And they are anxious to see you."

"Have they forced their way into our quarters?" Kol asked, his anxiety growing. "Where is Buchanan?" Kol asked, already moving toward the bedroom to gather his things.

"He's gone to see to his regular duties. Patroon Zhuxi is here with me and our guests." Elisher answered.

"Where are Zhuxi's security?" Kol asked.

"They're here, outside the door," Elisher answered.

"It sounds secure. If Zhuxi allowed them in, surely he knows them," Kol answered as he walked into the kitchen and leaned over to kiss Ada Jane's head.

"It appears he is at least familiar with who they are," Elisher answered mysteriously.

"I will contact you," Kol whispered to Ada Jane before rushing out of the cottage.

Ada Jane followed him out onto the porch, knowing he had a job to do, but feeling slightly pushed aside since they'd just completed their bond the night before, and it was kind of a big deal for her to be able to find that level of trust inside herself. She heard the tail end of their conversation just before he hurried out of earshot on his way to his cruiser.

"Kol, one of them won't get away from me. He keeps staring at me, and he follows wherever I go. I had to lock the door to my room just to be able to go into the bathroom alone. And he's angry! He keeps growling."

"I am coming, Elisher. I'll be there shortly. Do not allow Zhuxi to leave you alone with them. Stay near Zhuxi."

"I will. Hurry."

Ada watched as moments later Kol's cruiser lifted into the air and after only a split second to focus on it, it jetted off into the sky so quickly she couldn't keep her eyes focused on it.

Ada Jane went back inside her cottage and made herself a glass of tea, then went into her bedroom to get the tablet Kol had given her. She walked back into the living room and kicked her shoes off. She sat back on her sofa and put her feet up as she powered up her tablet. As soon as it was ready for her command, she spoke to it. "Hello, Missy."

"Hello, Ehlealah Ada Jane Ra' Don Tol."

"Can you get me information on Special Liaison Elisher?"

"I can. What type of information would you prefer? Birth information, personal information, professional information?"

"All of it," Ada Jane replied.

"Please allow me time to gather the information and organize it in an appropriate time line for you," Missy answered.

"Thank you, Missy."

"You are quite welcome, Ehlealah Ada Jane Ra' Don Tol."

Six minutes later Ada Jane's tablet spoke to her. "Ehlealah Ada Jane Ra' Don Tol? Your report is ready."

"Thank you, Missy. Please load it on my tablet."

"Uploading now."

Ada Jane spent the next several hours, reading the report Missy had provided for her, then searching for additional information on certain points she was particularly interested in. By the time she was done, she was completely convinced that Elisher was actually Elisha. The reason Ada Jane had mistaken him for a girl was because he was a girl. And he was living in Kol's quarters under the guise of being a male. And Ada Jane was not happy at all about it.

Ada Jane tried to com Kol using the communicator he'd left her. But it went unanswered. She tried again, and finally he picked it up. She was nervous about calling him, she'd never called a man before. "Kol?" she asked, waiting for him to appear on screen.

She watched as the picture blurred for a moment then snapped into focus. "Ambassador Kol Ra' Don Tol's quarters. May I help you?"

Ada Jane felt like snarling just the same way Kol did when he was irritated. Elisher was answering her mate's communicator. She plastered on a fake smile and pulled her manners together. "No, thank you. I'm trying to reach my mate. Is Kol there?"

"Yes, he is but he's not in our quarters at the moment. He's taken some new arrivals on a tour of the base. May I give him a message for you, or may I be of assistance?" Elisher asked.

"No. If you could just let him know I tried to reach him, it would be appreciated," Ada Jane answered.

"I'll let him know as soon as he gets back to our quarters."

"Thank you," Ada Jane said, ending the vidcom.

She ended the connection, then sat on her couch trying to control her temper. "Their quarters. There was a female sharing her mate's quarters and calling them 'their quarters'.

Her mind reminded her that Kol didn't know Elisher was a woman. He thought his assistant was just an effeminate male. Ada glanced at the communicator again, but knew if she tried to call again, Elisher would answer again and she'd be even more frustrated than she was now.

Ada grabbed her weapon from the side table and standing slipped it into her pocket, then after thinking about it for a moment, decided to leave her communicator where it was. If she took it with her, she'd be too tempted to look at it all day, or try to contact Kol again, and no matter how irritated she was, she didn't want to be that woman.

She didn't think for a moment he was doing anything wrong. She just knew that Elisher wasn't who he pretended to be, and she couldn't get in touch with Kol. Shaking her head to clear it, she walked out of her cottage, across the yard and into the side entrance of the church. She knew Pastor Douglas had a particular schedule for cleaning the church. Today was the day he polished all the wood with a lemon scented wax. She couldn't think of a better way to keep busy and her mind off Kol. "Pastor Douglas?!" she called. "Could you use some help in here today?"

Kol docked his cruiser and wasted no time rushing to his quarters. He unlocked his door and stepped inside only to come to a sudden halt. Then his face went from shock to one of delight.

"Blue Dude!" Kron called out teasingly.

"Kron! Ba Re'! Why are you here?" he said, greeting both in big bear hugs with lots of male patting each other on the back.

"Bart said you needed a small team for backup. We volunteered," Kron answered.

"He did not mention that he would be sending some of my own people, nor did he give any indication he'd be sending my friends and family. I am very pleased to have you here," Kol said.

"I am overly thrilled to be here," Ba Re' answered on a rumble while staring at Elisher.

"Kol!" Elisher said, moving quickly toward him. "Welcome back. Did you get everything finished that you needed to?"

Ba Re' snarled when Elisher got within a few steps of Kol.

Kol looked questioningly at Ba Re'. "Are you feeling well, cousin?" Kol asked, concerned. Ba Re' was never overly jovial, but he rarely snarled for no reason at all.

Ba Re's gaze moved from Elisher to Kol. "Of course, I am well. Where have you been?" he snapped.

Kol's whole demeanor changed. He took on the happy appearance of someone who had no issues or disappointments in life at all. "I have been with my Ehlealah! We are one!" he announced, smiling proudly, his chest puffing out.

"Congratulations!" Kron said, giving more ferocious pats on Kol's back. "I wish you many, many revolutions of happiness and many, many children. He looked at the closed door behind Kol. "Where is she? Does she not join you here?" Kron asked.

Kol shook his head. "No. She is still struggling to overcome the trauma she suffered. And I am doing my best to understand and give her the time she needs while also establishing my claim and our bond. She explained to me that she is not ready to enter a military atmosphere. And I believe that this many males in one place would frighten her greatly. We have found a small cottage not too far from here, and she lives there. I will move between the two places as I'm needed here and prefer to be there."

"It is a good plan, Kol. You are truly blessed. If she is still struggling yet accepted you, it shows that she realizes just how much you belong to one another. She realizes that you are her safety, her love, her male. You are much blessed," Kron said again.

"Yes, very blessed," Ba Re' said, once again glaring at Elisher.

"Zhuxi! Thank you for your welcome to my friends. I am in your debt," Kol said.

"Nonsense! And congratulations on your mating. It is a blessed day," Zhuxi said sincerely. "But, I must ask... Blue Dude?" he asked.

"A shortened name that our Sirena gave me long before she learned my true name. It has stuck," Kol said grinning. "And it is a blessed day, would be even more so if I were not here and my Ehlealah there, but, it is what it is, and we have both committed," Kol said.

"There will be time later to devote to strengthening your bond," Zhuxi added.

"There will," Kol answered, eyeing Ba Re' as he continued to glare at Elisher who was looking as though he'd like to run and hide.

"I believe I will provide my friends with a tour as I update them on our findings so far," Kol said, stepping back toward the door and opening it.

Kron followed readily enough, but Ba Re' stayed put.

"Ba Re', we are going on a tour," Kron said.

Ba Re' glanced at Kol. "Go then," he said.

"You are coming, too," Kol added.

Ba Re' pinned Kol with a pointed look. "I'll stay here."

"No, you will come with us. You need to be familiar with the layout of the base, and I have additional information to provide. Come along, we are waiting."

"I will stay here with Elisher," Zhuxi said, not sure what was going on, but aware that the big black and grey Cruestaci warrior was unusually focused on Elisher, and was making Elisher extremely uncomfortable.

"Thank you, Zhuxi. As soon as we return I will relieve you, and you can return to your responsibilities," Kol said.

"There is no rush. Buchanan and I have arranged our schedules so that one of us can be here to assist you and Elisher at all times. The other is covering our general duties about the base. We've got our tablets for communications with anyone outside the base, so all is taken care of," Zhuxi explained.

"How can I thank you?" Kol said.

"You already have. You're investigating questions we've had for years that have gone unanswered," Zhuxi said. "Now go, see to your friends, Blue Dude," Zhuxi said, laughing in his gurgling kind of way.

Kol, Ba Re' and Kron left, closing and locking the door behind them, with Kol chuckling at Zhuxi calling him Blue Dude.

Zhuxi turned to Elisher. "What is the problem? What is going on with Ba Re'?"

"I have no idea. You saw him! When you first brought them in, he was polite and shaking hands with Buchanan. Then the moment he looked at me, he practically charged me. If Kron hadn't called his name, I don't know what would have happened!"

Chapter 22

Kron and Kol walked down the hallway with Ba Re' grumbling behind them. "Why are you here?" Kol asked Kron.

"We already told you. Bart asked for a small team to support you," Kron answered.

"I know that, what I'm asking is who is standing in as Elite Force Commander if I'm here and you're here?" Kol asked.

Kron stopped walking and grinned at Kol. "You haven't heard..." he said chuckling.

Kron's response even earned a half-hearted grin from Ba Re'.

"What is so funny?" Kol asked, looking back and forth between them.

"Rokai ahl is acting as Elite Force Commander in our absence," Kron said, waiting for Kol's reaction.

"He what?" Kol shouted. "Has Zha Quin lost his mind?"

"He wouldn't be the only one," Ba Re' grumbled, rubbing at the back of his neck.

"Are you well?" Kol demanded, glaring at Ba Re'.

"Of course, I am well," Ba Re' snapped.

"Then why are you staring at my assistant like you wish to kill him? Stop intimidating him! He is not the male we are, and you are making him uncomfortable in his own quarters!"

Ba Re's face went from irritation and obstinence to surprise. "It was not my intention to unnerve him. I simply don't understand. It can't possibly be right," Ba Re' grumbled.

"What can't be right? He is my assistant. And he is a good assistant. I need him to concentrate on his work so that he can complete it and I won't have to!" Kol said, his voice raised to indicate his frustration.

"I will apologize to him. I did not mean to frighten him. I..." Ba Re' stopped talking, searching for the words.

"You what?" Kol asked.

"Nothing. Proceed. Are you going to show us this facility or not?" Ba Re' snapped.

Kol started to press the issue, but knowing Ba Re' as well as he did, he could tell the male was actually very upset, so he decided to let it lie for a while.

He and Kron started walking again, and Ba Re' reluctantly followed along. "I thought Rokai ahl was taking his Ehlealah to see all the wonders he could show her," Kol said dramatically, trying his best to imitate Rokai ahl's flamboyance.

"He was. Which is why it was funny. Zha Quin demanded he come back to Command Warship 1 without further delay. Told him it was a matter of life and death and that only he could make the difference. Rokai ahl showed up to help his newly reclaimed family, and Zha Quin advised him that he is Elite Force Commander effective immediately and until you or I return to relieve him."

"He willfully accepted?" Kol asked.

"Not exactly. It took some convincing, and Chairman Bartholomew had to promise to grant him a favor if needed in the future. We explained that he was the perfect fit because of his highly elevated skills, and because he had no interest in the job permanently. Then he accepted. He is now calling himself Rokai ahl Tel Mo' Kok, Elite Force Commander, feared the multi-verse over," Kron said.

Kol shook his head. "Rokai ahl certainly has the skills to lead the force. I just don't know if he'll apply himself and succeed, or be more of a hindrance because he doesn't actually want to be there," Kol said.

"I spoke with Jhan this morning. He said Rokai has actually taken pride in the new position. He said he can clearly be seen enjoying himself, and is seen taking meals from time to time with the Elite Force. I think it will be good for him, and possibly for them. He surely has a trick or two up his sleeve that he can teach them to be wary of," Ba Re' said.

“I’d have never dreamed of Rokai ahl leading Elite Forces. I do not believe there is anything that could surprise me more,” Kol said.

“Don’t be too sure about that,” Ba Re’ grouched from behind them.

<<<<<<<>>>>>>>

“Father, it is simply unacceptable!” Diskastes shouted, before swiping all the papers off his desk in a fit of rage.

“I do not care what you think is acceptable or not. What I am concerned about is why the Consortium believes it necessary to audit Base 28. I am concerned with why the Consortium has sent Cruestaci Ambassadors and a warrior team to assist with these audits! What have you done now?” the ruling monarch of the Planet Quisles demanded.

“I have done nothing but rule this Base as it should be ruled. I am offended that you would consider that I would have done otherwise,” Diskastes answered indignantly.

His father looked at him with an unmeasured amount of disgust. “I will make inquiries. But know you this, if you have engaged in any behavior that brings strikes against our family or our people, I will not stand beside you. I have removed you from incident after incident, the last of which left you on the planet you’re on!” he shouted. “The only reason I even consider lifting a finger in your direction is your dear mother! It is time you were responsible for your own actions! Being born into a monarchy does not mean you are guaranteed a life of ease. You must earn it!” his father bellowed at him before ending the communication.

Diskastes screamed his own frustration and kicked his desk. There was no other way. He absolutely had to be sure that this audit turned up nothing. He stalked from his office bellowing for his computer specialist. They’d have to corrupt all the computers on base in order to keep the Cruestaci from finding anything that would incriminate him. There was just no other way.

<<<<<<<>>>>>>>

Elisher sat at her computer tapping away at the keys, assembling spread sheets with the data she found as well as logging in the deliveries and expenses that had not yet been logged into the system. Each time she felt she'd made a little headway or found a discrepancy, she'd take a screen shot to record it, then dig even deeper.

Kol, Kron and Ba Re' had returned from their tour of the base and sat in the living room discussing options for containing Diskastes and his men should it come to that. And from the looks of the information she was finding, it would come to that. Elisher had no doubt that when the Consortium was made aware of all the evidence she was discovering, they'd come in and seize the base.

This was both good news and bad news for Elisher. The whole reason behind her decades long masquerade was the opportunity to go to space. She'd spent years finishing all the educational requirements, then applied to the aerospace program. Instead of receiving an invitation to train for the outer reaches of the universe, she'd been assigned as an envoy to all alien peoples visiting their planet.

She tried her best not to think about it. She still clung to the hope that with enough proven service and loyalty, they'd one day consider her for the job she dreamed of. Closing down Base 28, or reassigning all its personnel could possibly end in her actually moving backwards in her career, though she'd certainly be involved in taking down those who were abusing the people under their watch. Or would it? She wanted to speak to Kol about her uncertainties. She didn't want this to come back on her negatively. She'd given up far too much to have to be the scapegoat if all went to hell unexpectedly. But since his friends had arrived, he'd not been alone for even five minutes for her to ask.

Elisher's gaze drifted from the screen of her computer to the sofas the three of them sat on. Elisher's body shivered a bit when her eyes met Ba Re's, before she quickly looked away again. He'd apologized for making her uncomfortable when they'd come back to Kol's quarters. And he'd promised that he would never hurt her. But he still stared at her so intensely, it was difficult not to be nervous. And every time she got up to go to the bathroom attached to her bedroom, when she came back, he was loitering near her bedroom door.

Ba Re' looked away from her as she glanced at him again and caught him watching her. Elisher took the opportunity to really look at the male. He was intimidating, but he was impressive. His skin appeared to be a dark charcoal color from a distance, but up close it was easy to see that it was black with gray and ivory mottles throughout, giving it that charcoal colored appearance. His eyes were a deep stormy gray and framed with impossibly long lashes. His face was angular with wide high cheekbones and a hard chiseled jawline. His nose was strong and firm with a slight jog in the center of it that hinted that it was once broken. His neck was thick and the striations from the muscles as he turned his head often made her heart flutter.

His build was that of a professional athlete, times ten. His muscles had muscles, his waist was trim, his legs powerfully built and his ass flexed with every stride he took. She knew — she'd watched. Her eyes raised to his horns and she smiled slightly as she examined them from across the room. They were quite the crowning glory. They were just like Kol's, only Ba Re's were a deep gray instead of black like Kol's. They were gracefully curved back over his head as Kol's were and meant for protection in battle, but Elisher liked to think of them as a crown. Both males were practically regal in all their movements and mannerisms — except for when Ba Re' snarled at her, then all regalness went out the window.

Elisher smiled to herself as she took her time examining all Ba Re's features. She allowed her eyes to drift back over his face and startled when she found his eyes staring right back at her. Elisher quickly looked away as the growl she was pretty sure she could identify anywhere rumbled from his chest. This was his irritated growl, she'd come to know that one well.

Elisher went back to her data gathering and keying in all that she found, but her heart pounded. She'd been a fool to think Kol was going to tempt her into risking her cover. Not that he wasn't attractive, but he wasn't Ba Re'. And Ba Re' was, in her opinion, absolutely exquisite. Elisher glanced up at the male who unfortunately was still watching her, before quickly looking back down at her keyboard. Ba Re' was the example all males, no matter the race, should be measured by. That's all there was to it, she decided. He was, in her opinion, the epitome of what a male should be.

Ba Re' rumbled again.

Except for that damned growling, she thought to herself.

<<<<<<<>>>>>>>

Ada Jane sat up in her bed, her pillows propped behind her with her communicator in her hand. She wanted to com Kol, but her pride wouldn't let her. He should have contacted her by now. He promised he'd com her. He'd told her to com him, too, and she had, but apparently he didn't care enough to com her back. She knew he was busy, and that's why she didn't expect a com until this evening, but now it was well into the night, and he hadn't even attempted to get back in touch with her.

Frustrated, she tossed the communicator to the foot of her bed and slid down into her covers and snuggled into her pillow. And that just made it worse. "My pillows even smell like him!" she exclaimed, yanking the pillow from beneath her head and throwing it on the floor. "Stupid male!" she mumbled, curling into her own pillow and doing her best to settle in for the night. "I'm not contacting him," she whispered into her silent bedroom.

Kol was in bed, with Kron and Ba Re' also in his room on small single beds they'd brought into his bedroom for their use. All three warriors opened their eyes the moment Kol's bedroom door opened quietly.

"Kol?" a voice whispered.

Kron recognized it and turned over, trying to go back to sleep.

Kol recognized it and sat up in bed. "Elisher?" he asked.

Ba Re' noticed it and bit his own tongue to hold in the snarls he wanted to let loose on all of them.

"I meant to tell you earlier but with your friends arriving I forgot," Elisher said.

"Forgot what?" Kol asked.

Elisher moved through the darkened room until she was standing right beside Kol's bed. "Ada Jane com'd you earlier today. She didn't want to leave a message, just said if I could let you know she'd tried to reach you, she'd appreciate it. I forgot. I feel terrible. I'll contact her tomorrow and apologize."

"That won't be necessary, but thank you for offering. I got caught up in the days activities as well and forgot to contact her myself. I promised that I would, then I forgot until it was so late that I fear I'd awaken her if I tried now."

Elisher stood there for a moment then she shrugged her shoulders in the dark. "If I was newly mated and my mate promised to contact me and didn't, I'd feel better if he woke me to tell me he was busy and forgot instead of just not following through."

Kol smiled to himself. "Yes, but your mate would be female," he said.

"Hmm?" she asked. "Oh, yes! Of course, my mate would be female."

"Perhaps I will com her after all," Kol said, getting out of bed. He waited for Elisher to walk ahead of him then followed him out of his quarters, pulling the door to, but not quite closing it behind themselves.

Kol went to the coffee table between the sofas and picked up his communicator. He was almost ready to make the connections to Ada Jane when Elisher spoke again.

"I'm really glad we're alone. I've been trying to find a minute with just you all day," she said.

Kol looked up from his communicator. "Is there a problem?" he asked.

"Not exactly. I just, I was wondering. With all the auditing we're doing, and results being what they are, I'm concerned with my future with the government."

"It shouldn't affect your future," Kol answered.

"I know it shouldn't. But, my plan all along was to eventually be recognized for my efforts as a loyal and trusted employee. Eventually be chosen to go out into the universe. If I'm seen as one who can't keep secrets, then I may never be allowed to do that. I'd never be trusted."

"And if you're seen as one who allows others to suffer because you didn't want to be seen in a certain light, you would never be trusted either."

"Exactly. So, you see my point. I'm just wondering if you think this will affect my ability to leave Earth and represent Earth and her interests in the future," Elisher asked.

"I don't know, Elisher. But, I can promise you that our mission is an honorable one. Those entrusted with the welfare of others should perform admirably, and when they don't, when their actions affect their people negatively, they should be removed and they should have to answer for their actions. That is what we are doing."

"I know, I do understand that. And I'm in this until the end. I believe in what we're doing, and I know it needs to be done. I just wonder if it will affect my dreams. I'm not like you, I'm not this big, strong male that can run off to battle. I have to depend on my diplomacy to get me there, you know?"

"I do know. And I give you my vow that if I can I will see to it that you are given the opportunities you hope for."

"Thank you, Kol. But only if I earn it. I don't want anything I don't earn."

"Of course," Kol answered.

Elisher walked to her room before looking back at Kol. "Good night. Please apologize for my forgetfulness," she said.

"I will. Sleep well, Elisher, and do not fret too much over your future. I am sure yours is very bright."

"Thank you," Elisher said, smiling before disappearing inside her bedroom.

Kol swiped his thumb over his communicator. "Missy, please com Ada Jane," he asked.

"One moment, Ambassador Kol," Missy answered right away.

Kol stood there, waiting for some time. Then finally, Missy spoke again. "Ambassador, there is no answer from Ada Jane. I have left her notification that you attempted to reach her."

"Thank you, Missy. She is most likely asleep."

"May I be of assistance otherwise?" Missy asked.

"Not at this time," Kol answered. "Thank you."

"You are welcome."

Kol took his communicator with him and went back to bed. He didn't notice that Ba Re' rushed to get back in his own bed before Kol made it to the bedroom.

Ba Re' couldn't help it. He'd had to see the interactions between Kol and Elisher. And just that simple fact drove him insane. There was no way he'd ever claim a male for his Ehlealah. It made no sense. There was no record of a Cruestaci warrior ever taking a male for his Ehlealah. Then he arrived on Earth and was slapped in the face with Elisher, who is male, and who incites all the mating instincts Ba Re' does his best to keep hidden. It's not going to happen. He won't let it. Ba Re' punched the pillow his head lay upon and bit his tongue again to keep himself from snarling aloud.

"Ba Re'?" Kol asked, hearing him moving around more than he would be had he been sleeping.

Ba Re' didn't answer. He just lay still with a scowl on his face. He didn't feel like having to talk to anyone except Elisher, and didn't that just piss him off.

Chapter 23

Kol paced beside the table in his quarters with Elisher and Ba Re' both sitting opposite him, working on computers. Elisher worked feverishly on the computer supplied by the base, while Ba Re' typed away just as quickly on his own laptop brought with him from Command Warship 1. Kron stood to the side, his face tense as hc watched them trying to save the information Elisher had accumulated.

Buchanan wandered around the room his own tablet in hand trying unsuccessfully to log into any of his systems and apps. The damn thing would give him the log on screens to several, then when he typed in his passwords, it would cycle as though it was letting him in before going to a black screen and rebooting itself.

"Kol?" Bart asked from the handheld communicator Kol carried as he moved back and forth across the room.

"Yes," Kol answered as he glanced once more toward Elisher and Ba Re'.

"Any luck?" he asked.

"I think so. We seem to be making progress. Missy managed to grab several bites of information and lock the virus out as it began to infect the system. She took over that small bit of data and Elisher is working to transfer it to Ba Re's computer. But it has to be scanned and disinfected before it can be transferred."

"What is taking so long?" Bart asked.

"Because the fucking virus is attacking Missy. She's fighting it off as she helps to clean and transfer the information that Elisher transfers to her, and then sends it to me," Ba Re' snapped.

Kol looked down at the communicator in his hand and noted the surprised look on Bart's face at Ba Re's surly response.

"He is stressed. We all are. We cannot have Missy infected. Her mainframe is located on Command Warship 1."

"I understand. Is there any other way?" Bart asked.

"Only to abandon all the information to the virus and let it be destroyed," Kol answered.

"We need that evidence. If what you say is accurate, and I have every reason to believe it is, we'll need it to force his family to back off," Bart said. "It could be the only thing that prevents a military action on their part."

"I'm sure of it, the evidence will prove it. I know at the very least, he's misappropriated funds, channeling them to his private accounts. I know he's intercepted food deliveries and sold them for profit. I know he's denied medical treatment to those in our sector. I know he's falsely imprisoned any who dared to question his governing of the people under his guidance. And that's just having been able to dig into just over fifty percent of the documentation I was able to uncover," Elisher said.

"Then we need it. And once it's uploaded and safe, we need him taken into custody. As quietly as possible if we can."

"And if he fights?" Buchanan asked.

"You expect him to?" Bart asked.

"I do. I expect this to get ugly, fast. I have no doubt he'll make a run for it," Buchanan said decidedly.

"Then use whatever force is necessary. But, Kol, be sure you have your com mounted and live feed. Be sure your audio piece is in, too, just in case I have to call you off or redirect you."

"Redirect me?" Kol asked, surprised.

"I will not be the only member of the Consortium observing. This is for your safety there, as well as ours," Bart said.

"Quin?" Kol asked.

"Watching. Along with the rest of the sitting rulers who care to sit in and observe. Only I will have communication abilities with you, though," Bart said. "Quin has agreed not to interfere even though you'll be viewed and listened to through Missy's mainframe. Do not underestimate this male, Kol. He believes he is above the law. Hopefully, it will all go quietly. If not, be prepared to do what is necessary. But do it by the book.

"Whose book?" Kol asked. "I am not just military," he said.

"I know. Just make sure it's all justifiable," Bart explained. "And make sure those damn files are uploaded to me and not corrupted."

"We're at sixty-eight percent. We're more than halfway. We'll get it done," Elisher said firmly, loudly enough that Bart could hear her.

Ba Re' glanced up at Elisher working beside him, then he nodded his head and continued to type. "We will," he confirmed.

"If anyone can achieve this, it is Ba Re', and with Elisher at his side we are sure to be successful against this virus meant to destroy all the devices, and thereby the records on base. It's just a matter of time," Kol said.

"Have you determined the source of the virus yet?" Bart asked.

"We believe it to be installed by hand in the mainframe here on base. But until we finish the cleaning and transfer of the files Elisher has spent countless hours assembling, we will not be able to trace its actual source.

"I believe you will find it leads right to the person we suspect of all the questionable activity coming out of Base 28," Bart said.

"As do I," Kol agreed.

"And I," Buchanan added.

"How much longer?" Kron asked.

"Not sure," Ba Re' answered.

"Minutes," Elisher answered, concentrating on her computer screen and typing away so fast the rhythm of her striking the keys sounded like a hum rather than clicking of individual key strikes.

Ba Re' glanced toward her again where she sat beside him in her pajamas with her bathrobe wrapped tightly around her. He let out a snarl at the fact that he was so conflicted over this male.

"Stop growling at me," Elisher said, still typing away and not even pausing to look at him.

"It's not at you," Ba Re' snapped.

"Could have fooled me. You've been glaring at me since you arrived. I don't know you, don't know who you think I am, but I've not done anything to earn your ire," Elisher answered, not even breaking stride in her typing nor looking away from her computer screen.

"Ire?" Ba Re' asked.

"Irritation. Anger," Buchanan provided.

"Ninety-two percent!" Elisher shouted excitedly, a smile on her face.

"Yes!" Bart cried out from Kol's communicator.

"What's your percentage, Ba Re'?" Bart asked.

"Eighty-nine percent. I'm right behind Elisher. Soon as the data's cleared, I'm running it through my system to copy then uploading from Missy to your systems," Ba Re' answered, speaking to Bart.

"Didn't growl at him," Elisher mumbled.

Ba Re' shook his head in disbelief at the small male taunting him.

"Ninety-eight!" Elisher exclaimed.

"Kol, don't wait any longer! Elisher and Ba Re' will finish this up momentarily. Take Diskastes into custody now! Any who have even given a slight sign of being loyal to him should be taken into custody with him. And don't forget to go live so that a recording is made for any who may question our methods," Bart said, urgently.

"On it," Kol answered. "Where's Zhuxi?" Kol asked, turning his attention to Buchanan.

"Keeping eyes on Diskastes. He said and I quote, 'Tell Blue Dude we will be ready'. He's got our security with him or nearby. They'll know when we're moving in and be ready to support us as needed. We've been waiting for this for a long, long time."

"Let's go, then," Kol answered.

Kron, Kol and Buchanan moved quickly out of Kol's quarters. He paused at the door to look at Ba Re'. "Do not leave

Elisher unguarded. Diskastes would certainly try to hurt him because he's helped us amass evidence against him." Then he closed the door and their footsteps could be heard echoing down the hallway as they ran.

Elisher's system flashed one hundred percent. "I'm done! One hundred percent," she said, getting to her feet.

"I'm at ninety-seven percent," Ba Re' answered, still manually typing in the commands to accept each line of cleaned data as it hit his system.

"One hundred percent yet?" Elisher asked, watching from over Ba Re's shoulder.

"Almost..." Ba Re' answered, still typing.

Then Ba Re' jumped to his feet. "One hundred percent!" he said.

"Yes!" Elisher said, throwing herself against Ba Re' and hugging him.

Ba Re' hugged Elisher back, then almost immediately his face fell, and he pushed Elisher away with a scowl on his face.

Ba Re' didn't look at Elisher again, he simply retook his seat and began pulling up the spread sheets that they'd migrated from Elisher's infected system to Ba Re's laptop, which was connected to Missy, along with all the supporting documents and entries.

Elisher recovered from being pushed away by Ba Re' and readily took responsibility for the awkward situation on herself. Some people, aliens included, just didn't like being touched, and Ba Re' didn't like her when she wasn't touching him — she should have known better than to hug him, even on impulse. She walked over and stood behind Ba Re', watching as he assembled the already built spread sheets into one report to forward to Chairman Bartholomew. Elisher stood there, one hand on the back of the chair that Ba Re' sat on, as she leaned close to him and watched the screen as he worked.

Ba Re' ground his teeth and did his best not to react to Elisher, but it was hard to do. He was right there, just inches from his face. Elisher's scent permeated Ba Re's space and Ba Re' could feel the warmth coming from Elisher with his body so near.

"Move away from me," Ba Re' snarled.

Elisher jerked back like she'd been slapped. "I'm sorry. I'm just interested in the work. This is my work. I've done nothing but assemble this data since Kol arrived."

"Move. Away," Ba Re' growled, more deeply and threateningly than he had since he'd arrived.

Elisher moved away from Ba Re'. "You're a jerk. I've done nothing to you and you treat me like I'm an enemy. You don't even have the balls to explain what the hell your problem is," Elisher snapped, walking toward her bedroom to get away from the edgy male.

Suddenly Elisher was airborne, but not out of control. Strong arms held her securely as her body was spun and pressed to the wall beside her bedroom door. Ba Re' pressed the length of his body against Elisher's, allowing her to feel every taut muscle, the pulse of his heartbeat at his throat, and the steel like hardness of his swollen shaft as it pressed into Elisher's belly.

Ba Re' didn't speak. He pressed his hand against Elisher's throat and forced her chin up so he could glare down into her face, merely centimeters away from her.

Elisher was scared, as she should be.

Ba Re' scented his fear but he couldn't help it. He was nearly to the point of losing control. Elisher slipped his tongue out and licked his lips nervously and that was all it took.

Ba Re' descended on her. Grabbing Elisher's short hair in the fist of one hand while he held Elisher's body still with the other pressed against her throat. Ba Re's mouth covered Elisher's, his tongue forcing its way in as he slammed her head against the wall at the same time he drove his hips into her. Ba Re' plundered her mouth until she was actually dizzy from the contact.

Then just as suddenly, she was alone, her feet on the floor, leaning against the wall, trying to maintain her balance and Ba Re' was across the room watching her with a look that had it been possible, would have struck her dead.

"That's the fucking problem," he snapped. "Cruestaci warriors don't take males as life mates. And I sure as fuck won't be the first. You cannot be my Ehlealah! It is not possible!" he snarled, before stalking into Kol's bedroom and slamming the door behind himself.

Elisher stood where she'd been when Be Re' had released her and moved away. Her eyes were wide, her breath coming in short pants, and her mind whirling. Ba Re' thought she was his Ehlealah. And he thought she was a male. Elisher turned from where she leaned against the wall and went through the door of her bedroom, which was directly beside her. She quietly closed and locked the door, then went straight to her bathroom and locked that door behind herself as well.

Her hands shook as she turned on the water and waited until it warmed so she could wash her face. She looked up at her reflection in the mirror. Her heart was racing at the thought of this powerful male identifying her as his life mate. She was attracted to him, and had he not been so damned grouchy, she may have had a hard time staying away from him herself, but her mind kept screaming of all she'd sacrificed to get to this point. She couldn't tell him. If she did, her cover would be blown — all her plans shot to hell.

Her entire body jumped as she reacted to a roar coming from just across the common space she shared with Kol. Ba Re', no doubt, was screaming his own frustration. She really hoped Kol came back soon. She didn't have any idea of what to do if Ba Re' burst into her bathroom in search of her. She wanted him — badly. But she could never have him. She'd laid out her life to be lived as a male. And as he'd so clearly stated, Cruestaci males did not take males as life mates.

<<<<<<<>>>>>>>

Ada Jane had just finished lunch when there was a knock at her door. Her heart jumped at the sound of the knock. It had to be Kol — she just knew it was. She'd refused to call him all night long, or this morning, and finally he'd come back to her to explain why he hadn't returned her call.

Ada walked over to her door and didn't stop to peek out of the window because she was sure she knew who it was. She pulled her door opened and spoke at the same time. "It's about time you decided to remember me."

"I wasn't sure you wanted to be remembered considering how quickly you left the clinic," Jason said, smiling brightly.

Ada was surprised into silence. She'd not expected Jason to be here at all. She didn't even know for sure that he knew where she was. "Jason," she said, her unease evident.

"You were expecting someone else," he said, still smiling, though not as brightly.

"I... well, yes. But, that's not important. Come on in," she invited, stepping back to allow him entrance into her home. "Why are you here?" she asked, closing the door behind him. "And how did you know where I was?" she asked.

"I just wanted to check on you. To make sure that you were settled and acclimating well," Jason explained. "And the credits from your band show an origination of these coordinates. The pastor advised me this cottage is yours," he said, indicating Pastor Douglas's cottage.

"Oh. Well, yes. I'm acclimating quite well. I've got my own place, as you can see," she said, looking around her living room. "And I've got a part-time job, helping Pastor Douglas keep the church and the grounds up. I'm doing well," she said, sliding her hands into the back pockets of her jeans, as she smiled at him and waited to see what he'd ask next.

"I'm glad to see that, Ada Jane. I was worried about you when you rushed off so quickly with the alien male that showed up at the clinic with no warning at all," Jason said.

"Warning?" she asked, as she moved into the living room from the front door and with a wave of her hand indicated that Jason should have a seat. "Would you like a glass of tea or water or something?" she asked.

Jason sat down and nodded. "Tea would be nice. Thank you."

"You're welcome," Ada said, going into her kitchen. She came back into the living room and handed Jason his glass of tea before she continued her question. "What warning should he have given?" Ada Jane asked.

"It's more a statement of my own perception than anything else. I wasn't aware that you had friends here, so I was caught off guard when he showed up and whisked you away. Do you know him well?" Jason asked.

"I see. Because I didn't confide in you about Kol, you felt slighted?" Ada Jane asked.

"Well, no. It's not that. I just..." Jason stopped speaking, not knowing quite how to explain himself. Finally he just decided to go for a small amount of honesty. "I like you, Ada Jane. I had hoped that we'd have an opportunity to get to know one another and you would see that you can depend on me. I'd hoped that we could be more than friends."

Ada Jane nodded slowly as she let Jason speak until he felt he'd said all he had to say. "I like you, Jason. And I hope we can be friends. But, Kol and I are married — I think."

"You think?" Jason asked.

"He is mine. And he says that I'm his Ehlealah, I'm his mate. So, I think according to his people, we're married."

"Just to his people?" Jason asked.

"Well, to me too. It's just, right after we made it official, he was called away on business and I haven't been able to get in touch with him," she admitted, unable to keep the irritation from showing on her face.

Jason was not thrilled at the idea of the woman he'd set his sights on being committed to another. The idea that Kol had not been in touch with Ada Jane since they'd 'made it official' as she called it, put him in mind of men who would spout claims of love until they'd gotten what they wanted, then leave the woman high and dry while they moved on to greener pastures.

He watched Ada Jane and decided she wasn't so sure herself. The way her eyes focused on a spot across the room and she seemed to get lost in her own head after admitting to him that she'd not heard from him since he'd been called away.

"Ada, as your friend, I can take you to him if you like," Jason offered, hedging his bets that they'd find the male with another woman on the side, then he'd be able to soothe Ada Jane and guide her right into a relationship with him just as he'd originally planned.

Ada snapped out of her inner reflection thinking of her irritation at Kol not returning her call. "You know... let me try to call him again," she said, getting to her feet and going into her bedroom.

"Call him? We haven't called anyone in years," Jason said, chuckling.

"Call, com, you know what I mean," she answered as she lifted her communicator and smoothed her thumb over it like Kol had shown her. It came to life and she smiled when it greeted her. "Hello, Ehlealah Ada Jane Ra' Don Tol. How may I help you?"

"Hello, Missy. Can you com Kol for me?" she asked.

"Of course. Just one moment," Missy answered.

Jason sat in the living room, listening to the interaction between Ada Jane and whatever device she was using to com the alien she believed she was married to.

Moments later Missy was back. "Ehlealah Ada Jane Ra' Don Tol?" Missy asked.

"Yes, I'm here," Ada Jane answered.

"He is not answering his com. I took the liberty of coming his assistant, Elisher, but Elisher is not answering his com either. All communications are temporarily blocked. Shall I leave a message for them."

"Yes, please, Missy. For Kol, anyway. Please do not leave one for Elisher," Ada Jane responded.

"As you requested, a message is being left for Ambassador Kol. I will not leave a message for Elisher. Is there anything else I can help you with?" Missy asked.

"No, thank you, Missy," Ada Jane said, the disappointment clear in her voice.

She went back into the living room with the communicator in her hand and sat down. "He's not answering. He must be busy."

"Perhaps," Jason said.

Ada nodded and tried to hide her insecurities. "Are you hungry? Can I get you something to eat?" she asked.

"No, thank you. I'm more concerned that you look a little upset. Does your husband have an assistant you can call?" Jason asked.

"I tried. She isn't answering either. I'm sure they're busy, they were working on a big project together," Ada Jane said.

"I'm sure you're right. I'm sure it's nothing but business. Where are they?" Jason asked.

"Base 28. In Texas," Ada replied.

"Why don't you let me take you there. Put your mind at ease, then I'll bring you back once you know he's okay," Jason offered.

"Really? You'd do that for me?" Ada Jane asked.

"Ada Jane," Jason said, getting to his feet and walking over to her. He clasped her hand between his. "There is nothing I wouldn't do for you."

Ada gently pulled her hand free from his and offered a tenuous smile. "I suppose it couldn't do any harm," Ada Jane said. She got to her feet and slipped her communicator into her front left pocket, since her weapon was in her right front pocket. "Okay, well, I guess I'd appreciate that ride then. I'll just let Pastor Douglas know that I'll be gone for a little while. How long do you think I'll be away?"

"You'll be back by this evening, I'm sure," Jason assured her.

Jason followed her out of her home, pretty sure that he'd be bringing her back to his own home after she unexpectedly dropped in on her husband and his assistant, who were no doubt in the midst of activities other than business as were most aliens stationed here on Earth. It sickened Jason that so many human females were taken advantage of by the aliens that had invaded the planet. He took great pride in his status as a Purist, and had no doubt that Ada Jane would as well once she'd realized that the aliens were known far and wide for sexual escapades with human women. She'd soon see that fortunately for her, he'd intervened just in time to prevent her fully being taken advantage of by them again.

He smiled as he followed her out to his transport. She was about to have her heart broken, but that was okay. He'd be there to pick up the pieces and from this day on, she'd be a Purist just like him.

Chapter 24

Kol, Kron, and Buchanan were met by Zhuxi and the combined security forces of his own and Buchanan's, as they stepped into the corridor leading to Diskastes's official offices.

"We've been ordered to take Diskastes into custody," Kol said, a growl in his voice since his Psi had been engaged, knowing they were going into battle.

"Is all complete? We are ready?" Zhuxi asked.

"Yes. All data uploads should have been uploaded to Chairman Bartholomew as of now. Elisher is safe in my quarters, being protected by Ba Re', and all is a go."

"How do you wish to proceed?" Zhuxi asked.

Kol quickly engineered a plan that had several males proceeding down the corridor and forcing their way into the offices with himself and Buchanan. Kron took a third of their combined force outside to take out the electricity and to watch for anyone attempting to escape the base, and the rest of their force was sent on general patrol of the base and to take into custody any who'd been in Diskastes's employ and seemed to be loyal to him — better safe than sorry at this point. No one that had previously been associated with Diskastes would be allowed to go free.

Kol and those who were waiting with him and Buchanan stayed where they were, remaining quiet and undetected so Kron could have a chance to get into place outside the base.

Kol had heeded Bart's advice to activate the live feed on his com and clipped it to the strap over his left shoulder. Having slipped his ear piece in as he first left his quarters, he tapped it activating it as well. "Power's out. We're a go in five, four, three, two, one," Kol said, before raising his hand in the air, index finger extended as he pointed forward twice, signaling to the men behind him that it was time to move in. They began down the darkened corridor, crouching low, with weapons drawn.

Ten feet from Diskastes's office, they encountered the first of Diskastes's forces. "You are being taken into custody by order of the Unified Consortium Defense!" Kol shouted.

His announcement was ignored as the forces gave immediate resistance, completely ignoring, or not caring about, Kol's announcement that the Consortium had ordered their apprehension. A few short minutes and hand-to-hand combat moves later and the four males who'd been left to defend the exterior of the office were under control and in custody. Two males were left behind to oversee them as the remainder entered the offices.

They tried the knob and found it locked. Unperturbed, Kol kicked the door in and entered, his weapon drawn, shouting that Diskastes was to be taken into custody on charges to be determined by the Unified Consortium Defense. As the door was kicked in, more of Diskastes's males attacked. Shots were exchanged this time, and several on both sides of the confrontation were injured, but thankfully, the only two that fell lifeless were members of Diskastes's security forces.

Buchanan was having more fun than he should have been. He carried an antique shot gun, and was personally responsible for the death of both of the casualties on Diskastes's forces. Kol glanced toward Buchanan after the first shot with a surprised look on his face, and Buchanan grinned at him. "I prefer doing things the old fashioned way."

Kol returned his attention to the large office and the small skirmishes that were quickly controlled since most of the opposing security force in the office quickly realized it would be in their best interest to lay down their weapons and surrender. He realized as the remaining members of Diskastes's males were taken into custody, that Diskastes himself was missing.

"He's not here," Kol growled.

"Where is he?" Buchanan shouted, nudging one of the males from Diskastes's home planet with the barrel end of his rifle.

The male lifted his chin in the air, his mouth closed tightly, refusing to answer.

"Where the fuck is he?" Buchanan demanded, leveling the rifle at the male's head.

Kol shoved his way through his own security forces and reached down, grabbing the male by the throat, and snatched him into the air before slamming him against the wall hard enough to break the sheetrock.

Kol's Psi was fully engaged, he was almost eight feet tall, his shoulders widened to the point that they'd brushed the sides of the doorway as he'd kicked it in and ducked to rush through it. His horns had elongated, his claws had pushed through the ends of his fingers and become razor sharp, and his jaw had jutted forward while his mouth widened, very clearly displaying all the rows of his shark-like teeth. A snarl rumbled constantly from his chest and the saliva dripped from his mouth as his newly appearing cold, dead pupils pinpointed the male in his hand as a target.

He leaned toward the male now gasping in pain from being slammed into the wall, and gnashed his teeth. "You will tell me where he is, or you will die in his place when I rip out your throat," Kol snarled, the words barely understandable with his Psi so engaged.

The male's terrified eyes flicked to a wall displaying all the rulers Diskastes had managed to get photos with to further feed his delusions of grandeur. Kol shook him and dug his claws a little deeper into the male's throat.

He made gurgling sounds while quickly looking back and forth between Kol and the wall, as he clung desperately to Kol's wrist while still being held two feet off the floor. Kol realized he was trying to tell him that Diskastes's escape had something to do with that wall. Kol dropped the male to the floor and stalked toward the wall, glancing quickly over all the photos before getting irritated and beginning to snatch them from the wall, in search of anything that would show him where Diskastes had gone.

Kol thought it strange that photos covered the entire wall, even down at knee level. He reached out with a booted foot and kicked the photos there, causing the glass frames to shatter and the photos to fall to the floor. His kicks also revealed a small cavity built into the wall near the floor.

Kol leaned over and peered into it. He stood and inserted his booted foot into the space and stepped down. The wall shifted and swung open, revealing a small passage. Kol stepped into the passage on heightened alert, his weapon leveled and prepared to fire at anything that came at him. Those not responsible for taking the males they'd defeated into custody followed closely on his heels. They got no more than ten feet before Kol saw a body lying on the floor of the passageway. He approached cautiously, prepared to fire if it was a ruse. He nudged the body and on deciding that it was truly dead, flipped it over.

"It's Pomrance," Kol said in a hushed voice.

"Diskastes must have decided he was too much of a liability to keep alive," Buchanan said.

Kol didn't respond to Buchanan, instead he snarled in pain, bending his body in on itself as a piercing noise filled his head from his ear piece he wore. "Arrrrgggghh!" he growled, yanking his ear piece out and snarling at it before placing it back into his ear tentatively. There were voices arguing on the other end of his auditory device. And he knew them both. Bart and Quin.

<<<<<<<>>>>>>>

"Sire," Vennie said urgently to Zha Quin Tha Tel Mo' Kok, Commander of Command Warship 1, and Sire to the Cruestaci people.

Quin rumbled in response. He was intently watching Elite Commander Kol of his Elite Special Forces carry out what should have been a simple military operation taking the Consul of Earth Base 28 into custody for various offenses. But the male had run, and his security forces were providing resistance to Kol and those supporting his efforts to remove the Consul from power. Each representative of the governing planets of the Unified Consortium Defense had the option to sit in on the military operation if they so chose, and Zha Quin so chose. Not only was Kol Elite Commander of the Cruestaci forces, Kol was one of his best friends.

Quin had a private conversation with Bart prior to the operation beginning. As the technology Kol was using was of Cruestaci origin, Quin did have the ability to override the Consortium and step into the operation, figuratively of course, and affect the outcome. Bart had extracted a promise from Quin that he would not do that. So, he sat quietly on the bridge of his ship, watching as the operation unfolded from Kol's point of view, and listening, but unable to speak to Kol.

"Sire!" Vennie tried again.

"Quiet!" Quin snapped.

"Sire, you must see this!" Vennie insisted, sliding out of his chair and squelching himself via his tentacled body toward Zha Quin's command chair. He held a small tablet in his hand, and held it up for Quin to glance at.

"I said I am not to be interrupted!" Quin said, turning murderous eyes on his Communications Master.

"But, Sire. Missy has sent me notification of a face recognition."

Quin looked away from the main vid displayed in front of him and at Vennie. "Explain," he demanded.

Vennie looked to his left and his right, and took note of the warriors around them, some watching the operation take place, others listening to his conversation with Quin. "I can't, Sire. But, this will explain it for you." He handed the tablet to Zha Quin who wore a confused look until he looked down at the tablet and took a minute to absorb the information there. Then he was standing and barking orders at everyone, but especially Vennie.

"Block the Consortium's connection to Elite Commander Kol, now! Right now! I need to speak with Kol privately immediately! Contact Chairman Bartholomew on a private com!

Vacate this command deck at once! Only necessary personnel shall remain!"

Warriors ran from the command deck following Quin's orders at once.

Vennie was busy trying to block the Consortium's piggy-back link atop their own via Kol's audio ear piece, while one of Vennie's communication support people tried to reach out to Bart on a personal com line.

After a few seconds, Quin watched Kol's point of view vary sharply from the the path up ahead of him to a blurry view of the wall, then the floor beneath him as he heard Kol hiss.

"Blocked, Sire!" Vennie announced.

"Chairman Bartholomew is on a private live com, Sire," another communications officer advised.

"I want that bastard alive!" Quin snarled in his native Cruestaci language to Bart.

"What the hell is going on, Quin?" Bart answered.

"He's one of them! Missy is constantly running facial recognition software in the background of all communications. I will find all the males that assaulted my Sirena! Every fucking one, and they will wish they'd died!" Quin snarled.

"I still don't understand, Quin. What does that have to do with today's operation?" Bart asked, distracted from the military operation he was in charge of and wondering why it had come to a momentary stop.

"Diskastes! He's one of them! He was there, he's on the godsdamned video! I want him here, now! I will accept no less!" Quin thundered.

Bart was one of the last remaining relatives of Quin's Sirena, Vivian. He had in fact been instrumental in helping her heal and was one of the few that was well aware of the video that Quin referred to. "Let me get this operation completed. Take him into custody, then I'll petition to have him sent to Cruestace."

"No! I want him here now! He comes to us first," Quin demanded, his own Psi fully engaged. "If you get him first, it will be years before he pays for his actions!"

"Will you two stop the damned arguing?" Kol hissed.

Quin and Bart both stopped speaking and turned their attention to Kol who'd turned his com toward his own face. "Stop it! This is not the time. I'll take the bastard into custody and then you can decide what to do with him. But this is not the time!" he hissed.

"I've mistakenly brought the private call with Elite Commander Kol on line with the audio recorder he wears!" the communications officer said to Vennie. "Should I cancel the call?" he asked with a panicked look on his face.

"No!" Vennie, Quin, Bart, and Kol all answered forcefully, even though Kol was whispering.

"Do not end this private com unless you're willing to release the block you have on the general audio all the rest of the Consortium is attempting to listen to!" Bart shouted. "I need access!"

Quin ignored Bart's last statement, focused on his need to get one of those who'd harmed Vivi into his own hands. He just continued on with his explanation to Bart, trying to persuade him to see his point of view. "He was in the recording we found when we rescued Vivi. He was one of the males that assaulted her, tortured her," Quin growled. "He will answer for his actions."

"I will deliver him," Kol promised. "Now be quiet!" he snapped. He dropped the vidcom he was holding aimed at his own face to let it once again ride on his shoulder as he proceeded down the darkened passage again.

"Quin, unblock the audio feed. The other representatives are reporting a problem with the audio. They're figuring out they can't hear the feed properly," Bart said softly.

"I will speak to my Elite Commander as I wish, and I will not unblock the live audio. They do not need to know of the horrors my Sirena survived!" Quin shouted.

Kol snarled, then took the ear piece out of his ear and shoved it in the trousers of the BDU's he wore. He didn't need to fucking hear them arguing at the moment. He needed to concentrate on what he was doing. He needed to locate this bastard and do everything he could to get him back to Zha Quin.

This was no longer simply about duty, it had become personal. Vivi was his friend, one of his closest confidantes, and Diskastes had hurt her. Diskastes was going to pay.

Chapter 25

Ba Re' stood with his back against the wall nearest the only door that granted entrance to Kol's quarters. His weapon was drawn, and his left hand was flattened against Elisher in an effort to hold him still and quiet beside him. He listened carefully, heard the various weapons discharging, including the loud boom of the ancient firearm Buchanan favored. From time to time they'd hear footsteps running past the door, but as of yet neither had attempted to open it to look out.

Another particularly loud round of weapon firing had Elisher clearly frightened. "What should we do?" Elisher asked nervously.

"We stay here," Ba Re' answered, his eyes pinned to the door, weapon still at the ready.

"But isn't that just allowing them to come to us if it's their intention. Everyone at this base knows that I've been holed up in here, locked away with all the documentation I could find from every department. If anyone has it in for me, they're coming here!" Elisher said.

Ba Re' turned his head partially toward Elisher, before having to agree with her. "You're right. If they plan to come after you, they know exactly where you are." Ba Re' reached for the door and quietly unlocked it. When no one rushed the door, he very slowly eased it open. "Stay right there," he instructed Elisher. Then he stepped into the open doorway and looked up and down the hallway. Nothing but a little smokiness beginning to waft through the opposite end of the hall.

"Come on," Ba Re' said. He reached out and grabbed Elisher's hand, forcing her to follow him. "Stay as close to me as possible. Do not run off on your own, or make any noises that would bring attention to us."

"Where are we going?" Elisher said, crouching behind Ba Re' and staying so close to him she wondered if she hindered his progress through the building.

"Docking bay. Outside the building. Rather be there than trapped inside with nowhere to fall back to," Ba Re' explained.

<<<<<<<>>>>>>>

"You do realize that we aren't sure what exactly we'll find when we arrive at Base 28 don't you, Ada Jane?" Jason asked.

They'd been in the transport for some time now and since her initial expressions of appreciation, she hadn't made any effort to speak to him.

Ada didn't look over at Jason as he calmly maneuvered his transport toward Base 28 in Texas. They'd been on their way for about two hours already. They should be arriving momentarily, but at the rate Jason drove, which was maddeningly slowly, who could know for sure. "I'm sure what I'll find is that my mate has been unavoidably detained," she said.

"Perhaps. But, I just want you to know that no matter what we find, I will always be here for you. You will have me to turn to," Jason said, affirming his message.

"For what?" Ada Jane asked, finally turning her gaze to him.

"Well, for anything, Ada Jane. If your alien somehow turns out to be not all you expected him to be, it would not actually be the greatest of surprises, now, would it?" he asked, chuckling as though making light of it.

"I'm not sure I understand you, but I am more than sure that I don't appreciate you implying that Kol is less than honorable. He is nothing if not honorable," she said, somehow managing to maintain her calm.

"Oh, I'm sure he is. But, unfortunately, it's been proven time and again that no matter how honorable," he said, placing sarcastic tones on the word 'honorable', "these aliens are, they simply cannot resist the urge to copulate with any human female willing. And even some not willing as you unfortunately have learned."

Ada Jane's mouth worked like a fish, gasping for air as she searched for the right words to throw at Jason. She was angry, surprisingly angrier than she'd been since being rescued.

"Don't misunderstand me, Ada Jane. I'm simply saying it cannot be avoided, they have animalistic tendencies, you know."

Jason glanced toward Ada Jane and when she continued to look at him like he'd lost his mind rather than speak to him, he continued. "They are more attuned to their baser needs, and they corrupt our women. Sullying them so that even if they eventually figure out they've allowed themselves to be taken advantage of, those of us who see things as they truly are would never be able to see past their failings."

"Those of you?" Ada finally managed to get out.

"Yes. Purists. That's what we call ourselves. We are dedicated to keeping human blood human. We were not meant to blend our pure DNA with that of the aliens who are occupying our world. They have no right to be here." Jason glanced toward Ada Jane again to find her watching him, her eyes big, not even attempting to speak at this point. He misread her expression as concern and hurried to assure her he didn't see her as sullied.

"Oh, I know all the things you've endured are not your fault. And I do understand that you feel beholden to your alien for rescuing you. I also share your gratitude to the male. If it weren't for him, you may have never been brought home. But now that you're here, it's time to face facts. And the fact is, he's sure to have already broken whatever promises he's made to you. But I will be here to help you pick up the pieces. I'll be here to support you, and to help guide you through all the healing necessary to embrace the ways of our Purist movement."

"I want to get out. Now," Ada Jane said, realizing the doctor she'd believed was her friend, was actually quite warped, and had even joined a movement that believed all aliens were little more than animals.

"We're almost there," Jason said. "See that little silver dot up there?" he said, pointing through the windshield of his transport. "That's Base 28. I'll escort you in just the moment we land," he said. "I've been trying to ask for permission to land for the last ten minutes but no one has answered. It's shameful how unprofessional the remote bases are. We'll just land anyway. They mostly likely won't even notice."

"I don't want you to escort me. I'm going in alone," Ada Jane snapped.

Jason looked over at Ada Jane. "Oh come now, Ada Jane. Surely you knew what they were like. I understand the hero complex, but now that you're home, it's not necessary. I'm here. I'm your own kind, and I've decided to take you for my own and give you my name and all the regard that comes with it. You won't have to worry about how you're viewed, you'll be my wife, and as such an envoy and symbol of the Purist movement and an example of how the occupying aliens have abused our women for their own use. A constant reminder to women everywhere that they are not to be trusted and to stay with their own kind."

Ada Jane bit her tongue until Jason very, very slowly lowered them to the docking strip at Base 28. Then she unbuckled and moved toward the door, reaching out and being sure it was opened before she spoke. "My mate, my husband, is a good male. His friends are good people — all of them are. The occupying forces here, they're here so that we aren't enslaved and shipped off to other planets to live out our lives under another's rule. Maybe things aren't perfect, but those that are here now freed our world, and they keep it that way."

"Maybe at one time, but now... they simply occupy us, keep us from returning our world to the way things used to be. Go on, my dear. I'll wait here. You'll see shortly. I'll be waiting," Jason said, smiling at her pleasantly.

Ada Jane threw open the door on the transport and stepped out onto the scaffolding that surrounded all docking spaces and served as a walkway from the transports themselves to the ground. She hurried down the metal walkway the scaffolding provided and onto the ground. She was far enough away from the base itself that she'd have at least a seven or eight minute walk to get to the base. She started her walk with her temper flaring, but refused to allow herself to look back at Jason and flip him off. She was really, really tempted, but refused to lower herself. He was demented, truly demented.

Some minutes later as she approached the base, she took note of several teams of men moving about outside with their weapons in hand. Some were firing their weapons, while the opposing group took cover before firing back. She slowed her step as she realized this was not just a training session. She could hear the sounds of the weapons being fired. She could see the dust and the haze as a result of those weapons making contact with whatever or whoever it was they'd been fired at.

"Oh, my damn," she muttered, realizing that she'd stumbled into a battle of some sort. No wonder Kol hadn't com'd her back. He was in the midst of whatever was happening here. Just as she began to look around for something to get behind or under, she took note of a very large, very dark male, charging toward her, with a smaller male behind him. He was shouting her name, and waving his arms at her. Ada Jane stopped in place and watched him, unsure of what he was trying to say. Then she recognized him.

"Ba Re'?" she said, beginning to move toward him again.

"Go!" Ba Re' shouted at her again when he was only a few feet from her. "You need to leave, now. Go and take Elisher with you. He'll be a target if he's located. I have to go find Kol," Ba Re' ordered as he shouted at her.

"We can't! We can't go back with..." she tried to explain about Jason and the extent of his derangement.

"Get back on that transport and go!" Ba Re' ordered, grabbing Elisher and shoving her toward Ada Jane. "I do not care who is piloting it! Leave this place now! The Consul had additional troops stationed outside the base in the surrounding area. We have no idea where he is now, but his forces are not surrendering. Get out of here!"

"But, Kol?" Ada Jane said, her eyes filling with tears.

"He's here somewhere. He's leading his own team. Just go, now! Stop wasting time! And take Elisher with you!" Ba Re' said again, pushing both of them toward the transport that was docked so far away from them that they'd have to run back to it, and it would still take them at least four minutes to get there at a full run.

"I'll keep her safe," Ada Jane said, finally giving in and just doing what Ba Re' asked.

Ba Re' nodded and turned from them, running back into the melee, firing his own weapon as he ran.

Ada Jane linked hands with Elisher, and together they ran toward Jason's transport in the distance.

<<<<<<<>>>>>>>

Diskastes watched a lone, private transport fly over the base before hovering over the landing pad, then eventually docking. He watched a lone female get out of the transport and approach the base.

"That's it," he said to the males surrounding him where he hid a short distance from the base. "That's how we're escaping Base 28. Once we're away, I'll contact my father and he'll bring us all home. The Consortium can't touch us on Quisles."

As one group, Diskastes and his males began to move toward the transport. He slowed their advance and waited while one of the Cruestace warriors ran out to greet the female that had arrived on the transport. Then he snarled when he saw that warrior shove Elisher toward the female and run back toward the battle while the female and Elisher made their return to the transport.

"Take him!" Diskastes demanded. "Take Elisher into custody! He is a traitor to me and to our base! And take the female with him!"

<<<<<<<>>>>>>>

Kol and his team stepped out of the passageway, emerging above ground and behind one of the storage buildings, the one furthest away from the base in fact. Before he even had a chance to look for tracks and begin to follow them, he was fired on from a point off in the distance just over a small hill. He and his team dove for cover and thus the true battle started. Not only were they fighting with the main attackers in the distance, being held down by their unrelenting attacks, but Kol could also hear smaller skirmishes still taking place around the compound. Gradually they began to get the upper hand, picking off their attackers one at a time, until it was safer to move from the position they'd been forced into.

Kol watched as a transport approached the base from the north, skirting the eastern side of the base before disappearing from sight. "Unbelievable," he muttered to himself, wondering what kind of idiot would land a transport in the middle of a battle.

The constant fire they'd been taking was dying off as he and his males took out those intent on killing them. He was preparing to move his team when his enhanced Psi hearing picked up a sound that was familiar to him. A couple of his males spoke, urging him to relocate them all. He raised his hand to indicate he needed them quiet. His team immediately fell quiet, watching him, waiting. Then he heard it again.

"Fuck!" he shouted, getting to his feet and running as quickly as he could toward the voice he recognized as Ba Re's shouting Ada Jane's name. His team didn't know what was happening, but he was on the move and aggressively so, so they followed.

Chapter 26

Ba Re' was halfway back to the base when Ada Jane's words registered in his mind. Her. Ada Jane said she'd protect 'her' when referring to Elisher. He turned back toward them just in time to see a team of males surround them, taking them into custody only steps away from the transport.

A roar sounded in the distance, and Ba Re' had no doubt it was Kol's, but he didn't dare turn around to see if Kol was on his way or not. He couldn't tear his eyes away from Elisher, now in Diskastes's grip — literally. Diskastes was standing behind Elisher with a weapon pointed at Elisher's head as he screamed and rambled at her from behind. The forces with Diskastes had surrounded both Elisher and Ada Jane, and both were being physically held from behind.

Three of Diskastes's team moved toward the transport in what was an attempt to commandeer it to whisk them all away, but the transport lifted into the air leaving them all, including Ada Jane, on the ground to deal with their own fates. The transport lifting into the air was a good thing, though. It provided cover for Kol and his team to arrive, as well as Kron, who'd left the remainder of the clean up and the managing of those they'd arrested to Buchanan and Zhuxi.

As the dust cleared, Diskastes whipped his head around frantically trying to come up with another idea to save his own ass.

"Release them, Diskastes," Ba Re' demanded, his Psi making him scarier and growlier than usual.

"Release them now or die!" Kol snarled, leveling his weapon at Diskastes's head as he came to a stop beside Ba Re'.

"Never! This male is a traitor! He has betrayed his superior officer and the very base he was assigned to," Diskastes screamed at Kol. "He is sentenced to die!" Diskastes shrieked. "As are you! You will pay for the blemish you've wrought upon my record and my reputation!" Diskastes threatened. "You will all die!"

"By which court?" Ba Re' asked. "Is it not the Consortium's law that every warrior taken into custody is provided the judicial right of a court of his peers to decide their fate?" Ba Re' asked, doing his best to distract Diskastes as he sensed Kron taking up position right beside him, and heard the movements of the team that had been assigned to Kron assembling behind him. "These two are certainly not warriors, and I see no court here to decide their fate. Release them, they have no place in this," Ba Re' said calmly, trying to defuse the situation, to at least get Diskastes to talk instead of just beginning to shoot.

"By me! I do not need a court. This is my base, my people, and my laws!" Diskastes spat. "You will either move from my path, or you will die with them."

"You have no path. Your transport has left. You are out of options and this is most certainly no longer a place you have any power. Surrender, and you will not be killed this day," Ba Re' said, trying to talk down the obviously insane former Consul.

"You surrender! Or I kill this traitor here and now!" Diskastes insisted, pressing his weapon against Elisher's head. "You! You trade places with this female," he said, sneering at Kol, using his elbow to indicate he meant Ada Jane.

"Gladly, release her and I'll take her place," Kol snarled, stepping forward.

"Do you think me dim-witted?" Diskastes screamed. "You will not approach us. You will lie on the ground and make your males retreat!"

Ada Jane couldn't let Kol trade himself for her. She had to do something and she had to do it now. She was being held with her hands behind her back by one of Diskastes's men. She needed to find a way to get herself free, and to get the attention off Elisher and Kol and onto herself. She knew she could take Diskastes if she could just get her hand into her front pocket where her weapon was waiting for her.

Ada Jane stared at Kol until his eyes flicked quickly to hers once again. She focused on him and flicked her own gaze toward the lower half of her body. But there was no way to tell him she had her weapon without telling him she had her weapon. She'd just have to have faith that when she shot Diskastes, Kol would shoot as many as he could while she grabbed Elisher, and they went straight to the ground to get out of the way of what she hoped was a rain of weapons firing. Because this was the day she fully took her life back. No more victim. No more feeling sorry for herself. No more trying to find herself. She'd found herself here in this moment, and she was pissed off that this male would dare to use herself, Elisher, or any other woman in his bid to get away from the justice that was coming his way.

Ada Jane knew who Diskastes was and that he was at odds with Kol from the things Kol had told her when he'd spent time with her away from the base. She suspected Kol was behind this entire coup, and she was banking on Diskastes dropping his hold on Elisher and reaching for her instead. All she needed was the male holding her wrists to let go for just one second, so she could slip her hand into her front pocket and take hold of her weapon.

"Kol," Ada Jane said, making her voice sound weak and whiny, and interrupting him just as he moved to lie prone on the ground, so that he was on his knees. "Please, remember I love you. No matter what happens I love you. And this isn't your fault. I'm so sorry I didn't just stay away and wait for you," Ada Jane said.

"Shut up, female!" Diskastes screamed.

Kol snapped his gaze to her and it clearly said, 'shut up!'.

But she couldn't. She had a plan — no way in hell was she anybody's victim anymore. "I'm sorry I didn't spend more time with you. I'm sorry it took me so long to trust you. You are my mate. I love you, Kol," Ada Jane said.

Diskastes turned his head and looked incredulously at the tall, blonde female pouring her heart out to his nemesis. "You are his mate?" Diskastes screeched disbelievingly.

"Yes! Yes, and you'd better let me go, or you'll pay for holding me like this!" Ada Jane threatened, the whole while her eyes were pinned to Kol as she kept glancing down at the ground, trying to prepare him for the fact that she and Elisher would momentarily be on the ground — or at least she hoped so.

Diskastes shoved Elisher to the left and reached for Ada Jane's hair. She was taller than Diskastes was, and he yanked her head back to snarl in her ear. "You have just signed your own death warrant, worthless female!"

But Ada Jane didn't care, because in his unhinged state, he didn't think to control her arms and hands when his male released her as Diskastes grabbed her, all he did was grip her hair to yank her head back to his, and place his arm around her throat. Ada Jane slipped her hand into her front pocket and pressed her thumb down on the activation lines on her weapon at the same time she withdrew it from her pocket, and without hesitation in one fluid movement she slipped her own arm behind herself and held her weapon so that it was pointing directly behind herself and fired her weapon.

Diskastes screamed and let Ada Jane go.

Ada lunged for Elisher and together they went to the ground while the deafening sound of weapons firing overhead made their ears ring.

Kol watched as Ada Jane locked her gaze with his. It was almost as though she'd intentionally drawn attention from Elisher to herself and identified herself as his mate. And now, she kept glancing at the ground, then back up at him. Then he watched as she slipped her hand into her pocket at almost the same time Diskastes had grabbed her in place of Elisher.

Kol's eyes widened as he saw her remove her disintegrater from her pocket and move her hand behind herself all in one motion. In that split second he knew her plan. She was going to shoot Diskastes and go to the ground. As her hand slipped behind her own body, the disintegrater ready to fire from the looks of the green lights glowing on top of it, he fired his own weapon, hitting one of the males standing closest to Ada Jane.

At the same time Ba Re' and Kron began to fire as did the rest of the team behind them.

When there was no male left standing, Kol began to shout for the firing to end. He got to his feet and rushed to Ada Jane, grabbing her up off the ground while roaring his fear to the skies. Kol turned her to face him and on finding her smiling at him through her tears, he wrapped her in his arms and held her tightly against his chest.

"I thought you were dead," he said over and over again. "I thought you were dead."

"I'm okay," she said. "Look, I'm not even hurt," she told him, holding her arms out and taking a step back so he could see there was no injury on her.

Kol glanced quickly down her body, then his face became a mask of rage as he grabbed her and shoved her roughly toward his left while moving forward without warning. Kol bellowed his intent to kill when he saw Diskastes lying on the ground, half his pelvis missing, but his wound cauterized from the laser in Ada Jane's disintegrater. She'd obviously not had it set on full strength or there'd be nothing left of the male.

All Kol saw was the male that had only moments before been holding Ada Jane and threatening to kill her. The same male who was one of those responsible for the torture Vivi had endured — and he was holding a weapon weakly in his hand, aiming it at Ada Jane. The male needed to die.

Kol allowed his Psi to take over. He snatched Diskastes from the ground and literally tore him limb from limb, as Diskastes shrieked in pain, before Kol finally tore into the male's neck with his multiple rows of razor sharp teeth and ripped his throat out. Then he proceeded to destroy the male's torso so badly that there was little left of him. His adrenalin was pumping at the thought that Diskastes almost took his Ehlealah from him not once, but twice today. The second time while she'd been assuring him she was okay, and he just couldn't stop there. He looked around for anyone else that needed killing, and found one of Diskastes's males — still alive, but injured. Kol roared his battle cry as he advanced on the male lying helplessly on the ground.

The terrified male put his hands up in surrender at the same time he tried to roll into a ball to protect himself from Kol's onslaught.

"Kol!" Kron shouted, moving quickly to get between Kol and the now unarmed male. "Kol! Stop! He is not armed!"

Kol snarled at Kron and made to move past him, but Kron kept speaking to him. "Elite Commander!"

Kol stopped at his formal title and glared at Kron with his lip raised.

"He's no longer a threat. He is unarmed. Back down, Kol. Your Ehlealah needs you," Kron said, hoping Kol would listen since they were all being videoed and the last thing any of the Cruestaci needed was confirmation that they were as the rest of the Consortium believed, brutal at best.

Kol hesitated, but ended up moving back to Ada Jane instead of killing the unarmed male who immediately began murmuring thanks to Kron.

Kol lifted his arms, intent on pulling Ada Jane to him again, until he saw his own bloodied hands as they reached for her. He froze as he looked at them. There was no way he'd touch his Ehlealah covered in blood as he was.

Ba Re' stripped his shirt off and tossed it to Kol, who caught it and started wiping his hands.

Ba Re' stared at Elisher who'd gotten up off the ground and stood off to the side, tears silently slipping down her face. He stalked over to her. "You are female," he said accusatorily.

Elisher looked up at the magnificent male before her. She'd been wrong to ever think that Kol was the perfect male. This one, right here, snarls and all, was the perfect male.

"Answer me," Ba Re' growled.

Elisher gave a single nod.

That was all Ba Re' needed. He descended on her, placing his hand on her throat to turn her face up to his so he could ravage her lips while his other hand kept her body pressed tightly against him. He kissed her, until they were both practically dizzy from it. When he finally released her lips, he went in for another kiss, this one gentle and soft.

"You are mine," Ba Re' said.

Elisher didn't answer, but she eagerly welcomed Ba Re's kisses.

"Elisher..." Ba Re' said, a warning growl in his voice.

"Elisha," she corrected. "My name is Elisha."

"You are mine, Elisha," Ba Re' insisted.

Elisha nodded. "I don't suppose there's any way around it?" she said.

Ba Re' shook his head. "There is not. But you will not regret me. You will be happy. I vow it." Then he pulled her closer.

After all she'd been through, it was a relief to know the lies were finally over. She allowed Ba Re' to hold her to his chest and gave in to the relief of Kol's mate saving them both, and the fatigue of trying for so long to be someone she wasn't. Her dream was over now, she'd never be able to qualify for intergalactic travel and representation as a liaison, but, she had a growly, argumentative male on her side now. Elisha slipped her hands around Ba Re's naked waist and held him as the tears of so many reasons streamed down her face.

Ba Re' smoothed his hands over her short hair and down her back. "Shh, all is well. I am here, now."

Kol, still covered in blood, watched Ba Re' kissing his assistant. He looked confusedly down at Ada Jane who watched them with a smile on her face. "Why is Ba Re' kissing my assistant?" Kol asked.

"Because she's a girl," Ada Jane answered. "And she's his."

Kol looked over at Kron, then back at Elisher, then to Ada Jane. "Nooooo," he said.

"Yes," she answered. "How could you not have seen that?" she asked.

"I saw it," Kron said.

"Me, too," Ada Jane said.

Kol shrugged with one still blood covered shoulder as he watched Ba Re' with Elisher in his arms. "I did not see it. You are the only female I see, my Ada Jane."

Chapter 27

Bart paced back and forth in the main conference and media room of the Consortium's headquarters. He'd seen and heard every moment of the vidcom of the military operation at Earth Base 28. He understood every single moment of it, as did most of the other heads of state and the ruling houses of the various planets and worlds that made up the Unified Consortium Defense.

The problem was that the Planet Quisles and its ruler had watched Diskastes, who was also his son, be ripped to pieces on live vidcom feed. He was calling for the arrest of Elite Commander and Ambassador Kol Ra' Don Tol, and he expected him to be charged with war crimes. His argument was that honorably dying in battle was one thing, being ripped to pieces by the animalistic cruelty of a warrior race known for their brutality was quite another.

"Fuuuucck!" he shouted before pressing a button and waiting for his secretary to respond.

"Yes, sir," a soft feminine voice answered.

"I need to speak to Sire Zha Quin Tha Tel Mo' Kok, and I need it to be completely private and unscreened. Do not ask the computer to place the request for com. Do it yourself and advise that he will want to be somewhere private and secure when he takes my call.

"Yes, sir. I will begin the process now. Will you be in the media room when I have the com secured and on line, sir?"

"Yes. I'm waiting here."

Kol exited the shower in his quarters and found Ada Jane lying across his bed, waiting for him. He smiled and went to her as she raised up on her knees and opened her arms to him. "Are you well, my Ada Jane?" he asked, his voice still growly though his Psi had retreated.

"I am. A little shaky in the aftermath when I think of what could have happened, but it didn't happen, so all in all, I'm fine," she answered as he held her tightly in his arms.

"I am sorry you have had to go through so much in your short time home," Kol answered.

"I'm not. It showed me how strong I've become."

"I have missed you since I left your cottage," he said, releasing his hold so he could see her face and rub his thumb across her lower lip the way he liked to do.

"I missed you, too. When I didn't hear from you, I was worried about you. That's why I came," Ada Jane answered.

"I was fine, my Ehlealah. You should not have come, you put yourself in danger's way. I would have destroyed all in sight had you been lost to me," Kol said, his voice going gruff.

"No worries," Ada Jane said. "I had a plan."

"Your plan was terrifying," Kol answered.

A knock at the door interrupted them. "Kol, Zhuxi is here to see you," Elisha called to him through the closed door.

"I shall be right there," Kol answered, looking down at Ada Jane. "I still cannot believe she is a female," he muttered, none too happy at not noticing it himself.

"She is. And you were focused on other things. You've been busy and distracted," Ada Jane said as she watched Kol walk over to his closet and take out clothing before beginning to put it on. Ada Jane made a soft sound when he leaned over to pull his pants on.

Kol paused and looked over his shoulder at her, one eyebrow raised.

"What?" she asked.

"Did you moan?"

"Maybe just a little," Ada Jane answered, grinning at him.

"Why?" he asked, now standing and buttoning his pants.

"Because the view… the muscles in your back and legs and…" she stopped trying to explain as she suddenly realized what she was about to say. "Your body is just very beautiful when you move, okay?" she asked, smiling but slightly embarrassed.

Kol grinned at her while he pulled his shirt on and tucked it into the waistband of his pants. "I am very pleased that my female finds my form attractive. But I am not beautiful. I am handsome. Or, stunning perhaps. Or magnificence may even apply," he said teasing her.

"You're not the least bit sure of yourself are you?" Ada Jane asked, laughing.

Kol tapped his chin just to the left of the spike that grew out of his jaw there. "You know… god-like may apply."

"God-like? Really? What god?" Ada Jane asked, with an expression of disbelief on her face.

"Adonis, I believe. Is he not the most beautiful of the gods?" Kol asked seriously, before falling into a fit of laughter. "I could not hold back my smile any longer," he said, trying to catch his breath as he laughed at her expression.

Ada Jane giggled. Then she stepped off the bed and went to him, clasping her hands behind his neck as he held her waist. "Adonis wouldn't do."

"No?" he asked. "You said you thought me beautiful."

"Adonis is not beautiful enough. You outshine them all," she said, pressing her lips to his.

"As do you, my love. You outshine every female that draws breath. I am not even aware of them."

Ada Jane paused. "You called me your love," she said, smiling softly at him.

"You are my love," Kol answered.

"And you are mine," Ada Jane replied. "I love you, Kol."

Kol kissed her tenderly, sliding his hands up her body to hold her head gently in his hands as he took his time kissing her mouth. "I love you, Ada Jane. I will always love you."

Ada Jane kissed his lips then hugged him to her as she rested her head on his chest. She was tall for a female, so it was easier for her to reach him than it would be for most women.

Kol's attention was taken by the voices in the shared space of his quarters. "Are you ready to go see what's happening out there?" Kol asked.

"May as well. They don't seem to be going away," Ada answered, smiling when he let go of her to take her hand and lead her from his bedroom and into the living room.

"Kol," Zhuxi said, rising from the sofa he'd been sitting on.

"Zhuxi, thank you for your patience while I dressed," Kol said, switching Ada Jane's hand to his left so that he could shake hands with Zhuxi using his right hand. "May I introduce my mate, Ada Jane Andersen," Kol said.

"I am honored to make your introduction, Ada Jane," Zhuxi said, inclining his head to Ada Jane.

"And you," Ada Jane answered, smiling at the small light-brown alien with the slanted feline shaped eyes and shiny black hair. Zhuxi was only a little over 5'6" tall, but he gave off a dangerous air regardless. Yet, Ada was not the least little bit afraid of him. She liked him right away. His smile and his mannerisms indicated an honorable male.

"Kron is still working with those who were incarcerated until we can determine who is handed off to the Consortium and who is to be released?" Kol asked.

"He is," Zhuxi answered. "But for now, we were just about to hear Elisher's explanation of why she misled us all into believing she was a he," Zhuxi said, but there was no offense in his voice. He actually seemed rather entertained by the turn of events.

"Elisha," Ba Re' corrected.

Kol glanced over at Ba Re' and found him sitting beside Elisha, so close he had no doubt if they were any closer, he would have to be sitting on top of her. His hand was holding hers, and Ba Re' kept looking proudly at her as though he couldn't believe his luck.

Elisha, on the other hand, wasn't looking anyone in the eye except for Ba Re', and then only when he forced the issue.

"Of course, forgive me. Elisha, why did you perform such a grand ruse?" Zhuxi asked.

Elisha just barely shook her head, still focused on the coffee table between the sofa and the love seat. "I wanted to be accepted into the diplomatic corps. I wanted to get off this planet and see what all is out there more than I've ever wanted anything. And Earth stopped accepting female applicants for service off the planet when it became apparent that they were at risk of being kidnapped and worse. I didn't mean to hurt anyone. I didn't mean to lie to anyone. I just wanted a chance at my dreams," she said, pulling her hand out of Ba Re's. "Doesn't matter now. That's over."

Ba Re' reached over and took her hand in his once again. "Do not pull away from me, Ehlealah. There is no reason for you to feel as you do."

Elisha looked up at Kol. "I'm sorry, Kol. You were not only my employer, you were my friend. I lied to you. I willfully misled you. I'm sorry," Elisha said, just briefly meeting his eyes before glancing down at the coffee table again.

"You are still my assistant. You are still my friend. Stop this ridiculousness at once," Kol said, watching Elisha.

"But, I lied," she said, raising her eyes to his and daring to look directly at him this time.

"And I was so distracted that I didn't even notice. You performed your duties well beyond any assistant I've ever had," Kol said.

"Exactly how many assistants have you had?" Elisha asked.

"Beside the point. My point is, you never at any time abandoned your duties or your responsibilities. In fact, you went above and beyond that which is expected of you. You should have no shame. You have done well, Elisha. I didn't even notice you were female because I was so focused on my own mate, and trying to balance her, my duties here, and my pursuit of Diskastes. Who do you think has performed better?" Kol asked.

"You saved us all. You and your friends," she said.

"And you kept my responsibilities here addressed and performed perfectly."

"How did you make the Consortium believe you were male?" Zhuxi asked.

Elisha gave a half-hearted shrug and didn't seem like she wanted to answer.

"You do not have to say if you prefer not to, but I would like to know as well. I thought I was losing my mind when I arrived and could think of nothing other than you. I will confess I was much relieved when Ada Jane told me you were female," Ba Re' said.

"You knew?" Elisha asked, looking up at Ada Jane.

"I did. I knew when I saw you the first time on the vidcom with Kol. Or, I suspected. A little research later, and I knew," Ada Jane answered.

Zhuxi, Kol and Ba Re' looked from Ada Jane to Elisha, waiting for her to enlighten them.

"I had a twin brother," Elisha began. "When we were still in high school, he was killed in an accident. He always wanted to leave this planet just like I did. Once the Consortium changed their guidelines about accepting human females into their diplomatic corps, and I decided that I wanted to go — needed to go, to get away from this planet just as I always dreamed, just as he always dreamed, I started to plan. Our names are similar. I'm Elisha, he was Elisher. It was a simple thing to combine all our records, school, medical, everything. Taking out everything that was a reference to me being female, and assuming his identity. So, I did, and Elisher was reborn."

"And no one ever questioned?" Kol asked.

Elisha shook her head. "No. My family is gone now. Our parents had us late in life. I have no close friends. So, by all records available to any who may look, I'm Elisher. And I qualified to the diplomatic corps, and was on my way toward eventually proving my worth and achieving my dream."

"And then I found you," Ba Re' commented, finally understanding her obviously mixed emotions about him.

"It would be the same no matter. After I did all the research, I'm sorry to say that I was coming to tell Kol. I suspected you of lying about who you were for nefarious reasons. I am sorry," Ada Jane said.

"It's alright. It would have come out at some point, be it now or later. At least now I don't have to hide anymore," Elisher said. "But, I made sure I covered all traces of Elisha. How did you find out who I was?" Elisha asked.

"Missy. I asked for all information on you and that could even be associated with you loosely," Ada Jane explained.

"Ah, yes. Missy has access to all records. She is quite a bit more advanced than any artificial intelligence here on Earth," Ba Re' commented. "And once Kol told her you were his Ehlealah, she'd have given you access to anything that didn't reference Cruestaci security," Ba Re' said to Ada Jane.

"She already knew my Ada Jane from when she was on Command Warship 1," Kol said. "But, I did tell her that she should give Ada Jane anything she needed. I even left Ada Jane one of our tablets, not one of the base's tablets."

"That's all it took," Ba Re' added.

"So, basically, I'd have been found out as soon as I managed to leave the planet anyway," Elisha said.

"Yes," Ba Re' answered.

"I am sorry your dream is out of reach for the time being," Zhuxi said sincerely. "Perhaps with time, and recommendation from those of us who have worked with you, we can eventually obtain an exemption for you. Perhaps not all is lost."

Elisha offered Zhuxi a reserved smile. "It's alright. It was obviously not meant to be. And, not everything that's happened is sad," she said, lifting her hand still clasped in Ba Re's. "I'm not alone anymore," she said.

Ba Re' leaned toward her and kissed her lips — just a soft, gentle touch of his to hers. "I'm going home soon," he said.

Elisha's smile fell. "What? When?" she asked, feeling like she'd been gut-punched. "I am happy you're here. I just, I need a little time to adjust to my new reality."

"I know that. But, I am leaving as soon as this base is back to rights and I am given permission. I will be happy to get home to Command Warship 1. But, I will not be returning alone. You are my Ehlealah. You will be at my side," Ba Re' said, smiling ever so slightly, waiting for it to click in Elisha's mind. He could tell from her expression the moment she realized what he was implying.

Her eyebrows rose, her mouth fell open. "You mean... I'm going with you? I'm going to leave Earth?" she asked, her heart beginning to pound in her chest as her adrenalin pumped.

"Your dreams will all be fulfilled, my Elisha. I will see to it," he said, lifting her hand to kiss her knuckles.

Elisha gave a girly squeal and placed herself in Ba Re's lap, hugging him and kissing his face. "So, I get you, and I get space, too?" she asked.

"And I get you," Ba Re' answered.

"But, I falsified Consortium employment records," Elisha said. "They will end my employment with them."

"You don't need them, Ehlealah. You'll be aboard a Cruestaci warship. You'll no longer be under Consortium rule."

"Which reminds me," Zhuxi said. "I got caught up in the conversation here, and forgot the reason for my visit," he said, getting to his feet. "You are needed in the cafeteria," Zhuxi said, looking directly at Kol.

"Is there a problem?" Kol asked.

"Not at all. Buchanan and I are in the process of restructuring the base. We'd like your assistance," Zhuxi said.

"I'm not sure what I could add," Kol answered.

"You are the reason this base is now in a position to truly help the people in its sector. Every living thing in this sector now has a renewed chance at a better life because you decided to get involved. We have no doubt the Consortium will arrive soon to perform their own assessment. We plan to be prepared to present them with our vision and our plans for a fully functioning Earth Base 28. We'd be honored if you would join us and help us with the plans for our future."

"I will be happy to," Kol said smiling.

Chapter 28

"You cannot be serious," Zha Quin said, shaking his head in frustration as he glared at Bart through the vidcom in his personal quarters.

"I wish that I were not," Bart said. "But, I've had more than one inquiry. While I know all inquiries are made based on their association with Quisles, they are still officially logged in as individual inquiries."

"What do they expect to happen?" Quin asked.

"They expect Kol to be taken into custody. They expect him to be tried, found guilty and to serve time for war crimes," Bart answered. "I've drafted the first warrant for him to be taken into custody personally because I wanted it drafted with certain language left out."

"Such as what? Isn't the fact that you drafted it at all travesty enough?" Quin asked, his voice rising in irritation.

"Such as a death penalty. Such as a life sentence. Such as going before a judge who had full discretion in finding him guilty or innocent," Bart answered.

Quin sat quietly for moment absorbing Bart's words. "He did nothing wrong. All was done in battle. He hunted down a criminal Consul, incarcerated his criminal security forces, and in so doing liberated those who'd struggled under lack of provisions and proper leadership," Quin said.

"I am aware," Bart answered. "And were it simply my own decision, I'd laugh off the complaint as an emotional request by a grieving father. But I represent all peoples of all planets and all worlds. I have to address every complaint that is filed. And this one has video to support it," Bart said.

"I cannot believe this," Quin said. "I will not allow him to be imprisoned over this. He did nothing wrong."

"We are investigating Diskastes's past. We've expanded on Kol's investigation. We've found much illegal activity. We've confirmed theft, embezzling, failure to provide for and protect those in his quadrant, maleficence in office, and I'm sure there will be additional charges to be determined after the investigation of all evidence had been completed. But, there is nothing to support his violent death," Bart said.

"There is! He took Kol's mate, and Kol's assistant both hostage. He and his males were threatening to kill them, and Kol and the rest of those that had removed him from power. And you saw it yourself, he'd drawn his weapon after Kol's mate fired on him and was only seconds away from killing her as Kol rushed to her side."

"I saw it. I know," Bart answered.

"And there's so much more. The vid we saw of Vivi chained in that room. Those males…" Quin snarled.

"Quin, I know. I saw it. You showed me, remember?"

"Diskastes was one of them. He deserved to die. But he deserved to suffer much more than he did," Quin growled.

"Unless you allow me to show that vid to certain of the Consortium who will be hearing Kol's case, I can't even bring it up. It will be hearsay without the vid to prove it."

"I can't release that vid. I will not subject my Ehlealah to that horror again," Quin answered.

"I know," Bart agreed.

They were quiet about it for a few moments as both thought about their options. Then Quin's head came up suddenly. "Are there any missing females from the sectors under Base 28's protection?" he asked.

Bart looked dumbfounded for a second. "I haven't even looked. There are females missing from time to time. No matter how many restrictions we apply, slavers manage to get through to each planet, but humans are particularly desired. I'm sure there are some missing from this sector," Bart answered.

"More than on average in the other sectors?" Quin asked.

"I'm looking into it at once. Maybe we can tie Diskastes to their disappearances. If he was with Vivian at some point, it shows a connection to Malm. It's worth an investigation," Bart said excitedly.

"And Kol in the meantime?" Quin asked.

"He needs to turn himself in," Bart answered.

"So he can sit in prison while you investigate other possibilities?" Quin demanded.

Bart was silent while he simply sat and watched Quin looking back at him. "I'm not happy about this, Quin. I fucking hate this. I like Kol. He's like family."

"Then don't do it," Quin answered.

"I have no choice. With nothing to further justify his violent attack, I have to take him into custody."

"I will not put Vivi through that! I cannot release that vid!" Quin insisted.

"I know. And I couldn't either if in your place. Keep the vid hidden away. We'll argue his actions based on what is seen in the video footage of the battle itself. Keep Vivi's vid hidden," Bart said.

Quin nodded.

"I'll give him two weeks. He has two weeks to clean up the loose ends at the base, say his goodbyes to Ada Jane, and call me for an escort here. He has to turn himself in. It will look better for him, than me having to take him into custody."

"This is fucking ridiculous!" Zha Quin growled.

"I agree, Quin. I'm sorry. My hands are tied. He will have to stand trial," Bart answered.

"Two weeks before he contacts you. Then however long it takes you to send an escort," Quin replied.

"You're bargaining for just an extra three or four days, Quin," Bart said, spelling out the obvious.

"If they were your last days of freedom, wouldn't you want three or four more?" Quin asked.

"Fine. Granted," Bart answered.

"You will keep me apprised of every single minute element that is to be considered," Quin demanded.

"I will," Bart answered. "I'm sorry, Quin," Bart said again before ending the vidcom.

Quin sat back on the couch in his and Vivi's living room and scrubbed his hands over his face. He sensed a slight motion behind and to his right. He glanced over his shoulder and found Vivian standing there in the doorway of their bedroom, her hair still mussed from her nap. "Did you sleep well, my Vivi?" he asked.

Vivian ignored his question. She didn't smile. She stared right into his eyes. "What vid are you keeping hidden?"

<<<<<<<>>>>>>>

Kol walked calmly down the hallway leading from the new central offices of Earth Base 28. He and all those who'd stayed loyal to their duties at Earth Base 28 had spent the last week repairing the base and remodeling Diskastes's quarters into a large centralized area with several different desks and a private conference room for private meetings when needed, and a file room for all personnel and accounting files. All records were stored electronically of course, but after the attack on the Base's computer system, Kol felt the need to keep hard copy records as well.

Ba Re' and Elisha had spent a number of hours completely removing the software and virus it had been infected with from the base and installing new software and linking to the other bases. The Cruestaci had made a gift of an advanced software program to the Consortium for use in linking all the bases and making communications and traceability much easier.

The new base was functioning, and the males stationed on it, both human and alien, were happy to be there and be a part of it. Already the civilians living in that sector had begun to contact the base for support with things as simple as food and medical care. Things that should have been supplied to them all along.

Kol had given instructions for information to be gathered from all in their sector regarding any missing citizens. If

Diskastes had made people disappear, they needed to know about it. And if there was a chance that any of them had been sold into slavery, it was possible they may still be alive somewhere.

As Kol approached the door that would let him out into the docking area of the base, Buchanan called his name.

"Headed home for the night, Blue Dude?" Buchanan called.

Kol offered a smile he didn't feel as he turned to face his friend. "I am."

"Give Ada Jane my best, huh?" Buchanan asked. "I'll see you in the morning."

Kol nodded. "You have become a treasured friend, Buchanan. You and Zhuxi both," he said.

"You have, too, Kol. I'm proud to call you friend."

"Keep this base as we've restructured it, my friend. The people in this sector will prosper," Kol said.

"Oh, yeah. We all will. Just going to take a little time to shake off the reputation that Diskastes gave us. But it'll happen."

Kol nodded his head in agreement.

After a few awkward moments of silence Buchanan spoke again. "Well I won't keep you," he said, taking a step away. "I'm sure Ada Jane is waiting dinner on you."

"I'm sure she is," Kol answered. "Goodbye, Buchanan." Kol opened the door and walked through it for what could very likely be the last time. He stood still and looked around the docking area, returning the nods and waves of the males working there, before making his way to his cruiser and heading home to Ada Jane.

Ada Jane smiled as she served both her plate and Kol's. He'd requested his favorite for dinner tonight — her fried pork chops with mashed potatoes and peas. She caught her reflection in the kitchen window and smiled even bigger at her ever present smile. She always smiled now. She'd never in her life been happier, and it was all thanks to Kol. She loved him as desperately as he loved her, and she loved nothing better than being his mate, his wife. She waited for him to come home each evening, and he always did. Neither he nor she could sleep without the other they'd become so attached.

Her ears picked up the sound of his cruiser as it descended and was docked in place on the other side of the church, and she gave a little squeal of excitement as she placed the forks and knives beside the plates of food and glasses she'd already set on the table. She leaned over and glanced at herself in the reflection of the kitchen window again, then walked outside onto the porch to wait for him.

Kol walked past the church, waving to Pastor Douglas as he went by. Then he slowed in his tracks as he saw his female waiting for him up ahead on their own front porch. He smiled at her, his heart warming. "My Ada Jane," he said.

"I missed you," she called out, jogging down the steps and over to him where he met her half-way, kissing her lips and hugging her to him.

"I was just here this morning," he said, teasing her.

"I know. But I think of a thousand little things I want to tell you all day long, and I have to wait for you to come home to tell you," Ada Jane said.

"Is that all?" he said, draping his arm over her shoulder as they started toward their home.

"Well, I do kind of like your kisses, too. I mean, I do miss those," she said, teasing him.

"I will have to load you up on them this night, so that you can have plenty to last tomorrow," Kol said.

"Deal! I'll take them all," Ada answered as she proceeded to the table, and he closed the front door behind them before following her to the dining room table.

"My favorite," he said, taking his seat.

"You asked for it," Ada said, sitting in her own chair. "Ask and you shall receive," she said, placing her napkin in her lap.

When dinner was over, Ada Jane cleared the table and quickly washed the dishes before following Kol out into the yard where he'd moved one of their porch chairs so that he could look up into the night sky. As she approached him, he held out his arm indicating she should sit on his lap and watch the stars with him.

"So, when are you going to tell me what's wrong?" Ada asked as she rested the back of her head on his shoulder and looked off at the stars with him.

Kol hugged her to him for a moment before kissing her temple.

Ada Jane tried to turn and look at him but he stopped her. "It's easier if you do not look at me," he said softly.

Ada hesitated but she settled back against him, her stomach now doing flips at the unease his comment immediately sent through her. "Okay," she said.

"I never thought I'd call any place home but Cruestace, or Command Warship 1. But this is now my home. It is this cottage, this world, you, that I will dream of when I am not here," he said.

"Where are you going?" she asked, her entire body stiffening.

"I do not wish to leave, but I've been ordered to," Kol answered.

Ada Jane tried to sit up and turn to face him, but he held her gently, yet firmly in place. "Then I'm coming with you," she stated simply.

Kol shook his head, though he knew she couldn't see him since she still faced away from him. "You cannot, my love. Where I'm going you have no business being, and my heart would shatter if you were there with me."

Ada Jane slapped his hands away from her shoulders and spun on his lap to face him. "You can't leave me," she said, with tears in her eyes, though she fought them bravely.

"I do not wish to. And if I am able, I will return. But I cannot lie to you and tell you that I will," Kol answered.

"I don't understand. You said forever," she said, her lip beginning to quiver.

Kol cupped her face in his hands. "And I meant forever. I am forever yours. Always."

"And I'm yours, so I'm coming."

Kol shook his head. "I am making a mess of this." He sighed and pressed his lips to hers before starting again. "I have to turn myself into the Consortium tomorrow morning. Charges have been brought against me for war crimes."

"That's ridiculous!" Ada Jane cried out, jumping to her feet.

"The way in which I killed Diskastes is being questioned. It is said that I was overly violent and it was uncalled for. I must answer for my actions."

"No! All you did was protect me! And look what you've done with the Base in such a short time. Everything is so much better now," she said, her voice breaking as she still fought her tears.

"Yet, the sitting members of the worlds represented by the Unified Consortium Defense were watching. Charges have been brought against me. I must answer them. I must be responsible for my actions. If I was not willing to take responsibility for my actions, I would not be an honorable male worthy of your love."

"I don't care. You are worthy and you're not going anywhere!" Ada insisted.

"There is good news," Kol said sadly.

"There is? What?" she said, walking closer to him.

"Bart has written the warrant and charges himself. He did it so that he could leave out the possibility of a death penalty, or life in prison."

"Death penalty? Life in… What the hell is wrong with these people? Don't they realize what kind of male he was? Don't they realize that he was going to kill all of us given the opportunity?" Ada screamed.

"All they care is what they saw, my Ada Jane. They saw my Psi tear him apart when he leveled his weapon at you. They saw Kron have to turn me away from another male. They feel I acted uncontrollably."

"They're flipping idiots!" she shrieked.

"I will come back, Ehlealah, if I'm able," he said, his heart breaking as tears began streaming down her face.

"No. You can't leave," she said, on a sob.

"I have no choice. I have to go. It is the honorable thing to do," he said, holding her to him as she threw herself back into his lap.

"I don't care about honor. I just care about you, and us. And we deserve this," she said, waving her arms around them at their home and the night sky. "We deserve each other. It's not fair," she said sobbing.

Kol didn't try to dissuade her. She was right.

He let her cry for a while, memorizing the feel of her in his arms so he could carry it with him. Then he remembered he had more to tell her. "I have other news, Ada Jane. I have been working with Bart. He believes he can reclaim your land."

"I only want you," she whispered as her tears still soaked through his shirt. He sat there holding her until her sobs stopped, then he lifted her in his arms, got to his feet and moved them to their bedroom. "Where are we going," she whispered.

"I'm going to make love to you and I'm going to imprint every moment, every sight, every feel, every taste into my memory so that I can take you with me when I go."

"You are taking me with you," she answered.

Kol didn't argue with her. He didn't want her to leave her cottage. He didn't want her to see him in custody or at the trial. He wanted her memories of him to be loving and happy, not shadowed with the situation he was about to endure. Kol laid her on the bed, then started to remove her clothes. "I want the lights on. I want to see every beautiful curve of your body," he said.

Ada Jane nodded. "And yours too."

Kol nodded. "Anything you want, my Ehlealah.

Chapter 29

The early morning hours came quickly as Kol quietly slipped out of their bed and pulled his clothes on. He didn't want to shower and wash away Ada Jane's scent, he wanted to carry that with him today at least. Fully dressed he stood over her, looking down at her sweet face. His whole heart and soul belonged to this woman and he could not even say that he wasn't a lucky male. He'd been gifted with his Ehlealah, and she'd loved him, too. Quietly he left the bedroom and paused at the small table by the front door where they kept a bowl for keys, and Ada Jane always kept fresh flowers in a small vase there. He reached into his pocket and took out a letter Missy had printed for him from his dictated words. He'd signed it, but his mastery of the written English language left a lot to be desired, so he'd enlisted Missy's help.

Then he'd left his weapons beside the note and walked out of their home, closing the door softly behind himself. He started his walk toward his cruiser, knowing that if Bart's escorts weren't there yet, they would be soon. Before he got to the front of the church, he heard the screen door of his and Ada Jane's cottage slam shut as she ran out of it screaming his name. Kol turned toward her as she ran to him. "Ada Jane, go back inside, love."

"You can't do this! You can't!" she screamed, throwing herself into his arms.

Kol's eyes began to get misty as he held her tight. Then he heard movement behind himself and knew they weren't alone. He turned so he could see the four man escort standing and waiting for him. Kol made eye contact with them and nodded. Then he returned his attention to his sobbing mate. "Ehlealah, look at me. Hush, now. Stop crying and look at me."

Ada resisted, but she did manage to get her sobs slightly quieted and looked up at him.

"I am not leaving you. I will never leave you. My heart and soul live here," he said, placing his hand on her chest, "inside you. You will have me with you every day of our lives. And if the gods be willing, I will return in body as well."

"Take me with you," she begged.

"No!" he said firmly, leaving no room for discussion. "I will not have you see me as a less than honorable male. I will tend to these things. I will do whatever is necessary, and one day, hopefully, I will return to you. You will be here among the things that mean so much to you. In the place you call home. In our home," he said, gesturing to the cottage. "Kron has agreed to look in on you. I'm sure the others will as well. You will be strong for me. I need you to be strong for me so that I can do what I have to do."

Ada Jane couldn't even focus on Kol she was crying so hard. But she loved him, and she respected him, and if this was what he asked of her, she'd do it.

"Please, Ada Jane. Can you stay here and take care of our home?"

Ada nodded. "But I'm not going to be happy about it when you get back," she rushed out between her tears, trying to make him believe that she'd be okay.

Kol smiled at her. "I'd expect nothing less. I love you, my Ada Jane, my Ehlealah."

"I love you, Kol," she said, hugging him to her again.

"I have to go, my love. They are waiting."

Ada let go of him and took a step back.

Kol placed a kiss on her lips, each of her eyelids, the tip of her nose and her forehead before running his thumb along her trembling bottom lip. "I will see you again," he promised.

Ada nodded, then stood back and watched him walk toward the four males that waited quietly for him to join them. They didn't arrest him or cuff him, they simply fell into step with him as they all walked out of sight past the front of the church.

Ada stayed where she was. She couldn't feel her body, everything was numb. Her mind was racing and her heart was shattering. Her soul though, her soul kept whispering to her that she was strong, she could do what he asked and be strong for him, for them. She stood there, fighting the sobs that wanted to escape her until she saw the transport Kol and his escorts had boarded rise into the predawn sky and in the blink of an eye disappear from view.

Ada Jane collapsed to her knees screaming her pain to the winds, sobbing and pounding the ground with her closed fists. She had no idea how long she lay there, sobbing until Pastor Douglas found her and helped her back to her cottage. He got her settled on her sofa and made her a cup of coffee. "Do you want to talk about it, Ada Jane?" he asked.

Ada shook her head as she stared out of the front windows.

"Do you want company? I can stay with you if you need me to," he offered.

"You knew," she said softly.

Pastor Douglas nodded. "He asked me to watch over you until he comes back, if he's able to come back."

Ada's tears began to silently slide down her cheeks again as she kept staring out of the windows.

"You want to be alone for a while?" he asked.

Ada nodded.

"Okay. I'll be back in a little while to check on you. I'll be working close by today. If you need me, just call out," Pastor Douglas said.

Ada nodded, but never said another word as Pastor Douglas left her home.

Ada sat there, nothing making sense to her, as she continued to look out through the windows. Then she noticed something she hadn't before. She got up and walked over to the small table they kept near the front door and picked up a folded piece of paper that had been left there. When she saw what it was, she started to cry again as she made her way back to the sofa to sit and read it.

My Dearest Ehlealah,

It is my understanding that it was an Earth custom of your time to write love letters to your female when you go away. So, this is my love letter to you. Know that I am yours, Ada Jane. Know that until you, I was an empty male, wanting endlessly things I barely had any knowledge of. Once I found you, my true purpose was revealed — to love you, to cherish you until time ends. And that I will do no matter where I am.

I am sorry that I've been forced to leave you. Had I my way, I would never leave your side. But in my world, honor is valued, and I cannot become less than honorable. I have always acted with honor, even in battlc. I trust that all will be well and I will return to you soon. But if I cannot, do not think for one moment that it is my choice. You are the only thing that will ever bring me peace. You, your smile, your scent, your taste, your heart. You are my life, Ada Jane.

Kron is staying behind at Earth Base 28 to oversee its operations. He will be checking in with you. Do not hesitate to ask for anything at all you may need or want. Do not be surprised if Buchanan and Zhuxi make themselves available as well. It is my understand that Ba Re' and Elisha will be returning to Command Warship 1, but I'm not exactly sure at what time.

I've left my weapons here with you, and I've left my cruiser with you as well. Missy has been instructed to give you access to all things you may want or need, but she will not show you the legal proceedings of my trial. I have forbidden her from doing so. Because the cruiser is there, you may access it at anytime. It is stronger than most things on Earth and will shelter you from anything I can think of. It will open for you and only you. None other can access it. If you wish to activate the weapons I've left with you, Missy will help you assign them to your DNA. You will remember how to fire them from the days we practiced, I'm sure.

I love you, Ada Jane. I am proud to be your male and will carry you in my heart always.

Be strong for me, my love.

Your mate, Kol Ra' Don Tol

Ada Jane fell apart again, sobbing and crying as she clutched the letter Kol had left her. She fell over on the sofa and stayed that way for the rest of the day, alternating reading his letter, crying, then sleeping before waking and beginning the process all over again.

"We are arriving now, Elite Commander Kol Ra' Don Tol," one of his escorts advised.

Kol nodded.

"We are supposed to restrain you for arrival, but I believe that if you are allowed to willingly present yourself for processing, you will be better received by all who watch."

"Are there many who will be watching?" Kol asked, not really concerned with who watched, he was still seeing Ada Jane as she begged him to stay with her.

"Yes. Make no mistake, every move you make, every word you say will be recorded as evidence. It can work against you, or in your favor."

Kol nodded again. "I understand. Thank you," he said to the male, rising from his seat as his escorts did as well.

"No thanks necessary. I've seen the vids. I do not believe this is necessary, but I have my orders."

"Understood," Kol answered. He stepped up behind the two Consortium escorts who waited to lead him out of their ship and heard the other two step up behind him.

"We'll escort you in. We will be met by another escort and everything will be viewed and recorded. You have not much to fear, though. Chairman Bartholomew has made it known to each of us that is personable with him that you are a friend of his. Even those who are not particularly considered his friends respect him, and no one is willing to risk his anger. He has demanded that you be treated with respect."

"Thank you," Kol replied as they began to exit the ship. Kol looked around the landing pad and the docking spaces and realized they were about to walk up a catwalk toward the landing Bart awaited them on. He managed a bit of a smirk when he realized that Bart had mimicked much of the way Quin greeted visitors to Command Warship 1 in the set up of the docking bay, and the walkways leading to the astromegastructure the Consortium called home base. The large metal sphere was planet shaped, with different docking bays for shipping and receiving personnel, as well as dignitaries and goods.

It was basically a self-sufficient man made planet that orbited on the outer edges of Earth's solar system. It housed at any given time a minimum of three thousand people and all interstellar trials and legal proceedings took place there. It housed holding cells for the accused, their own military, the trappings of its own imitation of a small town with several various stores that offered a small selection of goods for purchase, medical facilities, offices for all dignitaries assigned to it, as well as accomodations and a few extra offices for those who may be visiting temporarily. But, it was for the most part the headquarters for the Consortium and was, therefore, a military based facility.

Bart stood above the docking floor, looking down over those who arrived with authority. Quin did the same thing, and it worked very well as an intimidation tactic. Kol approached Bart and several others who sat on the board of the Consortium under his own power, walking freely and keeping his eyes pinned to Bart as he approached.

"Elite Commander Kol Ra' Don Tol, we thank you for your willingness to remand yourself into our custody. We hope these proceedings will move forward expediently with the utmost accuracy so that we may all return to our previous assignments," Bart said officially.

"As do I," Kol answered.

"Please follow your escorts to your assigned holding cell. Your legal representation will arrive shortly to meet with you and lay out in detail all findings of the court so far."

"I haven't requested legal representation. Who have you assigned?" Kol asked, becoming concerned that it was someone other than a Cruestaci.

Bart smiled at Kol. "Me. I am your legal representation."

Kol realized immediately what it meant for Bart to be willing to represent him. It meant he was risking his entire career. Kol inclined his head one single time, and though he looked Bart directly in the eye, he offered no words. None were needed.

"I will see you shortly, Elite Commander," Bart called after him as he followed his escort to what was essentially his jail cell.

Chapter 30

Kol sat on his bunk and waited for whatever was to happen next. They'd brought him food and water, but he wasn't interested. They'd brought him blankets, bedding, and toiletries, and they still sat in a small stack on the floor. He just wasn't interested in anything, but getting this over with and getting back to Ada Jane. Kol's mind registered footsteps echoing down the corridor toward him, but again, he gave no indication that he even cared.

Moments later a male came to a stop in front of his cell, and he gradually turned his gaze toward him.

"Kol, how are you?" Bart asked.

Kol shrugged. "Want to go home," he answered.

"I know, but we can't release you to Command Warship 1 until we clear your name. Once that's done, we'll get you back to the ship as soon as possible, and send Ada Jane to you as well," Bart promised.

Kol's forehead creased as he processed Bart's words. Then he shook his head. "No. I want to go back to Earth. Earth is my home. Besides, Ada Jane and my friends are there. I don't want to go back to Command Warship 1. I fought to make something honorable out of Base 28, and I've fought to help Ada Jane find her place and heal her soul. She wants to live on Earth on her parents' land, and I want to live beside her," Kol said passionately.

"I don't know if that can be achieved, Kol. I may not be able to secure your place back on Earth. It'll be tough enough to prove your state of mind and gain your innocence for release back to Command Warship 1," Bart said.

"I understand. Do what you can," Kol conceded.

"I'm really sorry it's all come to this. But I have faith that we can at the very least get you released. From there we'll just have to see if they'll allow you back on Earth or not."

"Thank you, Bart. Have you any news of Ada Jane?" Kol asked.

"No, not yet. But, I'll ask, alright? I'll find out how she is for you."

"It's been what, two days since I left her?" Kol asked.

"About that, yes," Bart confirmed.

"Kron would have checked on her by now. He should have some news. If she asks of me, tell her I am positive and anxious to get back to her. Send my love," Kol said.

"I will, Kol."

Kol nodded, then seemed to lose any desire to talk, allowing his gaze to float away from Bart.

"You've not asked for me to contact Quin or anyone from Cruestace," Bart said.

Kol shook his head. "I've done nothing wrong. And if by some small chance, I'm unfairly found guilty of whatever they assume I've done wrong, I do not wish for it to reflect on my Sire or our people. I will be solely responsible. Not them," Kol answered.

"You know I've spoken to him. He's not going to just step away from you," Bart said.

Kol didn't reply, he simply stared straight ahead.

Bart sighed, then began to speak. "Tomorrow we're going to start going through the evidence. I'll send an escort to bring you to one of my meeting rooms. Our schedule will be the same each and every day. Breakfast, evidence, lunch, evidence, dinner, prepare a defense. We will do this each and every day until your trial, and if necessary, we will do it all over again."

"How long will this take?" Kol asked.

"You know how long it takes to have anything done in any world dealing with their government's bureaucracy?"

"Yes," Kol said dejectedly.

"Imagine having to go through all the bureaucracy of each of the governing members of the Consortium. This will not be a quickly moving trial. And I like it that way. It provides us time to slowly and methodically build your case, all the while preparing one against Diskastes post mortem."

"What do you think the chances of me going home are?" Kol asked.

"I'm not sure. But with the evidence we're gathering on Diskastes, I feel sure we can completely justify your actions, and have you freed. Where you end up calling home has yet to be seen," Bart said truthfully.

Kol nodded. "I will be right here waiting," he said, looking at Bart once more.

The next morning Kol wasn't brought breakfast. Instead, he was delivered to a conference room where Bart awaited him with an entire buffet of breakfast foods laid out for just the two of them and Bart's assistants. There were several computers and tablets lying about as well as a holovid podium for the viewing of any information that may need a closer look, and stacks of documents and photographs scattered across the large conference table.

"Good morning, Kol. Help yourself to any food you may like, and have a seat. I'll bring you up to speed on what we've found so far."

Kol glanced over at the food then at all the computers, and stacks of evidence. "I'm not really hungry," he answered.

"Eat. You'll need your strength," Bart answered.

Kol thought about it and decided that Bart was right. No matter what happened, he'd need his strength, and he'd need to be in shape to be able to be ready for whatever was required of him. He walked over to the buffet and served himself a plate, then took the seat Bart indicated.

"So, we've found that for every one human that disappeared without a trace, there are six more within Base 28's sector that have gone missing over the last ten Earth years."

"You believe he was involved in the disappearance of young females?" Kol asked.

"And males. I believe that he's been involved for a very long time. Especially since he's on tape assaulting Vivian," Bart said as he watched the images projected onto the white board. "Forgive the rudimentary slide projector, not all the documentation is adapted for holographic projection via the holovid podium."

Kol shook his head as he absentmindedly ate his breakfast and listened to Bart speak in detail on every single piece of evidence that he projected on the board at the opposite end of the conference room. By the time lunch rolled around, Kol found himself fully immersed in the evidence and actually feeling motivated to dig deeper. He looked over at Bart. "Thank you for all your help, Bart," Kol said sincerely.

"Don't give it a second thought, Kol. I have no doubt that this is all just bullshit. You've done nothing to be sitting here, but because the charges were filed formally, I have to recognize them and justify your actions. We'll beat this. Part of this is because of the stigma that follows the Cruestaci people as well."

"I am aware of the consequences for your career should we not win," Kol answered.

"Don't care, Kol. Right is right, and wrong is wrong. This is wrong. Besides, I carry quite a lot of weight behind my name and my office. They will only push so far before they risk provoking me. Me representing you is the best option we have. I will see you free."

As their lunches were served, Kol worked up the courage to ask about Ada Jane again. "Have you heard anything of Ada Jane?"

"I spoke to Quin. They are monitoring Missy for any attempt at access by Ada Jane, but there has been none. I am in contact with Kron and the others at Base 28. They are still outraged that you are on trial for war crimes. Kron has been to visit Ada Jane several times, but she tries to send him away each time."

"She is suffering," Kol said softly, looking down at his plate.

"She's missing her mate. But Kron is not giving up. He stays there and forces her to interact," Bart said.

Kol nodded. "Kron can be very persistent when he chooses to be. He can also be quite irritating."

"That's good. Get her blood boiling, get her to focus on something other than you being here."

Kol smiled and nodded again. He knew that Ada Jane was at least not alone. His friends were looking after her.

The days went by in much the same way. Some days there was no new evidence to process, so they worked on their defense and support of Kol's actions in killing Diskastes. And in their extra time they simply talked or sat quietly in each other's company. Bart did this in order to keep Kol out of his cell for as long as possible, and Kol knew it. He was well aware that his time there could have been much worse than it was.

On the morning of the last day of the second week of his stay in the holding cells of the Unified Consortium Defense, Kol arrived at the conference room and found a very excited Bart.

"Morning, Kol. I have good news for you!" Bart said, already eating his own breakfast.

Kol stood beside the table and waited. "Tell me, what is it?" Kol asked.

"Get your breakfast and then I'll tell you," Bart said.

"Tell me now," Kol insisted.

"Ada Jane's land... I got word late last night. It's being returned to her. My motion to have the storage facilities moved from it and it returned to her was defeated, but it has been returned to her. "Basically, Earth's government said, 'We're not paying to clean it up, but you can have it as is if you want it. I told them we did and transferred payment this morning."

"You used the funds I gave you in preparation for this day?" Kol asked, being sure that Bart didn't put himself out any more than he already had.

"I did. And I even owe you a small amount back," Bart said smiling.

"Put it in my account. Ada Jane has been added to the account so she can access all that is in it."

"I'll take care of it. The land's Ada Jane's, though. It's a done deal."

"That is great news! She will be so happy!" Kol said, truly smiling for the first time since he'd left Ada Jane.

"It is. And I've spoken to Kron. They're going to clean it up for her. I told them if they needed any help to let me know, and to ask for anything they come across that they may need. You never know what's stored in those old metal buildings."

"Of course, anything they want in exchange for helping my Ehlealah clean her land is more than fair. I hope they find something of value to them." Kol filled his plate with food and sat down at the table with Bart. "I miss her sweet face. I would give anything to see her, to hold her."

"We're working on that now. We have to get you out of here first," Bart answered.

"I know. Is she well?" Kol asked.

"As I tell you every single day. She is well. She is being looked after by your friends. Kron in particular is driving her crazy and refusing to allow her to become lost in the sadness of this situation."

Kol nodded his understanding. "I owe you much, Bart."

Bart shook his head. "No, you don't. It's what friends do for one another. Whatever is in our power to do to help the other out."

Kol held his hand out to shake Bart's.

Bart shook his hand then went back to his own meal. "Eat up, we have some work to get done today."

Ada Jane dragged herself out of bed and stumbled out of the bedroom and through the living room. Someone was knocking on her front door. They'd been knocking for so long that Ada Jane was seriously considering using her disintegrater on them — blast the whole damn door and whoever stood beyond it.

She didn't look to see who it was, she simply flipped the locks open, then grasped the handle and pulled the door wide open. "What?!" she snapped.

The male stood there smiling at her. His fine, silky, white hair lifting from his shoulders as the breeze caught and played with it. His happy smile matched perfectly his yellow mottled skin. It faded from a deep yellow to a pale almost white as the mottling moved across his body. Ada Jane allowed her gaze to travel from his smile and the tips of his fangs showing through, to his eerie yellow eyes fringed with white lashes the exact same color as his hair, yet she didn't return his smile.

"Hello, Ada Jane," Kron said, still smiling and showing the tips of his fangs as they peeked from beneath his full lips.

"Kron," Ada Jane returned.

"I came for a visit," he announced.

"Why?" she asked, turning and walking away from Kron, leaving the door wide open. "I told you the last time you came that it wasn't necessary. And I'll tell you just like I tell everyone though they don't listen to me either. It's not necessary, and I'd rather just be alone."

"Because it is what friends do, and who else do you tell to leave your home? Who else comes to visit you, Ada Jane? May I enter?" he asked, raising his voice to be heard in the back of the small house since she'd left his sight altogether.

"I don't care," she called back at him.

Kron stepped inside and closed the door behind himself. He glanced around the room and realized that for the few weeks Kol had been gone, she'd most likely not even left the bedroom. Other than a crumpled letter lying on the small table in front of the sofa, the room looked completely untouched as evidenced by the undisturbed fine layer of dust on all the surfaces. It was unlived in.

"Ada Jane," Kron called, "who else do you tell to leave your home?"

"Jason. He just won't take no for an answer!" Ada Jane complained.

"He has been here?!" Kron asked, disbelievingly.

"Yes. Deserted me to my fate with Diskastes and now won't go away. He's a Purist and thinks he can save my damaged soul from the likes of all the sinful aliens that can't wait to bed me," Ada Jane mumbled as she burrowed under her covers. "Go away, Kron. I'm not ready to get up and pretend I'm okay," Ada Jane answered.

Kron heard her words and followed them to the darkened bedroom that still scented of Kol and Ada Jane. He stood in the doorway and watched her outline hiding under the covers on their bed. "You must get up, Ada Jane. You cannot hide yourself away from the world like this."

"You don't understand. Just go back to the base and do whatever it is you're supposed to be doing. Just ignore me until Kol comes back, then we'll act like this never happened, okay?" she asked.

Kron grinned to himself. She was stubborn, and determined to wallow in her heartbreak. But she had a surprise coming. He was more stubborn. He stepped toward her bed and took hold of the edge of her covers, then yanked them off her body, off her bed, and dropped them to the floor beside his boots.

"Hey! What was that for? I told you to go, just go!" Ada Jane yelled.

"No. I am here as your friend, for my friend and commander. He instructed me to be sure you live your life — to force you if necessary. So, consider this me keeping a promise to a friend. Get. Up."

Ada Jane sat in the middle of her bed, legs splayed out before her, her hair a mess, her eyes bleary from weeks of crying and doing nothing but sleeping. "I thought I liked you. I don't like you."

"I don't care. Get up," Kron answered, still smiling at her.

"Why? What difference would it make? The only thing that will save me is Kol and he's not here. There is nothing that needs to be done! Just leave me alone."

"You can get up and dress yourself in something other than Kol's shirt, or I can take you just as you are."

"Take me where?" Ada Jane asked irritatedly.

"I have a surprise for you," Kron said.

"I don't want a surprise, unless it's Kol," she snapped, turning over and pulling Kol's pillow over her head.

Kron watched her for only a moment more before shrugging. "Okay. Have it your way." He walked over to the side of the bed, lifted her pillow and all, and tossed her over his shoulder. He turned and left her bedroom, then her living room, and carried her the whole way to his transport with her shrieking as he went.

Once he had her seated in his transport, he turned and faced her as she sat red-faced, practically spitting at him she was so angry.

"I don't want to go!"

"Yes, you do."

"No, I don't. I don't want to go."

"This is a surprise from Kol. He put this in motion long before he was called away. I heard from Bart two days ago; it's time for you to have your surprise. Kol doesn't want you to have to wait until he comes back to get it."

"Did you speak to him? Is he well?" Ada Jane asked, her anger turning into concern.

Kron shook his head. "He's not allowed to communicate with anyone other than his legal representative. Bart is defending him, and Bart is luckily friends with Quin, and most of the crew of Command Warship 1, and those of us who are running the base in Kol's absence. So, we get updates more often than most would. He misses you. He asked Bart to remind you that he loves you, and you should be strong for him until he sees you again."

"He's coming back?" she said hopefully.

Kron chewed a bit on his lower lip. "We honestly don't know yet."

Ada Jane's momentary interest visually deflated.

"Look, you can't waste your life away. He made you promise to be strong for him. He didn't want you lying in your bedroom sleeping away your life. He wants you out living it."

"It's hard," she confided.

"I know it is. Do you think that I am unaffected? I am so angry that he has to go through this over the loss of a worthless male that I want to rally our Elite team and go free him. Blast our way in and kill all who stand in our way. But I can't. The rest of his life he'd be tracked and hounded like a criminal. He deserves better. He deserves a life with his Ehlealah living every day to the fullest, not having to remain hidden every moment of every day waiting for someone to track you both down. So, he's got to go through this. We all have to go through this until he is found innocent, and can return to his life where he left off. You have to keep this life going for him so he comes back to a happy, strong mate. How do you think he'd feel if he comes back and finds that because of his absence you fell into a sadness so deep that you could not dig yourself out? He would feel responsible, and it would hurt him."

Ada Jane sat there, listening to Kron. He was right, she knew he was, but she still didn't like it. Finally, she conceded. "You're right. I know that. I just don't know how."

"Luckily, you have me. And all the rest of his friends," Kron said.

Ada Jane looked at him curiously. "I don't understand."

"You will. Sit tight and we'll be there in just a bit," Kron answered.

Chapter 31

"Where are we going, Kron?" Ada Jane asked.

"You'll see," he answered.

As the transport came up over the hilltop and started out over what were once fertile fields of corn and pasture land, Ada Jane sat up. She knew exactly where she was.

"Do you recognize it?" he asked.

"It's home," she said, her voice showing a trace of her excitement. "But, we were told that we didn't have access to it. We were told that we couldn't even fly over it!"

"That was all true, until Kol bought it for you. It's all finalized. He started the process before he was forced to turn himself in. And Bart finalized the formalities on his behalf a couple of days ago. It's yours, Ada Jane. The land is legally in your name."

Ada Jane was smiling so big it hurt and she pressed her hands to her cheeks. "I can't believe this," she said in awe as she looked out over the land. "Wait, who's down there?" she asked, trying to angle her head to see out of the windshield and the window to get a better look at the people she could see moving about on the ground.

Kron landed the transport and as soon as it was secure, he opened the doors and allowed her to begin to exit the transport. "Wait! You only have socks on your feet! And you need pants!" he called. He walked to the small storage cabinets in the back of the transport and dug around for a moment before finding what he wanted. They kept several sets of clothing and soft rollable shoes in the event they had to perform rescues of some nature. He walked back to the door of the transport and handed them to her. "Here, they're not boots, and they're probably a little big, but it's better than socks. And put these pants on."

"Thank you, Kron!" Ada Jane said excitedly, pulling on the pants that reminded her of sweat pants, and unrolling the soft-soled, elastic banded shoes and slipping them on her feet. Then she grabbed Kron and kissed his cheek. "Thank you so much."

"I have only done as requested. It is not me who should be thanked," Kron said, smiling at the first signs of interest in anything he'd seen in Ada Jane since Kol left.

"But it is. No matter how many times I sent you away, you kept coming back," she said, pausing in her rapid stride to get to the large aluminum storage buildings scattered about her family's property — now hers.

"When we are lost in darkness is the time we need the most encouragement, the most understanding. It is all I did," Kron said sincerely.

Coming to where the most of the activity was, Ada Jane was surprised to find Buchanan working on sorting through one of the buildings. "Good Morning, Viceroy," she offered.

Buchanan raised an eyebrow as he regarded Ada Jane. "Viceroy? I am not Viceroy. I am Buchanan."

"But you're a Viceroy, too," Ada Jane reminded.

"When I am with friends, I'm just Buchanan."

Ada Jane nodded in acceptance. "What is all this?" she asked.

"The government abandoned this place. It was used more or less as a storage facility for old or obsolete equipment and supplies they really didn't know what else to do with. They sold it to Kol with the understanding that it was being sold as is with all buildings and whatever was inside intact. They are not responsible for clearing the land, or cleaning it up," Buchanan explained.

Ada Jane looked up at the three story metal building stuffed floor to rafter with so much junk she'd never finish going through it all in her lifetime. And there were several more buildings just like it.

"That's where we come in," Kron added. "We're going through the buildings, sorting through it. If it's something you might be able to use, it goes in one stack for your input.

Something we as a base may be able to use, it goes in another stack. Strictly for disposal, goes in yet another. Those who wish to volunteer their time will be here anytime they get the chance. It'll take a little while, but we'll get it done."

"I don't know how to thank you. All of you have already done so much for me," Ada Jane said, eyeing the huge piles of what she'd label as rubbish, that they'd already removed from the first building. "And now you take on clearing all this from our land, too."

"You should know that our people wanted to assist as well, but in light of the proceedings taking place, the powers that be are hard-pressed to grant travel visas to the Cruestaci wanting to visit Earth."

"That's a shame."

"It is. But, picture a very large, very angry, very red male demanding he be allowed on Earth without further delay, and surely you can imagine their hesitance," Kron said chuckling, doing his best to make her laugh.

Ada smiled. "I can see how he'd frighten most people."

"In truth, I am only allowed here because my visa was granted previously. And, I was assigned to Earth Base 28 before anything occurred. I will stay here for the duration, if not longer," Kron explained.

"I truly appreciate you, and every one who's pitched in to help me and Kol."

"It's not a problem. If one of us was in Kol's position and he was still here with our mate, he would do the same," Kron said with conviction.

"Yes, he would," Buchanan agreed.

Ada Jane smiled at them, but didn't try to even speak. Her emotions were right near the surface, and she didn't want to break down in front of these men again. She'd been pretty inconsolable over the last couple of weeks, and she felt bad about it. Her eyes strayed to a spot on a small rise that was dusty and brown, the grass having died there a long, long time ago. Ada Jane started walking toward it.

"Ada Jane?" Kron said, calling her name. "Where are you going?"

Ada lifted her arm and pointed. "My home used to be right there," she said softly.

Kron fell into step behind her and just kept her company as she wandered around the site.

Finally after walking around the rise and deciding there was nothing there except the rise itself, Ada Jane took a seat right there on the ground.

She looked out over the land, the metal storage buildings, and watched the men working in one of them as they dragged large machinery out of it and left it there in the open before going back for more.

Kron sat beside her and was just there for her, not saying a word.

Sometime later she began to speak. "Where we are sitting right now, this would have been our front porch. Where that building is, that would have been our barn. The chicken coop was over there to the side," she said, pointing to her left, "but we let them run around free all the time. We had corn crops, and we had dairy cows and sold milk and cream. We could sit here and look out over most of our land, except for the pastures in the back behind the house, of course.

We'd get up early in the morning and feed the animals, collect the eggs, milk the cows. Then I'd go to school and Momma and Daddy would start the rest of their day. I used to think that I'd leave here one day and become something unbelievable. Now, all I want to do is get back to the life I lived here. I didn't know how wonderful it was."

"You have become something unbelievable. You are Ehlealah Ada Jane Ra' Don Tol. Mate to Elite Commander Kol Ra' Don Tol. You are highly respected."

Ada Jane smiled as she kept watching the men working. "Because I'm mated to a very good male?" she asked.

"No. Because of all you've survived to become the mate of a very good male. Your strengths are recognized as your own, as are his. Together, you are a force to be reckoned with," Kron answered, offering her a smile that flashed his fangs at her.

"I miss him," Ada Jane said simply.

"I do, too," Kron answered. "Hopefully it will not be very much longer. The trial is set to start at the beginning of the next revolution."

Ada Jane turned her focus to Kron. "What does that mean? How long is a revolution?" she asked.

Kron took a deep breath and let it out slowly. "It is difficult to explain. Time is calculated differently here versus the Consortium headquarters, versus Cruestace, and most other worlds."

"Can you guess at how long it would be?" she asked.

"When you were on Command Warship 1, that was approximately a quarter of a revolution," Kron said, thinking about it. "Yes, I think that's a close estimation," he confirmed.

"So it will be a while, then," Ada Jane said.

"Yes, but it is moving forward, and it usually takes much longer," Kron explained.

"Then I will be thankful. Do you have any other news?" she asked.

"Only that he loves you and misses you," Kron replied.

"He never sends me any word on how he's holding up, or what they think of their case, or anything about the upcoming proceedings at all," Ada Jane said.

"He doesn't wish for you to be burdened by it."

"I understand that. But I need to know how things are, I need to be kept abreast so that I can be prepared for whatever may happen," Ada Jane explained

Kron sat in silence for a moment before eventually shrugging and deciding to be honest. "The truth is, Ada Jane, that no one knows what to expect. The charges are ridiculous. The only thing that will make Diskastes's people withdraw their charges or to accept Kol's innocence is if they find damning evidence against Diskastes. If Bart and his people can find that kind of evidence, Diskastes's people will back off."

Ada Jane nodded slowly. She understood that. She didn't like it, but she understood it. And she understood that Kol didn't want her involved in whatever it was he had to go through, not simply for his own pride, but for her protection and anonymity, though he hadn't said as much she just knew him well enough to know that was part of it as well. She brushed her hands on her pants and stuck her hand out to help Kron stand. "How about a walk around the place to check the fences and see what needs mending?"

<<<<<<<>>>>>>>

Later that night Ada Jane actually ate dinner. She cleaned her small cottage, and sat for a while reading before she was tired. She did put on one of Kol's shirts to sleep in, but she'd probably always do that. Before bed she walked around her cottage, smiling as different places in the house reminded her of the memories she and Kol had already created in this small home. She loved this cottage. She smiled widely when she thought of her land and that he'd managed to have it returned to her. She stopped and looked around again; she was going to miss this place. Her brow creased and she began to move back to the living room as her mind worked.

Ada Jane sat on the sofa with the tablet that Kol had left her. She powered it up and swiped the option for audio. "Hello, Missy," Ada Jane greeted.

"Hello, Ada Jane Ra' Don Tol. I have been waiting for you to contact me."

"I am sorry I didn't think to do so sooner," Ada Jane answered, smiling at how lifelike the computer was.

"Apology accepted. How may I be of service?" Missy asked.

Ada Jane had a reason for contacting the Cruestaci artificially intelligent software system, but all she could think of at the moment was Kol. "How is Kol?" she asked, knowing the answer would be that she wasn't allowed to give that information.

Missy surprised her with a completely different answer. "I have a vid that I am allowed to play for you, Ada Jane Ra' Don Tol."

Ada Jane held her breath while the vid downloaded. Then she was looking at Chairman Bartholomew, speaking to her from what appeared to be his office. "Hello, Ada Jane. I can only guess how anxious and distressed you must be over this situation. Unfortunately, the laws are simple. While in Unified Consortium Defense custody, the accused are not allowed contact with the outside world. While it seems unfair, there is a reason for it. We have in the past experienced terrorist acts as a result of certain contacts — this is the reason for the lack of communication. Unfortunately, it is an all or none at all rule. And while I cannot allow contact, there is absolutely nothing addressing my ability to show you footage of myself and Kol as we work our way through all the evidence and prepare his defense. He is not aware that I'm sending you this recording. He loves you very much, Ada Jane, and you are always on his mind. I can only believe that you will be reunited at the closure of all this." Bart smiled at the vidcom recorder before the screen went black, then came back into focus with an obviously less focused camera angle. Ada Jane sat up straight and cradled the tablet in her hands as she watched Bart sitting at a large table. The door opened and two males escorted Kol in, then turned, leaving the room and leaving Kol alone with Bart.

Ada Jane's eyes were for Kol only, she looked closely at his face, his body, his hands. He didn't seem to be injured in any way. When they began to speak, she focused on their conversation.

"Morning, Kol. I have good news for you!" Bart told him.

Kol stood beside the table and waited. "Tell me, what is it?" Kol asked.

"Get your breakfast and then I'll tell you," Bart said.

"Tell me now," Kol insisted.

"Ada Jane's land… I got word late last night. It's being returned to her. My motion to have the storage facilities moved from it and it returned to her was defeated, but it has been returned to her. "Basically, Earth's government said, 'We're not paying to clean it up, but you can have it as is if you want it. I told them we did and transferred payment this morning."

"You used the funds I gave you in preparation for this day?" Kol asked.

"I did. And I even owe you a small amount back," Bart said smiling.

"Put it my account. Ada Jane has been added to the account so she can access all that is in it."

"I'll take care of it. The land's Ada Jane's, though. It's a done deal."

"That's great news! She will be so happy!" Kol said, truly smiling for the first time since he'd left Ada Jane.

Ada Jane listened to the rest of their conversation before rewinding it and watching it again. Just to see him sitting with Bart as they had breakfast and spoke of her land was enough to make her feel a little better. As the conversation went on, Kol mentioned her again, and she couldn't help but concentrate on that part.

"I miss her sweet face. I would give anything to see her, to hold her," he said.

Ada Jane stopped the vid on that particular part. In it, Kol's face was smiling and happy as he thought of her. She reached out and touched the image of his face on the tablet. "I miss you, too," she whispered.

That night she went to sleep with Kol's voice fresh in her mind as she watched the vid over and over again. It was the best night's sleep she'd managed to get since Kol left.

Chapter 32

The sky was dark and the docking pad of the repatriation center practically empty as Kron docked his transport and moved through the empty spaces through the medical center. The automatic doors opened at his approach and he stepped through them, pausing at the map mounted on the wall just past the information desk to locate the offices he was looking for. Smiling as he used his finger to trace the route to the lift, the office he wanted, then back again, he memorized the route and smiled to himself as he made his way out of the main lobby and toward the middle of the medical center where the particular lift he needed was located. He stepped inside and braced himself as he stared straight ahead.

Dr. Jason Cavanaugh sat at his desk, working late again, but not on anything to do with his patients. He was working on plans for the Purist movement he poured so much of himself into. He often stayed late at the medical center to take advantage of the online access to government websites he could sign on to here, that he didn't have access to at home. At the moment, he was making notes on all the most recent arrivals of aliens and their home planets. It was extremely important that he keep accurate numbers so that when the Purists rose up against them, evicting them from the planet, they were sure to get them all.

A knock sounded on his office door, and he looked up at it irritatedly. "My office does not need cleaning! Just skip it tonight," he shouted.

No one replied, but someone knocked again, more forcefully.

Jason got up and stalked over to his office door, yanking it open and preparing to repeat to whoever was standing there that they should leave him alone. "I said…" he began before the words stopped flowing from his mouth, probably because of the yellow hand that was now clenched around his throat and holding him up off the ground.

Jason kicked his feet and used both hands to grasp at the yellow one cutting off his oxygen supply and his voice.

Kron stepped into Jason's office and kicked the door closed behind himself. "Dr. Cavanaugh, we need to come to an understanding," Kron said, tossing the doctor across the room and allowing him to land half on, half off his own desk, his back slamming into the outer edge painfully.

"Who are you?! I demand you leave my office at once before I call security!"

"I've blocked your communication abilities. You can't call anyone short of running down the hallway and screaming for help. Though that would not surprise me as you are a coward," Kron answered calmly.

"I am no coward! You have no idea who I am," Jason answered.

"Oh, but I do. You are the male who deserted Ada Jane Ra' Don Tol on a docking pad at Base 28, knowing full well that she was being surrounded by violent, armed forces," Kron answered.

"It was too late to be able to help her. I had to get away while I could. I com'd the authorities as soon as I was away to have them send in assistance," Jason said defensively.

"No, you didn't," Kron answered. "You simply left her there to be taken hostage, die or worse. And as you are about to learn, there are worse things than death."

"You stay away from me!" Jason shouted. "I'm important! I'm needed here! I'm the reason most of the people in this facility have recovered from their injuries and survive!" Jason yelled.

"Really? If you weren't such a Purist, I may take that into consideration," Kron answered.

"What I do in my spare time is none of your business!" Jason said defensively.

"Oh, but it is. You see, it is my responsibility to watch over Ada Jane. And you've been stalking her home, trying to force her to interact with you. If you don't stay away from her, I'll make you beg for death," Kron threatened.

"You can't hurt me! I'm well known," Jason spat back at him.

"Test me. Please," Kron said calmly, then turned his back on Jason to exit the office.

Jason snatched his sharpened, bladed letter opener off the desktop and attacked Kron, just as Kron had hoped he would.

Kron turned and caught Jason by the wrist, snapping it in one single movement, then he beat him into submission until Jason was on his knees, sobbing and begging for mercy with both wrists broken, an eye swollen shut, bruises across his body, and blood falling from several cuts on his face. Kron opened his mouth and pulled his lips back tightly to expose his razor sharp fangs, then he leaned over until he was right in Jason's face. "You will stay away from Ada Jane, or I will come back. I will rip your body apart limb from limb, after I use my fangs to tear your arteries from your body. Are we clear?" Kron asked quietly.

Jason nodded while he continued to sob.

"Make no mistake, I know everything about you. Where you live, where you play, where you meet with your Purist friends, your family, your coworkers — all of it. I will kill you. It's only a matter of how many others you force me to send with you into death. You are a coward, you are less than a male. You will stay away from Ada Jane. You will not contact her, nor visit her, or I will be back. In fact, you will forget she even exists. Do you understand?" he asked with saliva dripping from his fangs.

Jason held his broken wrists up in front of him as he sobbed and begged for mercy from the yellow monster that had attacked him. The only way to survive was to agree. "Yes," he answered pitifully.

"Do not make me return. I may not be so pleasant if I do," Kron said. He straightened, turned his back on the broken and battered male, and left the medical center via the same route he'd used to find the doctor's office.

Jason let himself fall over onto the floor and sobbed uncontrollably. He'd get his revenge. Only it wouldn't be just on

Ada Jane. He'd take out the yellow alien that had beaten him, and broken his wrists. If he never achieved anything else in life, he'd take his revenge on the yellow bastard.

The next morning Ada Jane was up bright and early. She and Missy researched options for moving houses while she had breakfast, then went to Pastor Douglas's home to be sure that he was willing to sell her the cottage she lived in. Everything all ready to go. She com'd Kron.

After a moment his image popped up on her tablet. "Good Morning, Ada Jane," he said, smiling at her.

"Morning, Kron. I have an idea I was wondering if you'd mind helping me with."

"Of course. What can I do?"

"Well, first, I want to move my cottage to my parents' land," Ada explained.

"Can we do that?" he asked.

"Yes! Missy says that physically it's possible, and Pastor Douglas has agreed to sell it to me. So I need to transfer the money into the account for the church," Ada answered.

"Very well. We can do that," Kron answered as his attention was pulled away from somewhere off screen.

He stopped speaking for a moment and he was momentarily lost.

Ada Jane watched for a moment, waiting for his attention to return to her, but when it didn't, she called his name. "Kron?"

Kron looked back at her. "I'm sorry, Ada Jane. I'm a little distracted this morning."

"I can com you later if you're busy," she said.

"No, that's not necessary. Allow me to speak to Buchanan and see how we should proceed. He is going back to your land today with several males to complete emptying the last storage building. Once I speak to him, I'll be back in touch this afternoon," he said, his gaze again leaving her and getting lost somewhere in the room he was in.

"That's fine. Are you sure you're okay?" she asked.

"Yes, I am very well. Thank you for asking," he said, his brow creasing as he watched something she couldn't see.

"I'll wait to hear from you," she answered, and ended the com.

Kron ended the call on his end as well, and allowed himself the luxury of watching the small, pale female with the equally pale red hair as she waited for her father to return to his desk. He'd heard some of the other males call her hair red, but it was not red in the sense that Zha Quin was red. It was a softer color, almost a combination of the color of flames and the pale golden blonde of Ada Jane's hair. Whatever color it was, it was his new favorite. The tiny little spots sprinkled across her nose and her upper cheeks drew his attention almost as strongly as her hair.

He was so caught up in admiring the female that he didn't realize she'd spun her father's chair around and was now staring back at him. Instead of getting offended, she simply pressed her lips together in a smile and waited for him to notice she'd caught him watching her. After a few moments she laughed and raised her hand in front of her face to wave at him.

Kron startled, whipping his gaze up to hers.

"Hi," she said, grinning at him.

"Hello," Kron answered nervously, knowing she was aware of his having been admiring her.

"You sure Dad's coming back to his office?" she asked.

"Yes. He is," Kron answered, looking down at his own desk and starting to shuffle documents so he'd appear busy.

"Okay, I'll wait," she said, spinning the chair in a circle again. When she came face-to-face with him again, she smiled at him. "So, was that your girlfriend?" she asked.

Kron's eyebrows creased heavily over his eyes as he considered her question, a totally confused look on his face.

"The vid. The girl you were just talking to..." she reminded.

"Oh! No, no she's not my female. She is the mate of a friend of mine who cannot be here at the moment. So I continue to insure her safety until he can return," Kron explained.

"Ah, I see. Would that friend be Ambassador Kol?" she asked.

"Yes, she is Kol's female," Kron answered.

"I never met him, but my Daddy talks about him often. He said Kol's a good man and that without him we'd still be dealing with Diskastes."

"Your father is correct. He has been my friend and my commander for many, many years," Kron said.

"So, you're Kron, right?" she asked.

"Yes. I am Kron."

"I'm Ginger. I've seen you around, but you always seem so busy I didn't want to interrupt you."

"Baby girl!" Buchanan said boisterously, entering the open offices of Base 28.

"Hey, Daddy," Ginger answered, getting to her feet to hug him.

"What are you doing here?" he asked.

"You invited me to breakfast," Ginger said, smirking because he forgot.

"I sure did, didn't I?" he asked. "I'm sorry, baby. I got so busy I forgot all about it."

"Have you eaten?" she asked.

"I did. I was planning to go out to finish cleaning out those storage facilities I was telling ya'll about and just completely forgot."

"Which reminds me," Kron said. "Ada Jane would like to know if it's possible to move her cottage from the Church to her land. She has already gotten permission to purchase it, and would like it moved to her land," Kron explained.

"That's not a hard thing to do. Just have to get the permits to do so. And, seeing as how I'm headed that way today, I'll stop and apply for them. We can get it done by the end of the week."

"Thank you. I will com her back and let her know it will be done," Kron said.

"Very good," Buchanan said, then he looked from his daughter who was watching Kron intently, to Kron who was trying his damnedest not to stare at Ginger. "Hey, Kron? You eaten breakfast yet?" he asked.

Ginger's wide-eyed gaze flashed to his at the same time Kron's did.

"No, I have not yet eaten this morning," Kron answered.

"Excellent. I have to be off, I've got a lot to do and some men waiting on me, as well as the permit to move Ada's house now. You mind taking my daughter to breakfast so she doesn't have to eat alone?" Buchanan asked.

Kron looked at Ginger, who'd lowered her eyes and peeked up at him through her lashes. "If you do not mind the company, I would be honored to accompany you," Kron said with a slight smile.

Ginger smiled and kissed her Daddy's cheek. "Have a good day, Daddy," she said, before taking a step toward Kron.

Kron stood from his chair and walked around his desk. "Would you like to go now?"

"Yes, I would," Ginger answered, smiling up at Kron as they walked out of the office together.

Buchanan smiled to himself and shook his head. There were a lot worse males than Kron for his daughter to set her sights on. Kron was hardworking, he was loyal, and he had integrity. Besides it was obvious he was as smitten with Ginger as she was with him.

Vivian stood on the catwalk in the docking bay of Command Warship 1. She'd dutifully agreed to stay aboard their warship rather than attend the end of Kol's trial. But what Quin didn't know was that she had her fingers crossed behind her back the whole time she agreed.

She stood and watched as the Cruestace envoy left their dock via a small battle cruiser. On that ship were Quin, his personal guards, Ba Re', Jhan, and half of Kol's Elite Warriors. She wasn't stupid, she knew exactly what Quin was planning. If the final review of the judiciary board assigned to hear Kol's case did not find him innocent and release him, Quin was going to release him regardless, and he didn't really give a damn who he had to remove from his path to achieve it.

And he'd proved her guess correct when he'd left the entire ship on high alert, and the remaining half of the Elite Warriors stayed behind with Rokai ahl. She had no doubt they were to stand with General Lo' San should there be retaliation before Quin and those he took with him could reach Command Warship 1 with Kol in tow.

Vivian stood rigid and smiled, as they went through the process of flight check and eventually, launch. As soon as they were out of sight, she relaxed her body from her ramrod straight position. "Finally!" she snapped. "Got things to do, Kitty!" she said, turning and walking past her three assigned security guards for the day.

"Where are we going now, Sirena?" Kail asked, falling into step right behind her.

Vivian didn't stop walking, but she answered Kail. "Let me ask you something, Kail," she said.

"Of course, Sirena. Anything," Kail replied.

"Just how loyal are you?" she asked.

Kail's steps faltered. "As loyal as any, and more than most," he proclaimed proudly.

"Good to know. Good to know. What about the rest of you?" she asked.

Asl and Rel immediately agreed. "We are extremely loyal, Sirena."

"We've sworn our lives to you particularly!" Rel reminded her.

"Very good. You might want to go pack," she answered, smiling as they all got on a lift and she spoke to Missy. "Missy, please take me to the Command Deck."

"Yes, Sirena Vivi," Missy answered.

"Go pack?" Rel asked cautiously.

"Yes, we're going on a trip. Or, at least I am. Come with or not, I'm still going," she answered, stepping out of the lift and moving quickly toward the Command Deck. She smiled to herself when she heard Rel's voice behind her as he spoke into his communicator. "Zahn, you are needed here at once." Then Rel lowered his voice. "She is taking us on a trip!" he hissed, not at all impressed with the idea.

The hydraulic doors to the Command Deck slid open, and Kitty bounded through before Vivian even got there. As she passed through the doors herself, she smiled when she saw Kitty sitting at General Lo' San's side begging snacks. Vivian ignored everyone on the deck with the exception of saluting them in return when they acknowledged her presence with a salute, and made a beeline for Communications Master Vennie.

"Hello Vennie," Vivian said, smiling sweetly.

"Sirena! What a pleasure! How are you this fine day?" he asked.

"I'm as well as can be expected. But, you can make me happier," she answered.

"I can? But of course I will do anything you wish. Tell me what favor I may grant you," Vennie said.

"You can make a copy of that vid that you and my husband think I know nothing about. And you can do it right now. I need it portable, too. I'm taking it with me and I want to be able to control it," Vivian said, her smile shifting to a hard, no nonsense expression.

Vennie looked panicked. "But Sirena, I'm not sure exactly what..."

"Really? That's the position you want to take. Don't make me regret trusting you, Vennie."

"I have strict instructions, Sirena," Vennie explained looking truly pained.

"And I'm not supposed to know about it, protect the Sirena at all costs. Yeah, I get it. Thing is though, I do know about it. I heard Quin talking about it. And now I want a copy of it." She stopped talking and thought about it. "No, I don't want a copy of it, I need a copy of it. Leave it intact just as Quin ordered, I'm sure he has his reasons…"

"Facial recognition scans," Vennie said quietly.

"Makes sense. He's trying to find them all," Vivian said aloud.

Vennie agreed. "He is."

"I need you to highlight the part that he believes will save Kol. Whatever it is, whatever it shows, I need that part highlighted along with enough of it to give the gist of whatever is going on," Vivian said.

"Sirena," Vennie tried again.

Vivian decided to take a different approach. "Why is he hiding it from me?"

Vennie looked away from his Sirena. "He says that you have suffered enough. You barely survived for him to find you, and he will not ever subject you to the pain you had to endure again. He's right, Sirena. It is horrendous. There is no need," Vennie said emphatically.

"They can't hurt me anymore, Vennie. I'm here, I'm Quin's, I'm safe. But they can hurt Kol. There's no way in hell I'm going to allow them to hurt Kol if I can allow them to view a simple video. Do you understand?" she asked.

Slowly Vennie nodded.

"Make me a damn copy now!" she said.

Vennie slid from his chair, his tentacles supporting his body and giving him the impression that he floated above the floor. "It is not on the mainframe, Sirena. It will have to be accessed from another location."

"Well, carry on then, get it done!" she said, waving her hands flamboyantly in the air.

Vennie squelched his way from the room, and her personal guard prepared to follow her off the Command Deck as she followed Vennie. "Kitty! Come! We're going to save Uncle Blue Dude!"

Chapter 33

"Sirena, I cannot allow you to leave Command Warship! It is simply not possible!" Zahn insisted, facing off with Vivian at the docking bay.

"I didn't ask you to allow me to go, Zahn. I told you I was going. You can stay here, or you can come with me, but I'm going," Vivian answered.

"Do you have any idea what our Sire will do to me? To us? If I allow you leave this ship?!" Zahn asked.

"You know, at this point, I'd have thought you had just a little more faith in me than to think I'd throw you under the bus," Vivian said.

Zahn was as usual thoroughly confused by her use of Earth slang. "I do not know what a bus is, Sirena, but I do not wish to be under anything. You must understand, we are responsible for your safety. We cannot in good conscience allow you to leave the safety of our warship!" Zahn insisted.

Vivian saw the hydraulic doors slide open, granting someone else access to the docking platform they stood on. She saw a flash of orange and knew who it was without having to look any further. "You do realize the irony in that statement, right? You want me to remain safe on a warship, rather than go to a tribunal taking place on the very home base of the Unified Consortium Defense. The Consortium that maintains peace among all worlds."

"You do not know what is to happen there if Kol is not freed," Zahn insisted.

"Hello, Vor," Vivian said as Vor came to stand next to them. She didn't move her eyes from Zahn's as she spoke. "Yes, Zahn, I do. I know that Quin plans to bring Kol home one way or another. I know that he took half of the Elite Warrior team with him. I know that he took Jhan who is an assassin, I know that he took Ba Re' who is a computer freaking genius as well as an Elite warrior in his own right. I know that they plan to do whatever is necessary to get Kol out — override things, blow things up, generally make everybody do whatever they want things. Which is admirable. But, there's one problem. They are males. And they're going to start a damned war that is not necessary by any means. I am going to ensure his freedom the old fashioned way."

"And what way is that, Sirena?" Vor asked.

"By presenting the facts and letting them see the irrefutable truth that the male he killed was a piece of shit. I'm going to show them the tape that Quin thinks to keep hidden from me because he's afraid it will hurt me. And, you know what? It will hurt me, but it will hurt me a whole hell of a lot more if we lose Blue Dude. Like I told Kail, Rel and Asl, either come with me, or get out of my way."

Vor stood in place only a moment longer before giving her a single nod. "Missy!" Vor barked.

"Yes, Warrior Vor," Missy responded.

"Advise my Ehlealah that I was called away on business and I shall return as soon as I am able."

Vivian smiled as Vor spoke to Missy.

"I shall do so at once, Warrior Vor," Missy answered.

Vor held out his hand. "Come, Sirena. Allow me to escort you to the judicial hearing of the charges brought against Elite Commander and Ambassador Kol Ra' Don Tol."

Vivian grinned at Vor and reached up toward his face until he finally sighed and leaned over for her to be able to reach him. Vivian kissed his cheek. "Thank you, Vor," she said as she grinned at him.

"I suppose we're bringing Kitty, too," Vor asked as he followed the large shraler onto the battle cruiser.

"Of course. I have to make an entrance, you know," Vivian said.

Zahn stood outside the cruiser, looking at Vor who was waiting for him to board the cruiser and take his place among the rest of Vivian's personal guard that had already boarded the vessel.

"I cannot believe you condone this," Zahn said.

"Imagine it was you. Would you not want her to come to your aid? How much do we all at one time or another owe Kol? He has been a great friend to any who need it."

"Our Sire will have us executed," Zahn said.

"No, he won't. She won't allow it, and we will have prevented a war. She's right about that. He will yell a great deal though. Perhaps more than when she forced us to go along with her plan to kill Malm herself," Vor admitted.

Zahn shook his head and rolled his eyes toward the second level of the docking platform. "One day she will calm and our jobs will be easy," he said, taking the step to place him on board with the rest of the team.

"No, she won't," Vor answered.

"I simply want her safe," Zahn answered. "She has suffered so much already."

"I know that you only wish to protect her. But, sometimes it's easier to allow her to fight her battles herself and back her up if need be," Vor said.

"Wait! You cannot leave!" a familiar voice called out.

Zahn shook his head and simply moved further into the battle cruiser. "I am not dealing with him. You do it," Zahn said to Vor.

Vor stepped into the doorway of the open battle cruiser and watched Rokai ahl rush toward them.

"Where's Vivi?" Rokai shouted as he ran across the expansive docking bay of Command Warship 1.

"She is already aboard, Elite Commander Rokai ahl. We cannot be swayed from our journey," Vor answered.

"I do not wish to sway her from her journey, nor you!" Rokai snapped. "Vivi! Vivi, can you hear me?" Rokai called out as he stepped over the threshhold of the hydraulic door and into the already overcrowded battle cruiser.

"Rokai?" Vivian asked, getting up from her seat and moving toward him.

"You cannot go..." Rokai started.

"Do not even start trying to tell me what I can and cannot do. I will pull rank, bud!" Vivian answered, her hand on her hip and her small foot tapping a rhythm on the floor of the cruiser.

Rokai shook his head. "No. I didn't mean to stop you. Just to give you an extra bit of protection," he said, taking off his own golden bracelet and holding it up before him. "This will turn into a blade. Watch," he said, snapping the links of the band into a straight line, then pressing the clasp with his thumb once the links had become rigid.

Vivian's eyes rounded with surprise when a blade popped out of the end where the clasp was. "That's amazing!" she said, reaching out for it.

"Be careful with it, Vivi. The blade is very sharp," Rokai said, shaking the band out until it was once more pliable and fastening it around her wrist.

"Thank you, Rokai. I hope I won't have to use it, but if I do, I'll be very careful and be sure to bring it back to you."

"You are very welcome. Also, here," he said, holding out his disintegrater toward her. "This one is made of a material that will not register on most scans should you be scanned for weapons," Rokai confided.

"Plastic?" she asked, taking the disintegrater from him and testing its weight in her hand.

"I do not know what plastic is, but, it will not show on scans. Take it in the event you may need it and slip it into your pocket. None will detect it, and you will be able to kill many aggressors with it!" Rokai answered, smiling and then hugging her to him. "I've unlocked it so all you need to do is enter your own code into it to make it fireable."

"How do I do that?" Vivi asked.

"I am sure your guards can help you," Rokai answered.

Vivian looked over her shoulder at Vor who nodded to her.

"Excellent!" she said, excitedly.

"Sirena, it is a disintegrater. It will melt away anything it is fired at. People, buildings, cruisers," Rel said warningly.

Vivi glanced at Rokai who nodded his affirmation. "It is my favorite weapon," Rokai confided.

"Umm, maybe I'll let Rel carry it," she said.

"As long as one of you has it, it can be used for your safety," Rokai said, bowing to her. "Safe travels, sister-mine. Bring our warrior home to us."

"I will. Take care of everyone until I get back," Vivian said.

Rokai ahl stepped off the cruiser, then onto the metal scaffolding that led back to the platform Quin favored for welcoming all visitors as they arrived, and watched as the cruiser shot out of Command Warship 1, on its way to deliver a Sirena to a date with destiny that she refused to be left out of.

<<<<<<<>>>>>>>

Quin and his warriors who were actually an attack party incognito arrived at the headquarters of the Unified Consortium Defense, docked, were seated and awaiting the beginning of the trial when they heard the announcement of the arrival of a second party representing the Cruestaci.

Jhan leaned over to Quin and whispered to him. "Are your parents coming?"

Quin glanced at Jhan and gave a sharp shake of his head.

"Well, then who the hells?" Jhan asked at the same time the doors opened at the back of courtroom. A small, dark-haired human female, dressed in her signature white jeans and green silk shirt, her velvet green cloak and royal jewels, warrior boots, chain and dagger all properly in place, strutted through with a full grown eight hundred pound shraler on a chain padding along patiently beside her. Her personal guard in full battle gear surrounded and escorted her to the front of the courtroom where Quin and his party already sat as the courtroom was filled with murmurs and all watched Vivian with something of a bit of awe in their eyes. It was one thing to hear tell of the Cruestaci's Warrior Sirena and her shraler; it was quite another to witness it first hand.

Quin closed his eyes and ground his jaw as he prayed for calm.

He heard Ba Re' snort a chuckle to his right and gave him a warning look.

The Cruestaci people had been allowed the first five rows on the right side of the courtroom. Quin and his males took up three of them.

Vivian and her guards walked all the way to the front of the courtroom. When she came to a stop in front of Quin, he glared at her and stood to greet her formally. He leaned over kissing her lips as his males stood and began to rearrange themselves to allow Vivian's guard to blend in with Quin's guard and remain closer to her. The rest of thc Elite Warriors and the few males that overflowed the other rows moved back until they were comfortably filling all five rows alloted them.

"I thought you promised to stay home," Quin growled in Vivian's ear as he hugged her to him.

"I had my fingers crossed," she answered. "You were doing this wrong, so I had to come."

"Vivi..." he said, starting a warning.

The judiciary board chose that moment to call the trial to order, so Vivian took her seat beside Quin. "Sit, Kitty," she said softly and Kitty dutifully took his seat at her feet.

"Vivi," Quin leaned over to her and whispered.

"I know, Quin. I know all you have planned. It's not necessary," she answered, finally turning to look at him. She kissed him lightly on the lips then smiled sadly at him. "You greatly underestimate me, my love."

Quin's brow furrowed when she told him he underestimated her. "I do not!" he objected.

"Shh! They're starting," she said, patting his hand with hers before squeezing his fingers beneath hers and catching her breath when they finally showed Kol in.

Kol's eyes roved the courtroom, landing on all his people filling a large percentage of the available seats. He smiled when he saw Vivian sitting there with Kitty at her feet, and met Quin's eyes with a knowing look after he took a moment to realize which males he'd brought with him. His escort indicated a raised dais he was to sit on and opened the small swinging door for him to walk through. Kol stepped up and onto the dais before taking his seat and watching as Chairman Bartholomew, the most powerful man associated with the Consortium, exited his private chamber off the side of the courtroom and joined Kol on the dais.

The courtroom was filled with a soft rumble as all those familiar with the proceedings realized what this meant. Bart would be defending the accused.

Bart stepped up and raised his voice so that all present could hear him. "I am Chairman Bartholomew of the Unified Consortium Defense. I've recused myself from judgment this day of the charges brought against Elite Commander Kol Ra' Don Tol. Instead I have elected to defend him against the charges lodged against him. He will be judged by a judiciary panel in my stead."

One of the members of the panel called for order as Bart took his seat and began speaking with Kol. Kol nodded in response to Bart's whispered words, then raised his eyes to Vivian's.

Vivian smiled at him. She didn't know if he realized what she was about to do, or if he was even aware of the video she'd brought with her, but on the off chance he was aware of it, she was letting him know that she was there for that reason only. If it was necessary, she'd show it to the world to be sure that Kol was free. He was in her heart, her brother. These people were all her family, and she'd be damned if anybody was going to take one of them away from her. She was now in a position to prevent any of those she loved from being taken, and she'd do whatever was necessary to that end.

Chapter 34

After what seemed like only a very short presentation by the prosecuting side, the defense took over. They presented their findings on the occurrence itself — that Kol reacted as any male would have had his mate been in immediate danger.

But no matter how hard they argued the facts, Diskastes's people insisted he overreacted and that he could have simply disarmed the male and taken him into custody. Particularly effective was Diskastes's mother who sat in the front row on the left side of the courtroom sobbing continuously.

Kol even gave his version of that day. Explaining that Diskastes was crazed, insisting that they'd all die. But even that was met with disregard.

When it became apparent that there would be no easy ending to this trial, both sides holding fast to their points of view, Bart began presenting the evidence of Diskastes having been involved in the questionable activities at the base. He methodically laid out each and every charge: theft, embezzling, failure to provide for and protect those in his quadrant, maleficence in office, and then calmly faced the prosecution's bench and waited for them to reply.

There was much sputtering and denial of the charges by all three legal counsel hired by the Quisles people to try to convict Kol to win justice for their son as they saw it.

Bart calmly rose and spoke to several males who were standing just to the side of the Judicial Panel's bench where it sat facing the rest of the courtroom and raised a little higher as was the dais he and Kol sat upon. "Please provide the support documentation to the prosecution," Bart said with all professional manner.

After a short perusal the lead prosecutor rose to his feet and shouted at Bart and the rest of the courtroom. "All of the supposed offenses by Consul Diskastes were non-violent! They are non-threatening. And while we are still not fully convinced, these documents do seem to indicate they are valid. Nevertheless, he has always been a non-violent, loving child of the nobility of Quisles. The death he suffered is inexcusable!"

Bart merely smiled. "In addition, we are charging him post-mortem with activities including, yet not limited to, the kidnapping and selling of young females and males of the sector of Earth Base 28, into the multi-verse slave trade."

The court room erupted and there was shouting from all sides. Eventually the judicial panel gave up trying to regain control of the courtroom which left Bart having to do it. He bellowed as best he could, slamming his own chair down on the floor to get everyone's attention. "Though I am acting as legal defense on this particular case, do not for one moment forget who I am or my stature here! You will control yourselves, or I will have each and every one of you removed from these proceedings and this facility. Am I clear?!" he shouted.

A hush fell over the courtroom after which the lead prosecutor respectfully rose to his feet. "Chairman Bartholomew, these allegations are outrageous, and against a deceased individual who has suffered a senseless death, no less a violently imparted one. You cannot expect his poor mother and father to sit here and witness his name to be sullied in such a way without absolute proof."

Bart again indicated that the support males should once again provide the information gathered. "As you will see," he said as every word he said was displayed on the holovid at the front of the courtroom, "all evidence and inquiries support the facts that young females and males have routinely disappeared from the sector surrounding Base 28. Many of them after accepting employ at the base itself. The numbers far surmount those of surrounding territories. In fact, it's known among the people of this sector to avoid the base at all costs lest your children disappear shortly thereafter."

The lead prosecutor rose to his feet again. "Though a tragic occurrence, this does not prove that Consul Diskastes was involved in any way. Without concrete, irrefutable proof, we must insist that Elite Commander Kol Ra' Don Tol be found guilty and remanded to the custody of the military of Quisles to serve out his full life term in our penal system as punishment for taking the life of Consul Diskastes, Third Prince of Quisles!"

"This is the proof. The proof that we have provided is an example of the character of the male, and supports very clearly why Elite Commander Kol Ra' Don Tol was concerned for the life of his mate and reacted as he did. The tape clearly shows Consul Diskastes took two females into hostage and attempted to assume control of a civilian transport, which then had to flee in order to escape capture. It clearly shows one female being forced to fire on Diskastes in order to free herself. Elite Commander Kol Ra' Don Tol has testified that he clearly stated they would all die and insisted the Elite Commander give himself in exchange for the female. You can see for yourselves the battle was over. It clearly shows that Elite Commander Kol Ra' Don Tol was concerned for his mate and was checking her for injury. It clearly shows that Consul Diskastes, despite being injured, raised his weapon in preparation of firing on a female who was no longer a threat to him."

"All we see is that Consul Diskastes, Third Prince of Quisles, was afraid for his life and attempted to flee. We plan to press charges against the pilot of the transport as well for abandoning a royal noble in a time of need as soon as he is identified! Consul Diskastes, Third Prince of Quisles was not a danger to any! He was simply preparing to defend himself as he lay injured on the ground where he was subsequently attacked and literally torn to pieces!" the prosecutor shouted back. "Unless you have direct evidence that cannot be disputed, we demand Elite Commander Kol Ra' Don Tol be remanded to our custody without further delay!"

"The pilot you wish to bring charges against has been identified and accounted for. He is a doctor stationed at the repatriation base in Washington, D.C. He'd very kindly offered to take one of the females Diskastes took as hostage to visit with her mate. On seeing the armed security forces approached him with weapons drawn, he feared for his life and left the area. That in itself is additional proof that Diskastes was not simply protecting himself, he was the aggressor!" Bart answered.

"Still, there is no proof of his involvement in these vile charges you bring today. I demand they be stricken from the record, and Elite Commander Kol Ra Don Tol be remanded to our custody at once due to the lack of proof of your attempt to lead these proceedings astray!"

"I have proof," a female voice said shakily in the courtroom.

All eyes turned to Sirena Vivian Tel Mo' Kok.

Her mate, Sire Zha Quin Tha Tel Mo' Kok, reached for her hand. "Vivi," he rushed out, suspecting what she planned to do.

Vivian squeezed his hand in hers, then proudly she met all the eyes watching her, then she repeated herself. "I have proof. And it's irrefutable."

"Please introduce yourself for the accuracy of our records," the governing Judicial Panel speaker requested.

"My name is Sirena Vivian Tel Mo' Kok. I am Ehlealah and Mate to Zha Quin Tha Tel Mo' Kok, Sire to the Cruestaci people. I was abducted from Earth in the year 2041 and sold into sexual slavery. I was freed by my mate and his forces. While still being held captive, Diskastes is one of many who abused me horribly."

"You can't possibly prove this! You are simply making an effort to save one of your people!" Diskastes's mother shouted through her nearly hysterical tears.

Vivian smiled sadly at the woman, knowing she was simply reacting to the recent loss of her son. "I am indeed making an effort to save one of my people. But, I can without a doubt prove his actions." Vivian reached into the pocket of the cloak she wore and withdrew a golden shimmering disk. "Vor, if you would be so kind," she said without looking away from the woman.

Vor was immediately at her side, taking the disk from her and moving toward the Judicial Panel.

"This is a copy of a recording that my people found aboard the ship they freed me from. My mate is concerned for my welfare — he watched me struggle to even become half the female I am now. He made a decision to keep this recording private, allowing no one to see it in an effort to protect me from the pain I suffered.

I have been told that our technology is always running in the background of any visual communication we send, receive, or observe, as is the technology of most every world represented here today. It serves many purposes for each of us, but after this recording was located, another was added to our own programming. It's searching faces. It's been programmed to search for any face seen on this recording. On matching any face to those on the recording, our Sire, my mate, is notified. This is exactly what happened the day that Elite Commander Kol Ra' Don Tol encountered an unstable Consul attempting to flee his impending incarceration.

Diskastes was identified through facial recognition as one of those that brutally attacked me. Not just once, but several times. He had to have made the effort to return to assault me over and over again, which shows an understanding of the situation, and a conscious decision on his part to become involved. Further, the fact that he was acquainted with, and apparently extremely comfortable with those that held me and offered me for sale, indicates that he was involved in the slave trade of abducted individuals. Kol had been advised only shortly before they finally tracked him down, and he knew how dangerous this male was — how violent he was. He acted accordingly to protect his mate."

"This is ludicrous!" the prosecutor shouted.

Vivian shrugged one dainty shoulder. "See for yourself." Then she sat beside her mate again, and Quin immediately took her face in his large hands, forcing her to look at him.

"Vivi, you do not have to do this. It is too much. There is another way," he insisted, worry clear on his face.

Vivian kissed his palm, then gently pulled his hands from her face. "There is no other way. I won't allow them to take Kol. And I won't allow them to glorify the life of the male that did this."

"And I won't have you relive that horror," Quin said, his voice growly. "It could..."

"I will finally use that horror for good," Vivian assured him, interrupting him. "I'll be okay. In fact, I want the recording sent to all governments so that they can search their own data bases for facial recognition of their own people, then I want all of them to be outed. I want them all named publicly and shamed. I want them all to have to answer for what they did to me, for what they're likely still doing to others not so lucky as I am."

Quin pressed his lips to her forehead.

"It will be okay, Quin. Kol will come home, and we'll get help finding all the others on the recording."

"How much did you watch?" Quin asked.

"Only the part with Diskastes. It's hours long. I didn't have the heart for the rest. I lived it. I know what it shows," she said. "It will not own me, it will no longer affect my life. It will help me to free my friend, my family."

The speaker representing the judicial panel raised his voice once more. "We have the recording ready for viewing. If you'll direct your attention to the holovid located at the front of the courtroom..."

The recording started with a nude Vivian leaning against the wall in that dark, dank room that Quin never wanted to witness again. A small group of males could be seen entering from the other side of that room. Vivian pushed off the wall and limped toward the middle of the room, gathering her chain in her hand as she went. She went to the middle of the room and waited with her chain in her hand. The males made a game of it, taunting her from each side as she fought them, catching one or two unsuspecting and leaving marks on them with her chain. They even allowed her to 'escape' from them before lifting the chain near where it was connected in the center of the room and pulling her back to them as she fought it, kicking and screaming.

Then the real assault started. Quin turned his attention to those in the courtroom witnessing the video for the first time. The females who were in attendance cried out and covered their mouths and faces. Most of the males were shocked and appalled. Those of the Cruestaci warriors that had not seen it, who were not there the day she was rescued, began to rumble and growl.

Quin had to order calm and control of his males to be sure their Psi's didn't emerge. And through it all Vivian sat staring straight ahead with a single silent tear tracking down her face.

Kitty rose from his place on the floor and started nudging her with his huge head. Vivian patted him, but never once changed her position or her view. She stared straight ahead with Quin's arms around her until finally the Judicial Panel ruled it enough.

"It is our finding that Consul Diskastes is clearly identified on this recording. In light of the atrocities he subjected Vivian Tel Mo' Kok, Sirena of Cruestace to, the actions of Elite Warrior Kol Ra' Don Tol were more than warranted. What say you, prosecution?" The speaker of the Judicial Panel asked with vehemence in his voice.

Diskastes's mother sat almost catatonic watching the spot on the holovid where the tape had been played back. Diskastes's father rose from his seat and approached the Cruestaci delegation. As one, Zha Quin and all the warriors rose to their feet in a show of intent to kill anything that approached their Sirena.

He bowed to Vivian and was very humble when finally he spoke. "I offer my deepest apologies for the suffering you've endured at the hands of my son. There is no excuse for it. His name will be removed from all records and histories of the people of Quisles. No proof of his existence will ever exist. It will in no way make reparation for the pain you've suffered, but it will hopefully bring you some sense of closure that he will never be revered by our people."

Vivian didn't speak, she simply watched the male struggling with his emotions. "I was aware that he was never the kind of male he was raised to be, but I had no idea of the depths of depravity he had sunk to. Had I known, I would have taken his life myself. I owe you a debt that I can never repay, Sirena Tel Mo' Kok." He bowed again and returned to his place in the courtroom, though he didn't sit. He faced the Judicial Panel. "I formally withdraw all charges against this male. He acted with justified force and honor in the killing of Consul Diskastes. Please let the record show that Diskastes is no longer a prince of Quisles."

Vivian closed her eyes and smiled weakly.

"Vivi? Ehlealah" Quin said, worriedly at her side.

"I'm okay," she answered, with her eyes still closed.

"What can I do?" Quin asked.

"You can find out how long before we can take Kol home," she answered, finally opening her eyes to look at her mate.

"I am so proud of you, my Vivi," Quin said, caressing her face.

Vivian covered his hand with her own. She took a deep breath. "Better than starting a war, yes?" she asked, smiling at him.

"I am not so sure," Quin answered.

"A lot less fun," Jhan added from Quin's right.

Most everyone had already vacated the courtroom, or was in the process of leaving the courtroom, when Bart finally allowed Kol to reunite with Quin, Vivi and the rest of the warriors.

Kol strode toward them and caught Vivian up in his arms. "You didn't have to do that," he said, holding her tightly.

"Of course I did. I couldn't let the universe take anything else from me if I had the power to fight it. And, turns out, I had the power," she said smiling. "I'm pretty badass," she said, playing off the emotion that viewing the recording had brought forth in her.

"That has never been a question," Kol answered, finally releasing her. Quin pulled him in for a hug, as did all of the Cruestaci there. Even Kitty stood on his back legs to slap a huge front paw on either side of Kol's head and licked his face. Kol laughed and scratched Kitty's head. "I even missed you," he said.

Then he looked at all those who came to support him. "You will never understand the relief I felt when I saw you all here. Then I panicked when I realized you meant to break me out if I did not win!" Kol said, chuckling.

Bart shook his head. "I was thinking the same thing, right after I figured out what to get behind so I didn't get caught in the crossfire."

"Ba Re'! What news have you of Elisha? Is she well?" Kol asked.

"She is aboard Command Warship 1, training for a position among our diplomatic liaisons," Ba Re' said proudly.

"Mated?" Kol asked.

Ba Re's expression turned sour. "Not yet," he answered.

Kol chuckled.

Quin spoke to Bart while Kol visited with his warriors and his cousins. "When will he be released?" Quin asked.

"It will take a little time to finalize the paperwork, but he will not be returned to a cell. He'll be provided with a suite and access to communications and information from the outside world.

"I shall send a cruiser for him when he is released," Quin said.

"I'm not sure that's going to work," Bart answered.

"Why not? He has been exonerated," Quin said.

"Yes, he has. But I don't think he wants to return to Command Warship 1. I think he wants to go back home," Bart explained.

"Kol?" Vivian said. "Are you coming back to us when you're released?"

Kol shook his head slowly. "No, Vivi. I'm going home to my Ehlealah. I'll be there for a while. Maybe we'll decide to return to Command Warship 1, or even to Cruestace one day, but for now, we will call Earth home."

"What will you do for a living?" Vivian asked.

"I will continue to pay him," Quin said firmly.

"Won't be necessary. I'm planning to have him reinstated as Ambassador, then submit his name for consideration as Consul of Earth Base 28. He helped uncover the illegal activities there, he helped rebuild it. I can think of none better suited to lead and oversee the base and the people in its sector," Bart said.

Kol was smiling at Bart with a surprised look on his face.

"If that's acceptable to you, that is," Bart added.

"I would be very happy with that," Kol answered.

"You will still be representative of our people, Kol. You will receive a salary from us as well," Quin promised. "Though it will not be the same without you."

"I will speak with you all often," Kol promised. "If I get the commission," he said, looking toward Bart.

"I've already drawn up the submission of your name. I simply have to submit it," Bart said.

"You were very sure of yourself," Kol teased.

"I knew I'd never stop fighting for you. I just didn't know we had Vivian coming to our rescue," Bart said, hugging her to him.

"I would have freed him regardless," Quin insisted.

"Yes, but we'd all be at war now," Bart said.

Quin grinned. "Whatever it takes."

"I need to com my Ehlealah. I need to give her the good news," Kol said excitedly.

"Prepare yourself, Kol. It's been longer than it seems — almost six Earth months since you last saw her," Bart said.

"She will be waiting for me," Kol said confidently.

Epilogue

A luxury transport, clearly marked with the official seal of the Unified Consortium Defense, hovered in place just outside the docking bay of Earth Base 28. It was so large it would have to settle for a docking pad rather than the docking bay itself.

Once anchored in place, the exit walk was lowered from the huge luxury liner to the ground below. Several males dressed in the uniforms of the Unified Consortium Defense Military Unit exited the ship and took up their positions as security outside the ship. Then a smaller group of four guards led the way, followed by Chairman Bartholomew, and Consul Kol Ra' Don Tol, followed by four more guards.

With their first step onto the aluminum walkway, having been alerted by the dock workers, personnel began to exit Base 28 and move toward them. As Kol stepped out of the transport and into the sunshine, he heard his name being called and looked up to find Kron, Buchanan, and Zhuxi all clapping and smiling, hurrying along with others assigned to the base to greet him and welcome him home.

Bart chuckled when he saw the exuberance with which Kol was greeted. "Do not even attempt to keep his friends from welcoming him. It'll be a lost cause," Bart said to the guards around them, that were more pomp and circumstance than actually there to keep anyone away from them.

A grinning Kol stepped into Kron's embrace first. "Welcome home, Commander!" Kron said happily, hugging Kol then slapping him on the back.

"Consul Kol Ra' Don Tol… It's quite an elegant sounding name, don't you think?" Zhuxi asked, bowing deeply to Kol before mimicking Kron's behavior and patting his shoulder.

"Boy!" Buchanan shouted, striding right up to Kol, "You better give me a hug! None of that shy stuff!" he said. Buchanan embraced Kol. "Mighty happy to have you back, Kol. We're honored to serve under your command and look forward to it."

"I'm happy to be back," Kol said, full of smiles himself. He shook hands and hugged more than a few of the additional base personnel who were very happy to have him back.

"Come inside," Kron encouraged. "We have expanded the open offices and have quite a large meeting table in the center of the room that we will all be quite comfortable around. Bart, Kol, can we get you anything?" Kron asked as the acting Base 28 Consul.

"No, thank you," Kol answered.

"Thank you, but I'm okay for now," Bart answered.

"As you probably know, we've finished the rebuild and have several of the programs in place that you suggested before you left," Kron said, ready to make a final report to Kol.

"I'm sure it's all exemplary," Kol responded, smiling at Kron.

"You will be proud," Kron confirmed.

"We're the envy of all the bases we deal with regularly. They're starting to implement the same plans we have. Especially the food programs to all living in their sector. The preventative medical care as opposed to just when necessary. They're even looking into starting up farming programs like we are."

"Are the people receptive to that one? I didn't get a chance to see it at its inception," Kol said.

"Very. We supply the seeds and/or seedlings, they plant and harvest. They keep what they need to replant and to feed their own, then we host a farmers' market twice each month where they can trade, or sell the harvest they don't need. We supply animals when needed as well — cows, chickens, horses, pigs, any type of farm animal they may need. Every other farmers' market is more of an artisan's day. They sell butters and cheeses, and baked goods, cured meats, and eggs. We've even had a few of our citizens ask if they can sell hand made dishes and pots and pans and the like. It's very, very successful," Kron explained excitedly.

"Sounds like Base 28 may just become the model for all the rest," Bart said.

"We've all shared the responsibilities equally, so it's a group effort," Kron answered.

"Speaking of a group effort, I'm hoping to live at home, and commute each morning and evening. I was speaking with Bart and we decided that it would be best for me to have a counterpart to be here when I'm not. And, reciprocally, when I'm here, he wouldn't have to be," Kol said, a slight smile on his face while he looked at Kron as he spoke. "I know you came to assist me, and stayed on after when needed. I'm not sure how anxious you are to go home and would certainly understand if you'd prefer to return to Command Warship 1, but I would like to offer you the position as my second if you..."

"Yes!" Kron said, grinning that goofy grin of his that allowed the tips of his fangs to show through.

"You didn't let me finish," Kol said, chuckling.

"You do not have to say more. I've grown attached to the people here. Made lifelong friends that I would miss if I were to leave. Like you, I don't have to worry about the Elite Forces as Rokai ahl is covering that for us and from what I understand, adjusting very well. I'd like to stay here and be second to your position," Kron said.

"All in favor?" Kol asked.

"Here, here!" Buchanan said happily.

"I am very much in favor," Zhuxi said.

"Then it's done," Kol announced.

"Tell me, Kol. Is it as we heard? Sirena Vivi attended your trial and is the reason all charges were dropped?" Kron asked.

"It was exactly as you heard. She didn't hesitate at all. Zha Quin, on the other hand, arrived with Ba Re', Jhan, his own personal guard and half the Elite team. He planned to bring me home one way or the other," Kol said laughing.

Kron got a good laugh out of it, too. Then he became somber for a moment. "I am very happy that you're here with us again."

"As am I," Kol answered.

"It is a good day for us all that you have returned," Zhuxi said.

"Damn good day," Buchanan added.

"So, what do you want to do first?" Buchanan asked. "Surely you need a few days to get yourself settled."

"I do, if our schedule allows it. I have not yet been home," Kol said.

"You haven't seen Ada Jane yet?" Kron asked.

"Not yet. I've spoken to her via vidcom a few times, but she's located some distance from Missy's base of communication for her, which is my cruiser. It's still at the church. She is not always able to get a good reception."

"Well, go. Go see to your woman. You have a lot to catch up on. We'll be here when you're settled and ready to come back to work," Buchanan said.

The swinging doors to the office area opened, and a beautiful, young woman with light, strawberry-blonde hair entered.

"Hi, Daddy!" she said and walked right past them all to go to her Daddy's desk and pull out her laptop.

"Hey, baby," Buchanan answered before introducing them. "Kol, this is my daughter, Ginger. I didn't allow her up here before for obvious reasons, but now, she comes by quite often."

Buchanan looked over at Ginger. "Ginger, this is Consul Kol Ra' Don Tol. Just got back a little bit ago and he'll be resuming overseeing our base."

"It's very nice to meet you," Ginger said, walking over and extending her hand.

"I am pleased to meet you as well. I often wondered if any of you have families nearby," Kol said.

"Most of us do, just didn't want to bring attention to them with the element we had inhabiting the base before," Zhuxi said.

"Is your family near as well?" Kol asked.

"It is just myself and my female. We have not been blessed with children at this time. But, we are hopeful," Zhuxi answered.

"I will offer a prayer to our gods on your behalf," Kol offered.

"Kol, if you want me to drop you at your property, it's not an inconvenience, but I'm leaving shortly," Bart said. "I have to be in D.C. in three hours."

"Thank you, Bart. I will accept your offer of a ride. I am anxious to see my Ada Jane."

"We've been checking in on her regularly," Buchanan said. "Helped get her all settled in your new place over there."

"Yes, we often visit with her, do we not?" Zhuxi said, shoving Kron's shoulder with his own.

Kron had been lost in staring at Buchanan's daughter, and Buchanan's daughter was well aware of it, as she crossed and uncrossed her legs and toyed with a strand of her hair while peeking at him through her lashes.

Kol smiled. Now he fully understood why Kron had jumped at the chance to stay on Earth with him. Kron had his sights on this human female.

"Hmm? What?" Kron asked, looking around the large conference table they all relaxed around.

"Ada Jane," Buchanan said.

"Oh, yes, she's well, you'll find her much changed. Tells me to go away almost every time I visit," Kron said, glancing at Ginger and getting lost in her dimpled smile and the crinkle of her nose and its sprinkling of freckles again.

"Changed?" Kol said, immediately seizing on that one word.

Zhuxi and Buchanan shared a look before Buchanan returned his attention to Kol. He shook his head slowly, more like the bobble of a bobble head toy. "Yes, well. You could say that. She's definitely..."

"Changed," Zhuxi supplied.

"Yeah, changed," Buchanan finished.

"Is she well?" Kol asked, now alarmed for the welfare of his Ehlealah.

"Most days," Buchanan answered.

"Why wasn't I informed that she is ill," Kol demanded, getting to his feet.

"I wouldn't call it ill," Buchanan said.

"Ada Jane swore us to secrecy," Zhuxi explained. "She did not want you worrying about her when you had so much on your shoulders already. But I have no doubt she'll be fine now that you're home."

"Can you take me to her now?" Kol asked Bart.

"I can. But I think it's best if you get your cruiser first, then take yourself to her. That way you can take yourself anywhere you need to be," Bart answered.

"Very well, but please, let us go now," Kol begged.

<<<<<<<>>>>>>>>

Ada Jane sat on the old, antique tractor Buchanan had helped her buy. When she'd first told him she wanted one to start her own planting with, it had only been a week before he'd found one for her. He'd even had it delivered to her after she'd bought it, so she hadn't had to leave her property at all.

She got to the end of the field she was preparing for planting and made the circle turn to come back up next to the row she'd just finished. She laughed at her new babies — two very large, very clumsy, but very protective black and white spotted Great Dane pups. Well, pups was probably pushing it, they were full grown, brothers, each two years old, adopted from a friend of Pastor Douglas's who just didn't have the room for such large animals to run as they needed. They were currently playing tug-a-war with an old length of rope she'd tied knots in both ends for them.

Ada Jane looked out over the field she was plowing, and up the slight rise her home sat atop of. She sighed as she wiped the sweat from her face and the back of her neck. It was hot, and she was tired now. Exhausted all the time. Her heart began to tug a little at her when she thought of Kol, and she blinked back tears. Though it had been six months that he'd been gone, the separation never, ever got easier.

At least now she knew that he'd been found innocent, and it would only be a matter of time before he was able to come home to her. Or her to him. She looked out at the land again and thought about it. She loved her land, and her roots here. But if Kol wasn't allowed to come back to Earth, she'd go to him. One of her dogs yelped and took out after the other who'd won the tug-a-war and run off with the rope toy in his mouth.

She smiled watching them. They'd have to come with her though. She was not going to leave her babies behind. Then she became wary. As she watched her dogs playing at the other end of the field now, she saw them both drop the rope and stand together, facing the rise the house stood on. She watched them both go on alert, and they started barking.

Ada Jane reached into her pocket and wrapped her fingers around the weapon she still carried with her every single day. She let her foot off the brake of the tractor and shifted it into gear, driving it toward where her dogs stood together, barking a warning at whoever the male was that had just appeared, walking up and over the rise near her house. "Don't make me have to kill you," she muttered, more irritated than worried. She couldn't quite make out his form with the sun in her eyes, but she could tell enough to know exactly where to aim her disintegrater.

Kol landed his cruiser behind the house Ada Jane had placed on her newly acquired property. He knew from reports he'd received from Bart, and from speaking to Ada Jane in the last couple of weeks since being found innocent that she'd moved the cottage from the church and had it placed on her land. She'd told him that she'd also expanded it to add two more bedrooms and another bathing room as well. As he hurried up the ridge the house sat on, he admired the new shape of the cottage. His friends had done an excellent job in helping Ada Jane get settled on her land again.

Kol had knocked on the back door he found at the rear of the house and opened the door, calling out her name, but she hadn't answered. Then he'd noticed the loud sound of an engine coming from the other side of the house. He walked over the rise past the house and that's where he stood now, watching an old green tractor make its way toward him across a field that had been halfway prepared for planting.

Two very large, very loud dogs stood between him and tractor that was approaching, warning him away from whoever was driving the tractor. Kol whistled and knelt down on the ground, one knee actually on the ground, balancing him. "Come here, beasts," he said in the same tone he used with Kitty. "I will not hurt you," he promised.

First one dog approached, but was followed very closely by the second. "Hello," Kol said, holding his hand out for sniffing. The first dog sniffed his hand then immediately licked him and began wagging its tail as though it knew him. The second dog followed suit, licking his hand, then his face as they danced excited circles around him wagging their tails. Kol laughed, petted both dogs and got to his feet. "You are not very good protectors, beasts," he told them as he focused on the tractor that was just coming to a stop down at the edge of the field below the house he was standing in front of.

Then his stomach flipped, happy butterflies making him nervous with anticipation as the person driving the tractor removed her hat and all her long, blonde hair fell out.

The sun was coming from above and behind the house, shining directly in Ada Jane's eyes and making it difficult for her to make out more than a shape as the male stood near her home and watched her coming toward him. She wasn't worried, though, she had her weapon in hand.

Ada Jane squinted as she watched as whoever was standing close to her home kneel down and pet her dogs like they knew them. And didn't that just make her mad? They should not let anyone pet them, and were usually very protective of her and their territory. Her breath caught. Unless... She'd taught them Kol's scent. They slept with one of his shirts and she'd intentionally associated them with anything she had that had ever been his so that they'd not be threatened by him when they met him. Could it be Kol?

Ada Jane drove the tractor all the way up to the edge of the field, not caring that she'd just messed up the rows she'd made — she'd just fix them later. She turned off the tractor, removed her large sun hat from her head, allowing her hair to flow free, and slid from the seat of the tractor at the same time the male on the rise started toward her. He was coming at a jog at first, then finally at a full out run as she started toward him as well.

Kol was home. That was all that ran through her brain… Kol was home.

As he approached, Kol called her name.

"Kol!" she answered, sobbing and doing her best to get to him without falling. That was the worst thing about being as big as she was now, the clumsiness.

"Ada Jane!" he shouted as he got closer and closer, then when he was about eight feet away, he stopped in his tracks and just looked at her, wide-eyed.

"Kol!" she cried again, still moving toward him.

Finally his brain kicked in and he was suddenly beside her, taking her in his arms, kissing her so passionately that had anyone else been around, they'd have been embarrassed to watch. After kissing her and crying and laughing and assuring one another that they were both actually together again, Kol finally pulled his face away from hers to look down at her. "I missed you so much, my Ada Jane!" he said emphatically.

"I missed you, too! I'm so happy you're here! So happy!" she said again, hugging him as he pulled her into his arms again.

"But, Ehlealah," he said, dropping to his knees, "why didn't you tell me?" he asked, his face smiling, his eyes reflecting the joy and love he felt as he placed his hand on her huge, round belly.

"I didn't want you to worry," she answered, covering his hand with hers.

"They told me you were much changed," he said. "I feared you were ill. I never expected a youngling," he said as he reverently caressed her distended abdomen.

"I'm not sure, but, I think it's two younglings in there," Ada Jane said, laughing.

"Two?!" Kol said on a shout.

"Yes. Two. The doctor at the base says he hears two heartbeats," Ada Jane said, smiling down at Kol.

Kol looked up at his mate, then back down at her belly as he placed his other hand beside the first. "I will be a father," he said, looking up at her.

"You are a father," Ada Jane corrected.

Both the dogs bounded over to them, attacking them with kisses and wagging tails.

"What are these?" he asked, getting to his feet and laughing as they continued trying to get his and Ada Jane's attention.

"They are our furbabies. Billy and Bob," Ada Jane said smiling, while wiping the happy tears that had stained her cheeks.

"Which is which," Kol asked, smiling.

"Billy has two black ears, Bob has one black and one white ear. But if you just say, "Come on, Billy Bob!" They both come."

"They are not much protection," Kol said, pulling his mate to him and hugging her to his chest again as he ran his hands over her head and back, simply touching her and burying his nose in her hair, inhaling her scent.

"They sleep with your shirt and I've made sure they know your scent," she said, holding him back closing her eyes as she pressed her face to his chest.

"Ah, that explains it," he conceded.

"Ada Jane?" he asked.

"Yes," she answered, still holding him as tightly as he held her.

"I need you," he said.

Ada loosened her arms from around his waist and leaned back to look at him, a slight smile on her face.

"Is it okay?" he asked.

"What do you mean?" she asked him, completely confused. "Of course it's okay. I am yours, just like I always was," she answered.

"And I am yours," Kol answered, pressing his lips to hers again. "But, I meant with the younglings..."

"Oh!"

"I know nothing of a female when she carries younglings," he admitted.

Ada Jane smiled up at Kol as she cupped his jaw in her hand. "It's perfectly safe," she promised.

A fire filled Kol's eyes and he swept her up into his arms. "Kol!" she shouted. "I'm huge! You'll hurt yourself!"

"You are beautiful, and you weigh nothing at all," he responded.

"You're carrying three of us, now!" she said, laughingly.

"My world, every one of you, necessary to my very existence," he said as he strode confidently toward their home.

"I probably need a bath first. I've been outside sweating," she said.

Kol laughed and dropped a kiss on her forehead as he carried her through their front door. "Then I shall bathe you first, then I'm going to worship every inch of you for at least the next week. When we can no longer move, we will rest, then begin all over again."

"I'm so happy you're home, Kol," Ada Jane whispered, laying her head on his shoulder as he walked.

"I cannot ever leave you again, my Ada Jane. It almost killed me. I will never accept being apart from you again," he promised.

"Me, too. Many nights I wondered if I'd survive. I thought this land was all I needed to finally be home again. I was wrong, Kol. You. All I needed to be home was you. You are my home."

Kol placed her on her feet in their bathroom and looked down into her eyes. "You are my life, Ada Jane. All I will ever need is right here. I am home because of you, too. I love you, my Ehlealah."

"I love you, too, Kol. Welcome home, my love."

The end, for now.

From The Author

Thank you for purchasing this book. I hope that my stories make you smile and give you a small escape from the daily same ole/same ole. I write for me, simply for the joy of it, but if someone else also smiles as a result, even better. Your support is greatly appreciated. If you liked this story, please remember to leave a review wherever you bought it, so that more people can find my books. Each review is important, no matter how short or long it may be.

See you in the pages of the next one!

Sandra R Neeley

Other books by this author:

Avaleigh's Boys series

I'm Not A Dragon's Mate!, Book 1

Bane's Heart, Book 2

Kaid's Queen, Book 3

Maverik's Ashes, Book 4

Bam's Ever, Book 5

Vince's Place, Book 6

Whispers From the Bayou series

Carnage, Book 1

Destroy, Book 2

Enthrall, Book 3

Lore, Book 4

Murder, Book 5

Haven series

Haven 1: Ascend

Haven 2: Redemption

Riley's Pride

Riley's Pride, Book 1

Richie's Promise, Book 2

Standalone Novels

WINGS

Short Stories and Novella's

CAT

Only Fools Walk Free

Safe On Base: A Howls Romance

About the Author

My name is Sandra R Neeley. I write Paranormal, SciFi, and Fantasy Romances. Why, you may ask? Because normal is highly overrated. I'm 56, I have two kids, one 34 and one 14(yes, God does have a sense of humor), one grandchild, one husband and a menagerie of animals. I love to cook, and was a voracious reader, though since I started writing, I don't get as much time to read as I once did. I'm a homebody and prefer my writing/reading time to a crowd. I have had stories and fictional characters wandering around in my head for as long as I can remember. I'm a self-published author and I like it that way because I can decide what and when to write. I tend to follow my muse — the louder the voice, the greater the chance that voice's story is next.

I am by no means a formal, polished, properly structured individual and neither are my stories. But people seem to love the easy emotion and passion that flow from them. A bit of a warning though, there are some "triggers" in them that certain people should avoid. I'm a firm believer that you cannot have light without the dark. You cannot fully embrace the joy and elation that my people eventually find if you do not bear witness to their darkest hours as well. So please read the warnings supplied with each of the synopsis about my books before you buy them. I've got four series published at this time, Avaleigh's Boys - PNR, Whispers From the Bayou - Fantasy PNR, Haven - SciFi Romance, and Riley's Pride - PNR, a couple of standalone novels, several short stories, and much, much more to come. I'm always glad to hear from my readers, so feel free to look me up and say hello.

You can find me at any of these places:

authorsandrarneeley@gmail.com

https://www.sneeleywrites.com
https://www.sneeleywrites.com/contact
https://www.sneeleywrites.com/blog
https://www.facebook.com/authorsandrarneeley/
https://www.facebook.com/groups/755782837922866/
https://www.amazon.com/Sandra-R-Neeley/e/B01M65OZ1J/
https://twitter.com/sneeleywrites
https://www.instagram.com/sneeleywrites/
https://www.goodreads.com/author/show/15986167.Sandra_R_Neeley
https://www.bookbub.com/authors/sandra-r-neeley

Stop by to say Hi, and sign up to be included in updates on current and future projects.

Printed in Great Britain
by Amazon